I0783277

THE DRAKA &
THE GIANT

— · —

LIANE ZANE

AN IMPRINT OF ZEPHON BOOKS

This is a work of fiction. Names, characters, places, and incidents are products of the author's imagination or are used fictitiously and are not to be construed as real. Any resemblance to actual events, locales, organizations, or persons, living or dead, is entirely coincidental.

THE DRAKA & THE GIANT. Copyright © 2022 LeAnn Neal Reilly. All rights reserved under International and Pan-American Copyright Conventions. By payment of the required fees, you have been granted the nonexclusive, nontransferable right to access and read the text of this ebook on screen. No part of this text may be reproduced, transmitted, downloaded, decompiled, reverse-engineered, or stored into any information storage and retrieval system, in any form or by any means, whether electronic or mechanical, now known or hereafter invented, without the express written permission of the author. For information, email zephonbooks@gmail.com.

Digital Edition DECEMBER 2022 ISBN: 979-8-9850781-5-2

Print Edition ISBN: 979-8-9850781-4-5

Second Print Edition ISBN: 979-8-9850781-9-0

Cover design by Perla Enrica Giancola

SECOND EDITION

To my fans
Thank you from the bottom of my heart

<h1 style="text-align:center">ONE</h1>

A pulse-pounding dark techno beat drove the writhing, seething mass of bodies lit overhead by a kaleidoscope of color on the second floor of The Duplex, one of the most popular dance clubs in Prague. Which was saying something given that Czechs liked to party: Prague had more nightclubs and bars per person than London, New York, or Tokyo. Wednesday night or Saturday night made no difference. Dancing and drinking until five a.m. before stumbling into a rideshare or a taxi—alone or not—happened most nights for the city's singles.

It was the perfect environment for losing track of yourself.

It was also the perfect environment for assassins from Unit 29155 of the GRU, Russian military intelligence, to succeed in poisoning a target. All while enjoying a few beers and groping plenty of drunk, half-dressed women. It was their signature method for deniability while sending a message at the same time: we can get to you anytime, anywhere.

Not tonight, if she had anything to do with it.

Alžběta Černá, a captain in the *Vojenské zpravodajství*, the Czech military intelligence known as the VZ, had spent the last three years stalking the members of Unit 29155.

Beta wasn't going to let her quarry escape now.

Keen anticipation sharpened her senses and tightened her abdominal muscles. She resisted the almost overwhelming urge to slip her karambit, the wicked little hooked knife in her thigh boot, into her hand.

Instead, she flexed her fingers, imagining sending her internal heat into the turgid air. It might have been her imagination, but the temperature in the club seemed to climb around her. A smoky tang burned her nostrils and clung to her skin, mixing with the rich, sweet scent of her perfume.

The hard-driving industrial bassline kept time with the beating of her heart and the rhythm of her stride. The erratic flashing lights illuminated the staircase to the top level. There the Russians sat on two white velvet sectionals that let them watch the dancefloor below.

Beta didn't need the lights to see.

Her dragon vision recognized their infrared signatures. Even if that failed—and it wouldn't—she smelled them.

I've never been broken repeated an electronic female voice as she moved through the crowd.

It could have been her anthem.

Dancers pulled away from her, repelled by a dark invisible force, before closing in behind her and erasing her wake. Most moved instinctively, blindly as worms move away from painful stimuli. Those few aware enough to glance toward her saw an avenging angel dressed in black and stumbled, icy terror sobering them. One or two drifted in her direction, attracted to the danger emanating from her in refracted light waves like a shadowy mirage over desert sands.

She ignored them.

When she reached the top of the stairs, she turned left toward the bar. She felt the gaze from the Russian in the far sectional facing her. Even though she was more than half a dozen meters from him and surrounded by sweaty club goers who reeked of cologne, cigarette smoke, and alcohol, she scented the spike in the assassin's pheromones.

She saw the matching spike of white heat in his groin.

The smile that curled the corner of her mouth didn't reach her eyes.

Zatím to ujd. So far so good.

The men and women around her shifted to let her approach the bar. They gave her plenty of room to prop her forearms on the glossy blond wood. The bartender caught her gaze and hurried over.

"Trebitsch," she said. When he turned, she clamped his wrist. "Two fingers, no ice."

He nodded. "Understood."

A minute later he set the single-malt Czech whisky on the bar in front of her. The industrial bassline changed to dark synth with rhythmic piano chords interspersed with drum brushes on cymbal. The crowd on the dance-floor slowed and swayed, many individuals clustering in twos and threes.

She swallowed the whisky. Its silk slid down her heated throat. Lifting her chin at the bartender, whose gaze had darted toward her while he worked farther along the bar, she slid the empty tumbler toward him. This was new, this awareness of her incredible power over the attention of others. She'd always hidden in the recesses, the shadows of her assignments, but ever since she'd gone undercover on this mission, Beta had found herself growing beyond her psychic boundaries.

It wasn't confidence. It was something darker. Something she'd kept chained until she'd burned everything important to her to identify and gather evidence against the men who'd bombed Czech ammunitions depots and killed Czech citizens. The arrogant men who thought they were imper-vious to the laws of other nations, who acted with impunity.

Beta looked in the mirror behind the bartender and watched the Russians and their guests. Only two of the infamous Unit 29155 had come to the Prague meet.

That was wise.

It wouldn't do for the entire six-member team to be seen together. Which made it that much trickier for her. The 2014 bombings near the border with Slovakia had been carried out by a team of two. She'd spent the past three years building an extensive profile on the shadowy unit and tracking its missions.

To complicate her task, Beta wasn't the only one hunting Unit 29155 assassins. The British also wanted the Russian operatives who'd poisoned former Russian military officer Sergei Skripal and his daughter in England only a couple of months ago.

Beta had tracked two Unit 29155 assassins traveling under the names Ruslan Boshirov and Alexander Petrov to Salisbury where Skripal lived in exile. She hadn't realized what Boshirov and Petrov intended until it was too late. If, as her investigation suggested, Boshirov and Petrov had also bombed the Czech arms depots, the British would find themselves failing.

What would the Russian officer staring at her think when he realized that the bit of eye candy that he slavered over turned out to be the bodyguard of the arms broker they were meeting? As with everything in this murky, shifting world of espionage and hidden motives, not everyone or everything was exactly as it seemed.

The Russians would be wise to keep that fact in mind also.

The bartender set another whisky in front of her. She nodded and dropped a wad of cash on the bar. It didn't matter whether she kept drinking or not. Her metabolism burned alcohol as if it were fuel. She never got drunk. Not even tipsy. But she didn't need to spend any more time or money on this feint. Let her admirer wrongly assume that she'd been impaired, even a little, by the whisky.

It's all about humanity repeated a deep male voice over the sound system as the dark techno beat picked up again. The throbbing mass below moved faster.

A faint brush of energy—like static electricity before a thunder-storm—moved across her. She shifted her gaze to the reflection of the large male Viking now standing at her side. His shoulder-length white-blond hair accentuated his massive shoulders, which only led her gaze to take in his equally large biceps and chest. She was tall and afraid of no one, but his imposing height and mass made her feel vulnerable. Yet there was also something comforting about his presence.

For a moment she recalled another large male, equally massive at more than two-and-a-half meters and over 100 kilograms. More than twice her weight. A male with wavy brown hair and eyes the color of deep space. But nothing more came to her. A sharp ache pierced her between the eyes instead.

She shook her head. No time to think about the gaping holes in her memory.

The Viking's eyes focused on the mirror. Something shivered through her at their brilliant blue gleam. It was bone-deep recognition. And it terrified her.

"What are you looking at, my friend?" she asked, letting an aggressive note sharpen her voice.

He shrugged and turned away. Relief flooded her as though God's searchlight had moved on and left her in darkness once again. Sniffing, she rotated and leaned against the bar, propping herself on an elbow and staring back at the Russian officer. If she didn't know better, she'd wonder if being this close to her goal had jangled her nerves.

At that thought, Beta blew the Russian a kiss. He laid his hand on his crotch and raised his tumbler in a toast.

Vûl. Idiot. She smiled, imagining using her karambit to slice through the waistband of his jeans. Would he be so confident then?

"Marika."

While she'd been engaging the Russian, a male wearing a blazer and slacks had shifted into the opening where the Viking had stood.

That shocked her. Why hadn't she realized that the Viking had left? Scowling, Beta shoved the thought into a dark crevice at the back of her mind.

She looked over her shoulder and gave a short nod to acknowledge her cover identity. "Gordon."

Her voice sounded cool and detached. Good. She couldn't afford to let emotion distract her.

Drew Gordon, her new employer, smiled as he signaled for a drink. "I see you've attracted the attention of our buyers." He turned to address the bartender. "Chopin, neat and ice cold if you please. And leave the bottle."

The bartender nodded and turned to pull the Polish vodka from a shelf behind him.

Beta studied Gordon's profile as he waited. She'd heard his unfamiliar accent at their introductory meeting a week before. She thought it was American, perhaps something from the south of that enormous country, but it was new to her. As far as she could tell, however, Gordon was indeed the arms dealer that he purported to be.

"You drink Polish vodka?" she asked, truly curious.

Gordon had told her that he was meeting with members of the Ukrainian military, who opposed Russian-backed militia in their country. His vodka choice signaled ignorance about the buyers' true background. And intentions.

Or not.

She'd be a fool to think anyone operating in the international world of arms sales took anything at face value. Gordon was no exception. It had taken months of careful planning and a rock-solid legend to get the interview with him. And a job offer only after she'd defeated the other candidates in hand-to-hand combat.

Gordon smiled at her. It was mischievous.

"A little test, you see," he said.

And then she knew that he suspected who the Russians were. No self-respecting Russian would choose to drink Polish vodka when Russian vodka was available.

Beta nodded.

Gordon tossed back his shot before grabbing the bottle of Chopin and pivoting toward the Russians. "Come, let's introduce ourselves."

Beta fell into step at his side, her arm linked through his as though they were on a date. She let the fingers of her free hand skim the top of her boot. The karambit fairly hummed inside its hidden sheath.

Patience, she told the part of her that wanted to swoop in and snatch the Russian who'd stared at her before dragging him off to her lair. It was getting harder and harder to keep it chained.

Gordon stopped in front of the Russians and a half dozen other men and women seated with them. Beta scanned the low table between the sectionals. She glimpsed several plastic bags filled with pills among the bottles and glasses littering its surface. All of these, the people and the drugs, were props. The Russians were entirely sober. Their glittering dark gazes sharpened on Gordon and Beta.

"A drink before we get to business?" Gordon asked, waggling the bottle of Chopin.

Tension thickened the smoky air as the Russians looked at the Polish vodka. For a moment Beta wondered if the Russians would snarl and tell them to leave.

Instead, the bearded Russian nodded. The slight curl of his lips never made it past sneer to a convincing smile, however. The other Russian, the one whose gaze devoured her, slid over and patted the seat next to him.

Beta ignored the invitation.

When Gordon had poured everyone a measure of vodka, he raised the bottle in toast. "To new friends then. May all our transactions be as smooth as this vodka."

The bearded Russian lifted his glass. "*Na zdorov'ya.*" *Cheers*. In Ukrainian. Though his voice was friendly, his infrared signature blazed in anger.

Beta smiled.

And then the club exploded in chaos as thick smoke choked the air, and men in dark tactical gear erupted onto the dancefloor, sending the dancers scattering like water drops on a hot pan.

A little more than a kilometer northwest of The Duplex—a fifteen-minute walk for ordinary humans—a horde of *daemonia* materialized on the iconic Charles Bridge over the Vltava River at the same moment the strike squad breached the packed club.

Elioud warrior András Nagy, who'd tracked this particular nasty group of spiritual marauders from Munich, ignored the nano-origami perched in his ear tweeting at him. He didn't need the distraction right now.

Whatever the *zonjë* wanted to tell him could wait.

He eased under the Old Town Bridge Tower, which guarded the entrance to the city's medieval heart on the east bank of the river. He'd already shunted his internal heat into his specially designed tactical clothing, effectively cloaking his infrared signature. Now he adjusted his harmonics to match the tower's 700-year-old stone. To all but the most perceptive angelic senses, his signatures would read as inanimate. The *daemonia*, who'd siphoned enough harmonic energy to escape their underworld prison, were *not* the most perceptive spirits.

András grinned without humor.

Though it was almost two in the morning, old-fashioned carriage lights blazed along the 500-meter length of stone bridge in front of him. Except for the 30 statues of saints flanking both sides of the gothic structure, it was deserted at this hour. In a city that never slept, the nightlife danced and drank in modern clubs and bars instead.

András inhaled, his eyes narrowing.

He hadn't been in the capital of the Czech Republic for almost three years, not since he'd come on an *Elioud* mission to recover a stolen Caravaggio painting, *The Infatuation of the Watcher Angels*.

A mission that failed, leaving him and his partner, Alžběta Černá, a Grey *Elioud* and friend of the *zonjë*, gravely wounded. András had carried Beta to safety, never leaving her side as they were transported to his lord's estate to recover.

And then, after depleting the angelic manna stored in the Caravaggio, Beta had taken his heart and disappeared without a trace.

At that memory, András clinched his jaw and forced the spurt of heat it elicited into his boots. Miró Kos, his *Elioud* teammate who'd designed the boots, had guaranteed they wouldn't melt. Instead, the graphene material converted the heat into energy stored in lithium batteries in the soles. Just as András's tactical clothing collected his body heat and kinetic energy and transferred it to more lithium batteries sewn into the seams. The ingenious little batteries powered all of the electrical systems in his tactical gear.

Exhaling heated breath, András shrugged. Too bad he couldn't raise his temperature enough to melt the microscopic bullet fragments near his spine. The only physical reminder he had that Beta had ever been in his arms.

His nano-origami chirped again.

András fine-tuned the nano-origami's harmonics to transmit audio. Perfectly matched to his own harmonics, the tuning of the microscopic bots prevented unauthorized sources from intercepting transmissions between him and the rest of the *Elioud* team. It was almost as secure as flashing, their preferred mode for communicating mentally, with a wider broadcast range. Not necessary around the ethereal *daemonia* but a definite plus in their increasing engagement with living agents of the Dark angelic forces. Hence the *Elioud* maintained comms discipline while on every mission.

"Go for Giant." A hint of smoke tickled his nose as András spoke. He frowned.

"Giant, this is Harlequin. Stop ignoring me." The *zonjë*'s voice spoke in his ear. Olivia Kastrioti, his lord's wife, sounded irritated. "We have a situation. Do you copy?"

András locked onto the lead *daemon* that had come into view next to the statue of St. Francis Borgia in the middle of the bridge.

It appeared to be the restless soul of a Dark *Elioud*, one who'd abjured his duty to fight on the side of the *Angeli Fidelis* and died unredeemed. The souls of these humans with angel blood had a particularly tormented look on their countenances. The *daemon*'s gaze lifted toward the statues of two angels flanking St. Francis Borgia. It sneered.

András eased his foot forward.

"András." The *zonjë*'s authority crackled through the nano-origami. The molecular machines hummed as their harmonics responded, sending an electric jab into his flesh.

He shook his head at the stinging sensation in his ear. Olivia was the only *Elioud* who'd mastered that particular technique, thankfully. The irony was that she accessed his lithium batteries to make it happen. A 'love tap' she called it.

Olivia *really* loved him.

"A situation. Copy that."

The lead *daemon* halted, its alert gaze searching the bridge in front of it. The *daemonia* streamed past, oblivious to their leader's hesitation.

András paused. This one was more sensitive than the average underworld dweller.

"Aerie Two has picked up reports of a disturbance southeast of you not far from Wenceslas Square. Blackbird's close enough to sense significant harmonic discord."

András kept still as the unholy spirits floated on harmonic currents toward him like malicious spectral jellyfish.

Spectral jellyfish who would inject psychic poison upon contact with unwary souls.

Should the *daemonia* manage to infest anyone, they would feed on the victim's harmonic energy. As the dark spirits fed on their victims, they would grow in power and agency.

And so would madness, mayhem, and murder.

"Convenient timing," said András.

He shuddered as the *daemonia* polluted the harmonic plane around him.

Steady, steady, he told himself.

His harmonics stayed anchored to the stone tower, but his voice had resonated through the *daemonia's* dark chorus. As mindless as these beings were, they would still recognize the unmistakable sound of human speech.

"Fall back until we know more. The *daemonia* could be a distraction."

Before András could confirm that order, the lead *daemon* appeared right in front of him.

Hollow eyes and a gaping maw filled his vision. And then the creature lunged, wrapping its icy hands around his throat. Mutters, shrieks, groans, and cries of an entire mob battered his ears. Discordant vibrations surged through his harmonics. For a sickening moment András feared that he'd be swamped.

And then the lead *daemon* opened its mouth wider and swallowed him in a rush.

"Confirm last order, Giant," Olivia commanded in his ear.

András didn't respond.

"Confirm last order, Giant," she repeated.

When he still didn't respond, the *zonjë* gave him a love tap.

The harmonic jab jarred the *daemon*, who'd eagerly rushed into its human prey. Its spiritual assault wavered. Its malign intent shifted outward as it sensed something different in this human's uneven harmonic signature. Something *angelic*.

"What is this?" asked the *daemon* in a hollow voice, pulling back from András as if tasting something nasty. His German accent told a story about his former life.

In reply, András flared.

A brief intense lighting of the entire visual spectrum, angelic flares dazzled and confused humans and angels alike. *Elioud* warriors normally flared instinctively to protect the innocent and overwhelm the enemy.

In this instance, András's flare ripped apart the lead *daemon*'s harmonic energy with the force of a white phosphorous grenade. It scattered the mass of *daemonia* beyond the range of his angelic sonar.

Although of course his nano-origami had also recorded and transmitted it back to the local *Elioud* tactical operations center or TOC.

"Giant, this is Dragon Man. We registered a flare. What is your status?" The hard voice of Mihàil Kastrioti, his commander and Olivia's husband, confirmed that in fact his little stunt had been immediately registered.

Mihàil's call sign 'Dragon Man' came from the fact that he was part dragon. Or in other words, part angel. That's because early humans all over the ancient world had identified *Seraphim*, described as fiery, winged serpents, as dragons when these high-ranking angels had dominated history.

In Albania where Mihàil was from, demi-angels were known as *drangùes* or dragon men. In Mihàil's case, his father was also a *drangùe* and his mother an *Irim* or Watcher Angel. That made him three-quarters angel and almost 600 years old. Basically, awe-inspiring in the terror-inducing sense of the word.

Not that András cared.

"Dragon Man, this is Giant. The *daemonia* have been dispatched and won't be bothering anyone in Prague for some time. Over."

"Giant, would that be because you baited a *daemon*? And used my *zonjë* to free you?" Mihàil sounded angry. "Against my express command?"

"Affirmative." András paused. "What's the saying? Better to ask forgiveness than permission?"

"What forgiveness? Permission was already denied," Mihàil began when Olivia interrupted.

"Let's deal with this later, you two. Blackbird has arrived at Wenceslas Square. He's confirmed that something is happening at a club called The Duplex. People are fleeing into the streets. Local authorities have received dozens of calls from people on site reporting a well-armed team in tactical gear searching the club."

András had already begun jogging east into the Old Town. "ETA in 45 seconds."

His focus shifted to the new threat as if nothing else mattered. Because it didn't.

"All right, Giant, rendezvous with the team at the Můstek metro station, about a third of a kilometer northwest of the club. Aerie Two has sent building schematics and info on local law enforcement to our cellphones."

"Copy that," said András as he sped his harmonics so that he disappeared from human sight.

He ignored the turn toward Old Town Square where the Church of Our Lady Before Týn loomed like something out of a dark fairytale. Even so, the twin Gothic towers that inspired the Disney castle were unmistakable against the dark night sky. If he let himself, he'd remember what Beta had said about the iconic church the night she found him in the Admiral Botel farther south on the Vltava.

Her words invaded his thoughts anyway.

"Those two"—she tilted her chin towards the towers—"are ideal sniper nests. Position two shooters there, set a team at the Bridge Tower to block escape, herd all the tourists toward the square, and then"—here she raised an imaginary sniper rifle and sighted down an invisible scope, "*booomm.*" She imitated the explosive sound of a sniper shot from a large caliber gun.

Of course, the sharp-tongued, prickly Czech would talk about weapons and ambush instead of the nicknames for the towers, Adam and Eve.

András shook his head and ran faster.

The Můstek metro station popped into view on his left as he halted. Dozens of panicked people dashed pell-mell along the sidewalks and clogged the broad streets of Wenceslas Square. András scanned them, lips tight and hands fisted. All infrared signatures returned within normal ranges. No one had been shot at least. But their harmonics rippled like leaves in a wild storm.

Tires screeched followed by the sounds of crunching plastic and glass. Horns blared. Someone screamed.

Ahead heavy discord roiled the harmonic plane in Wenceslas Square, its locus centered on the distinctive glass dome of the nightclub. The timbre was all Dark *Irim*. Asmodeus, if András had to bet. And the fallen Watcher Angel hadn't come alone.

Miró appeared next to András. He looked grim.

"Have you seen the schematics?" he asked.

"Not yet."

"The main entrance on the ground functions as a funnel toward two elevators to the club. Very few patrons can exit at a time. There *is* a service entrance around the corner on Jindřišská Street."

"But not accessible to patrons. Most of them are still inside fighting their way out."

"Yes," Miró said, "Or being trampled."

Olivia and Mihàil appeared on the sidewalk next to them, their faces grim.

Mihàil's gaze touched each of theirs. "We need to bypass the front entrance to gain access to the club. Miró, you and András clear an entry point via the Marks & Spencer building next door. Olivia, you and I will take control of the main entrance. With luck, we will be able to get everyone out of the building faster with few casualties."

The *drangùe* paused and threw a look over his shoulder. When he looked back again, his face had grown harder, if possible. "Enough planning. Shots have been fired. Time to move out.

Two

The Russians shared a look, and then almost as one lunged for Gordon and Beta, dragging them backwards toward the glass door to the outside terrace. Each assassin had drawn a weapon and held it aimed toward the stairs. The rest of their group fell all over themselves trying to get up and move somewhere, anywhere away from the railing overlooking the dancefloor and the armed men. None of them followed the Russians, however. Even drunk and high, they hadn't lost all sense of self-preservation.

In the pandemonium, Beta realized a couple of things. First, that it's easy to be trapped on the top floor of a club with a single elevator and an open, winding staircase in the case of a threat one floor down. And second, the Russian who'd been staring at her like a hungry wolf also had the breath and rough paws of one. She rather regretted not showing him her karambit earlier.

Oh, well. There was still plenty of time for that.

The Russians pulled them outside and away from the door.

"Quickly!" ordered the older Russian, yanking Gordon farther along the terrace.

"Let go of me," hissed Beta at the other one, who gripped her so tightly by the upper arm her circulation had been cut off. She would have purple fingerprints later.

He responded by whacking her across the cheek with his weapon hand.

Stars exploded across Beta's vision. She tasted blood and ash.

"Hey! What the hell?" asked a male voice from somewhere beside them. He had an American accent. "Why don't you try hitting someone your own size?"

Her captor spun. Beta sensed him lifting his weapon, and an instant before he squeezed off a shot she elbowed him. She heard the gun spit and then the unmistakable sound of bullet hitting flesh followed by a groan.

She was so going to enjoy teaching this animal a lesson.

"Gun!" shouted a woman in Russian.

Sounds of running feet, shoving, furniture scraping, and panicked cries filled the terrace around them.

Her captor pulled Beta so roughly she stumbled and almost fell. A moment later he jerked her to the wall next to him. She blinked to clear her eyes. The scent of smoke clung to her, but she forced herself to breathe evenly and look at her surroundings.

The Russians had taken cover where the outside wall turned ninety degrees to create a shallow niche behind some rattan ottomans. It wouldn't hide them for long in a concerted search, but it would keep anyone glancing through the club's windows from seeing them. Muffled screams and crashes signaled the ongoing chaos inside.

Unfortunately, they weren't the only people on the terrace. Several patrons, initially curious about what was happening, had gone into the club only to return wearing terrified expressions. Beta surveyed their infrared signatures. Adrenaline had sent their temperatures soaring, and several shivered in the cool night air. A few across from them shielded the view, but Beta made out a woman kneeling.

The two assassins leveled their weapons at the other patrons, who shifted, revealing the wounded man sprawled in a rattan club chair. Hot blood spread across his midsection even though his companion pressed a tablecloth against it.

Beta compressed her lips and narrowed her eyes. Her would-be defender needed immediate medical attention.

"Now what?" Gordon asked the Russians. "Hope and pray that strike team doesn't come out here?"

Beta looked at her employer, who leaned into the corner behind the older Russian. He looked calm. Catching her eye, he smiled. What was he thinking?

Intuition niggled, but she said nothing. Instead, she let her hand drift toward the top of her boot.

Muted sounds of gunfire from inside the club raised the tension on the terrace. Beta's sensitive hearing picked out the distinct report of a shotgun among the gunfire.

That was very interesting.

The Russians ignored him and spoke to each other in low, heated voices. They didn't bother speaking in Ukrainian. They debated going back into the club and surprising the intruders before making a break for the stairs.

"I don't think you have many options," Gordon said. His smile confirmed that he knew exactly what they were talking about.

A moment later three men wearing full helmets with visors and tactical vests burst through the door to the terrace. Two carried the Heckler & Koch HK416 battle rifle. The third carried a Benelli M3T Super 90 combat shotgun.

Czech police special forces or URNA.

URNA was a rapid-deployment unit under the authority of the Ministry of the Interior. It provided protection at Czech embassies. It also rescued hostages, surveilled national threats, and engaged in counter-terrorism. URNA trained with Czech military special forces. It also trained with foreign units such as the British SAS and German and French special police forces.

Beta's night had just gotten a thousand times more challenging.

The two carrying the battle rifles spread out on the terrace, one going to stand near the group of club patrons nearest the door and the other heading toward the wounded man. The police officer carrying the combat shotgun stopped within a couple of meters of where they stood.

"*Odhod'te zbraně.*" *Drop your weapons.* He gestured with his combat shotgun before repeating his command in Russian.

So the Czech police had come for the Russians. Why?

Beta darted a glance at Gordon to see if he was surprised. His posture and temperature hadn't changed. Was it just his usual equanimity—necessary in his line of work—or did it signal something more? At the very least he didn't seem concerned that he would be swept up in URNA's operation.

The Russians obeyed the first law of intelligence officers everywhere: live to operate another day. They held their pistols high and visible and reached slowly for the ground, their gazes on their captors as they set the weapons down.

The lead URNA officer motioned for one of the other URNA officers to come and zip-tie the Russians, who said nothing. Another sign of well-trained operatives. Once at the police station, they would produce a card with the name of the local fixer at the Russian embassy. An embassy that all in Czechia knew was a regional base for Russian spies to operate throughout Western Europe.

"*Vy dva tam,*" said the lead URNA officer to Gordon and Beta, "*půjdeš s námi.*"

"Excuse me, I don't speak Czech," said Gordon in English.

Beta knew better.

"You two there, come with us," the officer repeated in English.

"Certainly," said Gordon. "Though I just met these two." He looked at Beta. "And I don't know her at all."

Beta could take a hint.

"They promised me a good time." She sniffed and touched her swollen cheek with a fingertip. "I do not think going to jail is a good time."

She stepped closer and reached into the jacket of the Russian who'd hit her and pulled out his wallet. "This is mine, *prase.*"

The Russian snarled and lunged at her, but the URNA officer jerked him back.

"Take what is yours and give him back his wallet," the officer said to her in Czech.

Beta dipped her chin and then pulled all of the cash from the wallet.

Time for a little distraction.

She riffled the bills with her other hand as though counting the amount before shouting, "*Ty laciný bastarde!*" and jumped on the Russian, conveniently tossing the wallet at Gordon's feet as she did.

As the bills fluttered in the air around them, Beta struck the Russian with open palms about his face and ears. She managed to hang on for a good thirty seconds while he roared and struggled trying to dislodge her. It took both

URNA officers to pull them apart. By then Beta had delivered an elbow strike to the Russian's jaw in her "wild" flailing. The sharp weights embedded in her sleeve opened a wide cut in his cheek. As the URNA officer tugged her free, she spit in the assassin's face.

Her dragon's breath meant that her saliva was hot enough to burn. Too bad she hadn't had the opportunity to use her dragon's claw.

Another time.

As the Russian screamed, an URNA officer dragged him away. More URNA officers had made it onto the terrace, and two came forward to escort Gordon and the second Unit 29155 assassin, who ordered his partner in harsh language to shut the hell up and act like a professional.

Gordon never looked at her as he disappeared into the club.

Beta surveyed the scene around her. Across from her, URNA medics treated the wounded American. Except for his date, most of the other patrons had been shepherded inside where they would be processed before being allowed to leave.

A moment later an invisible shockwave rippled through the night, sending the hairs on the back of her neck dancing.

And then the rumble of a detonation shook the pavement under her feet. Several windows cracked next to her.

The armed URNA officer stiffened, holding his weapon ready. He began speaking into his mouth mic. After a moment, he visibly relaxed.

Beta frowned. Whatever was going on, she was at a disadvantage on the terrace. The longer she remained here, the more likely someone was going to question her more closely. Not that she worried about her cover being exposed, but Marika Hubová wouldn't want to be caught anywhere near Russian assassins. It would hurt the reputation that she'd so carefully built over the past three years. A reputation that she needed to succeed in her mission.

She glanced at the medics, who'd finished stabilizing the American. She touched her cheek. It was still swollen, but the blood had dried. No matter. She could fix that.

Taking her karambit from the top of her boot, she slid it open with a *snick*. Then she sliced its tip across the scratch, reopening it. With a flick of her wrist, the karambit shut. She slipped it back into its hidden sheath. To complete the look, she took off the band holding her hair in a sleek ponytail. Dipping her fingers in a half empty glass of beer, she tousled her hair until it felt wild and tangled.

Done with her transformation, Beta pressed her palm to her bleeding cheek and wobbled toward the medics.

One turned and caught sight of her. *"Můj ty bože!"* *Oh my God!* "What happened to you?"

Not meeting his gaze, she muttered something as he urged her toward the other medic.

They spent the next five minutes cleaning the scratch and assessing her vitals. She let her internal temperature, already naturally hotter than the average person, rise, and stood shivering in the night air. Concerned, a medic wrapped her in a shock blanket and radioed that they had another civilian needing medical transport.

So it was that Beta was hunched and leaning against one of the medics when a giant came onto the terrace. Wearing black tactical clothing, he moved with the grace of a panther for all his size. And he was *huge*, with massive shoulders and defined pectoral muscles that his form-fitting t-shirt clung to as if it were a second skin. He wore his hair cropped short, and his eyes were dark and hard.

Warning shot through her like an icy arrow. Her heart began to race, and her breathing grew shallow. The medics, alarmed at her sudden downturn, urged her toward the door inside.

As they passed the giant, who ignored them to stalk toward the edge of the terrace, something like an electric current hummed through her.

It might have been terror.

As András approached the seating area just abandoned by the URNA medics, with his gaze locked on the night sky illuminated by turbulent emergency lights from the street below, the complex scent of a woman's perfume punched him.

Stunned, he halted and let it assail him.

Wild hints of vetiver and jasmine danced with the sweetness of vanilla and black currant. As soon as these notes hit his nose, they faded into the exotic floral scents of orchid, gardenia, and lotus sharpened by a tinge of citrusy bergamot and patchouli. These dissipated into the heavy, rich scent of chocolate.

Black Orchid.

It was familiar. Beta had worn that perfume.

András cursed his sensitive *Elioud* nose and his memory.

Whoever had worn that perfume had just been here.

Whirling, he turned toward the door into the club. The remaining URNA officers, ignoring him as expected, filed through the glass door. He surveyed their infrared and harmonic signatures, none of which were familiar to him. Looking back at the club chairs pushed into disarray from the recent emergency medical treatment, he narrowed his eyes.

The localized harmonic disturbance, though not as teeth-achingly jarring as the remnants of the Dark *Irim* who'd occupied this area not long ago, echoed with violence. Panic, fear, anger, and pain, like perfume notes, overlaid the harmonic plane. Traces of wild thermal spikes added to the picture of chaos and disharmony. If the melodious *musica universalis* served as the foundation of Heaven, then a little bit of Hell had ruled here only moments before.

"He is growing more powerful," said Miró from behind him.

András didn't reply. There wasn't much to add to the obvious. Asmodeus, a Dark *Irim* that Mihàil and Miró had struggled against for hundreds of years, had grown stronger in the past few years. It used to be that he played cat-and-mouse with them. Even András, a gifted *Elioud* tracker, had rarely caught the Dark *Irim*'s harmonic signature except as a tantalizing clue to the cause behind horrific events.

Now their expanded *Elioud* team raced to keep up with Asmodeus's overt crimes against humanity.

"I don't think he was the only Dark *Irim* here," said András, kneeling.

There were a few drops of blood here away from the seating area where the medics had worked. He dipped a finger into one.

"What? Are you certain?" Miró's voice sharpened.

András lifted his finger to his nose and inhaled. He rubbed his finger and thumb together, considering. Then he wiped the blood on his pants and stood, turning to Miró.

"Yes." He held the other *Elioud*'s gaze.

Miró, the team's intelligence officer, narrowed his eyes. András kept his gaze steady, never letting his harmonics waver. He knew that Miró, whose ability to read fine variations in harmonics and thermal energy allowed him to identify falsehood and deception, suspected that he wasn't sharing everything.

But that was nothing new. He'd stopped being an open book three years ago.

Miró sighed and turned to look toward the night sky where the harmonic intrusion slowly receded into the distance like clouds leaving after a storm. "What was the point here?" he asked.

"Point? Does Asmodeus have to have a point beyond mayhem and his own pleasure?" asked András.

"Normally I would say no, but something is different. It is more than his obvious presence. What did he get out of being here?" Miró gestured around them. "Hardly enough violence and bloodshed to titillate him."

"Perhaps the point was to meet with another Dark *Irim*."

"Or to test our response," said Mihàil as he and Olivia arrived.

"Or both," she said. She turned to András. "Don't think I've forgotten what you did back there with that *daemon*."

Even this late at night and after an intense, though brief, operation, Mihàil's *zonjë* glowed with vitality and confidence. She'd always been exceptionally beautiful, but ever since they'd learned that she was expecting a child, András thought that she'd grown into her role with power and grace. Already Olivia managed the Kastrioti estate as if she'd been born to the position. Given that the Archangel Michael had chosen and trained her, perhaps she had.

A tiny flicker of guilt niggled at her words. He shrugged. "I never expected you would, my lady."

Mihàil turned to Olivia. The hard planes of the *Elioud* general's face softened as he looked at his young wife. "Leave him to me, *dashuria ime*." He brushed a long strand of silky blond hair behind her ear.

It was a gesture of tenderness that stabbed András in the chest.

Clenching his fists, he walked toward the railing at the edge of the terrace before turning and saying, "Testing our response means Asmodeus knew we'd be here tracking the *daemonia*."

Mihàil looked at him. Something flickered in his general's eyes, but then the *drangùe* nodded. "It would seem that way. That alone is concerning. But I fear that he used the *daemonia* to lure and distract us."

"Something that he has not done in a very long time," said Miró.

He and Mihàil shared a look.

"What aren't you saying?" asked Olivia, looking between them and her voice sharp.

Mihàil put his arm around her and pulled her into his side. The *drangùe* had lost a first wife to a Dark *Irim* and had spent more than 500 years alone. No wonder he always seemed hyperaware of Olivia, unable to keep from touching her or keeping her close. Likely he knew that he didn't deserve her. He had, after all, at one time been Asmodeus's acolyte.

After a moment Mihàil's expression turned grim. He dropped his arm from Olivia and sat in a chair with a sigh. "Asmodeus prefers to work against individual humans. It is the easier path, after all, and the Dark *Irim* of lust is not known for patience."

The *drangùe* closed his eyes and pinched the bridge of his nose before looking at his wife. He looked tired. "It has kept us busy with the banality of evil and kept *him* satiated."

"But if he used *daemons* ...," said Olivia.

Looking unhappy, Mihàil shrugged. "Whatever his motivations or the specifics, if Asmodeus has made a pact with *daemonia*, then we are in for a bumpy ride."

Olivia shivered. She fingered the tiny St. Michael medal lying on her chest. "Bumpier than it already is?" At her husband's nod, she said, "That sounds terrifying."

"Because it is, my lady," said Miró, his arms folded.

András knew that the quiet Croat relayed the night's events to his wife, Anastasia, while they spoke. Stasia, whose call sign *Flower* came from the Italian for her unmarried name, remained in Rome where she maintained a cover with the Italian foreign security service. She, Olivia, and Beta had created a covert international group for missions against sexual predators before they learned that they had angel blood. Now she worked with her husband to manage the *Elioud* team's network of intelligence assets.

Olivia studied Miró. "Because *daemons* are like the Ebola virus?" she asked when he didn't elaborate. She turned to Mihàil. "You all told me earlier that they're mindless and burn through a small population too quickly to sustain themselves. That's why most of them can't escape the abyss where the archangels imprisoned them. Most of what we call demonic behavior is just humans being evil to one another."

"True," said Miró, inclining his head. "But *daemons* are lesser spiritual beings, not the human puppets that Asmodeus uses. They might behave like a spiritual virus, but that can change if a more powerful angelic being acts as a tuner, amplifying their power. Instead of a transitory surge in spiritual energy when they feed on humans, it will be more like nuclear fusion. The sum will be greater than the parts."

"And keep growing," said Mihàil. "Worse, it will not be transitory."

"The horde I faced earlier on the Charles Bridge had a *daemon Elioud* at its head," András said, folding his arms and leaning against the railing.

He wanted to pace instead. Or leave. He had somewhere to go.

Without glancing over his shoulder, he knew that the emergency vehicles had left and that the last few police officers herded the remaining bystanders and club patrons towards transportation and home. The night sky already lightened toward dawn. But for the moment he needed to pay attention to their onsite debrief. With effort he focused on the others.

Mihàil's narrowed eyes said that he was thinking about András's news.

"That is something new," the *drangùe* said at last. "Although I suppose that it makes perfect sense." He looked at each of them in turn. "Asmodeus has outsourced the tuning ability."

"But why a dispossessed *Elioud*?" asked Olivia. "Wouldn't the soul of an angel hybrid be less powerful than a pure *daemonic* being?"

"Pure *daemonic* beings take a lot of energy and focus to manipulate," answered Mihàil. "When they disobeyed the Heavenly laws governing their nature, they went mad. As discordant spirits, they naturally fight any attempt to yoke them. And they can be pulled off course at the first scent of human weakness. The soul of a Dark *Elioud*, on the other hand, is more biddable and takes little energy to put into motion."

"Especially if the Dark *Elioud* in question died as an acolyte," András added.

A sharp pain blossomed behind his right eye. He ignored it. Instead, he stood and stretched his tight shoulders as Miró took up the explanation.

"Because there would be a residual bond." Miró turned to Olivia. "My lady, the virus analogy is not quite right. Individual *daemons are* mindless. They seek out baser human nature more by sensory input than actual critical thinking. But that does not mean the horde has no ability to think."

"Like a pack of wolves?" asked Olivia.

"Or a swarm of wasps," said Mihàil, nodding. "A *daemonic* horde has a kind of innate cunning. However, I believe that a *daemonic* horde led by a Dark *Elioud* can be commanded instead of just unleashed."

Olivia tilted her head. "Let me guess: the soul of the Dark *Elioud* retains higher-level thinking abilities, probably seasoned with some vengeful passion."

"Correct." Mihàil looked at his lieutenants. "A *daemon Elioud* explains how the recent hordes are escaping from the abyss in the first place. András, did you notice any identifying trait for the *daemon Elioud*?"

András had all he could take of this debrief. Scowling, he crossed his arms again and said, "Besides being male, the *daemon* spoke with a German accent. He wore old-fashioned clothing, a black suit with a white shirt that had a wing collar and white bowtie. He also wore a waistcoat and had half a dozen large medals with ribbons pinned to his left breast."

"When you return to the TOC, work with Miró and Miles to create a portrait. Miró, once you have that, research our archives and see if you can identify which Dark *Elioud* Asmodeus has resurrected from the abyss. Once we know that, we should be able to disrupt his plans by locating the Dark *Elioud*'s grave and creating a harmonic sink."

András and Miró nodded.

Mihàil stood. He glanced over his shoulder at the sky. In another half an hour, yellow and orange would tint the gray, heralding sunrise.

"Thank the Archangel that there were only two casualties tonight, neither fatal. But our work here is not yet done. Except for you." The *drangùe* held his hand out to Olivia. "Come. You need to return to our suite and rest."

When she started to protest, Mihàil interrupted. "That is not a request, *dashuria ime*. As your commander, I am telling you to stand down. As your adoring husband, I need to know that you are going to take care of yourself and let the rest of us tie this off."

At that Olivia acquiesced and let her husband walk her to the car that he'd ordered.

András watched as the *drangùe* led his *zonjë* away. Then he turned to Miró, who studied him with a shrewd expression. "There's something I need to take care of. Tell Mihàil that I'll find the commander of the URNA tac team and charm him into believing he set the explosives for the wall we breached."

Instead of responding to his declaration, Miró said, "Be careful, brother. There is more than one ghost in Prague."

András nodded once, hard. "Meet you back at the TOC."

Turning, he climbed up the railing as if ascending stairs and launched into the twilight before dawn.

THREE

As human-angel hybrids, *Elioud* didn't have wings. They didn't fly.

That didn't mean that they couldn't fall gracefully.

András had learned this lesson only a short time after Mihàil had taken him in. He'd been an energetic twelve-year-old boy who still didn't understand what having angel blood meant. But he did know what it meant for someone to fling herself from the Széchényi Chain Bridge over the Danube. Budapest had, after all, become known as the City of Suicides in the wake of World War One. His mother was only one of many.

It had been more instinct than understanding that had led András to lunge after the weeping young man who'd let go from his perch over the icy brown water. And more wishful thinking than skill that led András to slow his harmonics down so that they glided on cold air currents. Even so, if Zophiel hadn't interceded, they would have both gone into the river where András would have been hard pressed to save himself let alone another.

But that was almost 85 years ago. András had long since learned to descend from a height as if he wore an invisible parachute, modulating harmonics and thermodynamics so smoothly that he stepped onto the ground without a stumble.

Which he did this morning as his feet touched the pavement in front of the entrance to The Duplex nightclub. Though it was late enough that anyone out for the night had already headed home and early enough that other businesses hadn't opened yet, Wenceslas Square was far from empty.

András didn't care. Anyone who happened to glance in his direction at just the moment he appeared out of thin air would believe he'd stepped from the dark club entrance.

And if they didn't? So what. Let the mystery of what had happened niggle at their subconscious. It made no difference to him one way or another.

He surveyed the harmonic plane around him in the still shadowy street. Already a tangled mess of vibrations from the life of a busy city square, it had ramped up into a polyphonic maelstrom from the previous night's URNA raid.

But András only needed to find the harmonic pattern that he'd identified on the terrace, the one synced to the blood drops he'd discovered. The one for the injured person of interest.

It took twenty seconds to isolate.

Interesting.

Slipping his cellphone out, András called Miles Baxter, the former CIA operative that Olivia had recruited to their team. Miles had taken on the role of the operations manager in their local TOC with the call sign Aerie Two. As a non-*Elioud*, his talents at asset management and logistics supported the *Elioud* members' increasing engagements against the *daemonia*.

"Aerie Two, this is Giant."

As he spoke, András began walking north toward the end of the square where the bronze statue of St. Wenceslas, the patron saint of the Czech Republic, sat on a prancing horse and holding a pike.

"Giant, this is Aerie Two." Miles's voice sounded a little rough. It had been a long week since András had caught sight of the *daemonia* horde in Munich. He'd likely been dozing. "I haven't gotten any intel back yet on the two Russians that URNA took into custody. But the commander of the URNA response team confirms that both men were armed."

"I'm not calling about that, Aerie Two." András stopped at the corner of Jindřišská Street. "I need more info about the two casualties."

"Copy that, Giant."

A faint sound of clicking and the squeaking of a chair filled the pause before Miles spoke again.

"The most serious was an American male named Ryan Helsing. Helsing suffered a gunshot wound to the abdomen from a handgun used by one of the Russians. Currently Helsing is being operated on. We won't know until later this morning if he's going to make it.

"The other casualty is a Czech woman spotted with the Russians only moments before the URNA team entered the site. One of the Russians hit her, which is what instigated Helsing's involvement and subsequent shooting. According to the medic who treated her, she sustained a deep laceration on her cheek and a likely concussion. But she gave him a false name."

András narrowed his eyes, considering the evidence at the intersection.

The unknown woman had separated from a larger group and headed northwest while the group's harmonics stopped at the curb, likely because the group entered a vehicle. The residual heat suggested that it had been larger than a sedan but smaller than a transport truck used by URNA. If he had to guess, he'd say the thermal footprint belonged to an ambulance.

Many of the streets between the iconic square and Old Town were pedestrian only. To get to the closest hospital, St. Francis, the ambulance would have had to continue around the square and head south before turning north again along the river.

"Let me guess. She chose not to go to the hospital," said András.

Instead, she'd walked northwest toward Old Town Square and the Vltava River.

"Tracking her, I take it?" Humor laced Miles's voice. "Police reports describe her as an escort hired by one of the Russians. Probably didn't want them to look at her more closely in case her services crossed the line into prostitution."

András looked east down Jindřišská Street.

The dark copper spires of Henry's Bell Tower, the highest freestanding Gothic bell tower in Prague, pierced the early morning sky. During the day, it was open to tourists who could ascend to the tenth floor to view the city panorama around it.

After a moment's thought, András walked toward the stone tower. The ornate facades of the buildings around him emerged from the shadows as daylight increased.

"Describe her."

"Hm. Give me a moment. I need to pull up some external files."

At the tower's entrance, András placed his palm against the lock on the heavy wooden door. He hummed, sending a focused band of harmonic energy into its keyhole. After creating a harmonic imprint of the opening, he manipulated the lock's tumblers. It clicked open. He stepped in as Miles continued.

"Okay, your mystery woman was a tall one. The medic estimated her between one-point-eight and one-point-nine meters, though on the thin side at around 60 kilos. She had dark-brown, shoulder-length hair. I think the medic wanted to make a love connection. He claims she had the most unique, dark-gray eyes he'd ever seen."

That detail hit András in the solar plexus.

"You okay, big guy?" Miles asked. That's when András realized that he'd made a sound.

"Never better," he said. He sounded strangled even to himself.

"Whatever you say."

András pulled the wooden door shut and headed for the elevator. "Tell me what you do know about the Russians."

"Yes, sir. No need to growl."

More clicking came through the cellphone's speaker.

"The names on their IDs are Ruslan Boshirov and Alexander Petrov. URNA got an anonymous tip about three minutes before they went in hot that there was an active shooter situation at the club. After they got in, someone opened fire on the rapid response team, but so far no confirmation that Boshirov or Petrov are responsible."

The elevator stopped one floor below the attic, which included windows in each of the corner spires. András ran up the flight of wooden stairs to the attic and made his way to the spire with the best view toward St. Francis Hospital, which faced the river.

"Where did URNA take Boshirov and Petrov?" he asked.

"URNA headquarters are at the Ministry of the Interior north of the Vltava River and outside Letná Park."

The view from Henry's Bell Tower left a lot to be desired. Prague, situated on seven hills just like its sister city of Rome, presented an uneven sea of mostly red roofs glowing in the rising sun. But András already knew the basic layout of the City of a Hundred Spires and just needed to confirm some details.

"Isn't the Russian Embassy about a klick and a half from the river?" he asked as he looked that direction.

"Affirmative. What're you thinking?" asked Miles.

"That Boshirov and Petrov will use their call to contact the embassy."

"Who will send someone almost as soon as they are processed to demand that they be released into the custody of the embassy representative."

"Agreed."

András had seen enough of the Prague skyline. He headed back down the stairs and then punched the elevator button for the ground floor.

"I'm going to prowl around the URNA headquarters. See if I can pick up more intel on these two," he said as he entered the elevator. "Something is very odd about this whole situation, not the least of which is that Asmodeus's fingerprints are all over it."

"Understood. I'll continue to work my sources for more information about Boshirov and Petrov. By the way, I've sent you images of both of them from the URNA intake process."

"Copy that. And Aerie Two, if you get any more intel on the mystery woman, send that to me as well."

"Wilco."

They signed off. András scowled as he exited the elevator. The mystery woman had gotten under his skin ever since he'd smelled her exotic perfume.

A mystery woman whose harmonics clashed with her fundamental frequency—a frequency that almost matched that of an *Irim*. Whoever she was, she was Dark.

Cracking his neck, András pulled a pair of dark-tinted sunglasses from a pocket in his tactical pants and stepped out onto the sidewalk in front of Henry's Bell Tower. Behind him the tower's medieval wood door swung shut on a harmonic pull. The lock clicked.

Then he set off at an easy jog toward the URNA headquarters only two kilometers north of the Vltava River. As he reached Stefanik's Bridge, the sun crested the monolithic Ministry of Agriculture to his east and glowed behind a fluffy blanket of clouds. It was barely 5 a.m., and what little traffic there was on the modern arch span consisted mostly of delivery and service trucks.

The route took him through a leg of Letná Park, a large green belt located on a bluff overlooking the Vltava and Old Town. He'd seen the spectacular views many times during the past century. But he'd grown intimately familiar with them searching for any trace of Beta in Holešovice, an industrial neighborhood north of Letná Park where she'd taken an unassuming apartment.

To no avail.

Holešovice had grown trendy over the last decade. Now art galleries, shops, cafes, clubs, and bars drew locals and tourists alike. When he'd asked Beta if she enjoyed the variety of new places to eat, she'd scowled.

"Of course, you would ask about food, *spratek*," she said, looking at him from the side of her eye. She pulled out the nasty little hawkbill-bladed knife she'd hidden in easy reach and began opening and closing it as she spoke. "I prefer to eat what I prepare. In a quiet place."

The word *alone* hung in the air between them.

Her words echoed in András's memory as he arrived at the Ministry of the Interior. Looking at the rectangular concrete-and-glass building that no amount of green trees and fountains could make attractive, he recalled that the Ministry of Defense, the headquarters of the Czech military intelligence, was only two-and-a-half kilometers west, in the direction that the mystery woman had headed after leaving the URNA medics.

Beta must have hated that her neighborhood had lost its anonymity.

A large black Mercedes sedan with tinted windows—and bulletproof body panels—drove up to the entrance. A man wearing an expensive gray suit got out from the rear.

A Russian envoy from the embassy here to get Boshirov and Petrov.

While the Russian embassy representative climbed the wide concrete steps to the entrance, another vehicle eased to a stop more than a hundred meters away on the other side of Milady Horákové Street. An older-model Škoda, gray and nondescript.

Two people sat in front.

Though shadows obscured their features, something about the tilt of the passenger's chin and the arch of the neck sent a tingle along András's skin.

"Our new friends should be released within the hour," said Gordon, who sat next to Beta as they watched the Russian emissaries enter the Ministry of the Interior.

He'd texted her minutes after she got free of the URNA medics. She couldn't say she was surprised, though they hadn't worked out a specific game plan in the event that they were separated. As a bodyguard, it was her job to stay at her principle's side.

Of course, Gordon had yet to explain his deception when hiring her as a bodyguard. Or how he'd been released so quickly.

She trained a critical gaze on him. She and her legend Marika Hubová shared a decided lack of patience for being played. And Gordon was definitely maneuvering her for unknown reasons. Reasons that might jeopardize her life—let alone her mission—in ways she hadn't bargained for. Her fingers itched to slide the karambit from its sheath and hold it against the soft skin of his throat.

"You knew full well that they are Russian when you hired me," she said in a husky voice instead. She tasted smoke. "It will cost you double for lying. *If* I stay."

Gordon laughed. Despite the tension thickening the air between them, he appeared at ease. His brown hair curled a little at the collar of his open sports jacket, which revealed a button-down shirt with the top two buttons open. He waved a nonchalant hand, whose long graceful fingers belonged on a concert pianist, not an international arms dealer.

"Now, now, my dear. Surely you suspected that this was a test for you?" he asked, smiling at her. His hazel eyes darkened with murky depths. Something alien lurked there.

Beta stiffened. Her dragon senses hummed in painful warning. The urge to open the car door and run almost overcame her—but not before slashing his throat and leaving his smirking grimace behind. She swallowed, tightening her fingers where they lay on her thigh.

Gordon's smile never wavered. Beta had the uncomfortable suspicion that he knew her thoughts.

"I will, of course, pay double once you pass the test. But I didn't hire you simply because your credentials and fighting acumen are exceptional. I hired you because of your innate nature."

"Which is?" she asked, no longer gazing at the Ministry of the Interior.

Gordon let his own gaze travel from her face down her body and back again before answering. When he spoke, he sounded admiring. And certain. "Ferocious."

"I see," said Beta, though she didn't yet.

Gordon cocked his head. "You're wondering how I can know that about you? I know a lot about you. For instance, I know that your name isn't Marika Hubová."

Beta's heart beat a frantic tattoo against her ribcage. But she only narrowed her eyes and tensed.

"Who do you think I am?" she asked softly, assessing the distance between her and Gordon. There was no thought of escape now.

"Alžběta Čermáková." Now Gordon's eyes had taken on the hardness of granite. He watched her with the cold focus of a basilisk.

Beta froze.

Čermáková. No one knew that name, she was sure of it. It meant *redstart*, a common European songbird that looked like a robin.

It was also a Czech euphemism for *devil*. An appropriate nickname for the bastard who'd sired her.

"How do you know that name?" she asked, shaking. Her voice stayed even, however, so she clenched her jaw and willed her nerves to steady. Even so, it had grown hotter inside the car, the scent of smoke heavier.

Gordon shrugged and lowered his window. The air cleared. She caught a faint whiff of decay before he spoke. "I've had my eye on you for a long time, Beta."

He lifted his chin toward the waiting embassy car. "You also knew that our friends are Russians. In fact, you were using me to meet them."

Beta unchained her dragon. In the blink of an eye, she held the tip of her karambit at Gordon's throat. "Enough games. Tell me what you want."

Gordon turned his face toward her. Though he smiled, it didn't reach his eyes. "You will want to rethink that move."

Beta felt the unmistakable edge of a muzzle against her side. She responded by pressing the karambit into Gordon's neck, drawing a thin bead of blood. For a moment their locked gazes sizzled. And then Gordon blinked. And smiled.

The pressure from the muzzle disappeared.

Gordon looked back at their target. "We want the same thing. Only in my case, I no longer follow orders to get it. I give them."

Intrigued, Beta slipped the karambit into her boot. She had to tread carefully here, even more carefully than she had when the URNA rapid response team caught her with the Russians. She couldn't let him lead her into betraying more than he already knew.

"Continue."

"We have a lot more in common than you might think." Gordon's expression turned pleasant as though they sat outside at a terrace café conversing over coffees.

"You were an American soldier," she said.

"Special forces," he said, nodding. "Where I got to know more than a little about Unit 29155 and Russian military intelligence in general."

Beta narrowed her eyes. "Now is when you try to convince me that you are not interested in selling arms to those two"—she jerked her chin toward the Ministry of the Interior where Boshirov and Petrov could be seen on the top of the steps, laughing with the man sent from the Russian embassy to retrieve them.

Gordon started the engine. "I am as interested in selling them arms as they are in buying them from me," he said as he watched the Russians get into the waiting car.

"Of course. They are removing anyone supplying the Ukrainians, such as Gebrev."

Six months after the first massive explosion destroyed a cache of ammunitions in the Czech forest, leaving a crater and blowing out windows in houses a kilometer away, Bulgarian arms dealer Emilian Gebrev was mysteriously poisoned in Sofia, the Bulgarian capital. Gebrev, who had a contract to supply artillery ammunition to Ukraine, had scoured former Warsaw Pact countries for the munitions and stored them in the Czech depots in transit to the Eastern European nation.

Gordon waited until the Russian car had pulled away from the Ministry of the Interior and disappeared before driving after it.

"The Brits have already been in touch with Bulgarian security services about the similarities between Gebrev and the Skripal poisoning." He looked at Beta. "But you already knew that."

Beta waited a moment before answering. Gebrev's poisoning by Unit 29155 had been an open secret in the Central European arms market. Until this point, she'd given nothing away in her answers, simply let Gordon talk.

Well, *almost* nothing. She'd unfortunately reacted to her name.

She shrugged and looked out the passenger window. "Everyone knows Russians love to poison their enemies."

"As well as anyone nearby who might accidentally come into contact with their nerve agent."

The embassy car entered a roundabout that would take it east. They would reach the roundabout in time to confirm that the Russians headed north toward the embassy.

"Novichok." Beta spat the word.

Novichok was a class of chemical weapons developed by the Soviet Union in the 1970s and 80s that had no antidote. It was a miracle that the Skripals had survived.

As they approached the roundabout, the embassy car turned north.

Gordon gestured toward it. "And two of the three Unit 29155 officers responsible for the attack in Salisbury, go free to poison anyone they want, anywhere they want. Even back to their comrades where they're celebrated as heroes."

Beta pulled the karambit from her boot and opened and closed it one-handed. The action soothed the burn that had risen in her chest thinking about the Skripal woman, Yulia, whom she'd seen collapsed on a park bench, the whites of her eyes showing and foaming at the mouth. Her father had been the ex-spy, not her. Yulia was just collateral damage.

Gordon glanced at her before saying, "These bastards need to know that they're not invincible. That's why I recruited you, Beta. I think you're just the candidate for tutoring our friends in a little rough international justice."

Something thrummed in Beta's chest at his words. She recognized it as a chord of dark joy. She didn't let it show, however. Just kept sliding the karambit blade into and out of the handle, smoothly and quickly. She missed practicing with her chain whip. She couldn't remember anything about the mission when it was destroyed. Nothing but flames leaping around her. Intense heat. And burning pain as she'd never felt before. The scar in her torso throbbed at the memory.

"What are you suggesting?" she asked.

Snick, snick went the vicious little hooked blade.

Gordon smiled. He reached out and touched the cut on Beta's cheek. She didn't need a mirror to see that it had already healed into a thin scab. And the puffiness from the blow had already disappeared. She healed extremely fast.

"I think our friend Petrov took an interest in you," he said. "Or at least an interest in paying you back. I somehow doubt *his* cheek has healed as quickly as yours."

Beta smiled to herself and transferred the karambit to her left hand. Where the small knife was concerned, she was fully ambidextrous.

"He will not mistake me for an easy target again." Her smile faded. "But as you already know, I have orders where Boshirov and Petrov are concerned."

"Those can be accommodated. After all, where best to get the information you need, except, as we say in the States, from the horse's mouth?" He grinned.

They turned west onto Ovenecká Street in time to see the embassy car get off at Coronation Street. Gordon took the right as well, but when the embassy car took the next right at Wolkerova he continued on. At this time of day, there was little traffic, and no way to hide their approach to the Russian embassy.

"What I do not understand," Beta said after several moments, "is how you would have approached me if URNA had not raided the club and taken Boshirov and Petrov into custody."

"Hm," Gordon said, letting a smile play at the corners of his mouth. "Do you really think two of Unit 29155's most decorated officers would risk drawing attention in a busy public place?"

Now it was Beta's turn to let her lips curl a little. "I see." She touched her hair. She'd pulled it back into a clip, but it was still sticky from the beer that she'd "styled" it with at the club. "I will need to prepare for my date with Petrov."

"Certainly," Gordon said.

Beta didn't see the otherworldly gleam that lit Gordon's eyes or notice the odd, harsh hum that emanated from him.

FOUR

By the time Beta realized that she'd picked up a tail, it was too late. She'd already entered her apartment building and gotten onto the elevator when a large hand thrust between the closing doors. They slid apart to reveal the large male from the terrace of The Duplex, a scowl darkening his already stern features. Despite herself, she retreated until her back touched the rear of the elevator. Her pulse quickened, and her temperature spiked. Her fingertips strayed to the top of her boot.

It got worse.

Said male stepped into the elevator as lightly as a stalking predator, but the elevator swayed from his weight nonetheless.

And then he'd trapped her inside the hot cage of his powerful arms. His dark-blue gaze pinned her. Worse, the scent of smoky balsam made her light-headed.

The door slid shut, and the elevator began to move.

Beta swallowed hard. She'd never been caught unaware like this before.

A long moment passed in which his heavy gaze never left her face. When he spoke, she expected his voice to be rough. Instead, it sounded like rich velvet. She heard a puzzling mix of fury and yearning in its tone.

"Gomba."

Mushroom? The way he said the Hungarian word sounded like an endearment. A memory stirred like a leaf in a slight breeze. She ignored it.

"Whoever you are," she hissed, "I suggest you take a step back."

She'd managed to pull the karambit from its hidden sheath and now pressed its wicked hook into his thigh near the femoral artery.

The male's eyes widened. Beta got the perplexing idea that they'd done so at her words and not her actions. Why?

She had no time to consider the undercurrents swirling about them because he hadn't moved.

"Whoever I am?" he asked. Now the fury dominated. Something sparked in the deep-blue gaze. She smelled smoke.

And then the stranger did something so unexpected it stole Beta's breath and all rational thought.

He leaned in and kissed her. It was as tender as his voice and gaze were hard.

Beta's lids drifted closed even as she stilled. His firm lips coaxed hers to soften and part, and then he pressed his advantage to encourage them to open farther. Images flashed behind her eyelids, swirling galaxies of stars and infinite deep blue space. She heard crystalline music. Something in her chest vibrated in response as though it were a tuning fork. She sighed and relaxed into him.

The elevator dinged and halted.

He stepped away, leaving Beta bereft and dazed. And inexplicably cold.

"You should watch what you do with this. Someone might get badly hurt." He smiled. His eyes stayed hard.

Shocked, Beta saw that he held her karambit up by one finger in the safety loop. He slid it closed as though familiar with its unique mechanism. Blinking, she looked at him as the elevator door slid open.

She swallowed, gathering her thoughts from where they'd scattered, and stiffened her spine. Even as she spoke, she analyzed the situation for an opportunity to respond. Something told her that she didn't have many options.

Still it didn't pay to project weakness.

"You should watch who you kiss. Or you may find that she is not so easily disarmed."

Then she turned and strode out of the elevator. He followed with his heat and bulk pressed against her. Beta whirled, her flat hand launching into his throat, catching the side against the hard edge between her thumb and forefinger. It was like striking a small tree trunk. He choked and bent, a hand instinctively coming up to his neck. Instead of following up with another blow, she danced back. As she'd anticipated, the giant didn't react to her attack.

He also hadn't dropped her karambit.

She *really* wished that she had her chain whip right now.

He straightened and narrowed his eyes. Then he smiled. "I'm well aware that you have other weapons, Beta. Just as you're well aware that I won't hurt you."

Her insides turned to water. How did he know her name?

More importantly, how *did* she know that he wouldn't hurt her?

She drew her shoulders back and let her chin rise. "You keep talking as if we know each other."

He tilted his head, studying her. After a moment she experienced the oddest sensation, as though invisible fingers ran down her back before warmly caressing her face and jaw. From the intent way that he watched her, she knew that he was somehow responsible for the unseen caresses. That was enough to send fury and terror shrieking through her.

The scent of smoke, the heat rolling off of him ... this giant was *not* a mere man. He was also a *drak*. A dragon. A *giant* dragon.

She tightened her lips. The gentle stroking turned into a jarring vibration that set her teeth on edge. From somewhere far off the faint tinkle of broken glass ended with a dull cymbal crash.

The giant's eyes widened. The inharmonious sounds faded.

"We did know each other. In another lifetime, it seems," he said.

Voices came from the apartment next to them.

He held out her karambit. "Invite me into your apartment, and we can discuss this further."

Beta resisted snatching the knife from his paw. Instead, she accepted it, its weight reassuring on her palm. But even if she'd wanted to use the karambit against him, she knew it would do no good. Wickedly curved though it was, the blade was too short to strike anything vital. And there was no way she'd get near his throat or his femoral artery again.

"Invite me, Gomba, or I'll carry you inside." His voice was pleasant, but his eyes had hardened to pure lapis lazuli. "Don't worry. I know which one is yours. I won't burst in on one of your neighbors."

Beta sucked in a harsh breath, and, spinning on her heel, hurried down the hall toward her apartment. He waited while she unlocked the door, leaning on the wall and watching. His predatory gaze made her nervous, but she kept her hands steady through sheer will.

She entered without saying a word.

Though spartan in its furnishings, the studio apartment had always felt spacious. Not now. The enormous male specimen standing next to the bar facing her galley kitchen where she ate her granola and yogurt took up most of the space and almost all of the oxygen.

A sharp pain stabbed her right eye, nearly blinding her.

Suddenly she was exhausted. It had been a long night. And she still had so much to do.

"Sit," she said, gesturing to one of the stools under the bar.

He sat, his massive glutes engulfing the seat and his broad thighs making the stool's legs look like toothpicks.

He wore the black tactical pants and black T-shirt she'd first seen him in at The Duplex, but instead of exhaustion from a long night, he radiated controlled power and vitality.

She still had beer in her hair.

Peevishness swept through Beta. Turning toward her espresso maker, she began making two espressos. She could feel the giant male's gaze on her back. On her *ass*. It didn't bother her as much as it should, which irritated her even more.

Pivoting, she brought an espresso to him and turned back for the sugar bowl. She didn't know how she knew, but she knew he had a sweet tooth. She set that in front of him as well.

"I do not have much for breakfast. Yogurt and granola." She shrugged at the gleam in his eyes. "You will forgive me if I do not offer to share."

To her consternation, he ignored the sugar bowl and picked up the tiny espresso cup, his large fingers graceful for all of their size. The demitasse cup looked ridiculous in his hand.

She'd rather not play the reluctant host, but she needed an espresso. And a shower. But that had to wait. Taking her cup up, she sipped the bitter hot liquid. Its familiar burn helped her get a handle on the rising heat in her core. She compressed it into a fiery ball, not examining the complex reaction she had to this male.

"No need to sigh, Gomba. This won't take long."

Beta shot him a sharp glance. "Why do you keep calling me *mushroom*?"

It was his turn to shrug. "You remind me of cat I had when I was a boy. I called her Gomba."

She set her empty cup down and folded her arms. "You claim we have met before, but I cannot recall you or your name." She lifted her chin in command. "Tell me who you are and how you know me."

He crossed his arms in imitation of her before leaning back on the stool, which creaked.

"The first is easy to answer: I am András Nagy. The second is not so easy." He paused. "Does my name sound at all familiar?"

There was that invisible rubbing again, this time along her shoulder and down her arm.

Beta wanted to arch into it. It felt *so* good.

Instead, she dropped her arms and widened her stance. The gentle rubbing transformed into irregular grating as though something sloughed her skin off. She gritted her teeth and hissed through them. The headache bloomed through her entire head, blinding her for a moment.

The foreign vibration halted abruptly.

"I'm sorry," András said in a low voice, concern softening his gaze.

That also felt good.

Which infuriated her.

András continued before she could tell him that she'd had enough and to get out. "We met almost four years ago on an operation in Vienna." He watched her closely as he spoke.

"Vienna?" Beta's curiosity got the better of her. That and a faint ring of familiarity to his words. "What was I doing in Vienna?"

"You came to support your friend Olivia Markham."

A clang resounded—entirely inside her head. Wincing, Beta threw a hand to her temple.

András was at her side in an instant. In fact, he'd moved so swiftly she hadn't seen him—which would have alarmed her if she could have formed a coherent thought. He slipped an arm around her shoulders and urged her to walk into the small sitting area next to her bed. When she would have resisted, he shushed her and hummed. He eased her into a chair before kneeling and removing her thigh boots. Then he massaged her feet.

Beta closed her eyes and focused on the stranger's hands and what he was doing to her. She felt every press of his fingertips on her soles, the warm, firm stroking over her arches, the light tug on her toes. When his palms wrapped around her calves and began kneading, she let out a small moan. On some level, she recognized his touch.

That thought caused her to sit upright and frown.

András, who'd apparently been watching her face, sat back on his heels and dropped his hands to his thighs.

"You have a scar on your lower right flank from a knife wound," he said.

Beta's mouth dropped open, and her hand flew to the spot.

"I was there when it happened three years ago." He spoke quietly, his gaze trained on her.

Confusion filled her. Large amounts of time prior to the current mission had faded from her memory. Since it hadn't compromised her legend as Marika Hubová—in fact, it had made it exceedingly easy to maintain her cover identity—she had consciously decided to ignore the memory loss.

Intuition told her that *she'd* blocked whatever it was that was missing. She didn't want to remember. Even now there was a painful prickling along her spine warning her to leave it alone.

She wanted to ask this giant man with the gentle hands if they'd been lovers.

"Did you follow me to The Duplex?" she asked instead.

Bright early morning sun entered the window behind András, leaving his face in shadow, but not before Beta glimpsed fleeting disappointment. She wondered if he'd known the question she hadn't dared ask. If so, doubly critical not to ask it.

"No," he said, shaking his head. Her eyes played tricks on her then because she imagined that dark waves swept his forehead at the movement.

That was insane. His short haircut and the tactical clothes telegraphed special forces. But that didn't match her admittedly vague sense of the man. Warrior, yes. Hungarian soldier, no.

Mercenary? That would certainly explain why she'd cut off contact.

But what could she ask him that wouldn't give away critical operation details? And what *did* he already know about her?

Fear spiked. What if she'd buried knowledge about this András Nagy before she went on her current mission, confident that he'd never find her? That was the only way she could explain knowingly putting herself in the dark.

She'd never thought to see him again.

The truth of that realization hit her like a tank. Followed closely on its heels with a grief so sharp it slipped inside her ribcage and plunged again into her unhealed heart.

And just as swiftly another hard truth echoed in her thoughts: *You must have had an insurmountable reason.*

Looking at András's chiseled features, the dark expressive brows over eyes that surely read all of her chaotic thoughts, Beta knew that she'd been so desperate to forget him that she'd tapped into her dragon nature somehow. Her dragon nature had saved her more than once.

When she'd been quiet for several long moments, András closed the gap between them to run a thumb across her injured cheek. "One of the Russians gave this to you." It was a statement, not a question. "Which one? Boshirov or Petrov?"

He knew. How? Beta didn't have time to figure out this new player in the game or even begin to guess what it meant. Perhaps he worked in Hungarian intelligence and not as a private military contractor.

"Why do you want to know?" she asked. She could hear the wariness in her voice.

"Because I'm going to beat him senseless." He said this so calmly it took Beta a moment to understand.

She sighed to herself. That's all she needed. A jealous interloper inserting himself into her operation. One that had already grown more complicated with Gordon's revelation and invitation to join *his* mission.

"Never mind which one."

She stood abruptly, forcing András to lean back. Even kneeling, his face was almost level with hers. Before she could meet his gaze, dizziness overcame her. She wobbled, reaching out and grabbing him to stay on her feet. Or trying to grab him. Her hand couldn't find purchase on the solid muscle in his upper arm, whose diameter was too large for her to wrap her fingers around. András caught her around the waist as her hand slid up to the top of his shoulder.

Dobrý bože! Good lord! The man was a *beast*. Large, hard, and hot.

Beta almost giggled at where her thoughts went after that. She clamped down on her reaction, narrowing her eyes at him instead. She swayed as another wave of dizziness washed over her. If she weren't so tired and stressed, this wouldn't be happening.

"You need to rest, Gomba."

"I need a shower, some breakfast, and headache medicine," she said through gritted teeth. "And for the uninvited intruder in my apartment to leave. Now."

He growled.

No, he did *not* just growl.

She stiffened, ready to elbow strike him in the throat and free herself. Well, a lightning elbow strike followed by a fast eye gouge and a vicious knee to the groin might work.

Those dark-blue eyes warned her not to try that. "You have a mild concussion. Your mission will have to wait. Our conversation will also wait."

Beta inhaled and regretted it. András smelled like smoky balsam with enticing hints of black currant and magnolia. His unique cologne made her woozy without the concussion. Why couldn't he smell like musk and sweat, as most of the men she encountered did? It was hard enough to think with his hand on her waist and his incredible chest inches from her own.

She shook her head and shoved that chest. Agh! That hurt. "I cannot afford to rest."

András released her waist but didn't draw away. "I'll tail Boshirov and Petrov for you." When she would have objected, he raised a large finger to her lips. "Don't worry. I'm trained, and I don't need to know the details of your mission."

She narrowed her eyes. He dropped his finger from her lips an instant before she could snap at it. "Why would you help me?"

András's gaze hardened. "Don't think of it as helping. Think of it as making sure you recover faster so that we can continue getting reacquainted. Besides," he shrugged, "I need to determine which of them deserves a beating."

His voice rang with truth. And subtle authority. She had no doubt that he meant what he said. She would just have to make sure that she stayed one step ahead. The first step would be to get rid of him. The second would be to use VZ resources to research András Nagy, if that was in fact his real name.

She hadn't planned to surveil Boshirov and Petrov anyway. Gordon had already contacted them for a follow-up meeting for later in the week when the furor over the URNA raid had calmed. Let this András waste time surveilling them. It would keep him out of the way until she could figure out how to deal with him.

Beta blinked and sniffed before returning his hard gaze with one of her own. "So be it. I am too exhausted to argue with you. Now please leave. You are stinking up my apartment like a big Hungarian bull."

He shocked her by laughing. "Of course, I am, Gomba. And you smell like beer." He winked as she bristled. "I will go, but only after I see you eat something. You're still a scrawny axe handle, all bones and no beef and potatoes."

This time when András smiled, it reached his eyes and brought dimples out in his cheeks, knocking Beta's breath from her chest. For a frozen moment in time, she remembered that expression. Then he got to his feet and reached out a hand to her. Bemused, she took it and followed him toward the tiny galley kitchen. He opened her refrigerator as she sat.

"You weren't teasing," he said as he looked at the mostly empty shelves. "You literally have no food here." He looked back at her, his expression darkening. "What do you live on? Air and Trebitsch?"

Beta started. He'd named her favorite Czech whiskey.

"And espresso," she added, watching him pull out a small container of yogurt and some raspberries.

András opened a cupboard where there were a few cans, boxes, and bags.

"Ah! You've been keeping something back from me!" He pulled out the unopened bag of *krupička*, or coarse semolina, stored there. "I will make *kaše* for you."

He replaced the yogurt and berries before pulling out milk, butter, salt, and a small pan and wire whisk. Beta watched as he expertly measured out the ingredients, whisking the semolina and salt with the milk as they heated over the stove. Then he transferred the porridge to a small bowl before sprinkling a blend of cocoa and sugar on top and layering several thick slices of butter over that.

"Eat," he said as he set the steaming dish in front of her with a spoon. "Or do you need something more with your *krupicová kaše*? Cinnamon? Honey? Raisins? Raspberries?"

Beta ignored him and picked up her spoon. It had been months since she'd indulged in her favorite breakfast. Fast though it was to make, *kaše* still took more time than opening a yogurt container and popping handfuls of berries and granola in her mouth while she ate. She was going to savor this as best she could while the big oaf hovered over her.

Pools of butter formed in the center of the crystalline sugar-cocoa mix, sending dark rivulets toward the edge of the bowl. Beta dipped her spoon on the side of the porridge and began eating tiny bites without stirring the topping into it.

"I see you are from the camp that eats in a circular motion, outside to center," András said, leaning against the far counter with his arms crossed.

She shrugged and touched the tip of her tongue to the corner of her mouth where she felt a few sugar grains. András's predatory gaze tracked the movement. Heat rose in her. Her breasts firmed, her nipples peaking. Thankfully she wore a lined red blazer over her black-sequined tank. All those layers of fabric would keep her body's response hidden.

She scooped another spoonful, this time getting a large mouthful of sugar, butter, and cocoa with the semolina. "And you no doubt dive right in without tasting anything," she said before eating it.

"Hm, I beg to differ," he said, shaking his head slowly as she inhaled and closed her eyes when the porridge hit her tongue. "Maybe once, but no more. Something may look sweet and filling only to burn the tongue so badly nothing tastes good for a long time afterwards."

Innuendo and warning sharpened his observation. Tension filled the air between them. And her headache spiked again.

Setting down her spoon despite the unfinished *kaše*, Beta stood. "Satisfied? You saw me eat something. Will you now go?"

András tilted his head, studying her. After a moment, he dropped his arms to his side and, straightening, nodded. "I'll go. I'll return this evening with an update on your friends Boshirov and Petrov. In the meantime, rest. And Beta?" He paused, holding her gaze. "No Trebitsch. Water or juice only."

She didn't respond. Instead, she watched as he left her apartment. Then she darted forward and locked both sets of locks behind him.

When she looked around the studio, it suddenly seemed much larger.

Then she sat and finished the *kaše*, whose warm temperature was just right and whose flavors melded perfectly on her tongue.

András waited until the series of clicks told him that Beta had locked the door behind him. As he walked toward the elevator, he called Miles.

"Go for Aerie Two."

"Aerie Two, this is Giant. I just texted you an image of a male I found outside URNA this morning when the Russians were released. Can you confirm that he's the same individual brought in with Boshirov and Petrov?"

"One moment." Thirty seconds later, Miles said, "Confirmed. URNA brought in an American named Drew Gordon. According to their intake report, Gordon and the female escort were both at the scene being held at gunpoint by Boshirov and Petrov. I haven't had any luck digging up any more intel on the female other than witnesses saw her with the Russians prior to the URNA raid and that the URNA officers on scene took her for a local."

"I tracked her to her apartment," András said. "I'll report back in person about what I found. When will Dragon Man and the Harlequin be there for debriefing?"

"Team leaders are scheduled to return at 1300. I've orders not to disturb them unless a legion of *daemonia* and a host of Dark *Irim* descend on Prague."

"Copy that. Can you contact your CIA sources about Gordon?"

"Got a feeling he's not an innocent bystander?" Miles sounded amused.

"Not even close," András said.

"Well, then you'd should know that I had a hunch about the weapon both Russians carried."

"And?"

"I was right. The GSh-18 Tactical handgun is a semi-automatic primarily used by Russian military and law enforcement."

"That explains the speedy visit to get Boshirov and Petrov released from Czech custody."

"Indeed. It also helps me target my research efforts."

András exited Beta's apartment building. He'd been stunned to find that she'd kept the same apartment. He'd set an angelic sensor keyed to her harmonic signature to alert him when she returned. It hadn't.

Meaning her harmonic signature had changed.

"Aerie Two, I'm heading in for a shower, food, and nap."

"Copy that. You might want to arrive at the TOC before team leaders get here. Blackbird has been waiting."

"*A fenébe is!*" András swore. He'd all but forgotten about the composite image of the *daemon Elioud* that Mihàil had ordered him to work on with Miró. "Tell Blackbird I'll be there at 1200."

"Affirmative."

Sighing, András sped his harmonics and disappeared from human sight.

He'd learned several important things in the last hour.

First, Beta's memory had been altered by an *Elioud* or *Irim*. Unbelievable as it seemed, she didn't remember him. Or more precisely, she remembered only submerged fragments. The good news: Beta might not remember him, but her body certainly did. He'd read every blaze of desire in her infrared signature and every time her harmonics had synced with his.

The bad news? Every time they'd synced, discord wrenched them apart almost immediately.

They were in disharmony.

Second, Beta already had plans where Boshirov and Petrov were concerned. She didn't need him to surveil them. She'd agreed simply to occupy him.

And third, Drew Gordon, her apparent partner, was the Dark *Irim* from The Duplex.

FIVE

When András entered the main room on the first floor of the team apartment overlooking the Vltava River, he found Miró and Miles seated on the leather sectional having a break. Miles, fully human, looked tired. Miró, on the other hand, had never looked better. He and Stasia would celebrate their third wedding anniversary in a couple of weeks. Ever since the couple had worked out their differences and gotten married, conjoining their *Elioud* nature, Miró radiated a vitality that made András envious.

He backtracked to the coffee station in the front hall. He could use a cappuccino. And a moment to stabilize his harmonics. Or try to anyway.

Returning with his cup, he remained standing. Though he'd only gotten a few hours of sleep, he felt restless.

Miró acknowledged András with a nod.

Miles ran a hand down his face before rising to his feet. "Back to work," he said. "Just let me get another cup of coffee."

While he was out of the room, Miró studied András. András had known the Croat almost as long as he knew Mihàil. However, while the *drangùe* had been a father to him, Miró had been the elder brother. He was the one who sparred with András during long, grueling hours in the gym, made sure he completed his academic lessons, and helped him navigate the complex social reality of being an *Elioud* among humans. And that was without taking into account Miró's *Elioud* status as a truthseeker. If anyone was going to discern András's conflicted state, it would be Miró.

András had no interest in bonding with his brother at the moment.

"I need new earwigs," he said to forestall any questions. "I blew the harmonics on mine out when I dispatched the *daemon Elioud* earlier."

Miró acknowledged this with a chin dip. "Your thermosensors are still collecting only eighty percent of your maximum output."

What Miró didn't say hung in the air between them. And that was this: why was András running so much colder now? András had never told the other *Elioud* that the surgeon had missed tiny bullet fragments next to his spine or that they pained him. Mihàil would want to remove these grains of metal, heating them himself when András failed. And Miró would want to test the material to determine whether the *bogomili* had used ammunition consecrated by Asmodeus.

András had been stabbed more than once by a consecrated *subulam*, the icepick-like dagger that the *bogomili* wielded. He'd know if the bits of bullet next to his spine poisoned him on a spiritual level. Removing them would only raise other questions that he didn't want to confront, especially as he had a pretty good idea what the answer was.

And constant physical pain distracted him.

Miles strolled back into the main room. Yawning, he ran a hand through his hair before sipping from his cup. Then he stretched, sighed, and moved into the smaller room next to the living room where a large monitor dominated a long wall. A long table with office chairs and laptops served as a desk. As András and Miró followed him into the TOC, Miles sat down at a clear space and pulled a large tablet and stylus towards him.

Miles looked back at them. "Let's hit it. I want to have at least a basic sketch ready for Olivia and Mihàil when they get here in an hour."

Miró sat on the other side of the former operative, who'd been trained on software used by the CIA and other law enforcement agencies. Among other restricted tools not available on the open market, Miles had stolen a copy of proprietary facial composite software and installed it in Mihàil's system. Miró, their resident tech expert, always took advantage of the opportunity to learn new tools.

András leaned against the doorframe.

"Okay, I've already added the basics about the *daemon Elioud*'s appearance that you told Miró and the others this morning: European white male from the late 19th century to about World War One given the clothing and medals."

On the screen behind Miles appeared a realistic black-and-white photo of a middle-aged male with thick, wavy dark hair, muttonchops, and a luxuriant walrus mustache. To the side of the face appeared a menu of features to specify when creating the sketch.

Miles looked at András. "How's that for a start?"

András nodded. "Not bad. But he was older with white hair and balding on top."

Miles adjusted the hairline and hair color before looking at András.

"No beard, and the mustache was trimmed in a more modern style, except for the ends made little wings."

"Like a variant of the handlebar?" Miles asked, modifying the mustache.

"A little sharper on the ends, but not points. And make it and the eyebrows black."

For the next hour, András directed changes to the shape of the face, eyes, nose, and mouth of the mystery *daemon Elioud*. After a few minutes doing so, his restlessness abated at the need to focus, and he took a seat next to Miles. He'd just recalled that the *daemon Elioud* had a cleft chin when Mihàil and Olivia entered the TOC. The *drangùe* and *zonjë* had purchased the entire building and taken the top two floors as their apartment. While András, Miles, and Miró stayed in the lower apartment, it also functioned as a general meeting place for the team.

"Rather reminds me of an Austro-Hungarian mustache from the late empire," Mihàil said as they halted behind Miles. "Not as ostentatious as Archduke Franz Ferdinand's, but that would not have been appropriate."

Olivia swiveled to study his face, her brow furrowed. "I don't see it."

Mihàil looked back at her, humor in his gaze. "What? Me wearing a mustache? I assure you, *dashuria ime*, I did. And cut my hair only once every three months." He laughed at the horrified look she gave him.

Miró said, "All the ladies found him rather dashing, my lady."

"Except for when they tried to run their fingers through my hair," Mihàil said. At Olivia's questioning look, he explained. "All that pomade."

"Made first from bear fat and then either petroleum jelly or beeswax," Miró said, smiling at his general's wife.

Miles joined in laughing at Olivia's wrinkled nose, but András only waited, his harmonics tightening.

Mihàil squeezed Olivia's upper arm before turning to his impatient lieutenant. "Given all the evidence, our *daemon Elioud* is either a German or Austrian active during the Imperial era. As an *Elioud*, he would have moved in society, so there is a very good chance that a photograph exists."

Then he turned to the other team members. "Miró, research our archives. Whoever this *Elioud* was, I did not run into him in a ballroom or a battlefield, but there are other places that he earned imperial notice. Miles, any information on the anonymous call about the active shooter last night?"

Miles swiveled to face the *drangùe* and Olivia. "URNA traced it back to the club."

"So the caller was inside," said Olivia.

"Perhaps Asmodeus himself called," said Miró. "Or the other Dark *Irim*."

At Asmodeus's name, a thrum of tension set the group's harmonics vibrating. András's own harmonics tightened even further, pulling at the otherwise balanced dynamics among them. He stood and walked toward the French doors opening onto a terrace where he looked out at the daylight with unseeing eyes.

"Not another Dark *Irim*," he said into the tense silence. "Beta."

A small harmonic storm swirled around them. András didn't turn around, but he read the shifting heat signatures. Everyone looked at him, but only Mihàil spoke.

"The female casualty." When András nodded in response, the *drangùe* continued. "She was with Boshirov and Petrov."

"So she's Dark then," said Olivia, regret and sorrow tinging her voice.

András shook his head. "Not entirely."

He turned around. Miles leaned back from the tablet, one hand propping his chin, watching the others. The man looked like he'd plumbed the dregs of his energy, but his sharp gaze confirmed that he knew how significant this news was. Miró's impassive face conveyed nothing, but András knew the other *Elioud* read more than he intended to share.

"You tracked her last night." Mihàil's eyes narrowed.

Olivia came over to András, laying her hand on his forearm. Warm harmonic caresses stroked up his arm and across his forehead. He closed his eyes for a moment as the tension left his neck and shoulders.

"You saw her." It was a statement so filled with understanding that András almost staggered.

From the first moment that he'd met Olivia during the attack on the Vienna Music Festival four years before, she'd won his admiration with her bravery, her loyalty, and her open affection for her friends—and for him. She'd gone out of her way to make sure that when she and Mihàil married she became a member of their team, befriending András and Miró. In his case, she'd learned to bake all of his favorite breads and pastries. He loved her for it.

Now Olivia would ask hard questions about the woman who'd broken her heart as well as his. András turned from her and the others. Olivia let her hand drop.

When he spoke, his voice was flat and hard. "I tracked her after I discovered her surveilling URNA headquarters. She wasn't alone."

"Asmodeus?" Mihàil's sharp voice could have cut glass. András actually saw a crack form in the French door in front of him.

He nodded. Silence reigned for a long moment. At last he swallowed around the thickness in his throat.

"I confronted her at her apartment. Her harmonics responded to mine. Temporarily."

András leaned his head on the glass of the French door, remembering the pure bliss of those few moments.

"What did she say about why she left?" asked Olivia.

"She didn't." He stood and squared his shoulders. "Asmodeus altered her memory. She doesn't remember me or you."

"Then all is not lost," said Miró.

András slowly turned back. His heart beat so hard he was sure the others heard it.

Mihàil now stood behind him and held his gaze. "If Beta responded to you, then Asmodeus's hold on her memory is imperfect. And that, my friend"—here he put his hand on András's shoulder—"is a testament to Beta's will and the bond between you. It is no small victory to keep a Dark *Irim* at bay for so long when she has never been fully apprised of her gifts or how to use them."

András nodded, bolstered by the *drangùe*'s conviction.

"I'm relieved to hear you say that, my lord," he said formally. "Because nothing and no one will prevent me from winning her away from him."

Beta surprised herself by how much it felt like coming home to be back in Prague. She'd never been particularly happy here, especially in the Old Town.

Maybe that's because she and this ancient city had so much in common.

She looked out the windows of the 26 tram as it crossed the Vltava at the city of her birth. The red roofs and beguiling mix of architecture from the Romanesque to the Rococo gave the impression she was entering a dark fairytale. Which made a lot of sense, given its history of intertwined mysticism and violence.

For thousands of years, people had lived along the Vltava, but Prague only became Prague when the first Czech prince built the castle atop the hill at the end of the ninth century. In the fourteenth century, Prague reached its apex. The Holy Roman emperor became King of Bohemia, the historic Czech lands. Under his dynasty, Prague not only became the capital of the empire, it was one of Europe's largest and wealthiest cities. The first university in Central Europe was established.

And then, like the fairytale of the sleeping princess, Prague fell under a dark spell.

Strife arose between brother and cousin, father and son, about what they should believe about God and redemption, salvation and grace. One faction tossed people out of windows and historical monuments were destroyed, the castle damaged.

The dark spell lifted for a hundred years. The Habsburg dynasty ruled, rebuilding the castle. Prague became a center of science and its dark twin, alchemy. After a fire, the Castle District and Lesser Town were rebuilt.

And then the darkness returned with vengeance. Religious animosity roared to life like a conflagration from long banked embers. More religious adversaries were again tossed out of windows, this time at Prague Castle in 1618. A word was coined from Latin for this very Czech method: defenestration.

And so the Bohemian Revolt started, leading to the Thirty Years' War which engulfed most of Europe, killing millions. Prague itself shrunk by more than half.

And the dark spell strengthened.

By now the city had become known as "Magic Prague." And the legendary Golem, a supernatural warrior born of the Jewish people's need for protection from pogroms and unpredictable Czech rulers, captured the city's imagination.

At the thought of Prague's Golem, a giant animated from Vltava river clay, painful prickles ran down Beta's neck and across her upper back. Was it superstition? Or was it something more? After all, the Slavic peoples had their own legends of supernatural protectors. Benevolent dragons and heroes born of the union between humans and them.

She'd always believed in these stories.

In fact, she'd pretended since childhood that she was the daughter of a dragon, a *dcera draka*. Better that than the daughter of a rapist.

Or she thought she'd pretended.

But the last time she'd lived in Prague she'd recognized that she had dragon traits. Like the ability to see thermal signatures. And there was the fact that her own body temperature ran hot—so hot that she'd always had to fake results for routine medical exams (she was never sick). Oh, and she sometimes exuded smoke.

The giant Hungarian had also been hot and smoky. A *drak*.

She shivered at the memory of his body imprisoning hers on the elevator, the intense blue of his gaze pinned on her.

More painful prickles vibrated through her. Beta shook her hands and rolled her head. It didn't help. It felt like her entire body had fallen asleep, and now all the muscles were waking up. As the 26 tram eased into the Republic Square stop, she stood and shrugged her shoulders. As she moved into the square, another passenger brushed against her arm. Electricity surged through her as if she'd been hit by lightning.

Or cast under a dark spell.

Beta halted and stared after the broad shoulders and white-blond hair. There was something familiar about him ... then she recalled the Viking at The Duplex. The memory of brilliant blue eyes reflected back at her sent terror rolling down her spine. She stiffened, widening her stance and pushing her heels into the pavement as she resisted whatever was rolling through her.

It didn't work.

In shock she realized that only moments before on the tram she'd remembered living in Prague before her deep-cover mission. Worse, as the electricity subsided, memories trickled through whatever block she'd put in her mind.

So Beta stood in Republic Square in broad daylight, frozen as she relived making love to András Nagy.

She padded down a silent hallway in the middle of the night, her dragon vision lighting the way. When she reached his door, she paused for a moment, hand on lever and forehead resting against the cool wood.

Her dragon senses heard his soft, even breathing in the room beyond. His infrared signature dominated the otherwise deep blue of the inanimate objects around him. She knew that signature as well as her own. Where her slender white core hid like a shining seed pearl among thin bands of yellow, orange, and magenta, András's core blazed like a white dwarf star. Brilliant yellow and orange encased it with only his outline in deep red.

Breathing in to steady a racing heartbeat, she pushed the lever down. The door opened with a soft *snick*, loud in the otherwise quiet room. András stirred as she shut the door with the finality of a *click*.

"Gomba?" he asked, looking toward her.

She came to him, the air suddenly chilly against her overheated skin. When she raised the sheet that covered his naked body, she realized that she too was naked. Her heart jumped like a swallow caught in a cage, but she slid in next to András, whose arms enclosed her. He pulled her against his hard, hot length, running one large hand down her back before cupping her buttock. Their legs entwined, she raised her arms to encircle his neck. He groaned. In the dark, she couldn't discern where his infrared signature ended and hers began.

András started to speak. She pressed a finger against his lips.

"Sh, *spratek*," she said.

Brat. She'd called him brat.

"*Dobrý?*" asked a female voice a meter from her.

Beta blinked and focused on the concerned face of a Czech police officer. The bright sun of a Czech afternoon dispersed the uncanny image that had captured her.

"*Dobrý?*" The officer again asked if everything was okay.

Startled, Beta couldn't speak for a hard heartbeat. Then reality crashed over her. She'd drawn notice while on her way to a clandestine meet. She'd never done that before.

Swallowing, she nodded. "*Je mi dobře.*"

A skeptical expression captured the woman's face. She took a step toward Beta.

Instinct took over. Beta let a sheepish look cross her features. She smiled a little at the same time. Whatever confusion she conveyed, it matched the turmoil inside her.

"I am fine," she repeated more strongly. "I encountered my ex-lover last night, and now he haunts my thoughts at bad moments."

The police officer studied Beta before nodding. The truth in Beta's voice worked. "Sleep with him again," she said. "Then you will either reconcile or forget him. Either way you will be unlikely to lose your wits when it endangers you."

Now it was Beta who nodded. "*Děkuji.* I will do as you recommend."

Then she strode away before the police officer could accept her thanks. She pulled her cellphone out and sent a text to her VZ handler, Major "Little Wolf" Vlcek. They'd planned to meet at the Museum of Communism, one of his personal favorite sites because he'd been among a network of students who'd brought about the Velvet Revolution ending communism in 1989. Best to switch to the backup site.

Havel's Market in five, she typed.

The nearby street market, also a favorite of Vlcek, had been around since 1232 but renamed after the Czech Republic's first president. Though originally it sold only fresh fruit and vegetables, the market now drew tourists in droves with its claim of being the oldest in Old Town. Somehow Beta doubted that the current version with its souvenirs prominently displayed among the brightly colored produce had anything in common with the medieval market except location.

But that didn't matter for their purposes. It was an ideal setting for a covert encounter. They'd be hidden in plain sight among the pedestrians moving among the stalls or entering the souvenir shops that lined the cobblestone street.

Beta hurried toward Havelská Street, where she strolled past the stalls featuring fruit and flowers, pretending to browse until she settled on a kiosk with souvenirs from the communist era. Vlcek took gleeful pleasure in seeing mock Red Army *ushanka* hats being sold next to decks of playing cards and marionettes.

She'd pulled one of the furred hats with its red star crest from a stack of hats of all varieties when her handler stepped under the awning. They were the only two shoppers.

"The anonymous tip on Boshirov and Petrov came from the club," he said without preamble.

Beta tried the hat on. "I know," she said without looking at him. "Gordon called it in."

She felt Vlcek stiffen before he picked up a set of coasters illustrated with Prague's medieval astronomical clock. "What is his game?" he asked.

She took the hat off and shrugged. She couldn't tell her handler that Gordon knew who she was or he'd pull her from the mission. "Another test for me. And a way to out the Russians. Now when we meet with them, he will demand more money not to sell to the Ukrainians."

Vlcek set the coasters back and picked up a small, brightly painted wooden carousel.

"That should both anger and impress them." He sounded impressed himself. "And give you a way in with the Russians, who will of course try to turn you against your employer. When did Gordon set the next meeting with Boshirov?"

"Thursday. Details are still being worked out. I think we may be taking a private Danube cruise."

"Smart." Again Vlcek sounded like he approved of Gordon's tactics.

Beta suspected that Little Wolf wouldn't have any problems with Gordon's plan to teach Boshirov and Petrov some rough justice, either. As long as the Czech Republic got the evidence it needed to tie Russia to the ammunition depot bombings, he wouldn't really care how she got it. That was one of the reasons the VZ had paired them: Major Vlcek had the surname meaning *little wolf*. Beta was known as a lone wolf. Together they'd formed a particularly effective hunting partnership.

Beta slid the furred winter hat back onto the pile of hats. "One more thing. Can you run the name of András Nagy for me? I think he is a mercenary. He has been making inquiries about Boshirov and Petrov."

Inquiries. Nice, Beta.

"I will leave it at the usual drop. This must be our last in-person meeting for some time. Follow protocol when signaling your reports. *Zlom vaz.*" After wishing her success, Vlcek took the carousel to the stall owner.

Beta slipped away while Little Wolf bought his pups a toy.

Six

The next time András Nagy approached her, Beta scented him first. Heady magnolia and sweet black currant followed by a smoky balsam teased her on the fresh air from the river.

Then her dragon sight identified his unique thermal signature.

Of course, by the time she'd recognized both of these signs, the giant Hungarian was already pulling a chair out from the table at which she was sitting. It was almost as if he'd appeared out of thin air. Perhaps he had. Maybe he had invisible dragon wings and could move faster than human sight.

Beta tucked that question away until she could consider it later.

András settled his large body into the chair across from hers. He overwhelmed the black steel frame, which looked fragile next to his massive shoulders and thighs. She could almost hear the metal groan. Dark sunglasses hid his magnetic blue eyes. Instead of black tactical clothing, today he wore a navy polo and light chinos. He could have passed for the handsome scion of a wealthy European family—if any of those had the genetics to breed a son two-and-a-half meters tall with the physique of an ancient Greek warrior.

"Dining al fresco at an Italian restaurant overlooking the Vltava?" His deep, rich voice matched the promise of his personal cologne. "I approve, Gomba."

Beta ignored him and picked up her glass of red wine, sipping it as she kept her gaze on the river.

The waiter hurried over with a menu and a water glass for András.

"Please bring me the same wine that she's drinking," said András to the waiter as he poured still water from the carafe on the table.

The man nodded.

After the waiter left, András continued his assessment of Beta's presence on the terrace at the Four Seasons Hotel. "But it can't be as simple as you following my advice to rest and eat, hm?"

She looked at him from the side of her eye. András sat with his elbows propped on either corner of the small square patio table, his hands steepled in front of him.

"Perhaps I was trying to hide from you," she said before returning her gaze to the view in front of her.

She sensed him smiling at that. Without confirming, she knew that dimples bracketed his generous mouth. A half-submerged memory of dipping a fingertip to those dimples surfaced.

"You've forgotten. You can't hide from me, Gomba."

Now Beta did look at her annoying stalker. "Apparently I did just that for three years."

András's swift mood change took her breath away and sent her heart tapping at its bone cage. First, he was grinning, and then he'd leaned into her space, his firm, full lips compressed into a harsh line.

"Not anymore," he said, low and furious. "Now I always know where you are."

Something niggled in the back of Beta's thoughts, but again, she didn't have time to analyze whatever it was. She needed to get rid of this interloper. He was seriously starting to interfere with her work. And the situation had only gotten more complicated since the URNA raid. She really needed to have all of her wits about her as the game heated up.

"Are you always going to show up uninvited then?" she asked, leaning toward him a fraction. She scowled. She sounded petulant even to her own ears. But she wouldn't back down.

Heat choked the air around them. Beta saw pinpricks of light sparkle in her peripheral vision. The scent of smoke grew.

Their waiter approached with András's wine, but when he got to the table, his eyes widened and the color drained from his face.

"Please," András said, leaning back and gesturing for the waiter to set the wineglass on the table. He never took his gaze from Beta, but the temperature dropped and the sparkles winked out.

After the waiter set the wineglass a little too hard onto the marble tabletop, sloshing the wine, he left without asking if they needed anything else.

"You can save me the trouble and invite me," András said.

Sleep with him again whispered the police officer's words. *You will be unlikely to lose your wits when it endangers you.*

Beta's heart raced, but this time it had nothing to do with anger or fear. Desire shot to her core so suddenly it shocked her. She shifted in her seat, uncomfortable at the fullness between her legs, and wrapped an arm around her midsection. Her fingers itched to pull her karambit from her jacket pocket.

As though he scented her reaction, András grinned and relaxed in his chair. His large white teeth under the dark lenses made him look like a celebrity. A soothing energy eased the tightness in her chest, and warm, invisible fingers brushed hair from her face.

"Stop that," she said. She picked up her wine and took a sip to hide the fact that she'd almost arched into that unseen caress. "Perhaps I *should* invite you to join me on my upcoming operation."

"The one in which you get closer to Boshirov and Petrov," he said, removing his sunglasses and laying them on the table. His deep-blue eyes glowed in the late afternoon sunlight.

They were dragon's eyes.

"Two of Mother Russia's finest assassins from GRU Unit 29155," he continued before drinking his wine. Fascinated, Beta watched the muscles move in his throat. "Otherwise known as the thugs of Russian intelligence, tasked with wet work and sabotage. You would be wise to invite me to cover your back."

"How do I know that I can trust you?" Beta asked, stalling. She was already trying to work a scenario in which she could kill two flies with one stone: clear her system of this stultifying desire and control the Hungarian's access to her.

András responded with a question of his own. "How do you know that you can trust Drew Gordon?"

A sakra. And damn. She should have anticipated that he'd know about the American arms dealer. She dropped her hand from the stem of her wineglass into her pocket where she could hold the karambit against her palm.

She stared at András. At last, she shrugged and said, "I trust that he can get me close to Boshirov and Petrov. If you are the operative you appear to be, you already know this." Narrowing her eyes, she held his gaze. "I repeat: why should I trust you?"

An emotion winged across his face too quickly for her to interpret. Instead of responding with heat, it was his turn to shrug. "We've had this conversation before, Gomba. You trusted me to lead you to the men who killed your friend Andrej and gravely wounded Eliska, his partner."

Something clanged inside her head. *Andrej and Eliska.* Beta remembered them. They'd all been recruited to military intelligence around the same time. Sharp pain threatened to crack her skull like a hardboiled egg. Wincing, she raised her free hand to her temple.

András waited while Beta massaged her head. Perversely, she wished that he was the one rubbing it.

At last, she looked at him. The sun reflecting off the Vltava turned his impassive face into opaque planes and shadows. He might as well have been wearing the dark sunglasses for how easily she could read him now.

"Andrej and Eliska were engaged to be married," she whispered. "They were the only friends I had in the VZ. I, I am not good at making friends."

She paused and swallowed. Gathered her burgeoning thoughts with a firm mental hand before they overwhelmed her. Still the words spilled out of her before she could control them.

"They were assigned to take a stolen painting—a Caravaggio—into custody at my request. Mercenaries from Skopje ambushed them and took the painting before they could complete their assignment. You led me to the mercenaries. Without you, it would have taken me months to discover who was responsible. By then, the painting would have been gone and the killers impossible to identify."

András nodded. "Indeed" was all he said.

Beta returned her gaze to the Vltava, but she didn't see the peat-brown river the medieval Germans had dubbed "wild water." Instead, images of feral-looking soldiers attacking her overlay the scenic view only to be wiped away by roiling flames.

She'd been stabbed, and András had carried her to medical help.

He'd saved her life.

She brought her gaze back to him, her eyes wide. She recognized understanding and something else in his expression. It was unfamiliar to her, whatever it was, but she feared that it was compassion.

Now András leaned closer, his intent gaze holding hers. "If you trust nothing, Gomba, trust this: I will always protect and defend you. Always."

This was going to be more difficult than she could have imagined.

Beta finished her wine and signaled to the waiter to bring more before speaking. "Gordon and I meet with Boshirov and Petrov on Thursday to discuss an arms deal."

András tilted his head. "Gordon has a strange manner of conducting business." He finished his wine as well.

When he didn't elaborate, Beta narrowed her eyes and asked, "What do you mean by that?"

"He's the one who called in the anonymous tip to URNA."

She clinched her jaw and didn't respond. She hoped that Major Vlcek dug up something useful on this giant Hungarian or she was going to be without options soon.

András shrugged and relaxed in his chair. The waiter, somehow intuiting that he needed another glass of wine, appeared with a bottle and poured them each a generous portion. A moment after that another server brought a selection of Italian cheeses and set it on the table between them along with two small plates. Before Beta could deny that they'd ordered it, András put food on a plate.

He held it out to her. "Eat while you tell me what you're planning."

Beta scowled but accepted the plate. She nibbled on a piece of cheese and bread together. When her stomach grumbled, she refused to look at András, who acted as if he hadn't heard it. She decided that she might as well tell him what she was doing at the hotel.

"We will meet here at the Four Seasons on Thursday evening. I have reserved the hotel's private riverboat for cocktails and hors d'oeuvres. One of Gordon's men will handle the boat, so there will only be five onboard."

"Clever. Everyone will be checked for weapons prior to boarding I assume?"

"Yes." No need to share more information than he'd asked for.

András didn't say anything more for several minutes, instead keeping her small plate filled. Beta surprised herself by eating it all quietly. She'd had the start of a headache when she arrived to the hotel, and the food had eased it. It was still there, but it hid in a corner licking its wounds. She knew she was pushing it by getting back into the field so soon after getting a concussion, but she'd always healed so quickly. And she wasn't exactly one for lounging around her studio apartment. Besides, she didn't expect to face any physical threats before Thursday—unless this big, stinking bull counted—so it had seemed reasonable to relax on the terrace here while making arrangements to deal with the Russians.

But if Beta were honest, she would have to admit that she would have eschewed food for several glasses of wine. Not exactly what the doctor or András had ordered.

After she'd eaten her weight in bread and cheese accompanied by a mouthful of apple compote, Beta allowed herself to drink more wine.

"That sigh tells me you're no longer hungry," András said.

He himself had mostly watched her eat, but this she knew only because of the amount of bread and cheese that he put on her plate compared to what remained on the serving platter. Every time she'd glanced at him, he'd either been staring at the Vltava with a faraway expression or gazing at her with a slight smile.

Beta shrugged. "I lost track of time."

"If that's the case, you have no sense of time at all by the looks of it."

"And by the look of you"—she lifted her chin in his direction—"you are always eating. I am surprised you have not ordered a full meal yet. And at least two desserts."

As she made this comment, Beta had a sense of *déjà vu*. Or was it?

"How do you know that I haven't?" he asked, his eyes twinkling and a dimple appearing. "The Black Forest cake or the plum mousse sound heavenly, though perhaps you yourself would prefer the salted caramel ice cream."

As soon as he said *salted caramel ice cream*, Beta wanted it. But damned if she'd say so. Instead, she drained her wine and stared at the river.

From the corner of her eye, she saw András raise his hand and signal for the waiter. "A dish of the salted caramel ice cream for her and two cappuccinos," he said when the man hurried over.

Beta felt her jaw drop as she stared at András. When she realized it, she pressed her lips together. Anger and something else—fear—silenced her for a time.

Then she asked, "How did you know that I wanted the ice cream?"

He smiled at her and said gently, "Sometimes you flash your thoughts to me, Gomba. You may not remember me or what you are, but some part of you does."

What you are.

His words were fraught with meaning. Then Beta realized what András implied. Her dragon nature. Of course. He knew what he was and recognized that she was the same. Just as she'd done in the hallway outside her apartment. In fact, he'd probably known it long before he trapped her on the elevator. He'd known her before.

Before she'd left him. Before she'd used her dragon nature to deliberately forget him.

She had the sinking feeling that the giant Hungarian also knew a lot more about his dragon nature and how to access it.

She was two steps behind him at every turn.

The waiter brought their coffees and two scoops of salted caramel ice cream. Beta didn't know how András had managed to get a double portion for her, but she wasn't one to sulk over something that couldn't be changed. She accepted the divine frozen treat and ate it the same way she'd eaten the *kaše* the day before. She didn't have to look at András to know that he grinned at that.

Beta had eaten half of the ice cream when András asked, "How long will your cruise last?"

"Gordon wants to convey that we are all friends now, so negotiations will not begin until after we have shared a drink and food."

"Long enough to be exposed to a Russian sniper on shore." His eyes narrowed as he studied the panorama in front of them. "Especially if the sniper hides behind the sun reflecting off the water."

He was good. He understood exactly her uneasiness about Gordon's plan. Even if Gordon stationed his own sniper along their cruise route, there were just too many potential spots for a good sniper to lie in wait, especially in the blind spot afforded by the setting sun. And they had no choice but to tell the Russians in advance about the details of the cruise.

András turned his dragon gaze on her. "I can help you with that."

It was Beta's turn to narrow her eyes. "How?"

"I'll be on sniper hunt."

Beta set her spoon down and held his gaze. "Let me rephrase that. How *exactly* will you handle a sniper hiding in any of dozens of positions?"

"*Exactly* I can't give you. But the field of play can be narrowed considerably. There may be dozens of positions, but some are better than others. If I were the sniper, I would set up on the western bank between the Mánes"—here he gestured toward the bridge a three-minute walk north of the Four Seasons—"and Charles Bridges. And hit you on the way back up the Vltava to the hotel dock before disappearing into Malá Strana. Even if Gordon delays the return until after the sun has set, that would be the ideal time."

Beta had determined as much herself. Nodding, she said, "No cellphones are allowed onboard, so Boshirov or Petrov will signal the shooter some other way if our meeting goes awry. I have some ideas about how to prevent that without making it look like they are in distress."

András smiled. His beautiful eyes remained cold, however. "Of course you do."

Beta had the odd feeling he knew that one part of her plan required her to sit on the lap of one of the Russians.

Well, why wouldn't I?

Sitting on a lap had the combined effect of making it look like the Russian was having a good time while affording her protection from the shooter. Although she supposed that he could shoot her through his teammate, if he didn't mind killing him, too. GRU special forces snipers had adopted the lightweight 50-caliber ASVK rifle early last year. Nothing could stop a 50-caliber bullet from ripping them both in two.

She shook her head. Why was she telling this *velka krava* her plans anyway? "Regardless, I would rather counter the sniper without relying on tactics on the boat."

"I have access to some advance tech toys that will let me surveil likely sniper positions in real time, including some nanodrones."

"Nanodrones?" Beta sat forward, intrigued.

Drones, of course, were very popular for surveillance and sometimes as aids for spotters, who identified targets and called out range and wind calculations for the shooter. But drones were easy to spot if the target looked for them. Nanodrones, on the other hand, would be invisible to the naked eye....

"What kind of camera works on something so small?" she asked, recognizing a fatal flaw.

"That's proprietary information, but irrelevant. The nanodrones will create a mesh network that collects ambient sound and temperature data."

"Which you monitor via your cellphone, which also acts as a remote control." Beta cocked her head. "Leaving aside the question about how these nanodrones can cover the target area, assuming the shooter is there and not somewhere else along the route, how do you plan to neutralize the threat?"

"That depends."

Beta snorted. "That depends? What does that mean?"

"On how close I am to the sniper." Humor colored András's voice.

The waiter chose that moment to arrive. Before Beta realized what was happening, András had paid their bill. She narrowed her eyes. Not only was there some silent communication happening between the giant Hungarian and the waiter, but András's covering the cost of wine and food had all the hallmark of a date.

Was he maneuvering her?

"Well?" asked András after the waiter left. "Do you trust me to find and handle your sniper?"

"I do not know," she said, recalling that Gordon had a team assembled, one that she would be introduced to on Wednesday—one day before they met with the Russians.

The trouble was that it was *Gordon's* team. And she wouldn't have much time to try to run background checks on them whereas Major Vlcek would have something on András by tomorrow, Tuesday at the latest. Perhaps she could temporize until she knew more. After all, unless he had dire motives beyond the apparent romantic ones, it would be better to have her own backup in such a delicate situation.

But Beta wasn't one for prevaricating.

"What do you expect to gain by helping me? Do you hope that we will be lovers again?" she asked, holding his gaze. She was shocked to find that she hoped he'd say yes.

Turbulence roiled those magnificent blue eyes. "You remember making love to me."

It was a statement but not an answer to her question.

Beta shrugged. "Let us cut the subterfuge, András Nagy. There is no need for this elaborate scheme to get me into bed again. I do not need chivalrous declarations or to be plied with sweets and alcohol. Nor do I need to worry that I will be distracted during my mission thinking about the chemistry between us."

She stood. "I was right three years ago." Now she held out her hand. "Come, then."

András looked at her hand and then again at her face. He too stood. Behind him, the setting sun limned his dark hair in a fiery halo and threw his features into deep shadow. For a moment, a presentiment of something both awful and majestic winged through her. Beta shivered in the warm evening.

At last, András spoke.

"No." He took a step closer, enveloping her in his scent and heat but not touching. "When we make love again, it won't be so that you can leave and forget me. It will be because you are mine, and I am yours."

And then he was gone, leaving Beta blinking in the fractured sunlight dancing on the Vltava.

SEVEN

Beta didn't see or speak with András Nagy over the next three days. It made her uneasy. She had very good instincts as an operative. They had to be or she wouldn't have survived three years undercover. She should have sensed him if he were following her, but she didn't. Yet her gut told her that he watched her. After Major Vlcek's background check, she was even more uneasy.

András Nagy was a ghost. Or more precisely a legend.

The Hungarian intelligence services had nothing official, but Vlcek's contact told him that unofficially they'd collected stories about an unknown player who fit the description of the giant that she'd provided. The problem was that some of the stories went back eighty years and seemed to have their genesis in the depression era before World War Two. Many of these early accounts described in breathless terms a shining, winged being that had saved countless people during the suicide epidemic that had gripped Budapest. Later accounts were remarkably consistent, though the details of heroic acts expanded. Given Hungary's role as the fourth member of the Axis, and after the war when it switched to communism, there were many opportunities for these.

Leaving aside the fact that András didn't appear to be thirty-five let alone eighty, the witness descriptions had the peculiar tinge of delusion common to a society experiencing mass hysteria. Surprisingly, it wasn't a fire-breathing dragon they saw. They saw an angel.

A tingle of recognition vibrated through Beta at that thought. That too made her uneasy. She didn't believe in angels and demons, only ordinary humans who were largely either self-absorbed and indifferent or actively engaging in offenses against their fellow humans. She wasn't so cynical that she couldn't see that some people fought their basic natures, trying to be kind or compassionate or just understanding. But she'd never encountered any angels.

Drew Gordon was no angel.

Major Vlcek had contacted a variety of sources in the intelligence communities in Central Europe about the American arms dealer. Selling weapons and other armaments appeared to be only one of Gordon's activities, and perhaps a front for more extra-governmental and paramilitary operations—though the secrecy in which he operated made that only a conjecture. Beta didn't like conjecture. She had every intention of expanding the slim VZ folder on Gordon as she worked with him.

Given the proposition that he'd made to Beta to teach some "rough international justice" to Boshirov and Petrov, she suspected that Gordon ran a well-funded and -equipped vigilante force. Someone who'd likely spent time in his country's military or intelligence service and had access to intelligence and connections. After all, he said he'd been watching her for a long time.

And he knew her last name. The one she'd tried to bury.

Čermáková had been on her birth certificate, but she'd been conceived on International Students Day—the first day of protests marking the Velvet Revolution. And her father had been one of the hardliners trying to prevent the overthrow of the Communist government. Beta hadn't known this until she'd been about to enter the army. Her mother, hoping to stop her, had given Beta her birth certificate along with the news.

It hadn't taken much to persuade the state registrar to modify the official record. Since her mother had enrolled her in school and all activities using the Černá last name, it had been simple to continue using it.

Beta had no idea how Gordon could have discovered it. But finding out how he knew gave her one more reason to work with him. It didn't mean that she trusted him, however.

They rode together this morning to a meet with his team in the small village of Chyňava, about half an hour west of Prague nestled among mountains. It was the first time that Beta had traveled with Gordon without a black hood. It had taken her months to get his attention through low-level arms dealers, and when she did, he'd shown her exactly how "rough" his courting could be. To be fair, she'd disrupted several of his deals and seriously injured some of his operatives in an effort to get his notice. So when she was taken by surprise, then drugged and hooded before being flown to an unknown site for debriefing, she bore the humiliation. She'd had no idea that Gordon had been aware of her identity all along. That certainly changed how she felt about his recruiting techniques.

Beta's hand twitched. She longed to pull her karambit out and practice opening and closing its unique gliding mechanism. It would ease the tightness in her shoulders.

Glancing to her side, she saw Gordon scrolling through a document on his smartphone. He'd spent the first fifteen minutes of the trip on a cryptic phone call. Whatever he reviewed now had arrived via messaging after he'd ended the call. Beta knew that Gordon's information security was impeccable. The message would disappear once he'd read it. And he used a burner phone for messaging her and likely everyone with whom he worked.

Of course, if she ever got her hands on his phone for even thirty seconds, she'd text the phone's number to herself. That would give her the door into Gordon's phone using a SIM-jacking program and a stingray—a fake cell tower the VZ had set up in Prague. Either or both would give her unparalleled access to his activities. Since the jacking program sent messages directly to a phone's SIM card, Gordon would never know she had access. And it was highly likely that the stingray tower had already forced Gordon's cellphone to connect, gathering data on his movements in Prague. In either case, as long as he kept his phone on, she'd be able to trace his location, listen into phone calls, read his messages—even check his Web browser history.

Turning back toward the passenger window, Beta studied their route. Though Gordon appeared to trust her in allowing her to know where the meet was, she suspected that was because it didn't matter. It was a pop-up site. The team would review whatever logistics Gordon had planned for tomorrow's meeting with the Russians and then disperse, leaving no trace.

They arrived outside Chyňava mid-morning. Lush green cultivated fields surrounded the bucolic village of eighteen hundred. Most of the houses had the same red-tiled roofs of Prague, but their architecture was simpler rectangles and squares. The site Gordon had picked was a large house two minutes' drive inside the village next to a large open field. There were three other vehicles already there, a black Mercedes, a gray Range Rover, and an Opel passenger van.

Four men stood outside of the vehicles, two leaning against them with arms crossed and the other two talking a short distance apart. All four watched Gordon's driver pull in next to their vehicles. Even from a short distance, these looked like hard men. One man wore sunglasses, but the eyes of the others were visible. Something dark and cold looked through those eyes. They didn't look quite human. Beta shivered.

She and Gordon got out of their car. Beta slipped her hand into her pants pocket and pulled out the karambit, holding it loosely in a curled fist. She crossed her arms and leaned against her door. She could be in motion in a heartbeat if necessary. She wouldn't consider whether her speed and skill would matter in the end against such a group.

"Gentlemen," Gordon called as he came around the front of the car. The two men leaning against their vehicles stood upright. All focused on the man who paid them. "This is Beta Čermáková. She's joining us for this mission."

It took all of Beta's considerable self-control not to startle at Gordon's use of her real name. She should have anticipated it. But it wasn't just the shock of hearing her name. There was something, some hint of authority in his voice that she'd never heard before. It echoed in the word *gentlemen*, but the way Gordon said her name had a power to it that clamped around her throat. Her dragon nature roared in response, sending her temperature soaring. She smelled smoke.

Beta shifted her stance wider, sliding the karambit blade out as she did. Her sensitive ears heard the soft *snick*. She gulped and gripped the handle so hard her knuckles ached. She recognized the signs of being on the verge of a bloodthirsty attack.

Gordon smirked at her as if he knew what had happened. "Beta, this is Todd, Jon, Wes, and Curt." Each man nodded as Gordon introduced him. "They've been with me for a while. You'll find that they're exceptional at what they do."

He turned toward the field, waving as he did. "Come, join me."

They strode thirty meters to a small tree that appeared to have been freshly planted at the edge of the field.

Gordon continued. "This, my friends, is a Tree of Liberty. The locals planted it to commemorate the hundredth anniversary of the independence of the former Czechoslovakia from the Austro-Hungarian Empire. We in the United States often quote Thomas Jefferson, who said, 'The tree of liberty must be refreshed from time to time with the blood of patriots and tyrants.'"

Beta didn't know how Gordon did it, but there was a magnetic quality to his speech—not the actual words, but the tone and timbre—that hypnotized. Even aware of the effect, she found that she didn't want to struggle against it.

"Today, right now, in Central and Eastern Europe, there is a dark and malign force at work. But that shouldn't stop you from working with me," said Gordon, grinning.

The mercenaries grinned back, easing their stances. Something creeped up the back of Beta's neck. She inhaled deeply through her nose, trying to regain control. Hot sweat trickled between her shoulder blades, nearly driving her mad. She pressed her heels into the ground and lifted her shoulders back.

Gordon's grin evaporated. He paced away from the group, running his hand through his hair.

When he turned back to them, his gaze held a feral gleam. "While governments search for evidence and proof, we act. Tomorrow, we get one step closer to Unit 29155, whose members have engaged in sabotage and assassination with impunity. Beta is going to be our way in."

Beta narrowed her eyes as the other team members turned to gaze at her.

Should it matter to her that Gordon was less arms dealer and more cult leader? His plan dovetailed quite nicely with her agenda. She didn't have to sacrifice her hard-won status with Gordon to continue her VZ mission. In her experience, it was always good to have options.

"Now then, let's run down logistics for tomorrow's meeting."

Gordon spent the next twenty minute going over assignments. His plan held no surprises for Beta. Jon would crew the boat while Todd waited on shore, checking the Russians for weapons and wireless communications. The other two, Wes and Curt, would be on either bank on overwatch as snipers. Gordon joked that meetings between arms dealers and clients were like two superpowers with nuclear weapons: they were always about deterrence. That is, both sides assumed the presence of unseen snipers.

Once details had been set, Gordon pulled Jon aside. While they were conferring, Wes, who'd worn sunglasses during the ops planning, followed Beta back to her car. She caught a whiff of something fetid. Pivoting without warning, she pressed the karambit's hooked blade against his muscular thigh. The wrong move, and she'd slash his femoral artery—not an injury even this hardass would survive without a miracle.

"Do you have a problem with me?" she asked, narrowing her eyes.

Wes didn't flinch. Or step back. Instead, he pressed against the karambit, which punctured his cargo pants and drew blood. "You'd better be prepared to use that if you're going to threaten someone."

Beta stepped forward, piercing the skin of his thigh. "Oh, I am," she said. Smoke filled the air between them.

His nostrils flared. After a moment in which blood darkened the area around the tip of her blade, he brought his hand, palm up, slowly to his shoulder before dropping it to the blade even more slowly. Then he carefully removed it.

He shook his head. "Then I have no problem with you. Just be sure you're as ready to act tomorrow or you won't have time to pull your funny little knife when I find you."

It was only after Wes walked away and Beta slipped the karambit back into her pocket that she realized that Gordon had seen the entire exchange. The unholy shine of his eyes and slight curling of his mouth should have sent a warning through her.

But Beta's dragon nature simply smiled back at her new boss.

A foul mood swamped András as he returned to the TOC after tailing Beta and Gordon more than 25 kilometers west to a tiny village among the mountains.

She'd met with a group of a Dark *Irim*'s minions. Asmodeus's minions.

These weren't the brainless puppets, the *bogomili*, that Asmodeus had used four years ago, humans who'd essentially given over their agency to a Dark angel. Those humans had barely deserved the name. They parroted gibberish based on a medieval heresy about Creation being fundamentally evil, and they acted on autopilot to kill at Asmodeus's whim. They did this in a gruesome way: they punctured the base of the victim's neck with a *subulam*.

No, Gordon's minions functioned at a higher level. They were still puppets, but they'd kept their higher thinking skills in order to fulfill their Dark leader's purposes quickly and efficiently. Asmodeus promoted the best of this group to acolyte, a full partner whose personal goals meshed so completely with the Dark *Irim*'s that he—or she—would act as Asmodeus's representative. Asmodeus expended angelic energy on all of these bonds with weaker human instruments, but if he could find a willing *Elioud*, especially an *Elioud* with more than a trace of angel blood, then Asmodeus would also receive energy.

It was like a twisted symbiotic angelic relationship.

András glanced toward his own leader. As a *drangùe*, Mihàil had been Asmodeus's most powerful ally. But he'd never been truly forsaken. András let his gaze travel to Miró, who sat in front of a monitor discussing something with Mihàil. They'd simplified the details of what had happened between them when the *drangùe* broke his bond with Asmodeus, but the two *Elioud* loved and respected one another. Those emotions would overcome any Dark angelic effort.

In other words, Dark *Irim* powers over humans and *Elioud* had limits. What those were mattered a lot in the long-running battle between the Archangel Michael's *Angeli Fidelis* and the Dark *Irim* and their forces.

The question regarding Asmodeus's limits related to his current avatar, Drew Gordon. Was Gordon actually Asmodeus embodied? Or a real human that Asmodeus possessed? Both situations required a great deal of angelic energy.

Possession was a singular mark of Dark *Irim*, who alone among the angelic species had the spiritual energy and proximity to humanity to engage in it.

It was also forbidden.

But the *Irim*, known as Watcher Angels, had already broken the divine law when they left their celestial choir loft to mate with humanity. What was the downside of possession after that?

Possessing humans, who had souls and wills of their own, further corrupted Dark *Irim*. The darkness of the Void literally ate at their spiritual essence. Rather than emanating a brilliant and pure radiance, Dark *Irim* emitted polluted light.

Dark static had disrupted Beta's harmonic signature after she'd been stabbed on their mission to Macedonia.

Asmodeus had possessed her.

Rage boiled through András. He'd been ignorant of the reason for Beta's unusual harmonics, but the *drangùe* had suspected. It was one reason he'd agreed to let András stay behind to care for Beta while he and Olivia went on a mission to help Miró and Stasia, who were engaging another Dark *Irim*. András didn't know if he was angry at Mihàil or himself. Probably both.

"You saw Beta again."

Olivia stood at his shoulder. Her arms were crossed and her long blond hair pulled back in a large hair clip. She looked tired this morning. He'd heard her throwing up twenty minutes ago. Morning sickness hit her at all hours of the day. András shoved his foul mood away. Olivia didn't need to deal with his bad attitude.

"Yes." He didn't want to talk about it. He did anyway. "I followed her and Gordon to a meet in the countryside with some of his minions."

Olivia knew what that meant. She frowned. "Did Beta's harmonic signature seem more unstable?"

András closed his eyes and pinched the bridge of his nose. Then he held Olivia's clear blue-gray gaze. "After he introduced her to the group as *Beta Čermáková*, she almost flared."

He refrained from saying that he almost blew the mission right then and there by going to her. As it was, he'd only managed to overhear Gordon's announcement because he'd treated Beta like a hostile target.

He'd planted some of the nanodrones on her at the Italian restaurant.

"*Beta Čermáková*?" asked Mihàil, who along with Miró, had joined them. He looked at his Croat lieutenant.

"What?" asked Olivia.

"*Čermáková* means *redstart*, a bird that looks like a robin, my lady," said Miró. "It is also a sobriquet for *devil*."

Olivia looked thoughtful. She studied each of the *Elioud* warriors in turn. "You think Gordon's nickname signals a change in her status?"

András scowled. Beta's reaction to Gordon's announcement terrified him. Olivia just gave voice to the reason.

The *zonjë* put her hand on his shoulder, sending soothing waves of heat and harmonics into him. Her gaze was filled with understanding.

"It could just be her last name," said Miró into the tense silence. He shrugged when they all looked at him. "I know that *Černá* is a common Czech surname, but there was always something about it that sounded false to me. Not quite a lie," he clarified at their wide-eyed reaction. "Simply not as authentic as a true name sounds when spoken by its owner."

András sighed loudly and ran his hand over his hair. He needed a haircut. "That sounds almost as ominous, if you ask me. Why would Beta not tell Olivia"—*or me*, he thought—"her real name?"

"Let us put this question aside for now. We will continue to operate to free Beta from Asmodeus's influence regardless," said Mihàil. "I want to know more about Gordon. Is he an avatar or a possession?"

"Possession," said Miró. He gestured toward the other side of the room. "If you will give your attention to the large screen, I will share the details on one Andrew James Gordon."

Everyone, including Miles, who'd been working quietly at a corner workstation, turned their gazes toward the large monitor on one wall of the room. A large picture of a younger Gordon wearing a military uniform filled the left side of the screen. On the right biographical details filled in a form that the *Elioud* kept on individuals outside their team, from assets to known agents of Dark angelic beings.

Miró delivered the salient points aloud. "Andrew James Gordon, born in Alabama in 1974, only son of Beauregard and Charlotte Gordon. Attended The Citadel in South Carolina before being commissioned in the U.S. Army, becoming a Ranger, and then a member of the elite Delta Force, the U.S. Army's counterterrorism unit."

"Otherwise known as The Unit by the operators," said Olivia, "the best-of-the-best. Hostage rescue, intelligence gathering, and eliminating targets."

Miró nodded. "Gordon then moved from The Unit to the Army's intelligence unit, simply referred to as The Activity."

"And from there to the CIA's Special Activities Division, I'd bet," said Olivia. She turned to face the *Elioud* around her. "Gordon is the American version of Boshirov and Petrov."

Mihàil scanned the information on the screen, his eyes narrowing. "It says here he was decommissioned with the CIA in 2015 after a failed mission." The *drangùe* looked at Miles. "Do you have more details about that mission?"

Miles cleared his throat and stood. "I do. Gordon led a SAD team into Syria. The team's orders have been scrubbed, but the end result is that only Gordon and one other team member, a former Unit colleague, returned alive. Josh Hendrix, the other survivor, claims that Gordon executed the rest of the team."

"Sweet St. Michael!" Olivia's sharp exclamation sent cold fingers of apprehension down András's neck.

But his temperature rose. Smoke scented the air around him. He was exceptionally aware of the bullet fragments next to his spine. Fragments that had melted enough at his response to pool under his skin.

Mihàil, Miró, and Miles all looked as thunderstruck as András felt. A commander killing his subordinates in cold blood felt like a personal betrayal to all of them. Asmodeus might or might not have perverted Gordon's own motivation, but the Dark *Irim* couldn't have convinced him to murder if Gordon didn't already have a broken moral compass. Each of the *Elioud* would carry the thought of those betrayed going forward.

The mission had just expanded to taking Gordon down.

András, his eyes narrowed and his mouth grim, spoke first. "Tomorrow's meeting isn't going to go exactly as Gordon plans."

<h1 style="text-align:center">EIGHT</h1>

Beta stood on the sun-bleached dock a short walk from the glossy blue wooden boat that the Four Seasons Hotel provided its guests for romantic private rides, her gaze searching the visible rooflines and Charles Bridge for anything out of the ordinary. Her dragon senses hummed. The Hungarian giant lurked somewhere, but she had no idea where or what his plans were. Much to her angry disappointment, he hadn't appeared to reiterate his intentions to back her up at this meet. She was angry precisely because she *was* disappointed.

And if Beta were honest with herself, she was angry with András for making her start to believe that she meant more to him than a casual sexual encounter. That he'd been hurt when she left him three years ago. His last words had led her to hope that he wouldn't stop pursuing her until she was his. But a small voice whispered that András wanted revenge, that she couldn't trust him with her heart or her mission.

He'd gone dark after her explicit invitation, and she was left with nothing else to believe.

Gordon, who also scanned the area around the boat, checked his Rolex. "Ten minutes until go time. My source at the Russian embassy confirms that Boshirov and Petrov met with their handler there yesterday. Someone has been asking around about me. And you."

Beta, who'd dressed in slacks and a blouse with pumps, looked at her boss. Something told her that he wasn't speaking of her cover identity. "You are not referring to Marika Hubová."

"No. I refer to Alžběta Čermáková. Of course, I may have let it slip that that's your real name and that you're a lieutenant in Czech military intelligence."

Gordon's sly smile told Beta that he knew this news caught her off guard. "Now, now, don't be angry. It makes you smell like an ashtray, and that won't do if you plan to lure these agents into trusting you. After all, the Russians invented the ploy of using beautiful birds."

Beta narrowed her eyes at the allusion to the Russian espionage tactic—still in use despite the end of the Soviet Union and the Cold War—of training and using agents to gather intelligence via seduction. Female agents using sex, intimacy, and romance were called *swallows* while their male counterparts were termed *ravens*.

She was no swallow. She was a devilish redstart.

"Why should I not smell like an ashtray when you burned me?" she asked. She hadn't changed her stance or looked anywhere but Gordon's face, but she was already reviewing her exit strategy. "Do you really think I will sleep with one of them, even to save my own skin?"

Gordon shook his head and gave a mock sigh. "Do you really think you can leave and find another way to get close to Unit 29155?"

Beta's shoulders tightened. Her core temperature rose. He was right, *čert ho vem—devil take him*. Her nostrils widened. She couldn't sacrifice three years of deep-cover investigation. She had to find a way to make this work. At the very least she had to learn what Gordon had told the Russians. She didn't want to test whether her dragon metabolism, which burned alcohol too swiftly for her to get drunk, could handle Novichok.

Gordon waited until she'd reached this conclusion.

"You see, Čermáková, I want you to work for me and only me, my beautiful redstart." He glanced up at the hotel, which overlooked the private dock. The gesture reminded her that it would be next to impossible to leave without passing Boshirov and Petrov. "Instead of pretending to let the Russians recruit your cover Marika as your VZ handler no doubt told you to do at Havel's Market."

He'd had her followed. Beta's heart battered her ribcage at the revelation. Ice water flowed into her stomach, but steam rose from her fingertips. Her dragon vision saw the hot pulse at Gordon's neck. She wanted to rip his throat open and taste it. Her reaction scared her.

He just laughed at her.

"What is our play then?" she asked, her voice soft.

He laughed again, looking at his watch. "I should think it's obvious, Čermáková. You left the VZ three years ago. You can make up whatever story you want to explain why you ended up out in the cold. Say it was for friendship. Or love. Whatever you say, I suggest you keep it as close to the truth as possible."

Beta's temperature lowered a degree, and her heart slowed as she practiced the breathing technique that she'd perfected while training with her chain whip. She could build on this. She turned her gaze back to Jon, who stood next to the boat. The mercenary wore a white jacket with epaulets, white pants and shoes, and a sailor's cap. Only his cold gaze suggested that he was something more than an employee of the swanky hotel. Next to the padded bench in the prow sat an open picnic basket with an assortment of cold finger foods and a bottle of Prosecco.

"Instead of a low-level player with minor intelligence on *your* operation, I am now a valuable asset who can tell the Russians about the Czech investigation into the bombings," she said. She glanced at him from the corner of her eye. "What if they want to cut out the middleman? The one who sent Czech special police forces after them last Saturday?"

"I'm leaving it up to you to improvise. Now it's time to meet with Boshirov and Petrov." Gordon nodded toward the two Russians approaching the pier that led to the narrow dock on which they stood.

Beta turned to face the newcomers as they were met by Todd, wearing sunglasses and an expensive suit—and a conspicuous earpiece. Gordon said that theater went a long way toward deterrence, and the earpiece served as a reminder that an unknown number of team members waited somewhere close by.

As Todd accepted the Russians' weapons and patted them down for others, Gordon leaned in. "And Beta?" His low voice was silky. When she glanced at him, his brown gaze had the quality of stone—especially jarring against the smile lines at the corners of his eyes. "Whatever you do, you're *my* redstart."

Beta shivered. She'd never been this untethered as an intelligence officer. Gordon had backed her into a corner. For all intents and purposes, she'd now gone dark. And the mysterious American controlled her future.

Boshirov and Petrov stopped in front of her and Gordon where they stood next to the boat.

"Gentlemen, good day," Gordon said, his Southern American accent heavier and reeking with charm. "So glad you could join us. I'm sorry that our initial meeting didn't work out." He gestured toward the boat. "Please, let's get started."

The Russians didn't move. Boshirov, his face impassive, studied them. "Tell me why we should get into a boat with you when you were the one responsible for the URNA raid?"

Tension clogged the air between the four of them. Beta shifted her stance wider and narrowed her eyes at the men across from her. Her fingers itched for her karambit, which Gordon had forced her to leave with Todd, who remained on the pier fifteen meters away.

It was fortunate that the heels on her pumps functioned much the same way.

Gordon smiled. He exuded an air of calm and unconcern. "Because you understand that it was a harmless maneuver to ensure that your real identities were revealed, Mr. *Boshirov*. Mediated by a neutral third party."

The way Gordon pronounced the Russian surname made it clear that he knew it was a cover name.

"Where we come from, state police are not a neutral party," said Petrov. His gaze raked Beta, undressing her. "And being led from a very public place with our hands bound and automatic weapons trained on us is far from harmless."

Gordon shrugged. "It couldn't be helped. I needed you to know that I'm not afraid to use resources available to me to set the terms of our negotiations." Beta heard the warning intended for her in his words. "Besides, I was confident that your superiors would resolve the situation before you suffered any harm."

Petrov growled and started to move, but Boshirov gripped his upper arm, stopping him. Beta noted this. Though the two Russian officers both held the rank of colonel in the GRU, Boshirov had led a previous Unit 29155 mission to extract a deposed Ukrainian president sympathetic to Russia, where he now lived in wealthy exile. His gesture provided a subtle clue that he commanded here.

Boshirov looked at Beta. "We don't need to drink the sparkling wine or eat the cheese and crackers offered by the Butcher of Syria. All we need is the Czech agent." He nodded at her.

Butcher of Syria? Beta scarcely had time to note the epithet.

"I'll determine what you do or don't need," said Gordon a moment before the boat exploded.

The blast sent Beta flying. She landed on her shoulder and hip. For what seemed like forever but was probably only ninety seconds, her thoughts swam in her already concussed head.

Rough hands seized her and pulled her to her feet.

"Move!" It was Petrov.

Beta swiveled her head to look behind her. Boshirov had grabbed Gordon, who pulled his arm free of the Russian's hand. Behind them the ragged shell of the boat dropped embers into the river and onto the gray boards of the dock, which had started to burn. A couple of meters ahead of them, Todd, his neck at an unnatural angle, splayed across the only exit. It seemed unlikely he'd broken it due to the force of the explosion. Jon was nowhere to be seen. He'd been close enough to the boat that parts of him had likely been thrown into the Vltava.

"I said *move,*" said Petrov, who shoved her.

Beta stumbled forward, caught herself, and rounded on the Russian, the heel of her hand connecting with his jaw. His head snapped back, but Beta was already lunging for the 9mm handgun in Todd's shoulder holster. Her fingers scrabbled to remove it, but Petrov yanked her free arm, swinging her around into his fist.

Bullets began to pepper the dock and pier, gouging great chunks of the weathered wood.

Stars danced in Beta's vision. She tasted blood at the corner of her mouth. Dizzy, she vomited as the pain in her cheek blossomed into her fragile skull.

Petrov swore in Russian and picked her up, throwing her over his shoulder and launching into a jog away from the river.

Voices shouted. Helicopter rotors beat the evening sky overhead. Petrov grunted. Panting followed as Boshirov's and Gordon's feet pounded the pier behind them.

A bright light blazed against the Charles Bridge, sending a glittering kaleidoscope of colors reeling through Beta's vision. The violence of the blast had jostled the contents of Beta's head until her thoughts resembled *kaše*. Because she saw a glowing angel with beautiful incandescent wings.

A tall, muscular angel with a stormy countenance.

They'd reached the end of the pier when the unearthly creature turned its gaze toward them.

It was András Nagy.

An angel. Not a dragon after all.

It was the last thing Beta thought before blacking out.

András felt the boat's explosion in the marrow of his bones.

That's because he'd positioned nanodrones keyed to his personal harmonics along the hull which would have allowed him to listen in on the conversation between Gordon and the Russian assassins.

That turned out not to be the best tactic because the detonation sent András's harmonics into a piercing flatline not unlike the sounds a heart monitor makes when a patient's heart stops. When his harmonics recovered their wavelength, he watched as Petrov shoved Beta away from the burning remains of the boat. She staggered, caught herself, and rounded on Petrov, the hard heel of her hand connecting with the Russian's jaw. In an instant she'd spun and dove for Gordon's team member lying on the dock, clearly going for his holstered weapon.

Triumph at the sight arrowed through András only to be replaced with shock and horror. Petrov hauled Beta toward him, punching her. She staggered and then vomited. Her harmonics oscillated wildly.

Petrov slung the dazed Beta over his shoulder as Boshirov urged Gordon to follow with a gun aimed at his back—the gun he'd picked up from the dead Todd.

András scarcely noted the start of gunfire except as bullets ripped through the soft wood of the dock, chasing Gordon and the Russians away from the flaming boat remnants. Overhead a helicopter's blades chopped the evening air. Chaos dominated the Charles Bridge around him as pedestrians shouted and ran in terrified clusters.

András's battle senses fully engaged, and he flared. While his thoughts remained coldly focused, his internal temperature soared as it hadn't for three years.

He'd become angelic magma.

His gaze connected with Beta's as she looked up from where she bounced against Petrov's back. There was recognition and terror in hers. Then she fainted.

The three men gained the shore. Bullets whined and buzzed, striking the pavement around them. András tethered his senses on Beta's thermal signature and the hidden nanodrone he'd planted on her days before.

"Giant, this is Aerie One. Sitrep." Olivia's normally calm voice held a distinct sharp note.

András ignored Olivia. He placed his hand on the bridge and leapt over the side.

Only to be met by a harmonic wind that buffeted him so badly on the heated air currents that he rammed into one of the bridge's stone arches, dislocating his right shoulder.

András ignored the excruciating pain and struggled to match his harmonics to those roiling the air around him even as he plunged toward the murky water of the Vltava. It was impossible. He caught traces of Beta's discordant harmonic signature in the wave pattern, but something amplified the dissonance. It was like trying to harmonize with anarchy.

Zophiel winked into view before him, her mother-of-pearl incandescence soothing the roiling disharmony around them. "You have got yourself into a pretty pickle, my dear boy."

András would have also ignored Zophiel, but the *Cherub* sighed and took the hand of his good arm, tugging him gently to the end of the pier.

He dropped and rolled to his feet, sprinting toward the group faster than human sight allowed.

"You are so very welcome!" said Zophiel, clapping her hands and disappearing in a shower of luminous drops.

Boshirov turned as András neared and managed to get off two shots before András plowed into him. András grunted as each bullet pierced his flesh but grabbed the weapon and melted it before flinging the misshapen lump away. Boshirov gaped and would have succumbed to András's hand around his throat but Petrov stopped him by calling out.

"If you want to save these two, you must let us go. Or she has no hope of surviving the poison I just gave her."

András went still. He felt the pavement soften beneath his blazing feet. The lithium batteries in his tactical clothing had been overloaded, forcing his boots to shed the incredible heat he generated. It shimmered in the air. Sweat beaded on the faces of the three men looking at him. Beta's own thermal signature showed that she was dangerously warm. It could have been her metabolism struggling against a poison, but other injuries already weakened her. Regardless, as long as she was unconscious, she was unable to help in her rescue.

"Or I can kill all of you and take her with me," said András in a voice silky cold with *Elioud* authority.

A visible tremor quaked through Boshirov, but Petrov only laughed. Gordon stood to the side, his expression closed and watchful. Asmodeus might possess the arms dealer, but he was also vulnerable while inhabiting a human vessel. Both of them knew that if the Dark *Irim* chose to sacrifice Gordon in order to free his angelic form, that would give the *Elioud*—especially the *drangùe*, who was moments away—brief power over him.

"Are you sure you'll discover which poison I used before she dies?" asked Petrov.

In response, András lifted Boshirov in the air and squeezed his throat. The Russian gagged and tugged on his hand, his legs swinging wildly.

"I do believe he'd rather kill you and your friend," said Gordon, humor underscoring his words. He looked over his shoulder at Petrov.

András felt the angelic charm in those words. Petrov wavered.

At the far end of Platnéřská Street where they stood, several men and women in civilian clothes came running, weapons held in a practiced grip with the muzzles toward the sky—until they halted ten meters from their group.

The lead newcomer, a hard-looking woman in her late thirties, gestured over her shoulder. The others with her surrounded András, Gordon, and Petrov.

"We seem to have come late to the party," the newcomer said in a British accent. "But we have the most party favors. Giles, McIntosh, restrain all of them until we can sort this properly."

At either end of the street, Mihàil and Miró appeared as if stepping from thin air.

This was starting to get complicated.

A massive hole opened up where the British commander's chest had been. Pandemonium reigned in the street as invisible snipers began picking off targets with impunity.

András dropped Boshirov and darted toward Petrov, who'd dashed toward the rear entrance of the Four Seasons Hotel with Beta dangling from his shoulder like a sack of grain.

Gordon stepped into him, using András's momentum aided by a harmonic shove. András, caught off guard, staggered forward, leaving his back open to the Dark *Irim*'s vessel.

As Petrov yanked the door to the hotel open, Gordon punched András in the kidney, leavening the organ-punishing blow with a harmonic jolt that turned András's vision into water.

By the time András pulled himself upright, both Russians and Gordon had disappeared into the hotel with Beta, who might or might not have been poisoned with Novichok.

<h1 style="text-align:center">NINE</h1>

Adrenaline surged through Stasia Kos's harmonics as she stepped from the iconic red Italo railcar onto the platform at the Santa Maria Novella station in Florence. Bright late-morning sunlight streamed through the open-air slit above the idling train, making it easy to keep track of the distinctive steel-gray hair on the woman who'd disembarked before her.

At least until they moved under the dimmer skylights over the entrance hall of the station, one of Italy's busiest.

That's because Gina Orlandi, the Grey *Elioud* who'd attempted to gain a previously unknown Van Gogh painting from a Dark *Irim*, could disappear in plain sight and move in the shadows.

Especially if she suspected that she was being followed.

Too bad for the older woman that Stasia had long ago put a nanotransponder on her that was keyed to her individual harmonics. It was impossible for Gina to discover and remove without her being trained in this new *Elioud* technology. Unfortunately, it didn't displace the need for Stasia's old-school covert abilities. Gina might not be aware of the nanotransponder or have the training to affect it directly, but she *did*, simply through typical *Elioud* harmonic manipulation.

As now, when the Grey *Elioud* modulated her harmonics to allow her to move through the tourists and commuters as if they weren't there. The microscopic machine, instead of sending out a steady signal to Stasia's harmonic pinging, disappeared at odd, unpredictable intervals, timed with Gina's maneuvers.

Stasia sighed when the other woman vanished ahead of her. She reminded herself that it had only been a few years since she'd even had the ability to track someone harmonically. As long as she stayed within a hundred meters of Gina, the device—too small for the naked human eye—would alert her to the Grey *Elioud*'s location, even in the medieval heart of Florence.

E lì! *There*! Just as Stasia's intuition had predicted, Gina's transponder pinged from the mezzanine shopping arcade. Fortunately, Stasia had already sped her own harmonics and gotten onto the escalator that led down.

What was Gina doing? She was no tourist pulling an awkward wheeled suitcase who wanted to avoid more than a dozen stairs outside the front of the 1930s building, a paean to modernism that thumbed its nose at the art and architecture of the birthplace of the Renaissance. Viewing its soulless fusion of futurism and fascism always sent a chill down Stasia's spine. She'd bet the architects were Dark *Elioud*.

Supposedly on a trip to the Uffizi Art Gallery to meet with one of the assistant directors, the senior officer of Italy's Art Squad should have walked out the main level and found the first taxi.

Despite the thirty shops and restaurants on the lower level, the Grey *Elioud* was more likely picking up intel, either through a meet or even a drop.

Stasia wove through the slower-moving humans, some Italian commuters mingled among a variety of tourists, and stepped onto the brown-and-cream striped tile of the mezzanine.

Which way had Gina headed?

The delicate chime of Gina's nanotransponder sounded from the new gourmet coffee shop, VyTA, located partway down the passageway. Stasia modulated her harmonics so that she remained invisible to the human eye and approached the shop, which gleamed with green marble, copper fixtures, and mirrored wall panels. Her *Elioud* senses heightened as the danger of being spotted by the other angel hybrid intensified.

Gina sat on a stool near the back of the bar that ran along one side of the narrow shop. As Stasia watched, nothing happened except that Gina drank her espresso and looked at her watch. After five minutes, the Art Squad officer got up, leaving her espresso cup but gathering up some papers from the bar. Stasia stood closer to the woman next to her, mirroring her harmonics in case Gina recognized them as she approached. The older woman threw the papers into the wastebin across from the coffee shop in the passageway.

Stasia hurried to the bin as Gina at last headed for the street and pulled the papers out. One had some cryptic typing, including the single word *Peretola* and a series of numbers and symbols. The other handwritten scrap said *Émile Bernard* and *Codex Angelicus*.

Stasia stuffed the papers into her pocket and sped toward the street, where she hailed a taxi. If she was quick enough, she'd be able to get to the small Amerigo Vespucci international airport ten kilometers northwest of Florence in Peretola before Gina flew to France.

Once inside the taxi, she pulled out the handwritten note and studied the words.

A cold thrill jangled her harmonics. Émile Bernard was a Post-Impressionist French painter who'd known Van Gogh.

She very much feared that the mysterious *Codex Angelicus* was the *First Book of Enoch*, the edition dictated by the Watcher Angels and ordered hidden by the Archangel Michael.

András gritted his teeth around the pain and blinked to clear his vision. His battle senses automatically identified and catalogued the harmonic activity around him. He ignored the chaos and lunged toward the hotel entrance. A moment later a large caliber bullet dislodged a fist-sized chunk of pavement behind him. András scarcely registered the near-miss from a sniper's bullet.

Gordon's tactic had bought the Russians a critical thirty seconds. Perhaps enough to escape.

Inside the luxury hotel, András followed the harmonic trail left by the three men as they ran through the lobby toward the main entrance on the far side. Stunned employees watched, open mouthed, as Boshirov commandeered a sedan from a valet. When the young man gamely tried to resist the unarmed group, Boshirov throat-punched him. The doorman raised his hands, palms up, and watched as the three men got into the car.

The valet still writhed on the pavement when András's heat tsunami melted the glass doors. He didn't bother slowing his harmonics to a visible wavelength, though he did modulate light waves along his path to magnify his nimbus. Whatever the humans saw, they would attribute it to a divine source if they believed in such things.

It really didn't matter if they didn't.

Boshirov hit the gas pedal as András reached the car. He slammed his heated hand through the steel of the rear side panel. For a moment, he even touched Beta, slumped in the rear seat across from Petrov. The vehicle fishtailed as András braced his weight, straining to rip the door from the car. The scent of burning rubber filled the air.

But the steel almost instantly cooled and began reforming into a panel. András managed to vibrate his harmonics enough to keep the door from taking his arm off. It removed the top layer of skin anyhow as he pulled his hand free. Off balance, he staggered as the car drove away, winking into visibility as his harmonic control wavered. Gordon turned to look at him, a smirk on his face.

She's mine, Elioud.

András almost fell backward at the revulsion that coursed through him at the Dark *Irim*'s invasion of his mind.

Not if I have anything to do with it, he flashed back. He pushed the message so that it would feel like a harmonic spear thrust, ignoring the Dark *Irim*'s disordered mind at the end of it. It was a technique that he'd developed fighting the *daemonia*.

Asmodeus's responding laugh echoed in András's head, reverberating until he thought it might explode. He'd never felt anything like it before in more than sixty years fighting Dark angelic forces. There was something strangely familiar in the harmonic signature, almost as though the Dark *Irim* channeled some of Beta's angelic energy....

Mihàil's hand dropped onto his shoulder. *András, are you all right?*

The *drangùe*'s mellifluous mental voice soothed the cacophony screaming around his thoughts until his vision had shrunk to a black pinprick. András swallowed and closed his eyes, letting the vertigo pass. He looked at the *Elioud* general standing at his side, the older man's gaze sharp and understanding. Mihàil probably had some idea of what had just transpired between his impetuous lieutenant and the demon of lust.

András nodded and started to run his damaged palm over his hair before dropping it. Instead, he said, "Well enough."

He didn't trust himself to flash a message at the moment. His dislocated shoulder hurt so much, now that the adrenaline from the chase had lessened, that he thought he might lose the contents of his stomach. The weight of the *drangùe*'s hand grew unbearable.

"Then you will not mind me doing this," said Mihàil as he stepped closer, tucking András's arm into his side.

Before András could ask what Mihàil intended, the other *Elioud* took his wrist and rotated the arm open ninety degrees. Because András hadn't tensed up anticipating the maneuver, the dislocated shoulder slipped into place. The pain resolved almost immediately. Mihàil sent a heated vibration through the injured tissue, soothing it further.

"Thank you," said András, looking away while he moved the arm through a full rotation. He'd forgotten for a moment who he was and why he was here.

Mihàil nodded. "You still need to have that looked at by our doctor. I did not sense any torn muscle or cracked bone, but you might still have greater damage. How did you hurt it anyway?"

"A few medieval stones got in my way."

"Ah." Mihàil didn't press further. Instead, he greeted Miró, who came up at that moment. "Time to reassess the situation before we do anything about Gordon and Beta. Miró, do we have any idea who the Brits are? My guess is that MI6 sent a team for Boshirov and Petrov, but how they knew where they would be this evening presents an interesting question."

"Definitely MI6. Miles intercepted their communications. That van that arrived as you left collected the casualties and their spent ammunition." He paused as the sound of sirens grew in the distance. "Local law enforcement will be here momentarily, but except for the physical damage, nothing remains of the firefight."

He left unsaid that he'd already picked up bullets from the street and gone through the Four Seasons lobby "adjusting" the memories of the handful of staff who'd witnessed anything, including the doorman and valet. There would be a more thorough sweep later when they returned to gather intel after the Czech police had finished.

"The snipers could have been either Russian or Gordon's," said Mihàil, "given the targets."

"Or both. I have the drones set to follow the trajectories of the shots to determine the sniper positions. Either way, it points to premeditation because of the site of the attack. Miles's team will scour the area for shell casings and anything else left behind. We should know how many shooters and what long guns were used by midnight."

"Petrov said he poisoned Beta," said András at last. It had taken all of his control to keep from shouting that as soon as his thoughts had cleared.

Mihàil and Miró both turned sharp gazes on him.

"Was there evidence of poisoning?" asked Mihàil. "Do you have any idea how he could have administered it?"

"What are the signs? She was unconscious. There's no other way she'd let him carry her like that."

"If it was Novichok, she would have been sweating, vomiting, incontinent, evacuating her bowels, and unconscious," said Miró. "Given the timing, the most likely administration would be via aerosol. I doubt Petrov would have risked his own exposure by applying it to her skin."

András exhaled loudly, turning from the other two *Elioud* so that they wouldn't see his expression. They'd see the scorched footprints and smell smoke soon enough. Then he turned back, scowling anyway.

"She vomited after the bomb exploded, but she *was thrown fifteen meters and already has a concussion*. She was also sweating, but I'd just melted Boshirov's weapon, so everyone was sweating."

Mihàil listened to his furious recitation before responding calmly. "I understand your frustration, but we must be smart about our next steps." The *drangùe* paused. The sirens came from the next street. "Let us regroup back at the TOC. Whatever the Russians plan, they also need to regroup somewhere safe first."

András nodded. The three *Elioud* sped their harmonics, winking out of sight as the first Czech police cars screamed into the street leading to the Four Seasons entrance. Half an hour later all three of them were back at the TOC where the team doctor evaluated András as he did his best to ignore the exam to participate in the mission briefing. The first order of business? Link the nanodrone on Beta to the *Elioud* system. While he could follow her on the ground, this was the best way to pinpoint her location on a map for the team.

And the nanodrone on Beta appeared in the district of Vysočany, an industrial area less than ten kilometers east of Old Town. Given the coordinates, Boshirov and Petrov held Beta in a warehouse near the district center. Miles and Miró had already discovered that the property offered configurable space for rent to startup businesses. While Miles checked ownership records and contacted the rental company, Miró piloted the nanosquadron to surveil the perimeter of the warehouse.

"That's likely one of the Russian safe houses in Prague," said Olivia from where she stood near the large screen displaying a map of Prague. She turned to look at them. "There's site security that the Russians will have reinforced, likely cameras over the loading docks, bulletproof glass on the windows, and biometrics on the security panels near the reinforced steel doors into the warehouse, including the lift doors on the loading docks. Whatever the rental pictures show, just imagine more impregnable. The question is how many armed people wait inside."

Mihàil answered her. "I cannot speak for the Russians, but Asmodeus will not want many other humans that he does not control present. They will require more energy outlay, and he has already possessed Gordon for some time."

"How do we know that Asmodeus is still there?" asked András. He looked at the doctor, a quiet man in his early fifties whose family had served Mihàil for decades, who percussed the muscles of his arm and shoulder. "That's good, Dr. Armand. I don't need any painkiller."

The doctor, fully aware of the *Elioud* ability to assess the health of their bodies to a fine degree, had accepted András's flat denial that there was greater injury to the muscles and tendons or a bone fracture, which if left untreated could have serious complications. He'd said nothing about the angry red on András's abdomen from the healing bullet wounds, simply cleaned them and applied antibiotic cream to discourage scarring. Now he nodded, turning to head to the bathroom on the other side of the apartment's main hall. Olivia followed him. András heard her thanking the doctor better than he had.

Which wasn't at all.

András ignored the niggle of guilt at being so brusque with Dr. Armand. He didn't have time to worry about a man who would serve the *Elioud* regardless of a word or two of thanks.

He stood, pulling a clean black T-shirt over his head as he did.

Mihàil answered his question about Asmodeus. "Because I sense him," he said, his blue eyes glittering dangerously. He held András's gaze.

András had a moment of clarity in which he felt the full force of the *drangùe*'s awe-inspiring *Elioud* authority—an authority tempered by the grace received after falling so far into the service of a Dark *Irim*. He didn't know how he'd ever forgotten it.

András didn't care. If anyone understood why he needed to be gone twenty minutes ago on a rescue attempt, it was Mihàil, whose own wife had moved heaven and earth to save him when Asmodeus's acolyte tortured him. And they hadn't even known each other as well as he knew Beta.

They hadn't been intimate.

"This is pointless. Beta could be suffering from Novichok. We don't have time to try to get into the head of a Dark *Irim*. All we need to know is he's enjoying whatever the Russians are doing to her."

Mihàil appeared to be on the verge of saying something when Olivia came to stand by his side. She linked her arm through his but said nothing. Out loud anyway.

Miró, who'd been standing with his arms folded, chose to speak now. "We have enough nanodrones to surround the warehouse."

Mihàil turned a sharp gaze on his lieutenant, who'd developed the increasingly useful technology. "We can amplify our harmonics," he said, smiling.

András felt his own ire settle a bit. "We can trap Gordon in the warehouse."

"I'm going with you," said Olivia in a voice that conveyed the finality of her decision.

"As long as you are at my side the whole time." Mihàil's hard voice, that of a commander, still held a trace of the husband's worry.

They both knew that Olivia's presence would add irreplaceable strength to the *drangùe*'s harmonics. Together, they were Asmodeus's equal, something they'd learned after Stasia and Miró battled and defeated another Dark *Irim*, Yeqon, as a bonded *Elioud* couple. It was one reason that Asmodeus had upped his attacks on humanity using *daemonia*. But it also meant that he would do whatever it took to separate them. If he suspected that she was pregnant....

It took them less than five minutes to gather their gear for the mission and coordinate an approach to the warehouse. Miles would remain in the TOC and monitor local law enforcement communications while piloting the nanodrone squadron using the interface they'd developed for non-Elioud team members. He could also deploy assets if they needed backup or exfil. Given the closeness of the site where the Russians held Beta, they would all speed their harmonics and go on foot, Mihàil and Olivia assigned the front entrance to the building that housed the space while Miró and András took the loading dock around the back.

The team, including Miles, gathered in the living room of the apartment. By unspoken agreement, they all looked at András, who recognized that he'd been given command. As he looked at each countenance, his *Elioud* eyesight sharpened. Each of the three *Elioud* radiated a warm nimbus, their harmonics so in sync that together they sounded like an angelic chamber music trio. Even Miles, solemn and alert, had steady harmonics and a healthy infrared signature. They were the only family András had known since his mother had jumped into the Danube.

András swallowed, a cold spear of premonition piercing his gut. Why had Mihàil chosen to give him command?

But he knew why. He had to choose where his loyalties lay.

He inhaled deeply, drew his shoulders back, and lifted his chin before addressing the team. "Objective is to recover Asmodeus's vessel, Drew Gordon. Once we've dampened the harmonics, we move on my command. Subdue all individuals in the warehouse and secure Gordon."

He paused, closing his eyes. Beta's ghostly harmonic outline transposed itself onto the back of his lids. She slumped in a chair, her head lolling. Her ragged form wavered as dark static devoured its edges. When he opened his eyes, the image floated in front of him as if it had been burned into his retina.

Why did it feel like he was diving wingless into the murky Danube?

Clenching his fists against an urge to howl, András nodded and said, "See you on the other side."

TEN

"*O na vesit bol'she, chem kazhetsya*," said a male voice near her as she came around, her head aching as if her skull had been split open with a rusty adze.

It took her long moments, her thoughts swimming against heavy, invisible currents, to translate the Russian. *She weighs more than she appears.*

She struggled to open her eyes. When she did, brilliant jewel-toned lights melted and slid against a deeper blue-black background. Figures emerged from the currents, their edges smeared and vague. A pale orb came closer. She blinked, trying to clear her eyes, but it didn't help. She raised her hand, to touch the orb or her own face, she couldn't decide.

The orb clarified as it grew closer. A face. Something was wrong with it. The eyes were where the mouth should be, the mouth on the forehead.

The forehead-mouth spoke. "*Vy dolzny sderzhivat eye.*" The muffled words came through water in her ears.

Her stomach hurt as she fought to understand the words from the misbegotten creature. Acid burned her throat and coated her tongue as she decoded the meaning. *You should restrain her.*

The creature flew away, leaving her eyes dazzled by the return of a million dancing colors through sheeting rain on a window pane. Her jaw dropped as she watched.

Language vibrated through her as if the air spoke. "*Ya dal yey dostatochno dlya kogo-to vdvoye bol'she yeye vesa.*"

Letters and words scrolled across the blue-black. She plucked them into order, bestowed them meaning. But she couldn't comprehend them.

I gave her enough for someone twice her weight.

"Are you sure you gave her enough then?" asked a third voice. "You just said that she weighs more than she appears."

The words, fiery sparks, hissed through the liquid air, leaving glowing trails. She clapped her hands over her ears. The ground under her shifted. More poisoned words dropped from the first voice above like acid rain, seeping between her fingers anyway.

"Are you worried that she will overpower both of us and then go for you after you betrayed her?" Hard fingers gripped her, digging deep into the bone of her arm. "She's too skinny to present much threat, even to you, the Butcher of Syria."

Butcher of Syria.

Bloody arms and legs and open mouths in eyeless faces erupted before her. She screamed.

Laughter cracked around her like lightning, doubling, then doubling again as though she hung in the midst of an echo chamber. Her head split open. She felt cold night air on her exposed brains and knew that demons had gathered around her to take turns dipping their claws into her skull.

Darkness swallowed her in deep black velvet. Something dragged her back up again by the hair, though her heavy eyelids refused to open.

The third voice wormed its way into her ears where it broke into a thousand different chords, hissing, whining, and grating as it spoke, the volume rising and falling erratically. But the words were remarkably clear and understandable.

"I'll hazard a guess that you didn't give the lovely Alžběta Čermáková, a lieutenant in the VZ, poison. Too risky if you plan to interrogate her. Perhaps something like Fantasy? Maybe you Russians call it something else, hm? Liquid X or G? A little aphrodisiac and euphoria paired with a loss of judgment and the ability to say no...."

Alžběta Čermáková. Beta latched onto that name like a drowning woman catches onto a tree limb protruding from a fast-receding river bank. Swaying, she sat upright and wrenched her eyes open. The dry air stung them.

A moment later, the pale orb descended from the static that clouded her. This time, however, when the face surfaced, the eyes had changed places with the mouth. The piercing gaze studied her as if debating whether to eat her now or wait until she was properly cooked. Claws scrabbled for her tender skin.

"She is feverish, and her pulse races."

The first voice, now distant and muted, spoke. "That is unexpected. They should both be lower than normal."

Rapid squeaks and the soft whisper of fabric rubbing against fabric sounded before rough fingers tipped her chin up where a brilliant light burned her eyes from their sockets. Beta hissed and blinked, fighting the brilliance until it submitted to her control.

A new orb hovered over her head, washed out and hairless with dark eyes like talons. It turned away, and the first voice spoke again. "You were right. I injected our lovely Czech spy with GHB. Did you know that it was first synthesized almost a hundred and fifty years ago by a Russian chemist named Alexander Saytzeff? Not the best choice, but something I had on hand."

Cool fingers felt at her wrist and neck. "As you say, I misjudged the dose. Perhaps I should give her more?"

The voice had a name. It popped into her mind in vivid, white script like smoke against a flawless blue sky: *Alexander Petrov.*

Contrails followed and resolved into more script: *Unit 29155.* Beta pulled at the white vapor, gathering it until more script filled her head, displacing some of the dizziness and confusion that ruled her thoughts.

"Sure, you do that. I'm sure she'll be coherent through the hallucinations and seizures while you question her."

That voice also had a name. *Drew Gordon.*

Beta pulled free of Petrov's hand and swiveled to look at the third person with them. This time the bearded face clarified immediately, along with the name. *Ruslan Boshirov.*

Gordon watched her from opaque brown eyes that nevertheless conveyed the impression that he was laughing at her. Or the situation. Her dragon intuition told her that he waited for something, something from her in fact. Cold uneasiness battled the lingering effects of the GHB.

GHB. A date rape drug known to arouse while simultaneously affecting judgment and memory. It was normally administered at clubs as a clear liquid in unguarded drinks. A shot, on the other hand, delivered the drug directly to the bloodstream, its effects faster and more severe.

Knowledge gushed like a rush of blood from a reopened wound. A second dose given too soon could lead to coma, brain damage, and death.

Beta's temperature soared, burning off more of the GHB.

Petrov had made a fatal mistake: he hadn't calibrated his dose to her dragon nature. Her fingers flexed without her conscious command, but she caught the gesture. She didn't have her karambit, but she was still wearing her pumps. The ones specially designed for hand-to-hand combat.

A tiny smile curled the corner of her mouth despite herself.

"Your sleeping beauty has awoken, Petrov," said Gordon, smiling at the Russian, who'd leaned back from his physical examination and now surveyed her through narrowed eyes. "She doesn't look too happy to be the guest of honor of your party."

Petrov glanced over his shoulder at Boshirov, who stood a few meters from Gordon with his arms crossed. Gordon sat on a folding chair near a support column, his legs crossed at the ankles.

"We can start," said Petrov. "She's alert enough."

Boshirov approached. He looked at Beta for a moment, and then he slapped her hard enough to knock her out of her chair. She fell to the concrete floor, landing on her injured shoulder and hip. A white star burst in her vision. Her ears rang.

Boshirov waited while Beta dragged herself clumsily back into the chair. She took her time, playing up the sluggishness that her dragon metabolism had already overcome. She touched the tip of her tongue to the corner of her mouth. Blood. The scent of ash hung heavy on the air between them.

Boshirov frowned. "What is that I smell? Smoke?"

"You are asking the wrong questions," she said even as her dragon nature catalogued their surroundings.

And added to her list of grievances.

There were no other infrared signatures with them. No other persons or living beings. Blues and greens delineated the dimensions of the large open space. On the far side stood a long table, and two other chairs on wheels. A window, still glowing orange from the last of the sun's heat, interrupted the warm magenta of the wall behind the table. A few items that she couldn't immediately identify sat on the table and the floor under it. She didn't read anything that said weapons cabinet, but if the Russians had any sense, they wouldn't have weapons in a room where their subject had been detained. She'd been out for some time, yet her gut told her it hadn't been long enough for them to leave Prague.

A Russian safe house then, *house* being a euphemism. It was obviously an empty warehouse. She'd note its location once she got free of the building and get word to Major Vlcek later.

Or not. She remembered that Gordon had set her up for a reason.

Boshirov struck Beta again. This time she'd caught the chair's seat an instant before his assault. Her head snapped to the side, jarring her already concussed brain.

"What questions should I ask?" He smirked. "How long you can last, my caged redstart?"

Redstart. He'd caught the meaning of her last name, one that appeared in Russian as well. Did he also know it as a Czech nickname for devil? Someday she would enlighten him.

She lifted her chin. "Who blew up the boat?"

Boshirov frowned again. Beta noted it. Though he didn't realize it, she had started to control the course of the interrogation.

"That is obvious. The British strike team. They have been after us since Salisbury. They saw their chance and took it."

Beta smiled at him. Whatever Boshirov saw in her expression, it caused him to take a step backwards.

She dipped her chin. "Mm, perhaps not so obvious," she said as coolly as if she sat sipping a cocktail in an upscale lounge.

As if her body didn't ache fiercely, from head to bruised hip.

She let her gaze stray to Gordon, who sat watching the interaction with a predatory gaze at odds with his relaxed posture. For an instant she thought she saw a wavering shadow behind him, a grotesque being whose outline jumped and danced like a flame in a steady breeze.

Ignoring what was likely a vestigial hallucination from the GHB, Beta brought her gaze back to Boshirov. "Gordon's boatman was a former Navy Seal. I saw Gordon pull him aside before this mission. He was missing after the blast. At first, I thought it was because he'd been killed, but then I remembered what Gordon said to you at the pier."

Gordon sat upright. Petrov, who'd gone to sit in one of the chairs at the table, looked over at the arms dealer. A thoughtful, focused expression came over the Russian doctor's thin face.

Boshirov narrowed his eyes and crossed his arms again. Oh, she definitely had the Russian colonel's attention now. And he would follow where she led. There would be no more strikes to her head or any other part of her.

"And that was?" asked Boshirov in a flat voice.

His infrared signature showed that he believed her. It had grown warmer by several degrees and, more importantly, yearned towards hers. Wispy orange fingers streamed ever so slightly from the front of his body on an invisible current flowing into her own heat.

Even better. The Russians had thought to use the GHB to impair her judgment. All she needed to influence *theirs* was subtlety and persuasion.

"That he needed you to know that he is not afraid to use available resources to set negotiation terms."

"As he used you?" Boshirov looked over his shoulder at Gordon. Already Beta could see a shift in his stance that suggested he had distanced himself from the American.

"Yes." She kept her answer short, simple, and honest.

She held his gaze. Let him conclude the obvious: *she* had every intention of using all of *her* available resources to set negotiation terms. And that included Gordon. If she were really lucky, she'd be free of the manipulative bastard and on her way to becoming a trusted insider with Unit 29155 within a few hours.

Gordon spoke. "She's just trying to distract you. I warn you. You should restrain her before she becomes fully alert. She took on three other candidates for the job with me. One ended up with a broken clavicle, another lost an eye, and the last one suffered a dislocated joint in his groin."

"None of them died," said Beta, keeping her gaze on Boshirov.

Silence reigned for a moment. Boshirov's face had gone blank. Without changing the focus of her gaze, Beta saw Petrov stand and move closer to Gordon, who was also not restrained.

"Why are you working for an American arms dealer if not undercover for the VZ?" asked Boshirov at last.

Beta lifted one shoulder. "Why not? I needed the job after the VZ disciplined me for an off-books mission." Which was entirely true as far as it went.

She'd been reprimanded for working with Olivia Kastrioti, which led to Andrej's death. Eliska had still been in the hospital when she got her assignment, the one that would rehabilitate her with the VZ.

A faint chime sounded in Beta's head, but she didn't have time to analyze it.

She could see that Boshirov believed her because he looked intrigued. He stepped closer. She'd never enjoyed this part of the mission, the one that relied on talking and coaxing. She'd rather dislocate the joint in their groins. But she played the resources she'd been given.

"Tell me more about the off-books mission."

Beta didn't know where the details came from, but the story fell out of her mouth as though she'd been waiting to tell it for three years. "I was part of a team with two other operatives. One was American, the other Italian. We handled sexual predators and traffickers that our agencies ignored."

"'Handled'?" Petrov's voice was sharp.

Beta lifted a shoulder again as she answered. "None of them died," she said, repeating her earlier explanation.

From the look on the *šašek*'s face, her nonchalance had the desired effect. No doubt he recalled the injuries the other applicants for the position with Gordon suffered.

"Was one of your targets important to the VZ?" Boshirov's question brought Beta's attention back to him.

Beta slowly shook her head. This part of the story was still fuzzy. "We recovered a Caravaggio stolen from the National Gallery Prague. I arranged for the VZ to take custody of the painting."

She paused to take a steadying breath. The scent of smoke hung in the heated air between them, but Boshirov didn't seem to notice. "The two officers assigned to deliver it were attacked, one killed and the other gravely injured."

Everything she'd said was true.

"Why would I kill my own man?" asked Gordon, disrupting the rapport she'd built with the Russian commander. "Even if Jon got away as you claim, Todd died from that blast."

"Boshirov broke his neck," said Beta, aiming her gaze at Gordon.

It was a calculated guess, but if she read the situation right, the Russians had also used their available resources to set negotiation terms. That included killing one of Gordon's men.

Gordon's eyes widened, and he shot from his chair. "What the hell?" He glared at Boshirov, baring his teeth and taking a step toward the other man. "Is she right? Did you kill my man?"

Even as he asked, Petrov gripped him by the upper arms and pulled him backwards. Strangely, Gordon's infrared signature remained steady.

Interesting. He only *acted* furious.

It was Boshirov's turn to shrug. "Of course. You would have done the same."

Beta realized that Boshirov now stood next to her chair. At her side. She stood as well. He didn't even look at her. If he had, he might have realized that she stood with all her usual grace.

"What will you do if he is the one who contacted MI6?" she asked.

Again, a calculated guess. But there had been no evidence of the Brits in Prague before today—and she would know because she'd asked Major Vlcek to keep her up to date on the British investigation. The Brits could have arrived in the Czech Republic using false passports, but then again, they had to know that the two members of Unit 29155 were in Prague first.

"Is this true?" asked Boshirov, anger clouding his features and raising his temperature.

Gordon shrugged, dipping his face to the side and grinning. "Would it help if I said my sniper took out the MI6 bitch?"

Boshirov glanced over his shoulder at Beta, and then he tipped his chin at Petrov. At the same instant, Gordon lunged free of the doctor. While both Russians grappled with Gordon, Beta took the opportunity to slip the heels from her pumps. Twisting each heel a quarter turn, she removed it along with part of the arch support, which now functioned as a handle for the sharpened heel. She slid the dagger-like heels into the special pockets in her slacks on either hip where she could draw them in a heartbeat.

She'd just managed to complete this when Gordon got close enough to grab her.

"Mine. You're mine," he said, a strange gleam in his gaze.

Before Beta could respond, electricity rolled through her, swamping her in suffocating darkness. Her eyes rolled up into her head. She sagged against Gordon.

A minute later, the two Russians pulled them apart. Beta's awareness returned in an exhilarating rush. In fact, she felt more alert and alive than she'd ever felt. Her dragon nature hummed. Her dragon senses had expanded beyond the empty warehouse into the surrounding night.

She saw more than heat signatures.

She saw the individual vibrations from everything in Creation, including those of the *Elioud* team outside. Without conscious thought of what she was doing, she slowed these vibrations around them. The *Elioud* would be unaware that they acted out of sync with the vibrations inside.

"We have visitors," she said. There was a strange hum bolstering the chords of her voice. "Head for the freight elevator. Leave him. Alive." Even she heard the *Irim* authority in her voice. She smirked before darting for the elevator.

Boshirov, who held Gordon in a chokehold, dropped him before following Petrov.

A moment later, the individual *Elioud* vibrations merged, and the vibrations around Beta and the Russians stopped. Four *Elioud*, three men and a woman, materialized in the warehouse.

Recognition made Beta's knees weak. She knew all of them.

András Nagy towered over the other three in a defensive line behind him. Almost at once the other two men surrounded Gordon, who was still unconscious. The woman watched them both. There was something unusual about her harmonic signature....

"Beta!" Command underpinned that deep masculine voice.

Too bad he couldn't command her.

What she did next shocked her as much as it did the woman, whom some instinct warned to flinch a microsecond before Beta threw both of the sharpened heels at them.

One bounced off the retreating woman.

The other pierced András Nagy high in the chest.

The last thing Beta saw as the doors to the freight elevator closed was the stunned anguish on his face as he fell to his knees.

ELEVEN

Pursuing Alžběta Čermáková was like trying to possess wild animals—who went berserk and ran squealing over desert cliffs into the sea, for example. Not unlike the difficulties in subduing her mother. Ah! *There* was a spirited human.

Too bad he'd had to sacrifice Gordon to get Beta where she was now. He would have loved to tame his little redstart the same way using his vessel. Though truth be told, even with Gordon's enthusiastic willingness, he'd been at the end of his strength when he'd jumped into her.

But he'd timed everything superbly, shackled and limited as his *Irim* strength was. Pushing and cajoling, and setting up all the conditions to bring Beta to the moment where she'd accept his presence had taken all the focus and patience he could muster after thousands of years on Earth. It was as close to a musical composition as his disordered *Irim* nature could achieve, yet still offbeat and tuneless. Despite that, it had all been worth it when he'd caused her to throw those vicious little daggers at her former *Elioud* lover and the *drangùe*'s mate. The agony and betrayal on the giant's face was priceless! He could feed on that discord for a long time.

Which was just as well because as soon as Beta realized what she'd done, her spirit had rejected Asmodeus's harness and thrown him off. At least temporarily.

The sheer power in this *Elioud!* Asmodeus basked in the possibilities for a moment. Of course, Beta was destined to be stubborn and willful. It went hand-in-hand with the level of angel blood coursing through her veins. Which was almost pure *Irim*.

Pure, faithless, and Dark.

Asmodeus chortled to himself, startling the nearby humans, whose terror fed him.

Michael's harmonics must be nearly set in fury. The arrogant right hand of *Elohim* looked on all *Elioud*, Dark, Light, and all shades of Grey, as his personal responsibility after failing to prevent the Watcher Angels from breaking Divine Law. But these particular *Elioud* he viewed as his special protégés. How could he not have grieved over the loss of Alžběta Čermáková? Or the grievous injury she inflicted on the giant *Elioud*, whose harmonic signature had never been the same since she broke his heart?

Yet as always Asmodeus truly didn't know. His ability to read the harmonic plane had been restricted to the Earth. Over the years even that had been slowly reduced as his *Irim* energy trickled away. It was the greatest punishment Michael could have inflicted on the faithless *Irim*: to strand them in their own chosen pursuits, forever unable to resist using their angelic energy to manipulate and use weak humanity only to find at the end of every immoral thing they did that they were weaker still.

Asmodeus's own fury spiked at the unfeeling justice, blowing the windows of the surrounding building out. The Russians cursed and hurried to leave the safe house in Lodz where they'd stopped for the night. One of them even surreptitiously crossed himself, as if his vestigial faith might protect him from the evil he so dimly sensed.

But that was all going to change. Ever since that audacious *Elioud* cunt had rammed her fingers in his vessel's eyes sending him into a coma, Asmodeus had burned for revenge. For that, he needed access to more angelic energy or manna. And there was a huge untapped reservoir hidden in the Shalë River Valley in the Albanian Alps. A real dragon compared to the puny *drangùe*. The Albanians called it a *kulshedër*, what they deemed a seven-headed dragon locked in an eternal battle against the *dragonj*, the semi-divine heroes of Albanian folklore.

A *kulshedër* who was actually one of the leaders of the unfaithful Watcher Angels named Kôkabîêl, the Star of God and commander of 365,000 spirits whom the Archangel Gabriel shackled deep underground until Judgment Day.

Asmodeus was going to free Kôkabîêl.

Did the Archangel, the Supreme Judge of the Heavenly Court, suspect Asmodeus's plans?

Asmodeus doubted it or he wouldn't be so aloof, relying on the pathetic *Elioud* to deal with Dark *Irim* and their followers, human and *daemonic*.

When his last acolyte had stumbled upon the Watcher Angel paintings that Yeqon had commissioned from his sycophantic *Elioud* painters, it had pulled Asmodeus from his coma sooner.

What was that human saying? Oft evil will evil mar? Ha! In this case, evil will had subverted the dumb luck of a Wild *Elioud*.

The fool Yeqon had captured his personal manna without any intent to use it beyond seducing more of humanity. He actually wanted humanity to love him. But any angelic being who possessed the paintings could tap into the stored manna. Just as Asmodeus had done the first time he'd possessed Beta, who took him straight into the heart of the *drangùe*'s lair and within the presence of his treasure, Caravaggio's *Infatuation of the Watcher Angels*. If Rembrandt's *Judgment of the Watcher Angels* had also been there, Asmodeus might have had enough manna to free Kôkabîêl.

Thinking about it now sent his harmonics into a wild oscillation. He sneered and gripped them tighter. The Russians, who'd hustled Beta into a car and driven away from Lodz like a bat out of Hell, said nothing as the temperature in the car rose to an uncomfortable level and smoke filled the air. Instead, as Boshirov gripped the wheel with white knuckles, Petrov lowered the windows and looked back at Beta with a gun pointing over his shoulder.

Beta, whose wrists had been manacled in carbon steel, stared back at Petrov undaunted. Likely her intuition told her that even these security handcuffs wouldn't hold her. She just didn't know yet how to use her nature to defeat them.

Asmodeus's good humor returned. He didn't need Yeqon's stored manna when he had a living source of angelic energy.

It was time to break her once and for all to his control.

Olivia Kastrioti drove into Fushë-Arrëz when she would have preferred to run. Even at seven months' pregnant, she could speed her harmonics and be in the small town in the valley below the Kastrioti estate within minutes. In fact, she needed the exercise. Mihàil would never forbid or restrict her from the gym, but she didn't need to read either his harmonics or his heat signature to know how much he wanted her to step back from vigorous training, and running through the mountains around the estate qualified in his book. Sparring she'd already given up after the raid on the warehouse in Prague in May. Now it was time to move to yoga and swimming and long walks—and runs on the flat track that he'd had installed in the gym facility he'd had built for the residents of Fushë-Arrëz the year after they got married.

Her body was telling her to step back from the challenges of navigating inclines and uneven ground with a growing belly anyway. And her mind wandered enough to make keeping her balance more than a little tricky. She wanted to daydream in the nursery more and review the security measures with their new chief of security less. Ryan Helsing, the American who'd been shot by one of the Russians in Prague, was more than capable of handling whatever they needed.

Ryan was a former Army Ranger who'd left the military at his fiancée's demand only to have her dump him. He'd been in Prague with Ranger buddies on leave, memorializing his newfound single state and considering his future plans, when he'd stepped forward to defend a woman being assaulted by her companion.

Mihàil and Olivia didn't need to discuss hiring Ryan as their chief of security. It hadn't even taken that long to bring him up to speed on the full extent of the job requirements for an enclave of demi-angels. He'd accepted that reality with remarkable equanimity. As he'd quipped, it was a Helsing who'd taken on Dracula. What were *daemons* and *bogomili* compared with the bloodsucking undead?

But even if Mihàil and their daughter—Olivia knew that she was having a little girl, though she'd kept that intuition to herself—hadn't preferred for her to drive into the small Albanian town this morning, Olivia would have. Though the denizens understood fully who and what lived above them, it was better to present herself as fully human. An ordinary human at that. No need to act like local royalty even if that's how the locals insisted on treating her.

Olivia had read a number of romances set in the Regency-era of England. Aristocratic ladies such as Jane Austen's Emma had duties toward the people living and working on their great estates, and the heroines always undertook to use their status to help them. As the *zonjë*, the *drangùe*'s lady, she certainly had the power to benefit the people living within a stone's throw of her. It was one reason that she made it a point to shop for as many items locally as she could and to order others through the shopkeepers. Not only did they get the profit, but when others saw what she was buying, they often bought the same. Of course, she'd also set up a wholesale company that sold goods at a loss to the Albanians.

She chuckled as she turned down the main street—once the only street—in her adopted hometown. *Stone's throw* meant something different when you were an *Elioud* who could adjust the harmonics of the stone's trajectory. At the far end of the shaded storefronts along the north side of the sidewalk, she glimpsed a towering figure whose loping stride and sloped muscular shoulders reminded her of András, and for a moment her heart caught on the hope that it was him.

But it wasn't.

As the giant moved beyond the buildings at the far end of the street, the bright sunlight lit his shoulder-length white-blond hair into a halo and seemed to limn his winged form.

Olivia halted her SUV in the middle of the street, her jaw dropping. There was something familiar about that profile....

The giant turned and headed behind the main street.

Olivia, unaware of the handful of cars stopped patiently behind her, began driving again instead of parking in front of the small clothing store that she'd come to visit. She turned at the corner where the giant had turned. The small side street was empty.

Heart pounding, Olivia drove slowly up the winding street as it climbed back into the lower hills behind Fushë-Arrëz. Most of the buildings on this end of the town were older, though several newer buildings had sprouted in the last year.

Where had the angel gone?

Because it had been an angel. And if her heart spoke true, it had been the Archangel Michael.

The St. Michael's medal lying on her bosom, the one that he'd blessed himself in the guise of her *sensei*, warmed, acknowledging her intuition.

And then Olivia's *Elioud* vision discerned the faint glowing trail to a small, rundown gray building wedged between two newer ones on the flank of the hill. She drove to the open space in front of it, her heart continuing to hammer her ribcage. When she got out, the plain wooden door, its paint peeling, drifted open a crack. Luminosity leaked through the narrow opening. Olivia, grasping the St. Michael medal, approached the entrance both tremulous and wary. A message from a *Cherub*, especially this *Cherub*, always held danger as well as promise.

Whatever waited beyond that unpromising door would change everything.

Olivia pushed the door open. The bare room smelled of oil paint, dust, and a sweet perfume that she'd come to think of as a mix of starlight and roses. What she thought the Heavenly choir loft must smell like.

Zophiel, the guardian angel of the male *Elioud* on their team, stood in front of a large easel, her fine white hair in a loose braid down her back. Wisps had pulled free and floated in a fine mist around her heart-shaped face. Unlike her usual haute couture, she wore a dull gray smock covered in paint splotches.

She looked over her shoulder at Olivia. "There you are, my dear. What do you think? It is far from done, but I believe it shall be my best work ever."

And then the *Cherub* stepped aside, gesturing toward the large canvas.

Olivia blinked, unable to process a thought. In her womb, the baby kicked as if it felt the harmonic emanations captured in luminous brushstrokes.

Later, when Olivia drove home, the encounter with Zophie had all the unreality of a waking dream. She had a slight headache as if dehydrated, and she was ravenous. Not unusual these days, but she'd already eaten the *qifqi*, a traditional snack in the form of rice balls seasoned with herbs and held together with egg, that she'd brought in her shoulder bag. She'd craved them ever since visiting Gjirokastra in Southern Albania last month where they were a staple. Mihàil had laughed at her deliberately cooking extra rice so that she'd have a reason to ask Adriana, their housekeeper and cook, to make them for her.

"You are going to turn into a *qifqi*," he said, kissing the tip of her nose before kissing her again on the mouth. "Or the baby will."

At the time, she'd responded crossly, "That's why I need to keep training."

Now she just thought about what Zophiel's painting depicted and wished she could still imagine calling her daughter *Qifqi* as a silly nickname.

Like the silly nickname that András had called Beta. *Mushroom.*

A sudden insight told her that *Gomba* might very well have had a less cutesy connotation for her beloved goofball. He'd certainly become a lot more serious since Beta had broken his heart. Colder, even. Impatient and withdrawn. And now he was gone, and none of the *Elioud* had seen him since he'd recovered enough from his chest wound to rip the IV out, rattling the normally unflappable Dr. Armand, and rise from his bed.

An unfamiliar Range Rover sat in the circular drive at the front of the house when she arrived.

Stasia.

Olivia felt relief ease the tightness in her shoulders. As she got out of her SUV under the lanai and murmured a greeting to Pjetër, who always seemed to know when she was about to arrive and waited for her, a memory of Beta kneeling next to her in the shadowed back of a moving tractor-trailer filled her with familiar sorrow.

Beta had been the first to join her—after rescuing her from her second harlequin mission which had gone pear-shaped almost as soon as it started. She would have survived, but she would *definitely* have been worse for the wear. And who knows if any of the young Eastern European women she'd intended to free would have been.

Olivia went into the kitchen where Mihàil leaned against a counter, holding a coffee mug in his long, graceful fingers. Miró stood across from him, his arms crossed. Stasia ignored the unhappy cook standing next to her as she deftly operated the espresso machine.

Mihàil's gaze caught Olivia's. The deep love and admiration there never ceased to hit her in the core of her being. He opened his arm in clear invitation, which she accepted as soon as she'd set her purse and shopping bags on the counter. His harmonics soothed hers as invisible warm fingers stroked over her forehead and down her back and thighs. Hints of warm cedar and musk relaxed her further as she pressed herself into his solid side.

"You have turned Mihàil into an Americano drinker," Stasia said, sniffing as she faced them with her demitasse cup. "Gulping down huge quantities *with cream.*" The mock horror in her voice made everyone laugh.

Mihàil squeezed Olivia to his side, winking at her before addressing the diminutive Italian. "Love changes you even—or should I say, especially?—in prosaic ways. What have you adopted because it pleases Miró, hm?"

Stasia, though exceptional at masking her emotions when on a mission, colored now. They all laughed again. It was an open secret that since marrying Miró Stasia had started singing arias as she cooked in the kitchen of their small Rome apartment. She sipped her espresso as Miró shifted closer to her, his thigh touching hers.

Stasia sighed and regarded her husband with such love Olivia's heart swelled. She was unbelievably happy for them both. Then her friend looked at her, her gaze now somber.

"András?" When Olivia shook her head, Stasia nodded as though it was as she'd expected. "I do have some news, *cara.* My contact at École des Beaux-Arts says that Gina has been found wandering corridors and rummaging around dusty storage rooms. She has also befriended most of the faculty and staff, including Alix Durand."

Stasia referred to the great-granddaughter of Émile Bernard, one of Van Gogh's pallbearers, who had taught at the French art school until his death in 1941. As Stasia had guessed, Gina Orlandi knew more about the secret society devoted to the Watcher Angel triptych than she'd shared with them. When Gina disappeared in May, she led them to a direct descendant of the most likely guardian of the final Watcher Angel painting.

The Grey *Elioud* also linked Bernard with the *Codex Angelicus*, which Stasia speculated was the original edition of the Watcher Angel story that had disappeared in the early Middle Ages. Which made sense because the secret society was rumored to have a copy of the *First Book of Enoch* when no one else in Europe had.

"Alix must not know where the *Codex Angelicus* is," said Olivia, glancing at Mihàil.

Mihàil nodded. "Good. That will give Stasia the opportunity to find it first."

"I have already made plans to travel to Paris after I leave here." She gave Miró an apologetic look. They had been apart more than together in the past six months.

Olivia swallowed and stepped from Mihàil's embrace. She went to the cabinet for a water glass, aware that her astute husband knew that something agitated her. She could feel his gaze on her, though he would wait until she was ready to speak.

After drinking enough to ease her suddenly dry throat, she turned back to the other three *Elioud*, who all watched her with concern on their faces.

"I have my own news related to the Watcher Angel triptych. When I was in town this morning, the Archangel Michael led me to an art studio where Zophiel painted *his* version of the final panel. It's titled *Redemption of the Elioud*. And features all of us." She held Mihàil's suddenly intense scrutiny. "Including our baby."

"What else?" Mihàil's growl sent a shiver down Olivia's spine. "Or are your harmonics this roiled over knowing that our daughter is part of the Archangel's plan?"

Olivia shook her head slowly without taking her gaze from her husband's. "No. It's because our redemption—everything, in fact—depends on the third couple in the composition."

Mihàil blinked in shock. "Beta and András."

Olivia nodded, and, her knees no longer able to hold her upright, sat on the nearest stool.

Twelve

Beta felt the change in the air from Petrov's approach a full five minutes before he opened the door to her cell. That was good. Her time was improving. That's all that mattered. She concentrated on developing this new skill. That and trying to raise her body temperature enough to lower the level of the water in the tank they put her in daily even more.

The door clanked open. Petrov stepped inside with a grin. Vibrations emanated from him in concentric waves. If she squinted and focused just a millimeter to the side of his face, they blossomed into a familiar three-dimensional whorl around his figure. She *saw* the resonance of his living cells. If she closed her eyes, she could still make out this unique characteristic.

Even if her head was underwater, and her ears ringing from blows.

"Good, you are awake," said Petrov as he stepped over to check the security cuffs. Currently they restrained her wrists on either side of her waist. "Perhaps we can start today without any drug enhancements, hm?"

Beta shrugged one shoulder as best she could. "I prefer more of the awful music blasted into my cell." She made a show of yawning. "Sleep deprivation works better than drugs. Or did they not tell you that at First Moscow State Medical University?" She was proud that she managed to say all of that in Russian without slurring.

Petrov's grin widened as he stepped back to survey her.

"No wonder our VZ friends recruited you. Your stamina is impressive for a Czech," he said. "Even for one so slight of stature. Though what you do have more than makes up for the lack of size."

Beta knew what came next.

Petrov ran a hand over her shoulder and down her arm, trailing painful static electricity along her skin. She'd long ago learned that the Russian doctor rather enjoyed the sensation and became aroused by it. She ignored the feeling. Instead, she concentrated on the hum and crackle rising from her in response. If she could only increase the intensity of her own resonance, she'd see just how much he liked being shocked enough to lose control of his bladder and bowels.

Her interrogator's hand rose to cup one breast. He didn't pinch the nipple as she expected. "Hm. I think we must put you on another course of intravenous feeding. We cannot have you waste entirely away."

Beta said nothing.

Petrov squeezed her breast once, hard enough to bruise, and stepped back. He squinted at her as if he could see into her. Could see what exactly would unmake her.

"Tell me, how is it that you are unbothered by the temperature in your cell? Or the water in the tank? Yet you wear no clothing."

Beta raised her eyes and let Petrov see the dragon in her gaze. He blinked.

"By all means, feed and dress me," she said, enunciating each word, "and you will learn precisely how unbothered I am."

A long moment of silence followed her announcement. Over the Russian's shoulder, the shadow in the corner grew darker.

The whorl of vibrations around Petrov, which had wavered at the vehement certainty in her words, steadied. "Ah, drug enhancement it is then."

He stepped toward the steel shelf bolted into the rough concrete wall. Beta ignored him to stare at the corner. Something waited there. She sensed it.

Something that waited for her mind to be defenseless.

The Russian turned back with a filled syringe. Beta forestalled him with a question.

"Why are you keeping me here?"

Petrov, in the act of leaning closer, stood upright. "Well, I should think that is obvious."

"Obvious? You already know why I left the VZ. This nonsense serves no purpose beyond titillating you." Beta paused. Despite her bravado, she tired easily and speaking as many words as forcefully as she did, brought her to the edge of her limits.

After she could be sure that she could speak without panting, she continued. "Is this how you recruit all of your assets? No wonder my former handler has a thick file on Unit 29155. All he had to do was follow the trail of broken bodies."

It was much the truth.

Petrov chuckled. It was an unpleasant sound devoid of real humor. He bent and inserted the needle into the catheter access port that he'd implanted on her upper arm. It was an unexpected kindness as it meant he wouldn't damage her veins from repeated injections or blood draws. Or the forced parenteral nutrition.

"Oh, we do not care what Major Vlcek does or does not have in his files on us. He has been chasing Russian ghosts for two decades."

He depressed the syringe plunger. A sharp, cold liquid invaded Beta's blood and was circulated quickly by her heart. She exhaled, flexing her fingers as she imagined sending the drug into the air around them before drawing in a slow breath and exhaling again. She found that this conscious gesture dulled the potency of the drug's first effects.

Petrov discarded the used needle in a portable biohazard container. They were clearly not in a sterile environment, but he maintained this aspect of his training at least.

Vůl. Idiot.

He looked back at her. As she watched in stunned horror, his face melted in thick oily strokes, becoming first a five-year-old's self-portrait in oil pastel and then a ghoulish clown.

When he spoke, his hollow voice drew gooseflesh on her reluctant skin. "I intend to own you, Little Redstart." His hot tongue licked her ear. "*I* am your handler. You are *my* asset. I control your recruitment. When you resist, I hurt you."

Beta struggled to contain a shiver of revulsion.

"You will never own me," she said, narrowing her eyes at the wavering, flesh-colored blob.

Laughter filled the cell around her, echoing and bouncing until her skull reverberated.

"I will own you as your father owned your mother." The timbre of the voice had changed. It was simultaneously harsh and pleasing, broken and melodic. It made her flesh crawl. "Is that what you really want? To be dominated in body and soul?"

Hands scrabbled at Beta's arms, yanking her from the chair. She stumbled and then was thrown to the concrete floor. Petrov's weight descended on her.

"This is how your father took your mother," he hissed into her ear. He bit her high on the breast, near her collarbone. Claws raked her inner thighs.

Beta's dragon nature broke its chains.

Her dragon sight, dimmed by the drugs, clarified as her body temperature rose. Inhaling sharply, she roared directly into Petrov's face. He screamed as her breath scorched his skin, his fingers fumbling for her throat.

Next her dragon nature harnessed her cells' fundamental frequency, converted the vibrations into electrical energy, and delivered a massive shock to the hands choking her.

Petrov thrashed on top of her. As she'd anticipated, he lost control of his bodily functions.

Beta flexed her fingers, imagining sending Petrov into the air as she exhaled. He flew from her and hit the wall. He lay still. The unpleasant scents of urine and feces filled the small, windowless room.

Beta sat up. Her hands had broken the links chaining her wrists at her waist. The chain running between her ankles had never been tethered to the floor. She placed a hand on the concrete, which had blackened and cracked under her, and levered herself into a shaky stand.

A wave of dizziness washed over her. She shook like a leaf in a hurricane.

With an effort, she steadied herself. Someone had locked the door after Petrov entered, but perhaps she could find a weakness in the door or frame to exploit.

A deep, inhuman growl resounded.

Beta's hands instinctively came up in a defensive position before her face as her feet shifted to approximate a fighting stance.

"Show yourself." Beta tasted smoke with her words.

"Here I am, Daughter." A ghastly form materialized from thin air next to her. The body was misshapen with skin like iridescent obsidian, the eyes deep set, and the skull overlarge. The eyes themselves sparkled in malice. When he spoke, his voice modulated unpleasantly from low to high, gravelly to squeaky. "Do you think you can withstand me?"

Beta's chin came up. "I already did, did I not?" She gestured with her chin toward the prone Russian doctor. A shudder rolled down her spine, but she kept her gaze steady on the monstrous figure.

The being laughed. It sounded like metal shearing. "I am enjoying breaking you to my will."

Beta felt her spine stiffen. Her shoulders, tired and bruised as they were, straightened and lifted. "That is not going to happen. You may as well set me free or kill me."

The being popped out of existence and then back in again close behind her. His foul breath seared her skin as he leaned in, slipping the hair from her neck with a long, sharp fingernail. "No."

Beta shrugged one shoulder. "Then we are at an impasse."

She pivoted and stepped away, managing to do so without staggering, and met the monster's hard gaze with her own. For a moment, their frequencies aligned, and something in her dragon nature leaped in joy.

The fiend smirked. "Are you sure about that?"

Instead of answering, Beta cocked her head and studied him. "Yes. You have no power that I do not grant you. And your puppet is out cold."

She turned away, intending to find a way out of the cell.

He snarled. Howling wind buffeted her. She ignored the maelstrom and proceeded to break the lid on the biohazard container by smashing it against the steel shelf.

Without turning, she said, "Your tantrum does not scare me."

The shrieking subsided to tiny squeaks and chirps as if there was a nest of rustling mice behind her. Beta had pulled out used hypodermics, for weapons or tools, she wasn't sure which, when Asmodeus spoke.

In a familiar voice that was not his.

"Beta, here you are!"

Beta whirled. Standing before her, in a cell in some Russian black site only God knew where, was an ethereally beautiful young blonde whose blue-gray eyes studied her with affection. A hand rested on a very pregnant belly.

Olivia.

Beta raised a tentative hand to the other woman's face. Warm skin met her fingers. Olivia smiled and pressed her cheek against Beta's palm.

"Let me rescue you from this place as you rescued me," she said.

Beta knew that Olivia could not be here. And yet …

She dropped her palm. "Be gone, Asmodeus."

In a blink, the Dark *Irim's* visage had replaced Olivia's. His malevolent gaze held humor. "Do you know, Daughter, that pregnant women are especially vulnerable to bad dreams and malign influences?"

And then he was gone.

Mihàil Kastrioti stood looking at the marker for the Soviet mass grave 32 kilometers southeast of Berlin. Prior to the Soviets burying thirty thousand of their soldiers between here and Seelow Heights eighty kilometers east in the last days of World War Two, it had been a German cemetery of no great renown. Georg Luger, inventor of the original 9mm semi-automatic handgun used for almost half the twentieth century, including the German army and navy in World War One, had been buried here.

Luger also happened to be the *daemonic Elioud* that led Asmodeus's *daemonia* hordes.

Sighing, Mihàil ran a hand through his hair. There was no way to tell where Luger's body had ended up. Or even if his bones still existed. The Soviets had emptied a lot of graves in their bloodlust, scattering the remains wherever the urge took them and burying their own dead there.

Desecrating the German dead in the name of justice when all they did was justify their own base nature.

A base nature that led Soviet soldiers to rape two million German women, killing many. Almost a quarter of a million German women died, some from suicide or venereal disease. Many were raped in public, in front of their families, and shot afterward. Soviet commanders gave their men three days to do whatever they wanted after they entered a German city. Age spared none. Pregnancy spared none. Religious orders spared none. Women and girls between the ages of eight and eighty were violated. Groups of soldiers gang-raped victims, who were assaulted more than seventy times on average.

Allied soldiers were little better. In fact, French soldiers in Baden-Württemberg matched the Soviets atrocity for atrocity. British military police had little power to investigate and punish the regular reports of rape in the months of Allied occupation. American soldiers managed to turn rape into coerced sex with desperate German housewives, who prostituted themselves to feed their starving families. And all because the Nazis had also done horrible things to their fellow humans, including systematically raping Soviet women in order to beget German children on them.

It was a very old practice, this raping of the enemy's women. Mihàil had seen it for hundreds of years and across many cultures.

Despair rose in his gorge.

He hadn't lied when he'd told Olivia that most of what humans called demonic behavior rightly belonged to humans. But the carnage and depravity of the twentieth century owed a great deal to empowered *daemonia*, who'd gone on a spiritual feeding frenzy. There had been more than one powerful angelic being acting as a tuner, and the result had been devastation and desecration such as the world had never seen.

Mihàil, Miró, and András had been virtually ineffectual. There had been just too many possessed soldiers and too many helpless women and children. For years it had felt like they bailed out a flooding rowboat with a spoon. But no one ever suggested quitting. Least of all András, who had been so young for such horrors. If anything, he'd been an indomitable, tireless warrior, whose energy and passion had inspired Mihàil and Miró whenever they flagged.

Olivia had never known this level of evil, only its long shadow. It frightened Mihàil that all the signs suggested that a day was fast coming in which his beloved, the woman he'd waited five hundred years for, the mother to his unborn child, would be exposed to it, even endangered by it.

And the Archangel Michael intended his wife to play a central role in overcoming it. Had, in fact, long planned for Olivia and her friends to be the second half of a celestial trio of couples, who together would form a harmonically linked triad against the Dark angelic forces.

A triad whose very existence would atone for the original disobedient Watcher Angels.

Mihàil's own mother, always and forever an *Angelus Fidelis*, had been sent by St. Michael to marry an *Elioud* for this reason. She'd never told Mihàil, simply allowed him to believe that she'd fallen in love with Georgj Kastrioti and left her place in a Heavenly choir to marry him. She, too, had been in the painting that Zophiel painted. The one that now hung over the mantel in his living room.

He didn't know whether to be relieved that St. Michael had a plan or angry that he hadn't told them until now.

The harmonic plane rippled with a familiar disturbance, one the *drangùe* hadn't felt in almost four months.

András had found them.

Thank Elohim. Mihàil's intense relief weakened his knees for a moment.

He turned toward his youngest lieutenant, who was like family to him, and his heart squeezed hard at the bittersweet sight.

András had lost weight. Dark shadows hollowed out his eyes. The coldness that had affected his harmonic signature for the past three years had grown, though his signature remained stable. The wound in his shoulder hadn't fully healed even after four months. And the bullet fragments from the Skopje mission, the ones that András didn't think that he or Miró knew about, had formed a hard mass on his shoulder blade.

"*Uram,*" he said, bowing his head.

Mihàil ignored the formal title of *lord* and pulled András into a hard hug. The big Hungarian stiffened and then relaxed, lifting his good arm to squeeze Mihàil back. Even with only one arm and clearly weakened, the strength of his embrace would have bruised a lesser man.

Mihàil stepped back but kept his hands on the Hungarian's upper arms. He held the younger *Elioud*'s gaze. "It is good to see you, *Stuhi*."

He hadn't used the nickname in decades. He'd given it to the twelve-year-old András after rescuing him from a gang of teenage thugs in the process of beating him within a hands' breadth of his life. *Tempest* had certainly fit the exuberant and undisciplined youth he'd taken under his wing.

András blinked. Mihàil thought he'd glimpsed a revealing shimmer in the other man's gaze, but when his lieutenant looked back at him, it was gone.

"Thank you, *Uram*" was all he said. Then he looked down at the marker and frowned.

"This is where Georg Luger, our *daemonic Elioud*, was buried," said Mihàil.

"'Was' being the operative word," said Miró, who'd been surveying the perimeter of the site and now stood next to them. He nodded at András. "Welcome back, *brat*."

Mihàil smiled. It always amused him that the Croatian word for *brother* had taken on the additional meaning of "annoying child" in other languages. Using it was Miró's way of showing humor and affection. András merely nodded back, but his infrared signature had warmed a little since he'd been welcomed by them.

"Then a harmonic sink is out of the question," he said, gazing at each of them in turn. "We're never going to get rid of this bastard, are we?"

The bleakness in his eyes made Mihàil's own despair deepen.

Miró, glancing at him, looked back at András. "The only way is through."

Mihàil, startled, looked at his senior lieutenant. András narrowed his eyes.

"What the hell does that mean, *brother*?"

"You know what it means," said Mihàil, squaring his shoulders to address the *Elioud* he viewed as a son.

András looked at each of them again. Whatever he saw in their expressions made him stiffen.

"I've already failed to win her. Twice."

What he didn't say, but both Mihàil and Miró knew, was that Beta had rejected him the first time after making love to him. Their harmonics and nimbuses had been forever changed after that. Her second betrayal had maimed András on a spiritual level even as her assault damaged his body.

"Then the third time will succeed," said Miró with no hint of humor.

Magma erupted behind András's gaze, but when he spoke, ice sharpened his words.

"I will track her until I find her." He paused. Mihàil saw him clench his fists. "What happens after that I refuse to speculate."

Mihàil tilted his head, studying the younger *Elioud*. "You did not mean it then when you said 'nothing and no one will prevent me from winning her away from him'?"

András said nothing. But his face grew stonier.

That infuriated Mihàil. He leaned closer to the bigger *Elioud*. The air between them heated. "Understand this, then, András. This is more important than how you feel. It is more important than the hordes of *daemonia* that Asmodeus commands. The Archangel Michael has decreed that Beta play a critical role in his plan to redeem the *Elioud*. So you had damn well better get your head on straight for this mission."

András glared back at him. Mihàil, turning away, ran his hand through his hair and dropped his temperature. He needed to keep his temper under better control.

"So now it's my *mission* to win Beta?"

The scorn in András's voice made Mihàil wince. He turned back to the other two *Elioud*, aware that he was failing as a commander *and* a friend. What would András think if he ever learned the truth about his mother and sisters, the truth that Mihàil had kept from him? Or what Mihàil suspected about Beta?

Given everything that had happened between them, the Archangel's plan would be for naught if András knew.

"Be the light that refuses to surrender," said Miró, putting a hand on András's arm, "so that she does not become the darkness that she endures."

Now András scoffed. "Endures? You speak as if Beta took a burden on instead of willingly making a pact with a Dark *Irim*."

Miró looked at Mihàil and then, dropping his hand, shrugged. "Something does not add up. When we found her again, her memory had been altered, but her harmonics responded to András. Perhaps Asmodeus has been trying to 'win' Beta as well."

András stared down at the grave marker. When he looked at them again, the anger had gone. "You think that I can prevail. But a plan is just that. Sometimes the bad guys win."

THIRTEEN

B eta's strength was almost gone. And with it, her confidence that she would outlast Asmodeus and the Russians.

She sat shivering on the thin mattress in the corner of her cell. It had no sheet or blanket, and the padding had compressed under her slight weight. At least it wasn't dirty. Unlike the loose tunic and pants that Petrov had given her some days ago after sneering that she resembled a survivor of a Siberian work camp.

Beta highly doubted that. Despite her ill treatment, she hadn't been flogged, raped, branded to the bone or had her nostrils and ears slit. She hadn't even been starved. Petrov—or more likely his dark master—had clearly realized that those methods would have just hardened her resolve. Instead, they kept her isolated in this sunless room twenty-four hours a day with no human contact other than Petrov and the countless, faceless male guards who brought her food, which they dumped onto the concrete floor, and water, which they watched her drink. Sometimes they even brought toilet paper. If she refused to eat or drink for more than three days, Petrov sighed and brusquely ordered a guard to chain her into a chair so that he could administer IV nutrition.

But the injections continued. And the frequent visits from Asmodeus, who tormented her drug-fueled hallucinations with dark visions and gleeful predictions. Beta wanted to believe that the Dark *Irim* visited only her and not her best friend Olivia, but she couldn't be sure. And in that doubt, she wavered. Which merely gave Asmodeus a wedge to crack her open.

She didn't even know how long she'd been held here. Months, her intuition told her. If Asmodeus suspected that she barely kept the memory of András Nagy and the moment her treacherous stiletto pierced his chest from dominating her thoughts, he'd compel Petrov to keep her drugged continuously as he replayed that horrible vision over and over until she went mad. Because nothing else tormented her as viciously as knowing that she'd killed the man that she loved.

There. She'd thought it. She'd admitted it to herself. She loved András, and it was far too late to tell him so. She'd *killed* him.

A long, shuddering sob escaped her before she could stop it. A hot tear trickled down her cheek, but she couldn't lift a hand to brush it away. She was too exhausted to weep.

Why does Asmodeus not take advantage of my great spiritual wound?

Before Beta could turn this question over, the lock to her cell clicked and the door swung open. She ignored the guard, not at all concerned that he would notice or care about the wet track on her face. She didn't register the tray he carried until he set it on the metal shelf that Petrov used for his implements. That got her attention. Looking up, she saw an actual bowl and plate on the tray. When she swung her gaze to the guard's back, she realized that he was larger than any of the other guards she'd seen before.

Turning toward Beta, the guard removed the cuffs from the belt at her waist. To her shock, he didn't stop there. He unlocked the cuffs and removed them before massaging her hands and wrists with surprisingly gentle fingers. Warmth and wellbeing rose up her arms and into her chest, where something frozen and dark had subsumed her dragon heat. Instantly she felt better.

When the guard's gaze rose to hers, Beta realized that she recognized those piercing blue eyes.

It was the Viking from The Duplex Club in Prague.

He studied her face for a moment before raising his hand and brushing the wetness with his thumb. "You are having a rough time, little one."

Beta cleared her throat, which had suddenly thickened. "Who are you?" she whispered.

"That you know already. I am Michael, the Commander of the Armies of Heaven and the Chief Justice of the Supreme Heavenly Court."

He turned and picked up the bowl and a spoon. Beta smelled something sweet and buttery before he scooped up a portion and offered it to her. She opened her mouth without thinking, and a moment later tasted *kaše*. Tears pricked her before streaming down her cheeks, but Michael said nothing. He simply continued to feed her until she was full. Afterwards, Beta felt better than she'd felt in a long time. Years perhaps.

"Are you going to free me?" she asked.

Michael shook his head. "No, that's not my role."

Despite his words, something in his tone gave her hope. She accepted the water cup from him and drank it all. It was pure and cold and cleared the ache in her head. The Archangel accepted the cup back and then, with an apologetic look, restrained her hands again. That's when Beta realized that the deep mottled bruises on her wrists had disappeared.

"Thank you."

"Of course." He stood upright. Shadows swirled in those startling blue eyes. "I have a gift for you, if you will receive it."

Nodding, Beta swallowed against the dumpling in her throat. The Archangel held out a slender chain whose silver links were so fine they could have been woven by fairies. On it a tiny silver medallion sparked in the single dim overhead light. It seemed to sway between his fingers, tinkling faintly. It made her breathless with longing for something pure and everlasting. Michael's gaze sharpened at her reaction.

He bent again, and Beta bowed her head so that he could fasten the pendant around her neck. She had no idea how she would keep this treasure from Petrov.

The Archangel, touching a fingertip to the medallion, murmured something. It warmed against her skin. Then he turned away to pick up the tray.

"What did you say?" asked Beta, her own fingers itching to touch the silver disc, which he'd tucked under the collar of the soiled tunic.

The Archangel turned partway toward her. Instead of answering, he said, "You have great power"—here he touched her forehead with hard fingertips—"and you know how to use it. I suggest that you counter his attack with a defense that he cannot take from you."

Later, when Petrov came to interrogate Beta for the hundredth time, she clung to the memory of that tall angelic form that had been at once terrifying and reassuring.

Her body had gotten so used to the drug that the Russian doctor gave her that he'd increased the dose several times. Today, after the reinvigorating visit by St. Michael, Beta found that the drug simply elevated her mood and softened the edges of cinderblock, concrete, and steel that defined her space.

"Where shall we begin today, hm?" asked Petrov.

He stood as far from her as he could inside the cell's narrow confines. Beta's nose assured her it was because she stank. It was also because she scared the crap out of him.

"Ah, yes. How about Salisbury? Did you know that we have confirmation that you traveled there in March?"

"When you and Boshirov poisoned Skripal and his innocent daughter?" she asked.

Petrov scowled. "Perhaps it was *you* who poisoned that traitor and his complicit spawn at the order of Major Vlcek to defame us."

Beta cocked her head. "I suppose I also sold you out to MI6 in your version of events? That makes me an opportunistic double dealer."

"Exactly what one would expect of a Czech." Petrov studied her. "Your answers are strangely lucid. Perhaps it is time to increase the dosage."

His shadow loomed large behind him as he filled the hypodermic needle, the whorl of his personal frequency as fractured and cutting as shattered glass. She heard it now as clearly as she heard the sound of her own disordered resonance.

Asmodeus.

Despite the Archangel's earlier visit, Beta's hands tightened into a fist. *Prosím, svatý Michaeli.* She had no idea what she asked for, strength or endurance or oblivion. Perhaps all three.

The tiny medallion warmed on the bare skin of her breast, drawing her attention as Petrov plunged the syringe into her catheter port. This time, the cold sensation halted when it reached that spot.

Beta narrowed her eyes at Petrov, who watched her, his gaze sharp with malice.

She inhaled deeply, imagining steadying her resonance as she released her breath. The St. Michael medal continued to warm. She smiled and managed to lift one shoulder slightly.

"*Naštvali jste se do bot*?" she asked innocently. She knew Petrov understood the underlying rude Czech idiom for bad luck when he flushed. "Perhaps your supplier gave you a bad batch."

Petrov's eyes widened. "What is that under your tunic?"

He lunged for her, ripping the tunic collar halfway down her chest. His fingers scrabbled for the pendant, and Beta knew a moment of sick fear that he would tear it from her neck. But as his fingers clasped the medal, it heated. He fell back, howling and sucking on his blistered flesh. Sweat had popped out on Beta's chest and ran in rivulets between her breasts, but she knew without looking that her own skin wasn't harmed.

"*Jste v rejži*," she said, letting mockery edge her words about being in trouble. She was having fun now, using familiar Czech idioms to show Petrov and his spiritual jockey that not only wasn't she witless, she was in control. "It was a gift. For me, not you."

"Then that will be the only thing you wear," shouted Petrov as he grasped the paper-thin fabric of the tunic with both hands and tore it to her waist.

A moment later, he yelped and blinked his streaming eyes against the piercing light that reflected from the exposed silver. He backed away, one hand swiping at the tears and the other frantic hand searching among his implements, for what she could only guess.

Beta waited for the inevitable. And there it was. Asmodeus had shed his vessel like a snakeskin. Petrov dropped to the floor of the cell like a bag of potatoes, hitting his head on the metal shelf on the way down.

She looked down at the unconscious Russian colonel.

"That will leave a nasty bruise," she said, pursing her lips in faux concern. "Soon you will need to find another puppet. This one is not so strong."

"Beta, you don't need to be high to speak with me," said Olivia, who stood near Beta's right shoulder. She looked solemn. And very pregnant.

As before, Beta's heart leapt in happy recognition. She squashed it ruthlessly and let her gaze drift out of focus. Olivia's avatar, who radiated a dark spectral light unlike the authentic Olivia, continued speaking. Except this time, Beta found that if she concentrated on the vibrations emanating from the false Olivia, she could cause them to flow around her own ears as a river rushes over a submerged boulder, blocking the avatar's words. Beta allowed the resulting white noise to mesmerize her....

"Get drinks," said Kacper, standing next to her at the bar. As usual, he smelled like curdled cheese and cigarette smoke.

Beta looked over her shoulder at him. Something in her gaze made the bar owner add, *"Proszę." Please.* Right. That didn't sound at all natural from his mouth.

She nodded, though the skin on her back prickled as she turned away from the newcomers who'd entered the club.

Jerzego, a cigarette dangling from his mouth, dumped ice into the bin under the counter as she came behind the bar. She ignored the bartender to pull liqueur glasses from the shelf along the back wall and then delivered the drinks to Kacper and his two guests, a large black man and a blond woman. The woman's gleaming blue gaze followed Beta.

A moment later—though it must have been longer—the woman trailed Beta into the bar's dirty bathroom. Before Beta could mutter and backtrack, the other woman placed her hand on her arm. Alarm shot through Beta.

"Are you here of your free will?" asked the woman.

She'd asked in Czech.

How did this too-beautiful creature know Beta's secret? Her alarm increased until her skin buzzed. She pulled her arm away and took a step.

The woman moved in front of the bathroom door. "You don't have any bruises that I can see," she said, her gaze searching Beta's, "but Kacper's too smart to damage such a lovely face. Is that why you're wearing long sleeves and jeans?"

Beta, irritated, scowled at the assertive questioning. "I am wearing long sleeves and jeans," she said—in Czech—"because that is what I like to wear. Now get out of my way. I have work to do."

The other woman ignored Beta's demand, crossing her arms instead. She held Beta's gaze. An electric current passed between them.

"I can help you," said the blond woman. "Get away from Kacper. You and the others."

A painful shock vibrated through Beta, tearing the vision of Olivia from her.

"Where did you go, Daughter?" hissed Asmodeus, clutching her shoulders with icy fingers that sent electricity vibrating through her. His hideous features filled her sight.

Beta, her teeth chattering, managed to answer the Dark *Irim*. "My day-dreams of Petrov with two black eyes and a broken nose."

Asmodeus roared and battered her face with a fist covered in horny scales, splitting her lip. Her eye swelled instantly, pain bursting in her head like an IED filled with nails and broken glass. Despite herself, Beta passed out.

When she woke, Petrov was gone and so was Asmodeus. She sat propped against the corner of the cell where the Dark *Irim*'s blow had knocked her. Clenching her jaw, she closed her good eye as the cell spun around her and rested her cheek against the cinderblock wall. The dim light from the single bulb burned through her uninjured eyelid. She didn't know if she could sit upright.

The lock in the door rattled as someone inserted the key and turned it. The door squeaked ajar. Beta cracked her good eye open as the visitor entered.

Not the Viking as her heart had hoped. Petrov.

Nevertheless, the medallion warmed on her breast.

She sighed and closed her eye. "Your face looks painful. I suggest you not risk any more injury and leave."

Petrov laughed. It sounded a little mad. Shrill notes frayed its edges until it broke. It ended on a deep and unnatural *chirrup*. He walked to the shelf, where gleaming instruments lined up next to vials and syringes, and picked up a pair of pliers. When he turned his head, Asmodeus gazed back at her.

"I should say the same to you," said the Dark *Irim*, opening and closing the pliers slowly, a smile deforming his bruised features. "Your strength is almost gone."

"The question is which one of us will break first." Beta paused, gathering her energy into her core, and sat upright without touching the wall.

Asmodeus laughed again. The sound reverberated around the cell. And then he came over and pinched the soft skin under her arm with the pliers. Beta swallowed a scream and imagined that she swung her long-destroyed chain whip around her. She *saw* the chain whip, which moved in time with the fundamental frequency of her cells, whose whorl arced around her in an incandescent path. She noticed the unevenness of its oscillation, which synced with her breath. Concentric color bands formed a rough shape where her body had been. A tiny white star blazed near the top of a dull red band.

The St. Michael medal.

You have great power, and you know how to use it. The Archangel's voice echoed in her memory.

Beta concentrated on controlling her breath and regulating her harmonic vibrations. As she did, Asmodeus, the pliers, and the prison cell all faded from her awareness.

She was back in Katowice, across the Czech border in Poland.

This time she rode in the back of a tractor-trailer. Sweat slicked her skin. Around her, silent women slumped or leaned against the swaying truck's sides. The blond American woman lay unconscious on her stomach on the dusty steel floor, her hands and ankles bound.

Beta knelt next to the American spy and shook her shoulder. As she roused, Beta said, "*Kdyby hloupost nadnášela, tak se tady budete vznášet jako holubička.*" *If stupidity floats, you will float here like a dove.*

"Better free my hands and feet then before I bump into the ceiling," said the American, her voice hoarse.

Beta sniffed and pulled out the small knife hidden in the special lining of her ankle boot before slicing through the blonde's zip ties. She helped the other woman sit up.

The American, wincing as she rubbed her wrists, looked around at the women steadfastly ignoring them. She wrinkled her nose.

"I was trying to rescue them. Something tells me you"—she lifted her chin toward Beta before continuing—"don't need rescuing. You look like a model but move like a trained fighter. Czech military?"

Beta scowled and refused to answer. Instead, she listened as the truck ground to a halt. Ignoring the blonde, she made her way through the huddled women to the unlocked lift gate at the rear. She raised the gate, jumped to the ground, and ran for the trees at the side of the road. Once she'd gone twenty meters, she turned to see the driver, an automatic weapon in his hands, come around the back of the truck where the blonde frantically urged the other women to follow her.

Beta yelled a warning, but no sound left her throat. The driver punched the gunstock into the American spy's head. She crumpled to her knees.

Beta hissed, spat on the packed dirt at her feet, and prepared to fight against terrible odds.

Only to find Asmodeus studying her through unblinking eyes. A wild profusion of spectral planes and lines jumped and spiked from his angelic form like a reactor on the verge of meltdown. Petrov was nowhere to be seen.

"Did you know that brainwaves are just harmonics?" asked the Dark *Irim* before he shrank and slipped through her pupils and into her brain.

Beta's heart raced. Fiery heat alternated with sharp cold in her body. Distant cymbals clashed. Rhythmic buzzing set her teeth on edge. Dull pain hammered her between the eyes until she couldn't see or think clearly.

In the midst of this turbulent dissonance, the St. Michael medal grew soothingly warm. Beta focused on that little bit of harmony until it grew into a quiet oasis.

Olivia sat next to her. This time she was neither a false avatar of Asmodeus or a dreamlike memory. Instead, she was a luminous harmonic being whose very essence sang, but her eyes were sad. She was indeed pregnant.

Beta laid her head on her friend's shoulder. "I am so tired, Liv," she said.

"I know, dear one." Olivia pressed a shining kiss to Beta's forehead. "You've taken on too much alone. You should have trusted him."

Beta felt another presence. Startled, she looked up to see another lambent being, a petite woman with honey-brown hair and hazel eyes, sitting on her other side.

"Stasia," she breathed, overwhelmed with gratitude. Tears pricked her eyes. She'd refused to allow herself to remember her other friend even after the memory had spilled from her when Boshirov interrogated her. "How?"

Stasia took her hands, tracing around the cuffs. When she looked up, tears glistened in her eyes. "We are connected, *cara*. You called me here."

"You called us both here," said Olivia. "We couldn't have found you otherwise. None of us could." She gently emphasized the word *none*. "Now we can help you."

Beta, slowly shaking her head, looked at each of her friends. "Why? I am a lone wolf. I went my own way." She swallowed, her throat so dry she had to whisper. "I seduced András and ..." She let her voice trail away. She couldn't bring herself to say *killed him*.

"We understand why you did what you did," said Stasia fiercely.

"It's time to come home," said Olivia. "Stay strong. And let yourself love and be loved. You *do* deserve it. Now rest. We'll see you soon."

Stasia kissed Beta's cheeks. And then both women faded from Beta's sight.

Beta sighed. She didn't believe that she deserved to be loved. Even if she did, it would take nothing short of a miracle to get her out of this prison.

Commotion roiled the harmonics outside her cell. The door burst inwards, slamming the wall before hanging from a hinge.

Gordon walked in. He smiled. "There you are."

FOURTEEN

Beta's mouth fell open before she could stop it. She closed it with a snap. "How did you get here?" she asked.

Gordon grinned. "I'm shocked at your appearance, too. You have questions. But answers will have to wait." He set the weapon he carried on the shelf and knelt next to her. As he unlocked one of the cuffs, he said, "It's a good thing that one of the guards was so cooperative and gave me his keys. Otherwise, you'd have to wear these cuffs a while longer."

Beta waited until he'd freed both hands. Then she struck one-handed against Gordon's throat, wrapping the webbing between her thumb and forefinger around his trachea. Gordon, gagging and choking, tried to pull her hand away, but Beta rose on her knees and sank her fingers deeper into his flesh. For several seconds, he struggled. Just as he sagged, she let go. He fell back against the wall, sliding down and coughing.

Beta, ignoring him, placed a palm against the wall and rose to stand on unsteady feet. She didn't know if she could get out of the Russian black site without help, but she wasn't stupid enough to trust Gordon, who'd sold her out to the Russians in the first place.

With that in mind, she grabbed the weapon, a new model SIG Sauer. Pointing it away from them, she ejected the magazine and checked. It was full. She pushed it back into place and brought the muzzle up toward Gordon, who'd stopped coughing and faced her. He held his hands up, palms out, and smiled.

"One answer will not wait," said Beta. "Why I should not put a bullet through your skull right now."

Gordon shrugged. "You could. It wouldn't actually make much difference to your escape. I was just the tip of the spear, though I'd like to think you'd fare better with me at your six."

Beta, who'd glanced toward the implements that Petrov left behind, focused on the American arms dealer again. "For whom are you working?"

"A colleague of yours." Gordon, despite an injured trachea and an unwavering 9mm aimed at his head, smiled. "He was most insistent when he recruited me."

Colleague? When she'd last seen Gordon, he was at the mercy of the *drangùe* Mihàil Kastrioti and his lieutenant Miró Kos.

Beta shoved the abrupt realization of who the *Elioud* warriors were from her thoughts. She had to focus on the here and now, not the past.

"Vlcek?" she asked.

Gordon's smiled increased. "You know, we *really* don't have time to discuss this. Let's just say that I had no choice but to come help you. Why else would I risk my life?"

He had a point. Best to get out of this *zatraceným* prison first and then find out what in the name of all that was holy was going on.

The St. Michael medal warmed at that thought.

"Then you lead the way out. There is no chance that I will allow you at my back."

"Fair enough." Gordon turned before Beta could motion him toward the doorway.

"But first, hand me the weapon you took off the guard outside."

Gordon blinked and then, laughing, pulled the Russian weapon from the small of his back where he'd tucked it. Beta took the gun and checked it. An actual Glock and not one of the Russian GSh knockoffs. It wouldn't accidentally discharge if it fell. She slipped it into the waist of her pants, grip-side slightly overhanging the fabric. It wasn't secure, especially as loose as the pants were on her, but she'd figure something out as she went.

As she followed Gordon, she snatched a couple of filled syringes with her free hand. Petrov had been careless of late, confident in her inability to free herself from her shackles. Beta had been conserving her energy for the moment she'd be able to get the drug and inject the Russian colonel. She'd known that she'd only have one opportunity given how weak she'd grown. Not that it was a perfect weapon, but she suspected that whatever dosage Petrov now gave her would incapacitate a large male.

Too bad she only had two syringes. And too bad Petrov was elsewhere or she'd inject both syringes into his carotid artery. At the same time.

Gordon waited for Beta outside her cell. As soon as she appeared, he jogged down the corridor, which was about forty meters long. Small rectangular windows appeared every ten meters on the opposite wall. By the color and brightness of the light coming through the dirty panes, Beta guessed that it was either very early morning or dusk.

As they turned the corner at the end of the corridor, Gordon swerved wide to miss the body slumped on the floor. Beta recognized him as one of her guards. Her gaze snagged on his feet.

"Wait."

Gordon, who'd reached the stairs, turned.

"Come back here and take his boots."

Gordon regarded her bare feet. "Of course."

He backtracked and, kneeling on one knee, removed the guard's socks and boots. Beta leaned against the wall while he slipped first a sock, and then a boot, onto each of her bare feet. Even that effort left her shaking. The thick men's socks helped pad her slender feet, which were otherwise long enough for the boots. Beta said a silent prayer of gratitude to St. Michael and felt the medal warm.

Gordon rose to his feet. "I got in unseen until this guy." He nudged the guard with his toe. "There's another guard on the first floor and two guards patrolling the perimeter, but the Russians are mostly relying on cameras and sensors to keep busybodies away from the property."

"Which appears to be an abandoned factory or other industrial site." She motioned Gordon to go on. "Where are we?"

"You mean, where outside of Russia would Unit 29155 assassins torture someone for an extended period?" asked Gordon as he started down the stairs. "That would be Babyrusk."

A city in Belarus. Of course. The former member of the Soviet Union often deferred to its larger, more aggressive neighbor to the east, especially in matters of state security.

Beta also knew no one in this country.

They made it all the way outside before the first Russian guard appeared. As soon as he saw them, he raised his weapon.

So did Beta.

She squeezed off a shot, but her hand shook enough that it went a little wide. The Russian answered with several shots of his own as he faded back behind the corner of the building. At the same time, Gordon pulled Beta back inside. A stinging burn in her upper arm blossomed into a bloody flower on her shirt. She pulled her sleeve up. She'd been hit, but it was just a flesh wound. Dizziness washed over her anyway. She leaned against the wall.

"You might want to give me that Glock," Gordon said, peering out the small window around the corner from the door.

Outside the Russian radioed the other guards. "*Zaklyuchenny sbezhal.*" *The prisoner escaped.* "*U nee yest pomoshch.*" *She has help.*

It was nice to know that Beta was the only prisoner in this appalling facility. One who'd merited four guards. She grimaced. One of those guards was on this floor, likely running like a demon towards them.

At the thought of demons, Beta's gaze darted around the dim hallway. Where were Asmodeus and Petrov?

She pressed upright and moved next to Gordon to look out the window. The other Russian remained hidden. Probably waiting for the other guards to converge on their spot and divide their attention.

"Did you come alone?" she asked Gordon. "Or do you have a team somewhere?"

"No team, just lone backup, though your colleague doesn't need a lot of help." He glanced at her. An odd light filled his eyes. "I got the feeling we're bait."

A frisson of unease rolled down Beta's spine. She lifted her chin in response. "I am no one's bait."

Before she could say more, massive disturbance roiled the harmonic plane around them. Something was happening on the far side of the building.

A moment later, a harmonic detonation shook the structure. Gordon's eyes widened.

Beta and Gordon looked out the window. The third Russian guard waited at the corner opposite them where he could cover the other outside guard. As they watched, that guard darted from his hiding place. Beta focused on the window in front of her. Its harmonic vibrations told her that it was ordinary commercial glass. The Russians hadn't reinforced it.

"Those are bonded rounds," Gordon said at her unstated question.

Beta nodded and, lifting the P320, fired two quick shots in the lower corners of the window. It shattered outwards. And the Russians responded instantly by firing at them.

Beta used both hands to steady the P320. Breathing in, she ignored the rain of bullets to focus on the three-dimensional whorl of harmonic vibrations around her. Manipulating the whorl, she deflected the incoming rounds. She didn't stop there, however. She consciously adjusted the frequency of her harmonic signature until she vibrated outside of the frequency around her. The harmonics of the P320 adjusted in sync.

Beta sighted the nearest Russian guard, suspended in a low run. Her first shot hit him high in the shoulder. She waited patiently for the impact to rock him back so that his torso became more visible. Then she hit him center mass.

By this time, Beta no longer needed to think consciously about how to adjust her harmonics. Instead, she pivoted and shot the third Russian guard in the head as he peered around the corner, almost before her last shot had connected with the other guard. The guards dropped to the ground one after the other.

Beta lowered the Sig, exhaled, and looked at Gordon, who for once stared wide eyed and speechless at her.

"Not bait," she reiterated. "And I am not giving you the Glock."

"Understood," said Gordon, a note of awe in his voice that irritated her.

"Then let us leave," she said, waving toward the door, though she had serious doubts that she could actually walk out it. Her arm stung from the graze wound.

"Actually, I prefer that you stay," said a hollow voice behind them.

Petrov emerged from the dark recesses of the corridor on the other side of the stairs. Spectral lines and planes pulsed erratically from his form, lending an eerie backlight to him, a kind of reverse nimbus. His eyes remained in deep shadow even when he halted only a couple of meters from them. He was unarmed.

Hundreds of invisible insects crawled over Beta's flesh, raising the hairs on the back of her neck. Her gut told her that Petrov had finally gone mad from Asmodeus's possession. She shifted toward Gordon, who seemed the lesser threat at the moment, and turned her hip toward him. He said nothing but moved a fraction closer. She felt his hand brush her thigh, and then he snatched the Glock from her waistband and raised it in one smooth motion.

What happened next happened faster than the human eye can comprehend. It could have escaped Beta's notice. Instead, she read Asmodeus's harmonics accurately and shifted hers in sync. Even so, Gordon proved his mettle as a former Spec-Ops operator, acting on instinct rather than visual confirmation. As Petrov reached them, Gordon managed to fire a round into the Russian colonel. An instant later Petrov's hands wrapped around Gordon's throat. They tumbled down, a writhing mass that smeared blood on the scuffed concrete, both floor and walls.

Beta let herself be distracted. Instead of shooting both men, she watched in fascinated horror as Asmodeus's harmonics sizzled and popped. It seemed that the Dark *Irim* had gone mad, too. His furious dark energy animated the human vessel beyond its proper limits. Given the amount of blood he'd lost, Petrov should be unconscious and dying. Or dead.

Gordon grunted as Petrov managed to get him into a reverse mount, sitting on his diaphragm as Petrov faced his feet. The Russian gripped both of Gordon's calves. Gordon bucked, trying to free his legs so that he could get out of the mount.

Bait, flashed a velvety deep voice in Beta's thoughts. A faint harmonic breeze caressed her cheek before a familiar figure joined the other two men.

And for the second time in ten minutes, a newcomer stunned Beta into temporary confusion.

It was András.

Her beloved stomped on Petrov's face.

Beta flinched.

Asmodeus screeched and tried to abandon his vessel's body for Gordon's.

András lifted the American arms dealer, her erstwhile employer, with one hand and dashed his head against the nearest wall. Asmodeus squawked. Harmonic energy spurted toward the ceiling and then fell abruptly before dying away.

Silence reigned in the corridor, but the harmonic plane churned and echoed from the violence.

Beta's legs gave out. She slid down the wall, dizzy and nauseous and overwhelmed.

András turned and saw her. Instead of hastening to her side, he narrowed his eyes and studied her. For her part, Beta drank in the sight of him. She didn't try to decipher the Gordian knot of emotions suffocating her. Whatever else was in the mix, joy comprised the largest portion.

Without saying anything, András came over and, stooping, slid an arm around Beta.

"Put your arms around my neck," he said.

Beta did as he ordered, setting the Sig Sauer on the floor first. He stood, lifting her against him. His other arm bent under her knees. A tremor went through him. Though he was as hard as she remembered, Beta's dragon senses saw that his thermal signature had cooled since she'd last seen him—and that had been much less white-hot than when she knew him three years ago.

The last time he'd carried her, wounded, from a conflict that she couldn't handle on her own.

Even as her nose scented his unique cologne—a blend of sweet black currant, smoky balsam, and a trace of rich magnolia—Beta recognized that something was wrong with András's non-dominant shoulder, the one on the arm under her knees. That's when she realized that his thermal signature was abnormal there. Cooler red trapped innumerable grains of fiery orange-white. Instinctively she knew that the injury she'd given him hadn't healed.

The one that hadn't killed him.

Pain stabbed her. She touched a fingertip to the injury as he felt for the door lever and then shouldered the door open.

András glanced down at her, his gaze opaque.

Without saying anything, he stepped outside. Beta tore her gaze from his stony profile and looked around them. As she'd guessed, the Russian black site was an unused industrial complex. She couldn't tell what the Belarussians had manufactured here by its chimneys and taupe stucco walls, but its condition suggested that it had been recently used. Given that industry in Belarus was state-owned, there was every reason to believe that the Belarussians knew what the Russians did here.

They needed to find cover as soon as possible.

"Belarussians watch this site," she said. "They will know what I am as soon as they see me."

András grunted. Beta waited, but he said nothing. His stride increased, however, along with his harmonics. Hers followed in sync.

"We are invisible to them now," she said, tightening her hold around his neck.

"Yes."

Beta's arm burned, but it had stopped bleeding. The dizziness had also passed. She thought that she might be able to walk.

As they got clear of the complex, Beta studied the landscape around them. It was now full morning, and the sun rose behind them. The complex sat isolated among fields, but she could make out other industrial structures along the horizon. She called up a memory of the Belarus map. Over the past three years, she'd followed leads here on Unit 29155 and the two colonels responsible for the bombings in her country. The Belarussians had in recent years tried to renegotiate some of their relationship with Russia, engaging in a brief and bloodless 'Milk War' with their sole market, but the two countries had always had close military ties. This wasn't the first or only Russian black site in Belarus. And Unit 29155 was both known and feared.

"Berezina is east or west?" The Berezina River bisected Babyrusk from north to south, with two-thirds of the city on the west side.

"West."

Beta closed her eyes and sighed. Of course. They needed to cross the river to get out of Belarus. And then make it almost 400 kilometers across the border into Poland. Almost seven hours of driving across sparsely populated land.

"You can put me down," she said. "I can walk."

"That's not what it looks like to me."

Beta wanted to argue, but she was too tired, and it felt so good—*so* right—to be in András's arms that she let it go and snuggled against his chest. She must have dozed because it seemed as though no time had passed before they arrived at the vehicle, an older blue Renault truck with an open bed. András jostled her a little as he reached for the passenger door handle. But he was gentle when he set her down on the worn bucket seat.

He pulled a box from the floorboard at her feet. A moment later he peeled the tunic sleeve from where it had dried against the bullet graze on her upper arm, wincing at her sharp intake of breath as the wound bled again. If she hadn't been watching him so closely, she might not have noticed because his movements gave away nothing.

He began cleaning the wound, his large fingers, slender for their size, encircling her arm to hold it steady. Those fingers fascinated Beta. She'd noticed everything about András before, of course, but only indirectly. She hadn't allowed herself to focus on him because that would have been too dangerous. Too honest. Now she saw his hands anew. For all their strength, they were elegant and aristocratic and sure. He could have been a pianist or a surgeon or a watchmaker.

He could have crushed her arm.

A memory of András teasing her four years ago transposed itself over Beta's view. Grinning, he'd told her that her mother had fed her only on axe soup and should have added beef and potatoes. He'd held her bicep, saying, "I thought so. Axe handle."

Despite every reason not to trust her—she, Olivia, and Stasia had attracted Asmodeus's notice as Wild *Elioud*—András had allowed her to leave his general's Vienna mansion.

Lost in her reverie, Beta missed András treating the wound using devices that she'd never seen before. Half a dozen pairs of white adhesive strips straddled the line of open flesh, which had been pulled closed with clips using long plastic ties. The wound edges had been so neatly and tightly matched that any scar would be as fine as a hair.

"Thank you," she said.

"Of course." András closed the medic kit and stowed it at Beta's feet before handing her a bottle of water. "Drink. Food will have to wait until we're safely out of Babyrusk. The Belarussians have dispatched a tac team. It will be here in two minutes."

He had yet to look her in the face for more than a fraction of a second.

He shut her door and came around to get into the driver's seat. The sound of a lock clicking made Beta look down as András started the truck and shifted into gear. That's when she saw that the truck, clearly a used vehicle intended to blend into the surroundings, lacked a door handle on the inside of the passenger door.

Instinct made her look at the seatbelt, which András had fastened after settling her in the truck.

It had been modified. There was no standard release button that she could see. And if she was right, the belt itself was made with a material that couldn't be cut.

She was a prisoner again.

As she studied András's hard profile while his attention remained fixed on the road ahead, the rest of what he'd said that day four years ago came back to her.

I extend trust so that you may trust. But word to the wise: broken trust cuts twice as deep.

She'd broken his trust twice.

Apparently András had been cut too deep.

FIFTEEN

They reached Lublin, Poland, by late afternoon. The safe house was about twenty kilometers south of the city in Jabłonna-Majątek. After a harrowing moment on the other side of the Berezina River where Belarussian soldiers had set up a roadblock that required all of his *Elioud* charm to finesse, András had driven the truck as slowly and deliberately as any farmer or delivery driver would, only stopping around midday so that Beta could eat, stretch her legs, and use a toilet.

Beta.

Just catching a glimpse of her ripped his insides apart. So he avoided looking at her as much as possible.

It didn't really help.

He could still feel her, read her harmonics and infrared signature, both of which he knew as if they were his own. He felt as if a long-missing part of himself had returned, now orbiting him as a binary star orbits its mate. It wasn't what he'd expected or even wanted to feel. Nor the pity and regret. Only the fury. That he'd expected.

He smelled her, too. Even after five months in which she'd been tortured to the edge of death, forced to wear filthy clothing and unable to wash herself, Beta's personal perfume dominated the rank scent of sweat, dirty hair, and bad breath. True, its sweeter notes of vanilla, black currant, and mandarin had been muted so much he wasn't sure that he smelled them. But the dark, rich aromas of gardenia, incense, and chocolate persisted, the sharper scents of vetiver and bergamot rising to the forefront.

András glanced over at the napping Beta, whose eyes had reflected understanding and resigned sorrow when she'd realized that he'd imprisoned her. Instead of spitting fire and finding the first opportunity to defeat her restraints, she'd sighed and curled into the seat as much as the tight belt allowed, instantly sound asleep.

That bothered him more than her appearance. And that nearly drove him mad.

Sweet Elohim, but Beta resembled a concentration camp survivor. She'd lost weight she couldn't afford to lose, though the Russians had apparently force fed her, if the intravenous port was anything to go by. Her milky skin, always fair, had a translucence about it that showed the blue of veins, lending her an otherworldly and fragile beauty that was nothing like the vital energy that she'd emanated previously. The worst part? The swollen, blackened eye.

Beta was only a shadow of her former self.

András would be relieved when they finally reached the restored granary house on the parklike grounds of a former palace for a long-dead Polish noble. As a safe house for reprogramming a Dark *Elioud* who'd just been recovered from a Dark *Irim* and Russian assassins, it was perfect.

It was also perfect as a haven for an injured *Elioud* warrior who didn't know if he could fight and win against Dark angelic forces.

His shoulder screamed at him. The intense burning pain was a constant under everything he did, a thread through his waking hours and a torment during his disturbed sleep. This morning's mission had only exacerbated it. He could read the small grains of inflammation inside the wound Beta had given him. They had spread into the shoulder joint itself, and now scar tissue had reduced much of its mobility. The cycle would continue, excruciating inflammation creating scar tissue in the joint, until the shoulder froze. Dr. Armand said that there was little to do except give him a cortisone shot. The condition would resolve on its own in time, perhaps as long as two years.

Unless András could control the inflammation himself.

He turned into the entrance of the long drive to the palace-turned-villa, set back among the old-growth trees. The sun was low in the sky, transforming the world into another time. He could have been riding in a coach pulled by a team of horses, protected from the bandits and wolves lurking deeper in the woods. Poland, where forests covered almost a third of the country, was a land of fairytales.

He'd forgotten that after his experiences here during World War Two when the monsters had rampaged unchecked. Lublin itself had lost all of its Jewish inhabitants to Nazi evil. In fact, a concentration and extermination camp located in its Majdanek suburb was now a museum thanks to the Soviets, who'd gotten to it in 1944 before the Nazi commandant could destroy the evidence of their crimes.

But the Polish forests had hidden more than monsters. They'd also hidden partisans and refugees, who blew up Nazi trains and bridges, stole ammunition, and killed collaborators and spies.

András inhaled the woodland scents of late autumn enveloping him from the truck's open windows. Up ahead in the distance, he saw the villa. To those Poles, Jews and Christians alike, who'd managed to escape into the woods outside Lublin, the villa had been a fairytale refuge. A refuge owned by a monster-hunter, an *Elioud* member of the secret resistance group Żegota.

Then, as now, András had brought survivors to the granary house where Mihàil's friend helped them travel on to safety in more impenetrable forests to the north and east. The Jewish refugees he sent to the Parczew Forest, where a large partisan band of Jews waged guerrilla warfare against the Nazis. The *Elioud* had been captured and killed by the Russians when they liberated Lublin. After the war, Mihàil had bought the estate and installed a caretaker.

András let himself relax as they arrived at the villa. The harmonics of this place soothed him until the pain in his shoulder had muted to a dull ache. When he parked the truck behind the villa and turned off the engine, he felt almost ready for what was to come.

Beta stirred and, blinking, sat upright. She even yawned.

"Where are we?" she asked, gazing around the landscape through the truck's windows.

"Someplace safe."

"Poland then."

"Yes."

Beta plucked the half-filled water bottle from her lap where he'd left it and drank, sighing. András was surprised at how his body reacted to that sound. Her obvious trust and lack of fear also surprised him. He found himself on edge, wondering when she was going to erupt. With that in mind, he popped the latch on his door and dropped to the ground, inhaling and stretching to get the kinks out of his muscles. He was even able to lift his weak arm more than halfway.

Behind him, Beta's harmonics had evened out. Her infrared signature, which had been much cooler earlier in the day, had steadied and even warmed a little. The feeling of her in his arms, her own around his neck, returned to him. Dropping his arms to his side, he closed his eyes and savored the image for a moment. A noise from the villa's back entrance broke his reverie.

"Right," he said, opening his eyes, "stop stalling."

He walked around the front of the truck to Beta's door, pulling it wide and leaning in to touch the seatbelt latch with his fingertips. It responded to the gentle harmonic nudge he gave and released the seatbelt pinning Beta in. She didn't move.

András, who'd half expected her to lunge at him as soon as the buckle slipped from the latch, allowed himself to look at Beta's face. They were centimeters apart.

For a long moment their gazes held. András scarcely became aware when her breath and harmonics synced with his. Instead, all he could do was take in her features, the unusual dark-gray irises surrounded with a black rim, the fine arched brows winging over the straight nose above lips too full for her finely-drawn face. Her high cheekbones stood out in sharp relief against her pallor, and there were dark-purple shadows under her eyes.

"I can walk," she said, breaking the suddenly fraught silence.

"Of course."

András leaned out of the truck and, taking a step back to hold the door, gestured for Beta to get out. She swiveled in her seat and, gripping the doorframe, began to climb down from the truck cab. He almost bit his tongue to stop the sharp exclamation that rose in his throat when she wobbled as her lead foot touched the ground. Instead, he put a steadying hand under her elbow.

Beta got both feet down before looking up at him. "Thank you."

Something in the sincere emotion that came from those two words conveyed to András how important it had been to her to negotiate her exit herself.

He nodded once and waited for Beta to take a few steps away before shutting the truck door. When he turned to face the villa, the caretaker, a matron named Roksana Jaśko, waited, her hands crossed in front of her waist. She bowed her head in brief acknowledgement.

"Welcome, Pan Nagy."

"Good evening, Pani Jaśko," said András formally in Polish. While his address was polite, hers held the respect reserved for nobility, which is how all the Polish assets viewed the *Elioud* no matter what Mihàil said.

Roksana turned to Beta. She bowed again. "Pani. Please let me know if your wardrobe is unacceptable. Pan Nagy told me that you wore a larger size."

He felt Beta shift closer to him, her harmonics undulating from fright or fatigue, he didn't know which. He slipped his hand to the small of her back, humming a little. Her harmonics harmonized with his. She nodded but said nothing.

"The truck will be gone by nightfall," said Roksana, turning back to András. "Everything in the granary house is as you asked. I left your dinner in a Dutch oven on the stovetop. Should you need anything else this evening, you have only to call."

"Of course," he said.

Aware that András had brought Beta here for an undisturbed retreat, Roksana pivoted and returned to the villa.

András glanced down at Beta, who fit into his side as if she'd been molded there. She looked up at him wide eyed.

"Now the real work begins," he said, as much to himself as to Beta.

And, squaring his shoulders, András nudged Beta to walk toward the stone granary house beyond the villa—their home for the foreseeable future.

For the next three weeks, András kept Beta inside the granary house whose warm gray fieldstone walls and wooden beams and floors exuded a soothing harmonic vibe that only natural materials could. Three times a day, he escorted her on walks through the woods on the villa's grounds. By now, all of the deciduous trees had shed their leaves, which lay in a deep-copper carpet at their feet. The evergreens, though judiciously harvested to keep the deciduous trees from being overtaken, added their green aroma to the woody decay. And throughout the day, he played music, classical or modern instrumental, but all of it incorporating subtle isochronic tones and binaural beats designed to train Beta's neural oscillations into more serene and steady waves. It was the same method that Mihàil and Miró had devised as music therapy for anyone traumatized by Dark angelic forces. Or for reprogramming human and *Elioud* agents.

Not unexpectedly, András found the music therapy soothing him, too.

He and Beta spoke little, even when they dined together. Roksana kept the kitchen stocked with freshly baked *povitica* and *drozdzowy*, two Polish sweet breads, and quick breakfast items like fruit and yogurt, so that they could eat breakfast without any intrusion. For the other meals, she either delivered a hot Dutch oven or large stockpot filled with soup or stew along with warm loaves of *ziemniaczany*, traditional potato bread, and *żytni*, sauerkraut bread. After a week, András began cooking dinner from scratch.

On the third day of his cooking, Beta asked for a second serving of the mushroom soup.

"This is very good," she said, spooning up a bite of the second bowl. "I like the paprika, but there is something else in here that is unfamiliar ... it is not Hungarian."

András, who'd already eaten two bowls and now tore off another hunk of potato bread to sop up the remains, nodded. "Tamari. It's a Japanese sauce made from fermented soybeans. It adds what the Japanese call 'umami' or a savory, rich flavor to dishes."

"Huh." Beta said nothing else for several moments.

András studied her from the corner of his eye. Her skin no longer had a milky translucence. Instead, it was a healthy strawberries-and-cream. Her lips, luscious as raspberries, no longer drew his gaze for their disturbing size in relation to the rest of her face. No, they drew his gaze because he couldn't stop think-ing—dreaming, actually—about kissing them. Every time he thought about it, however, he immediately relived the moment that she threw a dagger at him.

"I should have expected you to be an excellent cook," said Beta, "though you do not look like you eat as much as I recall. And your sweet tooth is nonexistent."

András shrugged. "My appetite hasn't been the same since you left three years ago."

The air grew heavy and warm around them. Beta stopped eating and began toying with the cloth napkin that Roksana felt they needed even in this rustic setting. The fire that András had made after they returned from their afternoon walk crackled and popped in the silence.

"I did not know what else to do," she said at last in a low voice. She kept her gaze on the bowl in front of her.

András had heard the thickness in her speech, however. Her harmonics trembled like a leaf in heavy rain. He reached over and lifted her chin until she looked back at him. There was no defiance in her gaze, bright with unshed tears, only pain and regret.

"Why?" he asked, his own voice husky. That one word encompassed so much more than her earlier confusion.

Beta blinked. He wanted to hold her hand, but she'd dropped them both into her lap. She licked her lips. András couldn't take his gaze from her mouth.

She opened it and then shut it again.

"You may not talk much," he said gently, "but I've never known you to be at a loss for words."

Beta breathed in deeply, watching him as closely as he watched her. She seemed to see something in his expression that reassured her. Her harmonics steadied and then synced with his. András felt when it happened. She began to play with her napkin again as she spoke, folding it into origami. It made him think of Olivia's paper eagle and the nano-origami that Miró had developed as a result.

"Asmodeus possessed me." She looked down again. "I had to leave to protect you. All of you, but especially you. But I wanted you so badly," she whispered, answering his unspoken question about why she'd made love to him, "I wanted a little of your sweetness to take with me."

András sat back. "It happened in Skopje." His voice was deadly flat. So was his gaze. "How?"

It was her turn to shrug. "Perhaps when I was injured." Now she looked at András, her fierce gaze an echo of her old self. "I would not have let him possess me so easily if I had been in my right mind."

He nodded, rubbing his chin with his thumb as he thought. "That explains the black graininess to your harmonic signature that Mihàil read as we flew back to his estate. It also explains why I couldn't find you. Your harmonic signature changed. And once you left, Asmodeus altered your memory. You couldn't remember us, so you didn't come back."

"I did not want to come back."

Beta's bald statement robbed András of thought. It was she who reached across the table and took his large hand in both of hers. The feeling of her slender fingers entwining with his moved him beyond words. He swallowed.

"*I* altered my memory. I did not want to remember you if it meant giving Asmodeus greater access to you. I did not want to be aware of how he hurt you," she said, her voicing breaking on the word *hurt*.

Her pain lanced him. Something opened up inside his chest and let heat pour through his body. It wasn't the same as the heat of anger or of passion, but it affected his thermal signature nonetheless.

"As he did when he possessed you again at the warehouse in Prague?" asked András quietly.

He began rubbing the back of her hand with his thumb, slow circles that transmitted a targeted harmonic massage. His nimbus blazed before hers radiated in response, blending and merging with his until he couldn't see where his ended and hers began.

A tear welled in one of Beta's eyes, slipping free as she spoke. András, fascinated, watched as it glistened on her satiny skin.

"He tried to kill you," she said. "Both you and Olivia. I was only able to adjust the aim of his throw, but until you showed up in Belarus, I thought that I *had* killed you."

"You did not."

"But I did cripple you, did I not?" she asked, crying so calmly that if he hadn't seen her face, he wouldn't have known that she did.

"No, you did *not* cripple me," said András fiercely. He raised a hand and wiped her tears with his thumb. "It is only an injury that will take some time to heal, but it *will* heal. I needed to come here, to this place, to focus on healing it."

He left unsaid that healing included confronting her.

Beta understood anyway. "By forcing me to face what happened."

She freed one of her hands to touch his weak shoulder. He wanted to feel those fingers against his bare skin, to feel her gripping him as if she'd drown in their passion without a firm hold.

"It seems to pain you less."

"Yes," he agreed to both statements. "And for long moments I even forget that it hurts at all." As he said this, he knew that he meant more than his shoulder.

Beta looked down at their joined hands. "I wanted to disappear into my work and forget all about you." She paused and then raised her face before going on. "I wanted to forget how I feel about you and what is between us."

Their gazes held. Beta's eyes lost their shimmery look. Instead, there was an awareness there that set his harmonics buzzing. The temperature in the room rose by fifteen degrees.

András leaned across the table and, cupping her cheek, kissed her. She sighed and opened her mouth to him. He groaned and slipped his hand to the back of her head, angling it so that he could devour her lips and tongue. She moaned and pulled her hand free from his on the table between them and grabbed both of his shoulders. Their conjoined harmonics danced, their familiar melody changing as their kiss deepened, inverting and slowing.

András pulled back from the kiss, turning it sweet instead of passionate. He pressed his lips gently to hers before moving to the tip of her nose and her eyelids. The air around them softened and lost its fiery edge. He rested his forehead against hers.

"What *is* between us, Gomba? Is it more than physical attraction?" Despite himself, a note of uncertainty wobbled in his voice.

Beta drew back, forcing him to look at her. Her somber dark-gray eyes held no fear or reluctance. But there was something behind her gaze that warned him before she spoke.

"What is between us, Spratek? *Everything*. Everything is between us." She leaned closer, sparks flaring along the edge of her nimbus where it tangled with his. "I tried to run away. I cannot. But neither can I promise you that what is between us will survive once we leave this place."

Though the woman across from him sounded like the old Beta, András heard the slight catch in her voice on the word *promise*. Dropping his hands, he leaned back in his chair. Already his shoulder had started to ache again. He tried to send soothing heat to it, drawing it from the air around them, but it went into his soles instead.

Nodding, he said, "Neither can I."

Beta nodded in return and stood, gathering their bowls and turning to go to the kitchen area, but not before András saw the grief in her eyes.

Sixteen

Stasia awoke before Miró and laid there, listening to him breathe and soaking in the feel of his arm around her waist, his back pressed against hers. He'd arrived in Paris in the middle of the night, his face careworn and tired. The gray hair at his temple had grown whiter and spread a little farther into the rest of his hair. It was only a microscopic change, but she, who knew his features better than her own, recognized it immediately. Her heart ached to realize that she wasn't with him more, to bolster his harmonics and tend to his physical needs.

As she'd done last night. Miró had scarcely entered her apartment and dropped his leather duffel before she'd been in his arms, pressing her body hard against his and kissing him. The world disappeared. There was nothing but Miró and her need for him. They'd made love, first as if starving and then a second time, more slowly and tenderly.

"When do you go back?" she asked, hearing the subtle shift in his breathing.

"This afternoon. We expect another attack, this time *bogomili*, but I had to see you." Regret roughened his husky voice. He buried his nose in the hair at her neck. "You smell divine, *Moja Duša*."

"*You* feel divine," she said, rolling over to kiss him.

She ran her palms over his shoulders and down his arms. The warm muscle responded to her caress in ways that never ceased to fascinate her. Even though she was fit and strong and capable of taking care of herself, lying within Miró's embrace made her feel sheltered. Cherished. Able to lay down her constant wariness and vigilance and trust that he would guard and keep her, with his life if need be.

As she would do for him.

Stasia, overwhelmed with the ferocity of feeling that accompanied that thought, braced her hands on Miró's shoulders and encouraged him to roll onto his back. He took her with him. Leaning above him, she studied his beautiful face, tracing its planes and contours, before moving down his neck to his chest. She ran her fingertips over his collarbones and pectoral muscles, humming as she did. He watched her intently, the love in his gaze closing her throat.

She infused her harmonics with all that she couldn't express in words, watching as they played over his skin, calling out his harmonics, which danced in response.

What had begun four years ago had continued until a whole new melody with increasing variations on that theme played in their unique harmonic signature. It was dense and strong and would cause unimaginable pain if severed.

Stasia kissed Miró, first softly and then with more urgency. And then she began to lay down more harmonic tracks to their epic love ballad, conducting the performance until it resonated around them.

Later, as they finished a leisurely breakfast, dawdling over what was likely their last shared meal for some time, Miró took Stasia's hand and played with her fingers while she gestured with the other as she spoke of Gina Orlandi.

"She and Alix just returned from yet another trip to Pont-Aven. She has personally inspected every rock on the coast for a hundred kilometers around the village and visited all of Brittany looking for the *Codex Angelicus*."

"It may be that Gina has learned to read trace harmonic elements from Bernard's early wanderings there. Having his great-granddaughter at her side would help boost and focus her efforts."

"Then how am I to discover the *Codex* ahead of Gina?" asked Stasia, frustrated.

Miró pressed his lips to the back of her hand, sending warm harmonic vibrations over her skin and up her arm. Stasia sighed as she relaxed.

"*Smettila!*" she scolded, smiling.

"I think that you are forgetting the bigger scene."

"That is?"

"That you are trained to think like an intelligence operative, not a treasure hunter."

Stasia narrowed her eyes at him, unsure for a moment whether he was trying to aggravate her or if it was just a by-product of his efforts. Sincerity mixed with a hint of mischief shone from his gaze.

"Are you suggesting that I interrogate Alix Durand myself?" She sniffed and looked away. "I have already. *È come cercare di tirare fuori un ragno da un buco!*" She punctuated the idiom with chopping motions, ending with a flourish on "spider from a hole."

"Surely she has something to say that you can work with."

"All she keeps talking about is *La Grandmère*, a portrait of Bernard's grand-mother, who raised him when he was young. It hangs in the Van Gogh Museum. Willem assures me that there is nothing angelic about it."

Miró shrugged. Stasia saw the jealousy waver through his harmonics anyway. Willem, the newest *Elioud* member of their group who was recruited three years before, had been sent from his post in Belgium several times in the past six months to support Stasia. In fact, he'd arrived last night just after Miró. The taciturn Dutchman had lost the woman he loved, Eva, during the same operation that brought Stasia and Miró together. Willem still grieved Eva, who had been a curator at the Van Gogh Museum until Yeqon the Seducer enthralled her. Miró knew this rationally. He'd even given Willem mission directives and trained the Dutch *Elioud* on the nano-origami technology that he'd developed. But what the mind knew the heart sometimes struggled to believe.

Stasia rose from her chair and slipped into his lap. Miró wrapped an arm around her waist and kissed her ear.

"Not everything useful has angelic connections," said her husband, feeding her a square of dark chocolate. "Sometimes the human ones are what is im-portant. For Bernard, his relationship with his grandmother was obviously of utmost importance. Why?"

Stasia thought this over. "Ah, *sì*. Bernard's grandmother recognized his talent. She owned a laundry and employed twenty people. Her support would have included money as well, something every artist needs."

"Hm." Miró nuzzled her. "Then I think you have all *you* need to get ahead of Gina."

"Are you saying, *amore mio*, that Bernard took the *Codex Angelicus* to his grandmother?"

"Why not? He must have trusted her judgment. For all that we know, his grandmother may even have had something to do with his acquiring the *Codex*."

She shook her head slowly, not convinced. "That may be. But Bernard's family moved to Paris when he was ten so that he could study at École des Arts Décoratifs. His grandmother moved in with them almost a decade later, not long after he met Van Gogh."

Van Gogh had been a Grey *Elioud* who'd painted in collaboration with Yeqon. His recently discovered *Infatuation of the Watcher Angels (after Caravaggio)* completed the Watcher Angel triptych by retelling Yeqon's role in the fall of the *Irim*.

"Which leads us back to Paris." Miró reached for his demitasse cup. "Perhaps the *Codex* is not in France. Where else did he travel?"

"Besides Italy? Spain and Egypt." She paused, considering. "Of course, Gina has already searched Italy. She has also made several trips to Spain in the past year."

Miró sipped the last of his espresso. "That leaves Egypt. Bernard hid the Van Gogh painting in Aix-en-Provence. I doubt that he would separate the Van Gogh painting and the *Codex* by hiding it on another continent, one with its own angelic tradition."

Stasia agreed. "That seems unlikely."

She blew out an exasperated breath and stood, reaching for Miró's empty plate and hers. It was time to clean up and acknowledge that their too-short visit was coming to an end.

Miró stopped her with a question. "Have you actually examined *La Grandmère*? There may be a physical clue on the painting itself. If I were Bernard, with only a trace of *Elioud* blood, I would probably rely on non-angelic methods to encipher the location of the *Codex*."

"That is if he left it somewhere," said Stasia darkly. "We only *think* that this mysterious society revolved around the triptych. What if Bernard simply handed the *Codex* to the next member?"

"We can worry about that later after you have gone to Amsterdam," said Miró, pulling her back to his lap. "But first, I need to say good-bye properly."

Then he kissed her as he slipped the strap of her nightgown from her shoulder.

Willem DeVries watched as the young couple, walking arm in arm, came into view across the Boulevard Saint-Michel and stopped at the corner, waiting for a break in traffic. They radiated happiness, the woman glowing as she smiled up at her husband, whose intent gaze seemingly had no room for anything else.

It was not entirely an act. They were truly, madly, in love.

But they were also apex predators who functioned as an exceptional hunting team who could have crossed the boulevard faster than the eye can blink.

The husband, who wasn't nearly as young as his features and muscular physique conveyed, saw—and assessed—everything in the nearly hundred eighty degrees in his field of vision. What he didn't see, his lovely wife did. And both of them read more than what the human eye could see, the unseen world of thermal and harmonic imaging.

But it was more than their extrasensory perceptions that made this couple formidable. No, that stemmed from their keen judgment combined with an exquisite sense of timing. Oh, and superb hand-to-hand combat skills.

Willem wanted to be like them. He already had excellent fighting skills, thanks to years of study with Miró Kos, the husband, and his *Elioud* teammates, Mihàil Kastroti and András Nagy. And Stasia, his wife, danced with Willem whenever they could steal time from a mission—something that Willem suspected Miró knew about and didn't like. Sparring and dancing had enhanced Willem's physical timing, but it hadn't given him the unquantifiable but undeniable edge that came with being able to read a room or an adversary.

It also didn't give him a bonded *Elioud* mate.

Dat zit wel snor. It was okay. Because his broken heart strengthened his eyes.

Willem may not have been a trained field operative for his country's intelligence services, but he'd always been preternaturally observant of people and his surroundings. It was what had protected him during childhood and led him to his career as an architect.

It was also what had led him to notice Eva, a quiet, willowy blonde who worked at the Van Gogh Museum when he'd been one of the architects on the team designing the new extension four years ago. He'd noticed the care with which she did everything, from presenting her vision of the space to the architects to the details she'd included in all of the exhibits she designed. He'd seen the genuine passion in Eva's face when she described Van Gogh's work or defended him from facile mockery for being unstable.

It was from Eva that Willem had learned that there was more to the story about the eccentric painter's severed ear: two German historians believed that Van Gogh had covered for the French painter Gaugin, who'd sliced it off during their last confrontation. Willem, who couldn't have cared less about his famous countryman, fell in love with Eva at that precise moment. He'd wanted to see passion for *him* transform her features.

Miró and Stasia crossed the boulevard, holding hands now and laughing. Despite this and the distance (which was too far for ordinary human perception), Willem saw the strain around their eyes and in the corners of their smiles. He raised his café au lait and sipped it, keeping his gaze trained on the other two *Elioud.* Though he could read their harmonics and thermal signatures, it was their emotional resonance, the subtle interplay among harmonics, heat, and nimbus against the more prosaic clues in their posture and expression, that intrigued him. Plainly their visit had been too brief.

They stopped at his table and sat in the open chairs. It was early November, still sunny and mild. Miró wore only a fine cashmere sweater in sky blue, but Stasia had on a leather jacket and silk scarf. Around them, Parisians enjoyed the relative calm of their city for a few brief weeks before the Christmas markets coincided with chilly, wet weather.

"*Café*?" he asked, opening his palm toward his cup.

They shook their heads.

"No, *grazie*. I could not drink another drop of *caffè* today!" Stasia waved her hand, dropping it to cover a yawn. "On another thought, perhaps I should." She gestured for the waiter.

"Do you still have connections at the Van Gogh Museum?" asked Miró, his icy blue eyes lasered on Willem. He looked tired, but Willem knew better than to underestimate this *Elioud*, who'd been alive since before Suleiman the Magnificent ruled the Ottoman Empire.

Willem nodded, glancing at Stasia. The Italian operative ran her fingers through her hair, smoothing the windblown strands with fine harmonics. "Eva had a friend in the research department with whom I've stayed in contact, a woman named Saskia Braam."

"Good." Without appearing to recognize what he did, Miró reached across the table and took Stasia's hand. His fingers played with her wedding band, a simple gold loop. "Introduce Ms. Braam to Stasia."

Willem said nothing for a moment. Instead, he picked up his café au lait, studying the couple's harmonics as he sipped. Miró would prefer not to send him with Stasia to Amsterdam. Stasia knew this. She ran fine harmonic fingers over her husband, smoothing his frayed edges.

"This is about *La Grandmère*?" guessed Willem. "I doubt that Saskia knows anything of use about a former friend of Van Gogh's."

"We need to read Willem in," said Stasia, giving her husband a pointed look.

Willem kept his own harmonics steady. No need to telegraph how badly he wanted to outwit Gina Orlandi, who'd been the one to introduce Eva to Zaccaria Angelli, the avatar of the Dark *Irim* Yeqon.

Miró sighed and sat back, pulling his hand from Stasia's. Willem noted that Stasia's harmonics hummed in disappointment, but she said nothing, simply watched her husband.

"Given Émile Bernard's relationship with his grandmother, I believe that she holds the key to discovering where the *Codex Angelicus* is."

Willem's gaze sharpened as he looked from Miró to Stasia and back. "You think Gina is looking in the wrong places."

Miró nodded, watching Willem closely. Willem recognized fine harmonic fingers testing the edge of his own harmonics. Miró wanted to know whether he could trust Willem's signature, and in essence, Willem.

"Anything that Ms. Braam knows about the painting itself or Bernard's relationship could be useful."

Stasia leaned forward, setting a hand on Willem's forearm where it rested on the table. "If she can give me access to the painting, I may be able to learn something from it. Perhaps Bernard used steganography to encode where he left the *Codex Angelicus* in the image itself. Or whom he might have given it to."

Willem allowed himself a moment to enjoy Stasia's *Elioud* charm as it warmed his skin, Miró's sudden stiffness notwithstanding. But then he pushed his empty cup away and crossed his arms. He hardened his harmonics. It was time to get the full truth about the *Codex Angelicus*.

Stasia blinked and sat back.

"That is very fascinating. But what I want to know is why you are tailing Gina Orlandi all over France when he"—here he nodded at Miró—"must stay to battle *bogomili* and *daemonia* in Central Europe. What are you keeping from me?"

Silence fell heavily between the three of them. Traffic from the boulevard and voices from the occupants of the nearby tables underscored the tension his words had caused. The arrival of the waiter with Stasia's café au lait broke it.

Miró started to speak as soon as the waiter turned away. Stasia put a hand on his forearm this time and held his gaze. Not for the first time, Willem had the distinct impression that the *Elioud* couple communicated nonverbally. He studied the flickers and turbulence in their joined emotional resonance. He guessed that Miró had wanted to shut him down and tell him to follow orders, but that Stasia argued to bring him farther into the fold.

Willem narrowed his eyes. Miró watched the world with a wolf's gaze. Was that all this was, his natural caution even after three years working with Willem, who'd done everything that the *Elioud* unit had required of him? On the other hand, the tension and dark strands in Miró's harmonics suggested something deeper than jealousy.

Stasia won her soundless argument with her husband. She turned toward Willem.

"The *Codex Angelicus* is the first edition of the *First Book of Enoch*," she said. "The one dictated by the Watcher Angels. I thought that was the case, but I was only able to confirm it by bugging Alix Durand's apartment."

Stasia said this so calmly that it took Willem a moment to process her meaning.

"Are you suggesting that Enoch could have captured some of the angelic energy of the Watcher Angels?" he asked, thinking out loud. "As the painters did in the triptych paintings?"

She nodded. "More than that. It is the full, *unabridged* edition."

She and Miró both watched him. Again, Willem had to take her words in before speaking. It was clear that both she and Miró wanted him to comprehend the weight of their search.

"The disobedient Watcher Angels brought forbidden knowledge to humanity," he said, looking from Stasia to Miró and back. "Some of that has been redacted from the current editions, which means that it is dangerous."

"Yes," said Miró, "which is why the Archangel Michael ordered it hidden. And when Dark *Irim* succeeded in having bastardized copies of the *Codex* created, he had faithful *Elioud* discredit these new editions."

"Making sure that they would not be included in canon and taught."

"Yes."

"How did the secret society get the *Codex*? Let me guess. Yeqon gave it to them." Willem couldn't restrain the bitter edge to his words. Yeqon's charisma had displaced any feelings Eva had had for him. She became Yeqon's cat's-paw, ultimately dying for the Dark *Irim*.

Miró shrugged at Willem's words. "Yeqon had already disobeyed St. Michael once. In this case, he stayed true to the letter of the law at least because it suited his own plans."

"To reveal his revisionist history to humanity to draw a mass of vulnerable people to him," said Stasia, a faint tremor in her voice.

It reverberated through Miró. He took her hand in both of his, sending soothing harmonics in a cascade over her. The tension and dark strands that Willem had noted earlier settled in the older *Elioud*'s signature, shielded from Stasia's harmonics through a complex web of continuous harmonic manipulation.

Willem toyed with his empty cup, thinking about whether he could have used the *Codex Angelicus* to save Eva—or at least force Yeqon into severing his hold on her—if he'd known that it existed.

Gina Orlandi couldn't be allowed to find it.

With that thought, he was about to say that he'd contact Saskia later this afternoon to set up a meeting when Miró's cellphone rang. Even before the terse conversation ended, Willem had pulled out his wallet and counted out enough cash for his and Stasia's coffees. Stasia waited, eyes wide, for Miró to finish.

"How bad?" she asked. There was no need to ask what she meant.

"They managed to stop seven heavily armed jihadis from coordinated attacks in Berlin, including a bomb at the jazz festival, individual attackers at the import tradeshow, and a car attack at the short film festival. But while they did, *bogomili* attacked and raped a dozen individuals including two children, and *daemonia* have possessed dozens around the attack sites." He paused. "And three innocents were killed along with a police officer."

Willem stood. He held Miró's intense stare with an unwavering gaze of his own.

"We can be in Amsterdam before evening," he said. "But I want to be included as a full member on this operation, not relegated to technical support."

Miró stood as well. If his icy gaze could have burned Willem, it would have left a massive hole in his forehead. Then he nodded once, sharply. "Very well."

Turning to his wife, who'd also risen to her feet, he murmured something, kissed her, and then sped his harmonics, disappearing from sight. But not before Willem recognized the senior *Elioud*'s hidden emotional resonance.

Not jealousy. Fear. Fear that he would be as helpless as Willem to save the woman he loved.

SEVENTEEN

*P**aprikás Csirke*. Three weeks after coming to the woods outside Lublin, Poland, that's all that Beta wanted to eat. Specifically, András's mother's signature recipe. The creamy vermillion sauce loaded with paprika, Hungary's national spice made from dried capsicum peppers, had ignited Beta's appetite. She was always hungry now and wanted only the heat and flavor unique to the iconic chicken dish. And she knew exactly when her ravenous drive started.

After she'd admitted to András that he was everything to her.

Meanwhile, there had been a subtle change between them. It began the next morning on their walk. Most of the deciduous trees had lost their leaves, blanketing the trails around the villa in dull copper that crumbled under their feet. András took her hand without a word, tucking her cold fingers into the crook of his arm against the wool flannel of his long-sleeved shirt. Her dragon senses saw the heatwaves that he exuded, bending the light rays around them so that the distant landscape wavered like a mirage.

Which is what she feared that their fledgling intimacy would turn out to be once they left the granary house: a distorted vision of reality.

Later that day, András made *paprikás csirke* for dinner. Since then, Beta had started to go mad with craving.

But more than a week passed, and she still couldn't bring herself to ask him to make the spicy chicken dish for her again. This morning, they had again walked in the woods, András holding her hand this time. The temperature had dropped overnight, and thick gray clouds lowered the sky. At midday, András heated up a simple lunch of *żytni* and *zupa pomidorowa*, a Polish tomato soup with egg noodles, when she said that she wanted something hot after the chilly walk.

He built up the fire and brought her tea afterwards so that she could sit in a comfortable recliner and read yellowing paperbacks from the previous century that had been left in a bookcase in the sitting area.

Following their afternoon walk, Beta finally asked András to make the *paprikás csirke* again.

He grinned. "Only if you make it with me, Gomba."

She'd had little choice but to agree.

The main room of the former storage house had been divided into separate spaces through the clever positioning of furniture. To create a kitchen area, cabinets had been built into a U-shape and covered in fieldstone like the walls. The durable concrete countertop provided plenty of room for both of them to prepare ingredients, cook, and load the dishwasher.

András directed Beta to chop onions and tomatoes while he cut up a couple of whole chickens. She stole fascinated glances at the powerful, sure blows he delivered with a cleaver, separating the thigh and leg as a unit before splitting the whole breast into halves. Fortunately, she'd remembered what she'd taught herself about adjusting her harmonics, so that she could speed through dicing the vegetables along with a handful of garlic cloves.

They worked in companionable silence assembling all of the raw ingredients for the *paprikás csirke*. Then András melted lard in a large Dutch oven and browned the chicken pieces before setting them aside on a platter. Next, he sauteed the onion and garlic before adding the tomatoes. To this mash, he added a blend of two different styles of Hungarian paprika, the mild and flavorful *különleges*, with an *édes*, or sweet, type.

"Did you know that there are eight different types of paprika?" he asked as he pulled the pot of hot onion and garlic from the burner and sprinkled the powdered capsicum over the vegetables, deftly mixing it in with a silicone spatula. "From the mild to the pungent. And the secret to my mother's *paprikás csirke* is this paprika paste."

He held up a small bowl containing a mixture that he'd made earlier in the week when he'd first started cooking for them. She'd seen him spooning dried capsicum from different tins into the bowl along with a generous pinch of salt, sugar, and a fine white powder followed by a dollop of softened lard. The resulting paste he now scooped into the Dutch oven. The combined scent of the fresh vegetables and dried peppers rose from the vessel in a thick, almost visible cloud.

Beta's stomach growled even as her eyes watered. She scowled and folded her arms across her chest.

"You do not believe in measuring spoons or cups, do you?" she asked. "Or written recipes?"

András grinned at her. It nearly took her breath away. It was the first time that she'd seen this boyish grin of his since she'd left him in the middle of the night.

"Nope," he said, sounding like her friend Olivia.

Beta shoved the resulting pang from that thought deep into a corner of her mind. Of course, András would have picked up a few of his *drangúe*'s wife's colloquialisms over the past three years. Olivia had a way of influencing those around her.

András slid the browned chicken pieces back into the Dutch oven with the seasoned vegetables, turning them around to coat them with a thick layer of the mixture.

"It's extremely critical to get a feel for the amount of paprika to use based on color and taste, not fixed measurements." He lifted the wooden spoon he'd been using and tasted his efforts. "Hm. I think that it needs more of Mama's special paste."

"What is in this special paste of your mother's?" asked Beta, slightly jealous of the unseen woman who elicited that special tone when András said *mama*.

He studied her, speculation narrowing his eyes.

"You aren't ready to receive that wisdom yet." He turned back to the Dutch oven before pouring in a quantity of chicken stock that Roksana had left them in the refrigerator. Beta saw that he covered the chicken but no more.

"Are you saying that I am not worthy of this secret?"

He shook his head, his face solemn, but his eyes sparkling. "I'm saying that I'll read you in when you've mastered the rest of the dish."

So saying, he plopped the lid onto the pot.

Beta, her arms still crossed, leaned against the counter and watched András as he returned items to the cupboards and moved dirty bowls and utensils into the sink.

"Why do Hungarians have eight different types of paprika?" she asked, not really caring about the answer, only wanting to distract him while she ogled his backside. And shoulders. And biceps. The rest of his body was, unfortunately, hidden under flannel and denim. "Two or possibly three seem like enough to me."

He shot her a mischievous glance over his shoulder. Something in his gaze made her think that he knew exactly what she'd been doing.

"Because Hungarians are more complex than you give them credit for."

Beta rolled her eyes heavenward and, expelling an exasperated breath, turned to load the dishwasher.

It had started to rain while they cooked, so they played cards by the fire. Soft music filled the background. Once or twice, András checked on the *paprikás csirke*, which he'd left to simmer on low. When he opened the Dutch oven, the scent wafted to Beta, who could almost taste the air.

She really was a dragon.

As the light began to fade outside, András finished their evening meal. Beta came to watch as he used tongs to transfer the cooked chicken to a platter. Then he whisked flour, sour cream, and a generous splash of heavy cream into a thick paste.

"Here." He handed her the bowl. "Blend that into the *paprikas* sauce. Keep stirring while it thickens. Taste it. If it needs more salt and pepper, add them. Then put the chicken back and make sure it's covered."

Beta blinked and stared at the bowl in her hands. András had turned away and was pulling something out of a cabinet. Despite a cold surge of panic, she grabbed a silicone spatula and shoved the cream mixture into the deep-red capsicum broth and stirred. When the cream broke into lumps that floated, the panic returned.

Without a word, András handed her a whisk. Beta applied the whisk to the mixture as if her life depended on it, letting out her breath when they merged into a creamy orange gravy. She stole a glance at András, who seemed engrossed in his own recipe.

He filled a large pot with water, sprinkling a liberal pinch of salt over it. While the salted water heated, he whisked together flour, salt, eggs, and water. Then he wetted a cutting board, scraped the dough from the bowl onto it, and used the back of a knife to cut little bits and guide them into the boiling water below.

"You might want to put the chicken back into the sauce now," he said, startling Beta, who'd forgotten to keep stirring the *paprikas*.

She looked down. The sauce had clumped in spots as the flour had cooked.

"Just put the chicken back. It will taste fine, especially with the *nokedli*."

Beta looked at András, guilt sitting like cold gelatin in her stomach. For the next few minutes, she concentrated on returning the chicken to the Dutch oven and turning it in the clumpy sauce. A few minutes later, András asked her to bring him plates from the hutch. Then he served his mother's *paprikás csirke* with the egg noodles that he'd made.

It tasted divine despite the lumpy sauce.

Beta ate two large servings even though the chicken was so spicy it left her tongue tingling and a fine sheen of sweat on her brow. As she sighed and pushed her empty plate away, a small smile played around the corners of András's mouth. He'd eaten little, instead seeming to find pleasure in watching her eat instead.

"Dessert?" he asked.

She shook her head. "I could not eat another bite."

He wrapped a hand around her upper arm. Lightning shot from his palm straight to her core. Her harmonics buzzed and jumped.

"Good thing that I'm feeding you, Gomba. You don't look as much like the starving kitten I saved when I was a child. She used to hiss and puff up, too, until I took her home and nursed her to health. And then she would curl in my arms for hours, purring and content."

She swallowed.

"I think soon you'll be ready for dessert, too." He smiled a slow, lazy grin that sent another buzz through her harmonics and a spike in her temperature. "Perhaps some *krupicová kaše*, this time with honey and cinnamon."

Beta watched him, wide eyed. She knew exactly what he was alluding to. It was so like the old András, and yet not like him at the same time. He'd been innocent three years ago, still so young in so many ways even though he was older than she was. Yet he'd never been anything but direct. This, this was something else, and it was setting her on fire. No, that wasn't right. It was calling to the heat that already boiled inside of her, the one that would scald them both if it ever spilled out.

Her heart began to thump against her ribs.

András slid Beta's sleeve from her shoulder while holding her gaze. His eyes never lowered as he felt with gentle fingers for the port in her upper chest.

"I can remove this." Her breath caught as he traced around the hard circular device under her skin.

"You are not a doctor," she said in a voice filled with gravel. She arched into his hand as it curved up and around her neck.

He shrugged. "This? This is battlefield medicine. I can manage that. Do you trust me?"

"Yes." She nodded without hesitation. "Always."

András nodded and went for medical supplies. Even though the room around her was hot from both the fire and their bodies, Beta felt colder as soon as András took his hand from her flesh. Yet he was back so quickly and kneeling at her side that she almost believed that she'd imagined it. Her head swam a little as if she'd had one of Petrov's injections.

She gripped his bicep. "Stay with me."

András looked at her, his deep-blue eyes penetrating. "Always."

He swabbed the skin of her chest before injecting lidocaine in the area around the port. She shivered as the cooler air dried her skin. He murmured to her as he worked, the words too low for her to catch their meaning, but something warm and angelic washed over her. She looked down as he made an incision with a scalpel. A moment later, he pulled out about six centimeters of tubing from her vein.

"You'll feel the next part a little," he said in a low voice.

Beta watched his intent face instead of his hands. *Ach, sladký pane! Oh, sweet lord!* He was undeniably, unbelievably gorgeous. High cheekbones and sculpted jaw stood out as if the last bit of adolescent softness had been erased in the past few years. Dark brows arched over expressive eyes that conveyed humor, intensity, and passion in a fascinating display. Right now, their calm confidence reassured her. A small dimple under full lips marked the slight asymmetry of his chin, the imperfection only increasing his attractiveness. His hair, which had been so short a few months ago, had grown longer since she'd seen him last, more like it was when she first saw him what felt like a lifetime ago.

She raised her hand and ran her fingers through his hair, brushing it from his forehead. "Please do not cut it so short again."

"As you wish," he said, lifting the port high enough for her to see. "There. Now I can close you up."

She continued speaking as he applied more of the specialty clips that he'd used on her arm in Belarus. "You have gotten hotter since we came here. More like you were before."

She didn't define 'before,' but they both knew what she meant.

Now he looked at her. She couldn't have looked away if she'd tried.

"It seems my thermal signature responds to yours. My harmonic signature and nimbus as well and vice versa. See?"

András hummed. Strong vibrations played over Beta's skin. A moment later, her harmonic signature sang. A distant chime sounded. Golden light burned along her skin, softening and warming it. To her astonishment, a similar warm glow emanated from András. She hovered her open palm along his forearm, never touching him, but his warm glow blazed wherever hers passed over it.

"What are we?"

"You have forgotten?" Now András's eyes had hooded. His expression was hard to read. "What do you think you are that you can sense and manipulate heat, sound, and light?"

She shrugged and looked away under his probing gaze. "I think of myself as a dragon."

"Of course, you do, Gomba."

He turned away and began to pack up the medical kit on the table next to her.

"Why do you say that?" Beta heard the peevishness in her voice and sat up in the dining chair.

"Because you are a Slav. Dragons are in your blood." He looked at her. "Did you never wonder where the dragon mythology began?"

Now it was Beta's turn to close her expression. "No."

András stood.

She gripped his arm. "Perhaps I can help you heal your shoulder."

"Because my thermal signature responds to yours?"

She nodded.

András tilted his head, studying her while he considered her offer. "Very well. I don't see any harm in letting you try."

He pulled out a dining chair and sat down.

Beta's breath came a little faster, and moisture slicked her palms. She didn't have any qualms about using her dragon energy with an intent to wound or destroy. She also never worried about testing it to see what she could do, as she'd done in Belarus. Her gut told her that she'd never harm herself. But now she wanted to use it to mend some of the damage that she'd inflicted on the one person who mattered more to her than life itself.

Taking a deep breath and letting it out slowly, Beta rose and went behind András. She focused on the distinct whorl of his harmonics, aligning hers with his until they vibrated in unison. Her human sight and hearing now muted, the concentric color bands of András's unique heat signature absorbed her attention. In his affected shoulder, tiny white grains clustered among orange patches gluing the joint partly immobile.

Ignoring the way that András smelled and the feel of his muscles under her hands, Beta placed a palm on his upper arm and the other on his shoulder. Humming, she imagined moving the white grains and orange patches into a pliable mass. As she watched, the inflammatory particles merged into a larger band centered on the shoulder. She inhaled, drawing the excess heat into herself, and then exhaled over her shoulder. Heat and smoke clouded the air around them.

That's when she noticed the cool, hard mass on his shoulder blade.

"What is this?" she asked, tracing it.

András didn't answer immediately. Instead, he lifted his restored arm straight and rotated it several times forward and backward. Then he swiveled at the waist, tugged her into his lap and kissed her breathless.

"Thank you, Gomba," he said, pulling back to look at her, the look of love and gratitude on his face stealing her breath as thoroughly as his kiss.

His gaze dropped to the front of her tunic sweater, and his expression transformed. Suddenly she knew what had caught his attention. He hooked his finger under the delicate chain and lifted the small medal free of the fine cashmere.

"St. Michael."

Beta lowered her chin and saw András rubbing the medal between his finger and thumb.

Looking up, she said, "He came to visit me at the black site." Her voice broke as she went on. "I would not have survived without him."

András slipped a hand into her hair to cup her face. She leaned her cheek into his warm palm. His other arm held her close. It felt so good. So right.

"You may be a dragon, my love, but you are also an *Elioud* warrior chosen by the Commander of the Angelic Hosts himself." Unbelievably, pride filled his voice.

Elioud. A soft chime rang in recognition. She knew what that was. A descendant of angels and humans. Not a dragon, but what her Slavic ancestors had believed were dragons with their powerful, fiery natures and wings. And she remembered everything again.

"Is that why Asmodeus hasn't found me?" she asked. She ignored the words *my love*. "Because the Archangel Michael chose me?"

"Partly." András paused, his gaze searching hers. When he spoke, the pride had been replaced with something else, something more tentative. His harmonics wavered and then steadied. "But it's also because your harmonic signature has been permanently changed."

Fear stabbed Beta. She smothered it. "What does that mean?"

"It means, my love, that no matter what happens between us, our fates have been joined." He paused again. "Because we share a harmonic signature now."

And then he demonstrated so that Beta had no reason to misunderstand him.

Eighteen

Asmodeus always knew where to look for his brother Yeqon when he wanted to find him.

It was the same place that Asmodeus went when he needed an energy boost. Someplace where human lust dominated.

While opportunities for gratifying his insatiable appetite abounded, Yeqon had a few favorite places to replenish his empty angelic reservoir. And the Seducer had been left quite diminished these past three years by the match-up against that luscious Italian *Elioud* and her mate, the right hand of Asmodeus's old acolyte, the Dragon of Albania's whelp.

Asmodeus chortled imagining it. He himself had faced the pair in a cemetery in France. Of course, he'd never admit to anyone that they had stunned him with their conjoined harmonic signature. Who knew that an *Elioud* pairing could match an *Irim*? Or at least a fallen *Irim* left to muddle through with humanity?

Truth be told, Asmodeus hadn't been certain that he could match them. Besides, his vulnerable redstart had awaited him.

But that prize had eluded him. Now he needed his own angelic boost. And he needed a new plan to release the Star of God and his army of 365,000 spirits located inside Albania.

Inside the *drangùe's* defenses.

Asmodeus had to accept that it was time to recruit another Dark *Irim* to his cause if he wanted to succeed in freeing Kôkabîêl. As soon as he did, he saw the logic in it. *Irim* were by nature choral beings. The fallen Watcher Angels had just allowed themselves to forget that in their Earthly prison.

Which is exactly what Michael the All Powerful and Righteous took advantage of.

At the thought, Asmodeus sneered as he watched the panorama of human lust and disordered desire before him in the dark erotic theater.

Michael had ensured that the unfaithful angels lost the power of their cohort. He'd sent other angels, and later *Elioud*, like celestial will-o'-the-wisps to draw them away from humanity using their own deceitful and selfish intentions. The unfaithful *Irim* followed these agents into angelic energy sinks, farther from the Heavenly choirs and their angelic brethren. It's where many of the lesser disobedient angels had gone.

Once upon a time, Asmodeus and Yeqon had roamed Creation together. Their proclivities dovetailed nicely. Most of the time anyway.

But there had been no need for Michael's agents to split up their happy collaboration. After all, lust and desire were fundamentally opposed, if often confused by humanity.

Lust was about power, control, and consumption.

Desire was about intimacy, connection, and hope.

Yeqon wanted to be intimately connected with humans. The problem was that was a disordered desire. *Elohim* had expressly forbidden that relationship.

And here he was in Amsterdam, forced to act the incubus in order to siphon off the smallest amount of energy. It took almost as much angelic energy to collect as he expended. No wonder Yeqon had been stuck here for three years.

The Seducer sat at a center table next to the stage where a couple copulated, his attention transfixed on the woman next to him watching the act with open-mouthed admiration. Asmodeus, whose own weakness and hunger had been slaked over the past few weeks in Amsterdam, smirked as he observed his brother Dark *Irim*, who wooed the vulnerable tourists attracted to the sexual license in the Dutch city. He'd managed to collect a few people to feed from, installing them in a small warehouse in the Red-Light District. It was a futile endeavor. Most of the people Yeqon charmed into joining his enclave, not deeply bonded by desire but the shallow urges of lust, left at the first new opportunity to fuck.

The woman Yeqon seduced this evening, unfortunately for him, was going to leave the Dark *Irim* in the lurch.

Asmodeus flew to their table and sat next to her. When she turned to look at him, he said, "Boo!"

She screamed. Asmodeus drank the sound from the air, getting a little harmonic jolt from it.

Yeqon, sighing, took her hand. "Giselle, please, my love, listen to your heart. You asked me to bring you to the most titillating show in Amsterdam because you were afraid to come by yourself. Ignore any qualms to which your fear has given life, no matter how real it seems."

His narrowed gaze sent fiery arrows at Asmodeus, who just grinned at his brother *Irim*.

Giselle stared at Asmodeus in horrified fascination. She lifted a tentative finger and touched his cheek. He smiled.

"Even when it looks like a hideous, yet strangely compelling, being?" she asked, wonder coloring her voice. She stroked upwards, running her palm over his head. Then she caressed his shoulder and down his arm.

Asmodeus blinked. *This* was unexpected.

When he looked at Yeqon, he saw shock followed quickly by understanding and then something else, something dark and decisive. Yeqon, his features now nonchalant, raised his forefinger and lifted his chin toward the nearby waitress, who hurried away to fill his standing order. The Seducer finally turned his attention to Asmodeus.

"I wondered when you would foul my harmonics with your presence," he said in a dry tone. "It has been almost a month since you arrived in Amsterdam."

The stupid *Irim* prided himself on almost achieving a concordant harmonic signature. It was a shabby performance, however, at the best of times.

Tonight was *definitely* not one of those times.

"I hate to tell you, Brother Dearest, but your timing has slipped. Your harmonic frequencies clash almost as much as mine do." Asmodeus grinned. "I rather like it."

He felt Giselle's hand on his crotch. *Little minx*! He growled and gave her better access, picking up her drink and gulping it down as she continued her exploration. His avatar had been minimal until this point, but the human female encouraged him to fill out his form, so to speak.

Yeqon scowled. "Why are you here, *Brother*?"

"I have a proposition for you."

Yeqon turned away, a sour expression on his handsome face. What vanity it was to take most of his failing energy to prop up such a shallow veneer when apparently his current companion not only didn't mind a hideous countenance, she seemed quite turned on by it.

"She has been primed for lust," Yeqon said, accurately guessing Asmodeus's thoughts. Irritation sharpened his voice until it broke disharmoniously on the word 'lust.' "You have me to thank, not your ugly visage."

"True, true," said Asmodeus, relaxing as Giselle's lust flowed into him.

Of course, he should be agreeable and show a little gratitude to Yeqon. It would speed up this negotiation.

His thoughts drifted for a moment.

He'd forgotten what it felt like to have humans gift him their lust instead of his own being sated through control and domination. He could get used to this.

His eyelids lowered until they were only slits. He watched the female on stage come to a climax, but the male continued to grind and thrust. He was likely drugged to continue beyond the normal human male's limits. The lust from the surrounding audience flowed into Asmodeus, making him almost sleepy.

"What is this proposition of yours?" asked Yeqon, who seemed much more relaxed now that he had a fresh drink in his hand.

"Hm? Oh, yes. I propose that we work together to wipe the *drangùe* and his *Elioud* cohort from the face of the Earth." He paused to swallow as his lust built. When he spoke again, his gravelly voice almost vibrated in a rough harmony. "Giselle, my dear, you have a very fine touch."

"In our current state?" asked Yeqon, ignoring the human female's antics. He sounded skeptical. "You expend a lot of energy on your playthings. These *daemonia* have done a lot of damage, true, but they swallow up most of the harmonic energy that they release. Your human minions are simply a waste of energy."

"Yes," said Asmodeus, nodding, "but they have run the *drangùe* and his cohort ragged these past few years. And as the *daemonia* grow stronger, we can feed from the possessed humans. Unless that is beneath you, Brother."

Yeqon wrinkled his nose as if he smelled something rank. "*You* may be able to glean enough energy from your sorties against the *Elioud*, but I am as weak as a newborn kitten. At the rate I am refilling my reservoir, it will be decades before I have enough to tilt the outcome to something I desire."

"What about your paintings?" asked Asmodeus, groaning at Giselle's ministrations. "The manna would make a very satisfying meal, would it not?"

"That little Italian temptress depleted the manna from my Van Gogh." Yeqon scowled and drained his drink, raising his hand to signal for another without looking at the waitress. "And you, *Brother*, stole the manna from the Caravaggio."

Asmodeus waved a languid hand. "I needed it to possess an *Elioud*."

"And how did that work out for you?" asked Yeqon, looking at him from the side of his eye.

It was Asmodeus's turn to scowl. "There is still the third painting. The Rembrandt. Surely you know where it is. Or know someone who knows where it is."

"I do." Yeqon fell silent.

Asmodeus, normally impatient when he'd decided on a course of action, thought the current conversation held less urgency while he enjoyed Giselle, who'd climbed into his lap. In fact, he'd rather Yeqon kept his mouth shut until she'd satisfied him.

Yeqon apparently didn't like that prospect because he started talking again. "But I have a better solution."

"What. Is. That." Asmodeus panted between words.

"First tell me what you are holding back, Dear Brother. After all you propose—how did you so elegantly phrase it?—'that we work together to wipe the *drangùe* and his *Elioud* cohort from the face of the Earth.' As it stands, there is not enough manna stored in the Rembrandt to enable either one of us to accomplish that, let alone both. You have something else in mind."

Asmodeus looked at Yeqon only to see amusement glinting in his gaze. The other Dark *Irim* looked revitalized in a way he hadn't only moments before.

Realization thrummed through Asmodeus's harmonics. He'd mistaken Yeqon's little sycophant as a harmless human target. Damn Yeqon! He'd masked his control of the woman, who'd do anything that her master desired. As she pleasured Asmodeus, Yeqon fed on his brother's response.

In fact, the Seducer fed on most of the audience around them, whom Asmodeus now realized observed them intently. Though lust had been a part of the members' response to the show that Asmodeus had unwittingly provided them, their ultimate desire had been to please their master.

Asmodeus had been caught in a harmonic sink of his own making.

"Kôkabîêl." He ground out the name.

"Ah, of course. Of course. The Star of God." Yeqon appeared thoughtful.

Giselle moved into position over Asmodeus's erect member, her adoring gaze on her master's face, waiting for confirmation to continue.

"Well, Dear Brother," said Yeqon, smiling, "you are most fortunate because I happen to know that there is an original copy of the *First Book of Enoch* extant." He nodded at Giselle, who lowered herself onto Asmodeus. "And the last keeper of the *Codex Angelicus* encoded its whereabouts in a painting here in Amsterdam."

A jolt of pure harmonic pleasure surged through Asmodeus. He'd manifested a body for this visit with his brother, and now it solidified with heavy muscled flesh. Lust and disordered desire clouded the harmonic plane around him. He little cared at the moment that Yeqon had deceived and yoked him to his will. Again. It felt so good to be aligned with another *Irim*, one who rewarded his most basic hunger.

One who knew where to find the secrets of the dispossessed Watcher Angels.

"It is time to go, dear boy."

András felt his guardian angel at his shoulder, but he didn't look at Zophiel.

"I know," he said.

It was mid-morning, the sky cold and clear above them. He'd left Beta at the granary house after breakfast, speeding towards Lublin and the two sites that he wanted to visit. Alone. Now he dawdled in the woods on the villa's grounds, soaking up the peace and solitude. It would be a long time before he would be able to lay down his duty and tend to his spirit again.

Zophiel adopted his pace as he walked back to the granary house. Her harmonics radiated from her in pure concordance, each higher harmonic frequency in her signature aligned with her fundamental frequency—a frequency tuned to the celestial key signature.

She was unadulterated music.

"How can you stand it here?" he asked. He didn't elaborate, but she understood him anyway.

"Majdanek?"

"Mm," he grunted. The museum of the concentration and extermination camp had been one of the two sites that he'd visited this morning. The sight of the children's shoes always made him weep.

"I too have duty."

András looked at Zophie. The *Cherub* often took on a playful avatar, though in the past few years she'd adopted the form of a British aristocrat who loved high fashion. Today she wore a white cable-knit sweater under an open gray wool jacket and charcoal wool pants tucked into riding boots. She could be slight or muscular, petite or tall, depending on her mood. It had taken him some time to realize that Zophie embodied the physical form she sensed that her wards needed to see. Apparently, right now he needed a companion who strode shoulder-to-shoulder with him.

She looked at him. Her blue eyes, usually so vividly arresting, matched the dull gray sky. Without explanation, she adjusted her harmonics until András caught the threads of lower chords running through her signature, flats and sharps and missing notes standing out like boulders in a smoothly rushing stream of sound. Sadness, grief, and pain snagged at the angelic composition, roiling and spoiling its perfection.

András was shocked.

He'd never considered how the heavenly music of the *Angeli Fidelis* intersected with the impure harmonic plane of Creation. But then, how did his guardian angel manifest in the lives of her wards? How did she mentor and comfort them if not by intwining her harmonics with theirs?

Shock reverberated through András again.

There. Those diminished chords and minor keys threading through Zophiel's cherubic harmony, those dissonant notes in her sweet melody.

Those were from András.

Compassion radiated from his guardian angel. Her gaze warmed to a brilliant blue. Their harmonics shifted together, Zophie integrating his into hers more fully. She smiled. A weight lifted from András's shoulders.

"You also visited the cathedral."

He nodded. "Yes."

Though the ornate Baroque interior held little appeal, the soaring, arched ceiling with its ethereal paintings lifted his spirit after visiting Majdanek. He'd missed hearing the organ music.

Almost as soon as he thought that, organ music surrounded them, filling the woods.

Zophie stopped. So did the music.

András halted and faced the *Cherub*.

"You can't promise that Beta will choose to stay with me," he said.

She shook her head, watching him. "No, dear boy, I cannot." She laid her hand on his upper arm. Soothing vibrations ran through him. "Only she can do that."

András sighed. "Which is the point, isn't it?'

She nodded. "But you know who you are. And what *you* can choose."

"Yes."

Zophie studied him. He felt as if she read him down to the marrow of his bones. And then she smiled, a brilliant smile that transformed the gray day. She touched the hard mass on his shoulder blade, the one made from the bullet fragments left in his body after the Skopje mission.

"Let me help you with this," she said.

András tilted his head, hesitating. Gifts from his guardian angel were rarely straightforward. Zophie waited, silent and patient. After a moment, he decided to trust her. She smiled again.

"Good man! Right, then. Let me see what I can do."

Stepping behind him, she ran a gentle fingertip around the mass, which began to warm. And then she began to sing, her mellifluous voice swelling around them. It resonated within his chest. As she sang, the liquid alloy spread in a thin layer under his skin. To his surprise, she traced an intricate design, manipulating it harmonically as she worked. A few moments later, it was done.

Zophie stepped back. András looked over his shoulder at her.

"Some of my best work if I say so myself. Have a look."

András started to quip that he didn't have a full-length mirror stashed in the woods. Something in Zophie's expression made him pause. He closed his eyes and focused on the molecules of lead, tin, and antimony threading through his skin cells, the harmonics of the alloy synced perfectly with his. He saw a luminous tattoo of a bird.

"A robin?" he asked softly.

"A redstart."

He turned to face Zophie. She waited for him to realize the connection. When it came, András wasn't sure whether he was angry or fascinated.

"Čermáková," he said in a flat voice.

Zophie nodded, watching him.

"What does it mean that you've transformed the bullet fragments from our failed mission into a symbol of her last name. Her *real* last name?"

"What it means, dear boy, I will leave for you to puzzle out. However, it is past time for you to collect your beloved and return to the other *Elioud*. They need you." She leaned in and, grabbing his face, kissed him on the forehead. "Go in peace." Then she disappeared.

She'd drawn a sigil for Beta. Into his flesh. Whatever else it was, it appeared permanent.

András didn't need to wrestle with what that meant.

Putting the thought of the sigil away, he set off for the granary house. By the time that he arrived, the sky had cleared into a fine late November afternoon. A Range Rover sat behind the villa. Ryan Helsing, the Kastrioti chief of security, leaned against it. He lifted his chin in greeting as András came out of the woods.

Thank you, Zophie, for the notice, he flashed.

You're quite welcome, she flashed back.

Ryan waited for András to get within a couple of meters before standing.

"Hey, how're you doing?" he asked, stepping forward with an extended hand.

András shook it. Ryan's grip was sure and confident. The former Army Ranger, though not an *Elioud*, was almost as tall as András and as massive. He trained with the *Elioud* as often as they could spare the time. András had discovered that he was a formidable foe who didn't quite understand what it meant to go toe-to-toe with demi-angels. But he was a fast study. And not all battles were won by those with the best weapons. Something Ryan understood.

"Sitrep." András didn't wait for the other man's answer. Turning, he headed to the granary house.

Ryan fell into step at his side. "Mihàil has pinpointed the location of Luger's spirit, not far from Stuttgart. And there's been increased *daemonic* activity around Paris."

That sent alarm jolting through András. Stasia and Willem had left Paris for Amsterdam a couple of days before, but if Asmodeus had any idea that they'd been there looking for the *Codex Angelicus*, he would send his *bogomili* after them. And while Stasia had impeccable fighting skills and an unbelievable amount of *Elioud* charisma, she'd need more than Willem, a former civilian and inexperienced *Elioud* fighter, to keep from falling into Asmodeus's control.

András didn't want Stasia to suffer as Beta had suffered.

"Where are we going, Paris or Stuttgart?"

Ryan stopped before they reached the door. "Neither."

Before András could say anything, the door opened. Beta stood, a duffel in her hand. She wore unfamiliar dark jeans, a heavy gray sweater, and tactical boots, which shocked András. Either Roksana had already been briefed about their departure or Ryan had been here for some time.

An awkward moment of silence descended.

"We are going to Fushë-Arrëz," said Beta. She lifted a cellphone. "Olivia called."

András looked at Ryan, who nodded. "My orders are to fly you. The *zonjë* will debrief you both once you arrive."

"Lublin Airport?" asked András. After Ryan nodded again, he said, "Give me five minutes to pack my gear."

"I already packed for you." Beta pushed another duffel into the doorway with her foot. "Roksana loaded the Range Rover with food and a thermos of coffee."

András glanced between them. "Well, then, I guess it's time to head out."

Fifteen seconds later, the villa exploded in a massive fiery ball. András reacted, pulling Beta from the granary as Ryan, a weapon materializing in his hand, scanned the area around them. Black-clad figures carrying weapons ran towards them from the woods. András sensed dozens of other humans running from the other side of the destroyed villa.

Bogomili.

Asmodeus knew where they were.

"The Range Rover!" shouted Ryan, tossing the keys to András.

András, pulling Beta after him, sped his harmonics. He scarcely noticed that her harmonics followed in sync.

Bullets whizzed past them, pinging off the Range Rover's armor plating. András buffered the air around him and Beta using a tight band of harmonics. It prevented any bullets from reaching them long enough to reach the Range Rover. Behind them, Ryan returned fire from the corner of the granary, covering their sprint to safety.

András ran around to the SUV's driver's side. Beta, who'd already jumped into the passenger seat, pulled Ryan's backup handgun from the glove compartment. Starting the Range Rover, András threw it into gear as Beta leaned out the window, firing at the nearest *bogomili* as if she'd been born with a weapon in her hand.

Every shot found a target.

Ryan plunged into the gap Beta's shooting gave him and ran for the rear passenger door as András threw the Range Rover into reverse. Ryan made it into the backseat as *bogomili* got within ten meters.

András hit the gas, ramming into *bogomili* behind them, and shifted into drive before plowing into the *bogomili* in front of them. For the next two minutes, he focused on driving as Beta and Ryan shot at the *bogomili* from both sides of the Range Rover.

When they'd cleared the long-time *Elioud* sanctuary—the one the Nazis hadn't destroyed—András finally spoke.

"Either you just saved us with your miraculous arrival ahead of the *bogomili* or you led them to us."

At his harsh assessment, Ryan's startled gaze replaced the heavy black smoke from the burning villa in the rearview mirror.

András kept his tone hard. "Either way, we aren't heading back to Fushë-Ar-rëz with you."

Nineteen

Ryan Helsing wasn't easily intimidated. Not by a cold stare or an unspoken threat of violence.

András Nagy might be a large, well-trained warrior, but so was Ryan. Hell, almost all of Ryan's Ranger buddies were as large and menacing as the Hungarian giant and just as lethal, with or without weapons. And he didn't give a crap about the man's angelic abilities. If there was one thing he'd learned in Special Forces training, it was that the measure of a man was between his ears—his own as well as those he faced. In that case, Ryan knew who he was and what he was capable of. And he had a pretty good take on the Hungarian, whose gaze kept returning to the slight woman in the passenger seat next to him.

So he held András's stare without flinching.

"Fair enough," he said, nodding. He glanced toward the woman, who'd relaxed against the seat. "You can keep the handgun. It looks like it was made for you. There's a mag in the center console and a few more in the cargo hold."

She looked over her shoulder at him. He'd never seen such intense dark-gray eyes before. They filled her delicate face. Even after nearly a month recuperating in the Polish countryside, she seemed almost fragile. A strong wind would knock her on her ass. No wonder András looked capable of eating a bucket of shrapnel, followed by ripping the sonsofbitches who'd held her limb from limb.

She narrowed her eyes and sniffed before turning back to the front. "Of course, I will keep the handgun, though I prefer the CZ-75 Compact."

Ryan grinned. He liked her. Instead of showing gratitude for the gift of a Czech weapon, the P-10C he'd tested for the U.S. Army, she'd made it clear that he had no choice *and* that his taste in guns left something to be desired.

All at once he knew exactly how she'd survived five months in a Russian black site. He doubted that Arly, his ex-fiancée, even knew the difference among the various weapons he owned. Arly would *not* have lasted more than a few days being tortured.

He looked out the side window at the flat farmland, the fields long harvested and brown. There weren't many vehicles on the highway in either direction. In the distance, they heard sirens. After a few minutes, András turned north onto Route 835.

He was taking Ryan to the airport.

"I'm Ryan, by the way," he said to the woman. "Since we missed introductions."

András kept his gaze on the road and the surrounding countryside. "Helsing is the new security chief for the Kastriotis." He didn't introduce her.

She glanced back at Ryan. "You were at The Duplex."

Ryan studied her. "You're the woman the Russian struck?"

She dipped her chin. "Thank you." A tremor, so slight that he almost missed it, shook her voice.

Ryan didn't need to ask her to what she referred. Instead, he gave a sharp nod. She turned back to her own window, clearly scanning for threats like András was.

He turned his attention to the silent Hungarian. "Is he still a factor?"

"No." The coldness in András's voice left little doubt that he'd been the one to end the Russian.

"Good." At Ryan's curt response, the other man looked in the rearview mirror. Understanding passed between them.

The woman spoke without looking back at Ryan. "I am Captain Alžběta Černá, Czech military intelligence." She paused, glancing at him. "My friends call me Beta."

"Nice to meet you, Beta. That was some impressive shooting back there."

She lifted a shoulder. "*Bogomili* are not particularly hard to hit."

Ryan blinked. She seemed sincere. "Where I come from, hitting moving targets from a moving vehicle counts as hard."

"Staszek supply the Range Rover?" asked András, bringing them back to the matter at hand.

"Yes. I picked it up earlier at the airport." Ryan considered the question. "How trustworthy is Staszek?"

"Very. I trained him myself."

They'd arrived on the outskirts of Lublin. András got off Route 835 and headed east through more farmland. The airport was twenty minutes away.

"What're you thinking happened?" asked Ryan.

"*Bogomili* are Asmodeus's personal playthings, but they're human. They require a mastermind to direct them." András paused. He appeared to be thinking out loud. "Asmodeus dangerously depleted his reserves trying to break Beta, or he would have sent them after us weeks ago."

"Asmodeus has recovered." Beta's husky voice drew András's hand. He took hers. The air between them fairly hummed and glowed.

"And he tracked Beta's harmonic signature here?" asked Ryan.

Of all the angelic talents, the power to discern and pinpoint the unique cellular movement of living beings fascinated and worried Ryan the most. It was like supernatural biometrics. The *Elioud*, of course, knew how to play with their harmonics, but their human assets couldn't. He'd been working with Miró and Willem on nanotechnology to level the playing field. But they weren't there yet.

András glanced at Beta, whose wide eyes told Ryan all he needed to know.

"It's possible," the Hungarian *Elioud* said, answering Ryan's question about tracking. "At least before her signature changed. He also has agents everywhere. Whether we headed west to the Czech Republic or south to Albania, we would have to come through Lublin. Perhaps he's known where she was all this time and waited for the energy to launch an attack."

Ryan was surprised at how relieved he felt that András didn't list him as a possible intel source for the Dark *Irim*. Then again, the Hungarian probably would have pulled over at the first opportunity and beat him to a quivering pulp if he believed that.

Or tried. Ryan might not be a *daemon*, but he could fight dirty when necessary.

"New plan?" he asked.

Beta said nothing while he and András talked. Instead, she opened the center console and removed the spare clip for the CZ P-10C and reloaded it. The clip slid into the weapon with a determined *snap*. She laid the gun in her lap and returned to her survey of their surroundings.

András ignored her. "We'll take the jet; you take the Range Rover," he said to Ryan. "I'll call Staszek and have him send a couple to ride with you as decoys for us. Head toward the Czech Republic. Slowly. Erratically." He paused. "Obviously."

"Like an injured animal?" Ryan knew the tactic.

"Exactly. Best-case scenario, the *bogomili* didn't spot you until the attack, so they don't know about the jet. You and Staszek's people ditch the vehicle and make your way to a Czech safe house before any *bogomili* catch up to you."

"Worst case, I find myself fighting for my life with a couple of strangers."

"Worst case, we've only split whatever *bogomili* forces are still in the area. No telling what Asmodeus's minions can pull off if they suspect we're flying instead of driving." András's hard gaze held Ryan's in the rearview mirror. "Whatever you signed up for, know this: Asmodeus will do whatever it takes to eliminate Beta and me. So I need to know right now if we can rely on you."

Ryan clenched his jaw. "I'm a U.S. Army Ranger, *sir*. I don't quit. I don't surrender. The enemy will never succeed while I breathe."

Whatever András saw in his gaze, the *Elioud* simply nodded.

They took the next exit, which Ryan knew was less than ten minutes from the airport. The two *Elioud* had continuously checked their mirrors for a tail. Ryan himself had watched over his shoulder. Nothing. The *bogomili* seemed to have been taken off guard by his arrival at the granary. Ryan's neck itched anyway. It was the calm before the storm.

They pulled into a McDonald's where András called Staszek while Ryan called Mihàil's pilot, Daněk, who waited on standby on the runway. Beta, who'd jumped out as soon as András parked, went to the back of the Range Rover where she pulled out the extra magazines for the CZ P-10C and stuffed them into a duffel. Then she began rifling through the rest of the gear. When Ryan came around to help her, he saw her studying the tactical knives that he'd packed.

"What's your poison?" he asked.

"Hm?" asked Beta, selecting a knife from the stockpile. Its designer called it a 'morphing' karambit whose blade slid out smoothly from a locked position with a thumb press.

She swirled the loop around her forefinger. The next instant, she deployed the hawkbill blade, her grip sure on the handle, the wicked curved steel extending away from her. She hefted the karambit in a practiced jab before disengaging the locking mechanism and pushing the blade back into a folded shape with her free hand. In a blink she repeated the maneuver with the other hand. She ended by clipping it to the beltloop of her jeans and hiding it under her sweater.

Ryan whistled. *Damn.* And here he'd thought the Czech handgun had been made for her grip. But this was even more impressive. If a bullet didn't take out an attacker, she'd gut him. Ryan suspected that these were the least of Beta's lethal weapons. All that and drop-dead gorgeous.

He was in love.

András came around the tail of the Range Rover and stopped close to Beta. Sliding a possessive hand on her lower back, he lifted the duffel she'd snagged onto his shoulder. Something in his hard gaze made Ryan wonder if his admiration had been a little too obvious. The big Hungarian had nothing to worry about. Ryan had resolved after Arly dumped him to ignore women. Beta was just the exception that proved the rule.

András turned to him. "Staszek's people will be here in twenty minutes. We'll go the rest of the way on foot. I suggest that you wait in the Range Rover."

Ryan had no problem with that idea. They'd parked in the corner away from the direct line of sight of the windows, and most of the traffic at this hour used the drive-through.

András continued. "Miles will coordinate with you from the TOC. Remember: the longer you can distract the *bogomili*, the better our chances."

"Copy that." Ryan held out his hand. András shook it. Beta, who'd never stopped scanning the highway or area around them, simply nodded.

Ryan watched as the couple headed toward the road before disappearing in a blur. He needed to get his head on straight and focus on the mission. Something told him that things were about to get kinetic.

Five minutes later Beta and András were at the airport and walking toward the Embraer Phenom 300 light business jet that Kastrioti Industries owned. Five minutes after that, they'd stowed the duffel, taken their seats, and engaged their seatbelts. Now they sat waiting for the tower to give the pilot permission to taxi.

"That was too easy," said Beta, looking out one of the jet's windows. The new karambit was in her hand. She opened, closed, and transferred it between each hand repeatedly.

"I agree." András checked his smartphone. "Helsing just rendezvoused with Staszek's people. He'll send updates on the road."

Beta looked at him. Strain deepened the lines at the corners of his eyes and mouth, the ones that had almost disappeared over the last month. András no longer looked as young as he had when she'd met him. Before she'd seduced and betrayed him.

"Do you really think the *bogomili* will pick them up?"

"For their sake, I hope not," he said.

"But for ours, you do." It wasn't a question. "Why? Surely we are safer now unless they manage to assault the runway before we take off."

He shook his head. "I won't feel at ease until we're in Albania."

"Because Mihàil has more power there?"

He nodded.

"But that does not mean that Asmodeus will not try to strike at *me*," she said.

Before András could respond, Daněk, Mihàil's Czech pilot, opened the cockpit door and came back to them. He smiled and greeted her in Czech before telling them that he'd been given permission to take off after the next commercial flight. They would land at the private Kastrioti airfield in northern Albania in an hour and twenty minutes.

Beta surprised herself with how glad she was to recognize the self-possessed pilot, who'd skillfully flown a mission to rescue Mihàil before Olivia had become his lady. He'd also flown the helicopter that had medevacked her and András from Skopje. It was strange starting to feel like part of a team, one made up of friends, and not just Olivia and Stasia.

The Phenom had climbed to cruising altitude before András returned to their conversation.

Picking up Beta's free hand and playing with her fingers, he said, "As long as I've been one of Mihàil's lieutenants, Asmodeus has been unpredictable in his assaults on humanity. Of course, Mihàil is one of his favorite targets, but he'd rather strike at the *drangùe* by setting his vicious henchmen on innocents. He doesn't have the power to destroy Mihàil alone, especially now that he and Olivia are married."

He raised his gaze and looked at her. "I've never seen him obsessed with anyone until now. And that worries me deeply. It's almost as if he thinks he owns you. But you are *mine*."

A shiver ran down Beta's spine at his words. She wanted to be his. Yet doubt lingered.

The jet had a small refreshment center as well as lavatory. While András fixed them both coffees, Beta found some packaged pastries in one of the drawers. The Kastriotis stocked gourmet treats, but they wouldn't compare with the pastries that Roksana had baked and packed for their trip.

Roksana. Maybe not a team member, exactly, but a member of the *Elioud* family. And now she was dead.

Beta waited until András had taken a seat opposite hers before lowering a tray table between them.

"Here," she said, piling the pastries on its glossy veneer along with two plates, real porcelain ones.

András grunted and handed her a cup, also porcelain. He'd made the coffee just the way she liked it, black and sweet. She sipped it, realizing as she did how shaky her harmonics had been since the *bogomili* surprised them. András opened two of the pastries and set them on the plates.

He handed her one. "Eat," he said. "You need something after this morning's excitement."

Beta didn't argue. Instead, she picked up the tasteless croissant and ate the whole thing in quick, small bites, washing them down with sips of coffee. At least the coffee was excellent.

"Will Roksana's family be taken care of?" she asked after she finished, toying with her empty cup.

Almost all she could think about the whole time they were driving away from the estate was the fact that the kind, self-effacing woman had perished in the explosion.

András leaned across the tray table, lifting her chin until she met his gaze. She saw pain there. He'd known Roksana since she'd been a young woman.

When he spoke, his grief roughened his voice. "Yes. A team has been dispatched to recover her body, if possible. As soon as we're able, we'll all gather to honor her sacrifice."

Beta nodded. András slid from his seat and cleaned up their plates and the empty pastry wrappers before pouring them more coffee. While he did, she looked out the window at the brocaded landscape below. She thought they'd passed over Budapest while they ate. Idly, she wondered if they'd crossed into Serbian airspace yet. It was impossible to tell. Funny how fourteen kilometers above ground erased manmade political boundaries.

After András slid back into his seat, graceful as a panther in the constricted space, Beta asked, "Why do you not like Ryan?"

He glanced out the window, his profile rigid. She waited patiently until he spoke. "*Azt hiszi, hogy bombahéj vagy,*" he said. *He thinks you're a bombshell.*

Beta took his hand, entwining her fingers with his. "He thinks that you are a *bomb*. He respects you, Spratek. I do not think he does that lightly."

"He was there when you were hurt, and I wasn't." His low voice conveyed the depth of his self-castigation.

Now it was Beta's turn to move András's face to meet her gaze. "Yes, Ryan Helsing risked himself without hesitation for me. Because he is like you." She searched his gaze. "Until I met you, and Mihàil and Miró, I was blind to men with heroic qualities. Now everything—*everything*—looks different to me because of you."

András placed a large hand over hers where it cupped his jaw. "And to me as well."

Heat spiked between them. Beta's eyes widened at the intensity of it radiating from András's core, an intensity that matched hers. His own eyelids drooped as he looked at her mouth. She swallowed, desire for him roaring to life. He dropped her hand to lift and fold the tray table out of the way, and then she was in his lap and he was kissing her as if he would never, *ever* have enough of her.

Beta inhaled, pulling his unique smoky sweet scent into her until her thoughts swam from the heat, and the scent, and the taste of him. Their harmonics intertwined, linking them together until her breath was his and his breath was hers. The glow of their nimbuses warmed her eyelids.

Her hands dropped to his chest, then lower to the bottom of his shirt. She slid them under the material and pressed her palms against his sculpted pectoral muscles, a soft moan escaping her as electricity hummed along her nerves and spiked need in her groin.

She was aware of nothing else. Only András.

Until Daněk opened the door to the cockpit.

And even then, she missed his presence until András pulled away, gently setting her back in her seat before turning to look over his shoulder at the pilot, whose face remained politely blank.

"What is it?" András sounded alert and in command, unlike her.

"Sir, Serbian air traffic control alerted me to an aircraft flying the same heading in our flight path."

András frowned. His harmonics tightened, drawing Beta's tighter in response.

"Range? Altitude?" he asked the pilot. "Can you get a visual on it for markings?"

Daněk shook his head. "It's at our radar limit, about 65 kilometers. Altitude is thirty thousand meters."

"With its transponder off," said András.

Daněk nodded. All aircraft had transponders to alert other aircraft and civil ATC of their position. While commercial airliners cruised at thirty thousand meters, only military aircraft could turn their transponders off.

"Serbian military?" asked Beta, grasping at an answer. Civil air traffic control would have closed airspace to them if the military had notified it about training flights. "A Mil Mi-8 helo?"

The Mil Mi-8, one of the most popular helicopters in the world, was a medium-size twin-turbine Russian-made bird that could fly almost as high as many commercial airliners. This in and of itself wasn't worrying. Helicopters flew much slower and lower than the private light jet. They also didn't have the range. But it could signal that their whereabouts were known. Mercenaries of all sorts numbered among Asmodeus's bogomili hordes, many of whom had access to weapons that they shouldn't, like combat helicopters and surface-to-air missiles.

"Maybe surveillance or a mobile command op," said András, thinking out loud.

"Or an escort," said Beta. Her neck itched.

Daněk waited for them to run through all the theoretical possibilities.

At last, András asked, "How much longer before we're vulnerable?"

Neither Daněk or Beta had to ask what that meant. A bogomili on board a Mil Mi-8, which could carry three crew and twenty-four mercenaries, could launch a missile, likely a Russian Igla-V, once they got within eight kilometers laterally and four-and-a-half kilometers vertically. The Igla-V was a heat seeker, requiring little in the way of targeting. It had been used in combat zones to bring down civilian aircraft for decades.

"Ten minutes." Daněk paused and then went on soberly. "That's when we'll be over the Dinaric Alps."

Beta looked out the jet's windows. Below them, she could see the jagged mountains against the darkening November sky. In twenty minutes, they'd be in Albania, descending through the Accursed Mountains to the Kastrioti airfield.

Or not.

"What kinds of countermeasures does this jet have?" she asked as soon as Daněk had slipped his headphones back on and began radioing Serbian ATC for help.

"None." András's voice was grim. "Though Miró has been working with the manufacturer to develop an emergency landing sequence in the autopilot program if something should happen to Daněk."

"Parachutes?"

He shook his head.

"Then we better hope Serbian air traffic control diverts us to a different airfield. What range does this jet have?"

The strain on his face told her what she needed to know.

"If we'd waited to refuel ..." he said.

Before Beta could respond, Daněk looked back at them. His face was white. "Sir, someone has hijacked control of the digital autopilot."

Almost as soon as he finished speaking, the Phenom began slowing. A moment later, the nose tilted precipitously, dropping Beta once again into András's lap. He wrapped one arm around her and braced his other against the fuselage until the plane leveled off. Beta, her heart pounding, looked out the window at her shoulder.

They were much closer to the ground.

András called to Daněk. "Can you override the autopilot?"

"Affirmative." There was silence for several moments before he continued. "I now have manual control, sir. But we're also in range of the helo."

Beta's dragon sight saw the spurt of heat and smoke from the tiny aircraft.

"Missile incoming," she said.

TWENTY

S askia Braam was a hot mess as Olivia would say.

Well, more accurately, her friend would call the Dutch art historian *a flaming dumpster fire.*

Stasia narrowed her eyes at the other woman, who sat at a table in one of Amsterdam's infamous sex clubs, drinking a cocktail and openly salivating over the show on the stage in front of them. She'd clearly already taken something prior to meeting Stasia and Willem. Her glassy eyes, mussed blond hair, and unkempt clothing suggested that she'd been flying high for some time, maybe days.

Which would explain why it had taken her three days to respond to Willem's phone call.

Saskia waggled a bill in her outstretched hand until the stripper sashayed over and let her wedge it into her thong. She looked up at the performer through drooping eyelids and pouted. The woman tossed her head, her long teased hair resembling a lion's stiff mane, and lowered herself onto Saskia's lap where she bent and kissed the other woman.

Stasia exhaled and rolled her eyes. She glanced over at Willem, whose closed expression and stiff harmonics confirmed that Saskia's behavior didn't align with their previous encounters. Not surprising, as Willem seemed pretty buttoned up. Unlike Stasia, who often had to waltz confidently into a covert operation amongst all types of hot-mess behaviors and act as if it were nothing more out of the ordinary than a thunderstorm at a garden party.

Stasia took pity on the architect and swiveled to address Saskia, whose flushed cheeks betrayed her intoxicated arousal. The stripper pulled back from the teasing kiss and began to stand. Saskia clutched at her, trying to keep the other woman from leaving.

"*Per favore*, what is in that drink? I *must* have one, Signorina Braam," said Stasia, feeding *Elioud* charisma into her words so that the other woman wanted to look at her more than she wanted to stop the stripper. When she did, Stasia waved her left hand, the diamonds on her wedding band sparkling in the light from the stage. Saskia seemed mesmerized as Stasia intended. "I am a little nervous about being out on my own without my husband."

Willem cleared his throat, but Stasia ignored him.

They'd agreed to meet Saskia in the less graphic club side of Bananenbar in order to convince the art historian to give them access to *La Grandmère*, which was currently in restoration. Willem hadn't mentioned the painting in his voicemail, just said that he was in town with a colleague who worked with the Italian Art Squad. It was too loud in the Bananenbar for a real conversation, so Stasia and Willem directed a fine array of nano-origami around their table to deflect sound from their ears that wasn't keyed to their trio's voices.

Saskia laughed. "It's a Porn Star Martini. You know, like the James Bond drink? But with passionfruit, pineapple, and vanilla. You'd need more than one of these"—here she waggled her glass and smirked—"I fear. You look like your husband fulfills *all* of your needs."

Stasia squelched her irritation, widening her smile to underscore her answer. "Indeed, he does."

For a moment she held the other woman's glazed stare. Saskia blinked, swallowed, gulped her drink, and swallowed again.

Finally, Saskia set her glass down and sat up a little straighter. Her gaze had sobered satisfactorily. "Why did you want to meet, Agent Kos? Willem didn't share any details other than that you work for Italy's Art Squad."

Stasia, who'd signaled for a waitress instead of a stripper, waited until she'd ordered her own favorite cocktail, a *negroni*, before answering. Willem shook his head when the waitress asked if he wanted to order something. Stasia sighed internally. He needed to work on his technique if he was going to stay in the field. First and foremost, not drinking a cocktail in front of you was a lot less obvious than not having a drink in front of you at all.

She smiled again, this time with less *Elioud* power. Nodding and easing a tiny breath of *Elioud* charisma into her words, she answered Saskia's question. "That is true."

She'd captured the art historian's attention and now must navigate the conversation in such a way that she didn't lose it—or give away more than she intended. "But let us just say that the Art Squad is not my primary employer."

Stasia's instincts proved correct. Even though Saskia's senses had been dulled by drug, drink, and self-indulgent sexual desire, her eyes narrowed. "Don't tell me that you also 'acquire' pieces for interested individuals on the side?" Cynicism colored her voice.

Stasia didn't allow her surprise to show. Not only were Saskia's wits intact, she'd conveyed a decided hostility toward illicit art activities. She could use this. It was always easier to work with an asset's deepest values than to try to deceive or compel them. Willem wisely said nothing, simply shifted in his seat and crossed his arms.

"No," said Stasia, moving her head from side to side, watching as Saskia took in the deliberate movement. "You misunderstand the situation entirely. My cover is with the Art Squad, but I am actually assigned to Europol's counter-terrorism center."

Saskia accepted a fresh cocktail from the waitress, who'd also brought Stasia's *negroni*. She didn't drink, however, simply held it up as she tilted her head, considering Stasia. The other woman's harmonics definitely said that her curiosity was piqued. There was something else familiar about them....

"I'm sorry," said Saskia, not sounding sorry at all. "Then what do you need from me? I'm not a terrorist or date one."

Stasia refrained from looking at Willem. Excitement thrummed in his harmonics. He clearly understood that this was the pivotal moment in their approach.

"I need access to Émile Bernard's *La Grandmère*." Stasia said nothing more. As always, on covert operations, the less said the better.

Saskia laughed, wide eyed. There was something more to her humor, how-ever, than generic disbelief that a Post-Impressionist painting held any interest for a counter-terrorism investigator.

"What is it?" Willem asked sharply.

Stasia shot him a quelling look, but he leaned across the table, his hands gripping the edges.

Saskia shrugged and tipped up her Porn Star Martini. She swayed a little on her seat as she sipped in that careful way a drunk has when trying to simulate sobriety. "The dour old woman is very popular this week."

Willem and Stasia shared a look.

"Was it a woman from the Art Squad?" Stasia asked, leaning forward like Willem.

Saskia shook her head, her lips pressed together in mock consideration. "No, not a woman. And not the Art Squad. An art lover." She giggled.

Stasia wanted to shake her. Instead, she asked, "Who did you give access to *La Grandmère*?" She spiked her words with *Elioud* authority, forgoing the charisma altogether.

Saskia blinked several times. Then she looked puzzled. "You know, I don't know. But he was most decidedly worth my time, if you know what I mean." Her wink was grotesque. "He and his ugly friend."

Ugly friend? Stasia shoved that question to the back of her mind for later. "Did you ever leave them alone with the painting?"

Saskia shook her head again, shock widening her eyes followed by swift out-rage. Stasia could tell that it was authentic. "Absolutely not."

Stasia groaned and closed her eyes for a moment, pinching the bridge of her nose. The dark noisy club and gyrating, nearly naked women disturbed her harmonics in a way that nothing else had in a long time. A headache pierced her through her right eye.

Willem placed a hand on her forearm. When she looked at him, he dipped his chin toward Saskia in clear question. Stasia sighed and nodded.

"Did they discuss the painting in front of you?" he asked. His calm tone soothed Stasia's jangled nerves.

Saskia nodded and sipped her drink, letting her gaze wander toward the stripper gripping the pole a few meters from them. She'd clearly lost interest in the conversation.

Willem persisted. Stasia noticed a quiet thread of *Elioud* authority in his voice. "Do you remember anything they said?"

The Dutch art historian appeared not to have heard him. But then she answered as if unaware that she spoke. "They found the old woman's eye inordinately fascinating. Apparently, if you look close enough, you can see a tiny map or something in microscopic dots."

Sweet St. Michael! Stasia forgot her fatigue and edginess as excitement surged through her harmonics. "I need to see that painting."

"That can be arranged." Saskia turned a shrewd gaze on Willem. "For the same price that I charged the art lover and his friend." She put her hand on his where it rested on the table between them. "I always did envy Eva."

Willem sat back as if bitten by a viper.

Before he could speak and ruin their progress, Stasia said, "No negotiation, no payment." When Saskia turned to argue, she continued in a pleasant tone that belied the hard look she gave the other woman, "Our time is limited, and you have already allowed access to unknown individuals."

Stasia held Saskia's gaze until the other woman shrugged. "As you wish." Then she raised her hand to flag a waitress.

"Now, Signorina Braam," said Stasia, nudging her harmonics. When Saskia didn't respond, she zapped her with a quick flick of her nano-origami blackbirds.

"Ow!" Saskia blinked, rubbing her breastbone. She didn't look tipsy or high anymore.

Stasia and Willem stood, waiting until Saskia led them from the club. As they passed out into the dark November night, Willem held back. Stasia slowed her steps to match his. Without spoken coordination, they both buffered the harmonics around them so that their speech would be unintelligible to anyone who happened to listen.

"What good does it do to examine the painting?" he asked. "She clearly described Yeqon. It also explains her behavior." He paused, staring at the woman a meter in front of them. "The same thing happened to Eva." He sounded bitter.

Stasia put a hand on his forearm, sending soothing harmonics into him. "I have found, *caro*, that it is always wise to decide for myself what is and is not valuable intel. Where these Dark *Irim* are concerned, it is doubly true." She looked up at him, afraid her worry showed. "Otherwise, we must assume that Yeqon has the *Codex Angelicus*."

Beta reacted without thinking.

Or more precisely, her dragon nature broke its chains.

She fixated on the heat trail of the Igla-V, her own temperature rising in response. Dimly she sensed objects on the harmonic plane around her. They vibrated faster and faster, glowing in a white-hot constellation.

Then she launched them toward the missile on an intercept path.

A moment later the microscopic flares disrupted the Igla-V's infrared tracking. The missile exploded a kilometer from the Phenom, the blast wave rocking the jet.

"*Mi a fene volt az, hogy?*" András asked. *What the hell was that?* He sounded shaken.

Beta let out a smoky breath. "I don't know." It hurt to speak.

She'd gotten tangled in András's arms and between his thighs. She pushed against his hold. He didn't try to stop her. She stood and lurched into the opposite seat. Their skin glistened in the heated cabin air. Next to them, the fuselage had blackened. The white leather seat beneath András had charred and split. His tactical pants had scorch marks.

But that wasn't all. The cabin pressure had fallen. Oxygen masks had dropped from overhead and now dangled above them. Head swimming, Beta pulled a mask to her mouth and inhaled. Her arm shook with the effort.

Daněk had already donned his aviator mask. He spoke via the comm system. "Sir, we're too low. I don't have time to clear the mountains. I'm going through the Valbona Pass instead. It's going to get bumpy."

"Copy that," said András before pulling his oxygen mask over his mouth. He reached for his seatbelt and fastened it.

Beta did likewise. As she did, she looked out the window next to her. Her heart kicked at the sight. The helo, more maneuverable among the mountains, had gained on them. It was only a matter of moments before another Igla-V was launched.

Can you mask the heat trail from the jet? she flashed, scarcely aware that she did so.

I can try.

An orange-white flare and spreading smoke warned of a second Igla-V speeding toward them. This time, however, András's gaze hardened on Beta.

The *Elioud* tracker had caught the scent.

Holding his gaze, Beta focused her *Elioud* senses on their entwined harmonics. She bolstered András as he inverted the thermal wave pattern of the jet's exhaust. What had been blazing white on the infrared spectrum flipped to a deep cool blue.

The Igla-V sped past the Phenom and hit the rocky mountain next to them.

An instant later, shockwaves exploded into the already turbulent air currents swirling around the mountains. The jet lurched and rolled, pulling Beta hard against the seatbelt. The nose dipped, but Daněk fought with the yoke and brought it level again.

Harmonics!

András's mental shout brought Beta's thoughts back from the wrenching pain in her shoulder. She concentrated on the harmonic maelstrom around the jet. Violent whorls rushed against the metal fuselage, threatening to tear it apart.

A teremburáját! Lord of Creation! András gritted his teeth. Veins popped in his neck. His hands clutched the armrests.

Beta exhaled and, closing her eyes, stepped into the harmonic plane next to András, tuning her harmonics to the jet's. She slowed her breathing, forcing their combined harmonics to slow. It was like wrestling with a firehose with the hydrant fully open.

András managed to pull the Phenom out of the invisible whirlpool.

Only for it to come under fire from the helo's guns.

Two 23-mm twin-barrel autocannons mounted on the Mil Mi-8's weapon stations rapid-fired shells. Several ripped through the cabin. An engine cut out. The Phenom bounced and then steadied.

"We've lost an engine, sir," said Daněk. His calm voice contradicted their situation. "The helo is coming around again."

András lowered his mask. "How much longer before we reach the airfield?"

"At this speed in the pass ..." Daněk's broadcast trailed off. "Twenty minutes." He didn't have to say that they weren't going to make it.

András looked at Beta. Fatigue lined his eyes and flattened his mouth.

Before he could respond, Daněk pulled his aviator mask off. The plane's altitude was low enough now that the masks were unnecessary anyway.

They were out of time and out of options.

"Sir, you have to jump." Daněk's steady gaze belied the meaning of his words.

A moment later, the helo's side-mounted PK machine gun strafed the side of the jet opposite of Beta and András. As Daněk swiveled back to the yoke, the autocannons boomed. The rear of the Phenom tore away. The plane bucked like a wild animal. Beta's heart choked her as she was thrown around inside the restricting harness. Releasing his seatbelt, András jumped up and lunged for her.

She pulled her oxygen mask off and unclicked her latch, rising to meet him. He took her hand and pulled her toward the cabin door. Daněk pushed the yoke forward and to the side, causing the Phenom to roll as it descended. She fell into András, but the Czech pilot had bought them a few moments. Beta spared a glance through the nearest window to see the helo struggling with the jet's backwash. It spun away across the pass toward the rugged mountain on the other side.

András planted a palm on the door latch. It vaporized. He shoved, and the door flew from the jet. He looked over his shoulder at Daněk.

"We will not forget." His voice rang out in the cabin with *Elioud* authority.

Daněk didn't look back or take his hands from the yoke. Beta's last view of the Czech pilot was of a proudly upright head and straight shoulders, his knuckles white.

Before Beta could consider what András was doing, he launched from the jet as it rotated with them.

As they plummeted, Daněk dropped the plane, shielding them from a burst of machine gun fire.

Beta clutched András, her heart beating against her ribcage like a trapped swallow. The craggy base of the mountain loomed larger as they hurtled towards it.

Gomba. András's calm voice in her head halted the mad whirl of her thoughts. *Do you trust me?*

Always, she flashed.

Then stop fighting me.

What are you doing?

Falling gracefully.

Beta had no idea what he meant by that, but she relaxed into his arms. Instantly András took control of their combined harmonics.

Above them, the helo had circled away from the Phenom and now headed back toward them, its blades beating the air like a deranged metallic insect. The autocannon began firing, belching 23-mm shells at András and Beta.

Daněk, who'd anticipated the move, had already angled the jet in its path. The remaining engine whined as he pushed the throttle wide. Seconds later, the jet exploded, sending a massive fiery plume of oily smoke to the peaks dominating the valley. Metallic debris and human body parts rained down. The shockwave knocked the helo sideways, stalling its engines. It dropped like a boulder. András hunched over Beta, pressing her into his chest and wrapping his arms around her as he did his best to protect her.

She closed her eyes and leaned against him, sickened. Her *Elioud* senses told her that András fought to slow their descent with all of the energy of their combined harmonics. Her temperature fluctuated as he modulated it in response to the shifting ambient temperature. As the ground rose up to meet them, his arms began to shake. They tilted and swung about on an invisible axis.

Beta, whose heart rate had steadied, didn't slip the reins from him. Instead, she imagined their harmonics taking the shape of incandescent wings. And then she unfolded them like a winged predator—*a dragon*—gliding the two of them to clear ground beyond the evergreens bordering the base of the mountains.

András gave out at the last moment, and they tumbled to earth, flying apart as they hit. He ended up beneath her and took most of the impact. Beta rolled, knocking into icy outcroppings and scrub until the ground leveled.

The helicopter pilot managed to restart an engine, the helo bobbing up and down and pirouetting like a drunken ballet dancer as he wrestled to regain control.

Only to smash into the unyielding face of the mountain on the opposite side of the pass.

Beta groaned and pushed herself upright enough to scan the area for András, who'd come to rest twenty meters above her on the hilly terrain among some evergreens. She got to her feet, a mass of bruises but no broken bones, and stumbled to him. As she reached András, her *Elioud* senses caught something across the valley. She glanced over. While she couldn't see the wreckage of the Mil Mi-8 among the evergreens blanketing the opposite slope, she knew exactly where it was from the plume of smoke curling up into the clear November sky. The acrid fumes scorched her nostrils as trees and dry grass caught fire around the wreck.

She detected infrared signatures. *Moving* signatures. Six of them, to be exact. The burning mass of the wreck and scattered glowing fragments remained stationary.

They weren't alone.

András's big body lay sprawled on the grassy turf. Beta knelt and took his hand, holding it to her cheek. "András! András, my love, please. Can you sit?"

"Why are you disturbing my nap, Gomba?" Even with her *Elioud* hearing, Beta strained to hear the words. He didn't open his eyes.

"Sit up! You must sit up! Six *bogomili* survived the helo crash." She swallowed around her dry throat. "And I hear more aircraft engines."

"Leave me."

"What?" Beta couldn't believe what she'd heard.

András opened his eyes and glared at her. The dark-blue irises had hardened into agate in his lined and bruised face. If she didn't know better, she'd think that he hated her. He rolled to his side, groaned, and then pushed himself into a sitting position.

"I said, leave me." This time his voice was audible. "Head northwest toward the village of Valbona. Stay under the tree cover and off the trail. Find Davud and tell him you're one of the *drangùe's* warriors. He'll drive you the rest of the way to Fushë-Arrëz."

Beta's dragon temper roared. She leaned forward, getting within a hands-breadth of his face. She narrowed her eyes. "And what exactly will you be doing?" Smoky heat swirled in her words.

András's own eyes narrowed. A vein pulsed in his jaw as he scanned her face. "Distracting some *tutyimutyi* men."

"Elvesztetted a fejed, Spratek," she said in Hungarian in a low voice. *You've lost your mind, brat.* "We should get to Valbona together."

He shook his head, holding her gaze as he said, "Our last joint mission didn't end so well. You're better alone with me covering your back."

Hurt zinged through Beta like a lightning strike. Did he blame her for Skopje?

She brought the karambit to his jugular; it was as much dragon instinct as training. "You do not always have to rescue me."

Steam rose from their skin, clouding the chilly air around them. Beta thought she might choke on it.

"If you want to help me, stay off my tail." Then she nicked the tender skin under his chin to underscore her command.

Fury melted the agate in his gaze. Perhaps now he did hate her a little. He blinked slowly several times before answering. "As you wish."

Beta stood, swiveling on her heel while hooking the karambit to her belt loop. As she headed for cover under the trees, tears blurred the last view she had of András.

Twenty-One

András watched Beta stalk away with only a swift backward glance.

That, however, had been enough to drive home the hurt echoing through their combined harmonics. Even from a distance, he'd recognized the glisten of tears on her cheeks.

András grimaced and shifted his weight on his buttocks. Falling gracefully. Right.

The nick she'd given him with her dragon's claw stung. He swiped a thumb across the blood, wiping it on his pants. He didn't bother trying to seal the cut via thermogenesis. He'd tapped his energy stores out keeping the jet airborne and then getting the two of them to the ground whole.

At least he thought he was whole. He scanned his body and signatures for any alerts. Then he wiggled his toes, and when they moved freely rotated his ankles. He worked his way up his legs, confirming that they were uninjured. The effort left him shaking. He needed food and water, but there hadn't been time to grab even a go bag before jumping from the jet, leaving Daněk to die.

Daněk.

Grief swamped András. He'd known Daněk for more than two decades after meeting the Czech pilot who was serving at the time on the U.N. Protection Force during the Croatian War of Independence.

The rumble of aircraft engines broke into András's reverie.

He shoved his grief down with his anguish over losing Roksana, who, despite being younger than him, had mothered him almost as long as he'd known Daněk.

He looked up. Two more Mil Mi-8 helicopters buzzed the valley in an offset formation. They flew north-to-south along the same route that Daněk had flown. They'd likely already flown past Beta. He'd help her escape by moving into the open. The Valbona Trail was closed this time of year, which was fortunate. He wouldn't have to worry about protecting any hikers who strayed into the battle zone.

It also meant he'd stand out for the bogomili mercenaries.

In fact, a helicopter passed over his location. His battle senses told him that it swung around after a few hundred meters, flying lower towards him. András came to his knees, gripping the trunk of the pine nearest him and exhaling as he pulled himself upright. Somehow, he succeeded in getting to his feet as the helo came overhead. The pilot and another *bogomili* looked right at him from the cockpit. The gunner manning the PK machine gun from the open bay door also had eyes on András. He couldn't read their expressions hidden under helmets and sunglasses, but none moved. The helo began to swing wide as it flew around his location, clearly looking for something else. Or someone.

Beta.

Adrenaline surged through András. He modulated his harmonics to pinpoint his shout inside the helicopter. "Hey, *gyengélkedő*, where are you going?"

The gunner looked back and flipped him off.

That was a mistake.

Leaving András alive was a bigger mistake.

The helo that had spotted him joined its mate across the valley where it hovered while crew members descended ropes from the hold to the ground.

András scanned a radius around the wreck of the lead helicopter. Most of the scattered debris, though still too hot for human touch, had cooled on the thermal spectrum to orange-red. The main bulk of the aircraft still blazed white to his infrared vision, with cooler pockets inside from charred dead bodies. The non-metallic gear had already burned. Red and orange sparks jumped between the surrounding trees, catching branches and grass on fire. At this time of year when everything was so dry, a forest fire seemed inevitable.

He frowned. Where were the six surviving *bogomili* that Beta had identified?

He got a partial answer when two of the new arrivals ran toward separate body-shaped lumps, kneeling and reaching a hand to one end. From the rapidly cooling infrared signature of the shapes, he knew they were dead *bogomili*. Either Beta had misread their signatures or they'd died since she'd looked.

He widened his scan radius. There were three other bodies fifty meters south of the crash zone, one leaning against a boulder and two twenty meters on either side of him collapsed against tree trunks. Several new arrivals from the hovering helos ran towards them.

That left a single *bogomili* from the six survivors. Where was he?

András widened his focus.

His heart sank. He recognized Beta moving through the tall, yellow grass south of the crash site. Moving *towards* the burning wreckage and newly arriving *bogomili* mercenaries.

What the hell are you doing? he flashed.

Attacking bogomili, she flashed back.

Two helos full?

That was your plan, was it not? They are not expecting me. She paused a beat. *Just as the survivors from the first helo did not expect me.*

A fenébe! he swore to himself. He should have expected the lone wolf to go for the injured *bogomili* on her own.

His temperature rose higher than it had in months. He welcomed it. It drove away the frigid mountain air chilling his limbs and warmed his muscles.

It didn't banish the cold completely, however. Icy clarity settled in his mind.

Ignoring his exhaustion, András forced his body to do what his will wanted. It was just another weapon for his use. He took a few lurching steps, speeding his harmonics so that he moved faster than the surrounding landscape. Adjusting harmonics took no energy, but being out of sync with the material world caused a slow energy drain. He didn't know how long he had before he collapsed.

Then he remembered the lithium batteries in the seams of his tactical clothing and the soles of his boots. If Olivia could access them to give András a love tap, then he should be able to draw on them enough to keep his harmonics stable.

Thank you, brother, for your techno-geek ways, he thought. He'd never give Miró a hard time again for insisting that the *Elioud* team add high-tech weapons to their angelic arsenal.

Setting off at a run on the trail, András headed to intercept Beta, praying to all the *Angeli Fidelis* that he'd make it before she engaged the new *bogomili* arrivals.

His angelic sonar took in the entire field of engagement. One helo hovered, dropping *bogomili* to the wreck site. The second helo, however, had moved off and set down on the trail farther south where armed *bogomili* were dropping out and rushing north toward their comrades.

You've got bogomili *on your six approximately two hundred meters back*, he flashed.

And you are a hundred meters behind them and closing rapidly.

András didn't know whether to be relieved or furious. He settled for peremptory. *We're going to discuss this when we have more time. For now, stay clear of the wreck and don't engage any* bogomili *unless you have to.*

Yes, sir. Sarcasm edged her flashed message.

I mean it. That's an order.

A squad of *bogomili* cleared the helo and formed up into two fire teams of four commanded by a hard-looking man wearing sunglasses. He directed them with sharp hand gestures to flank the trail and head south through the tall, yellowing grass.

Of course, they'd miss András.

Invisible to the human eye, he passed through the two squads and right by the commander's shoulder. The man must have sensed something, perhaps residual heat, because he turned and continued walking backwards as he scanned the area behind them on the trail. There was always one of those sensitive to the supernatural among the *bogomili*.

András ignored him. He had an idea.

He neared the second helo. Its pilot had powered down and the rotors slowed as they continued to turn. The gunner on the PK machine gun, the one who'd flipped him off minutes before, leaned out the open bay, yelling something to his mates in Serbian.

Something about making sure to save some of the target's scrawny ass for him. András flared.

So much for sneaking onto the helicopter unnoticed.

Several things happened at the same time. The yellowing grass, so tall that it bent over along the shoulders of the trail, burst into flames for several hundred meters on either side of András. The squad of *bogomili* behind him yelled. Most of them fell, their weapons clattering to the earth. The squad leader stumbled, falling to a knee. But then he raised his weapon and began firing back at the helo. The machine gunner swiveled the gun around and began unloading on an arc around the helicopter.

Too bad for him. András had already stepped inside the gun's range. He sprinted toward the gunner, launching the short distance into the helicopter and grabbing the man by the shoulders. He ripped the *bogomili* from the weapon's pistol grip, causing the gun to career wildly and spray dozens of bullets, some of which struck the inside of the helicopter. The man, his movements uncoordinated from the flare's effects, struggled.

It didn't matter. András, burning through his stored energy, had gone into battle mode. He twisted the man's neck and discarded the body, turning to grapple the pilot, who'd opened the cockpit door and led with a handgun. András shoved the pilot's arm up as he squeezed off several rounds, knocking his chin up with an elbow strike. Then he disarmed the pilot, shot him, and swung the gun around to shoot the co-pilot.

Outside the cockpit window he saw ten of the forward *bogomili* racing back to the helo. *Good.* They'd been drawn from Beta.

He flung the pilot's body into the cabin and plopped into the pilot's seat. It took only an instant to find the trigger for the autocannons and unload them on the advancing men. Then he powered up the twin-turbines. The radio crackled to life as the other helo pilot radioed for a sitrep.

András picked up the comm and radioed back in Serbian. "Target has acquired helo. And oh, ten of the others ran into the autocannon."

His battle senses alerted him to an approaching *bogomili*—the rear squad leader—a moment before the man shot the weapon he aimed. András flung himself into the other side of the cockpit. The bullet whizzed across the trajectory where his head had been and smashed into the cockpit window. András, speeding his harmonics, leaned around the cockpit door and fired his captured handgun three times in a tight grouping. The squad leader dropped to the ground, with two holes in his chest and one in his head. Already behind him, one of the teams stumbled and lurched toward the helicopter, half more recovered from the angelic flare than others. All carried their weapons.

András dropped the handgun and dove for the machine gun's pistol grip to strafe the advancing *bogomili*. Two managed to make it through the growing conflagration on the trailside to take cover among the trees, but the remaining two fell, seriously injured if not dead. The second team remained behind, crouching east above the trail. András could almost feel the rifle scope on his head. Across the valley, the second helicopter had already swung around and now flew towards him.

András sank to his knees. He'd finally drained the lithium batteries, but he didn't have time to pilot the helicopter out of range from its companion.

Then the squad leader's comms chirped. "Laughing Wolf, this is Angry Wolf. We have the female."

Mihàil was bone tired. Perhaps he was getting soft. Or aging faster. There was a time when being out on an *Elioud* campaign against Dark angelic agents would have energized him. Now all he wanted to do was go home to Olivia, whose beauty had only increased as her pregnancy advanced, kneel at her feet, and listen to the twin heartbeats within her.

He closed his eyes, calling up the image of her at the last director's meeting for Kastrioti Industries where she'd presented a domestic initiative to develop the minerals on their Albanian holdings, particularly licensing medical magnesium-alloy technology and magnesium-ion battery technology. Magnesium, she said, was the mineral of the twenty-first century, and Albania had vast stores of it. Kastrioti Industries must ensure that Albanians benefited by controlling the resource from raw ore to finished products. She proposed partnering with a German medical equipment maker to make biodegradable implants in an Albanian factory. She also wanted to manufacture magnesium-ion car batteries for the burgeoning electric vehicle market. And that was just a start.

Olivia had worn a pale-pink linen dress, her long blond hair brushing her shoulders. At eight months pregnant, she no longer wore the Christian Louboutin heels that she'd worn when she interned for her unofficial cover at the Austrian business incubator. Roses kissed her luminous skin, making her blue-gray eyes more striking. If Mihàil had thought her stunning before, now she took his breath away.

When one of the board members, aware of the rising *daemonic* incursions and the risk from Asmodeus and his *bogomili*, had asked Olivia why she pressed forward with such optimistic investing plans given the possible bleak future, she'd tilted her head and said, "That question smacks of the one thing we must not do: despair."

The board member had blanched at that statement. Despair, after all, was proscribed by *Elohim*.

Then Olivia had gone on to explain that it was her job.

"Mihàil and I are a team. He needs me to take care of business at home while he's fighting *daemons* abroad." She'd paused before delivering the *coup de grâce*. "Besides, everything we develop for commercial use can be used by our *Elioud* forces, including our recent human recruits."

She'd said this so matter-of-factly that not a single member of the board questioned her. That's the moment that Mihàil had determined to elevate Olivia to the position of chief executive of the new businesses that she proposed. Until then, he hadn't been sure how much she wanted to be involved in managing the business side of their lives, but she'd left no doubt. She'd also freed him to do what he did best: fight the Dark angelic forces.

She'd never been more desirable or precious to him.

He'd taken her home and made love to her as tenderly as if she were made from spun glass. And yesterday he'd gotten up at o'dark o'clock as Olivia teased so that Pjetër could drive him to the airfield where Daněk waited to fly him to

Stuttgart in southwest Germany near the border with France. This morning he'd arrived at Mosbach on the outskirts of Odenwald, the wooded uplands north of Stuttgart where Luger's spirit had settled with *daemons* that boldly attacked cities in the Neckar River valley. The harmonic plane over Odenwald rumbled and churned. Ominous off-key tendrils forked west toward Paris and east to Budapest and Prague.

Deep unease plucked a harsh chord in Mihàil's harmonics. More than one Dark angelic being now tuned the *daemonia*. *Daemonia* that numbered in the thousands.

A legion.

A second-level knight of the Order of Malta waited for Mihàil at the Tempelhaus in Mosbach. The Order's earlier incarnation, the Knights Hospitaller, had built the medieval complex's hospital and chapel at the end of the thirteenth century. Since accepting his duty as a *drangùe*, Mihàil had found many of his assets among the Knights of Malta. Though the modern organization focused on diplomacy and humanitarian aid, some members discreetly lived the warrior aspect of the knight ideal.

That's why Mihàil asked Elias Klum, a knight of magistral grace in obedience, to rendezvous with him at the carved altar of St. George. The central image of a mounted knight shoving a lance down a dragon's throat called to mind the image of St. Michael crushing Satan.

In other words, a fitting rendezvous point for this critical mission against the *daemonia*.

Elias, a tall, good-natured man in his early forties, stood with his hands crossed behind him at Mihàil's side. He wore the red-bordered black scapular of his rank over a black choir robe. The familiar white Maltese cross gleamed on his chest. "If you ever decide to resurrect the Order of the Dragon, know that I will transfer my allegiance in a heartbeat."

Mihàil, whose father Gjergj Kastrioti had been a member of the chivalric society that included Vlad the Impaler, just grunted. "I will keep that in mind."

His nano-origami chirped, pulling his attention away from the red-and-gold angels watching over St. George. He tuned the comm to transmit. "Go for Dragon Man."

"Dragon Man, this is Aerie One." It was Miles Baxter, who manned a mobile communications center while the *Elioud* and Ryan Helsing were in the field. "We received an automated distress signal from the Phenom just inside the Albanian border. Then twenty minutes later, Giant flared. His transponder pinged on the Valbona Trail, but we can't raise him on his comms. In fact, they don't register a signal at all."

"What about *Vir*? Have you had any direct communication?" Mihàil didn't want to think about what it meant that Daněk had triggered a distress signal. The man flew like he had *Elioud* blood, hence his Czech call sign *Whirlwind*.

"Negative, sir." Miles paused again. "Sir, the autopilot system registered an engine failure three minutes before the Phenom entered the Valbona Pass. Five minutes after that, it stopped transmitting."

He left unsaid that the jet had clearly gone down.

"Demon Slayer?" Mihàil had thought Helsing's call sign was a little ambitious, but he'd said nothing at the time. Now he wished it were true. "Did he and White Eagle's team make it to the safe house?"

"Affirmative. However, the *bogomili* strike team they picked up north of Ryki abruptly broke off twenty minutes outside of Warsaw. There may be other teams inside the city, but they haven't spotted any signs of one." Miles paused. "Demon Slayer says his neck itches, sir."

"I know the feeling," said Mihàil, rubbing his own. He glanced at Elias, whose alert expression told him that he'd listened to every word. "Get air transport and have them fly the route that the Phenom took. Send a ground team to the Valbona Pass. I want a sitrep as soon as anyone has eyes on the area."

"Teams already in route, sir. Sitrep estimated in thirty minutes."

Mihàil looked at Elias. His jaw ached already. "Asmodeus has learned some tactics since allying with Luger's shade."

The German knight had a thoughtful expression. "You think the *daemonia* have served to draw you away from your border in accordance with the Dark *Irim*'s plans?"

"I do."

"Then you should return posthaste and leave the *daemon Elioud* to me."

Mihàil shook his head. "No, my old friend. You cannot handle the *daemonia* on your own, despite the power that your order lends you."

He paused, his vision turning inward as he surveyed the harmonic plane for leagues. "For once, Asmodeus has the upper hand. Another Dark angelic being has joined Luger. The *daemonia* are legion and reach across Europe. They are a greater threat to humanity than the threat Asmodeus poses to my lieutenant."

Elias nodded toward the altarpiece. "Then slay the dragon here, sire, so that Asmodeus must withdraw his minions there. And trust your lieutenant to succeed."

Twenty-Two

A half an hour later, after Elias introduced Mihàil to the dozen *donats*, the lowest rank of the Order of Malta who'd waited in the knight's hall in the upper story of the Tempelhaus, they set out. Mihàil wanted to drive one of the two armored Range Rovers that Elias had procured for the operation, but Elias assured him that two of the *donats* had tactical driving skills in case the *daemonia* had *bogomili* or possessed humans among them.

Mihàil shrugged. It seemed highly unlikely that the drivers would get to test their skills in the Odenwald, a twenty-five-hundred-square-kilometer region dominated by low mountains, dark forests, and river valleys. He got into the front passenger seat of the rear SUV while Elias strode to the lead vehicle. They drove north for about an hour to the heart of Odenwald where Mihàil sensed the highest concentration of Dark angelic discord. As they got closer, the harsh, roiling harmonics retracted from their wandering across the countryside and formed a dense mass overhead.

Elias's Range Rover headed west on Route 460 toward the Marbach Reservoir, and Mihàil's driver followed. They passed signs for Fáfnir's Trail.

Fáfnir was the name of a dragon. Luger knew that Mihàil had come for him.

The question was, who was the dragon in this encounter? After all, Fáfnir, who'd been transformed from a greedy dwarf prince, had been killed by a hero named Sigfried, whom Wagner immortalized in his operas known as the Ring Cycle. Georg Luger had been Austrian, but even so, he would have been very influenced by the heroic epic poetry of German-speaking people.

Mihàil looked outside at the lower Mossau Valley. Dormant yellow fields hedged closely by bare trees hugged the state road next to the reservoir. Fog clung to the surface of the reservoir, blurring the edge of the dark water and gray sky.

Luger would see himself as Sigfried.

Mihàil activated his comm as he stepped out of the Range Rover. "Aerie One, this is Dragon Man. Is there a spring on the Fáfnir Trail where legend claims Sigfried was killed?"

"Dragon Man, this is Aerie One. Let me check."

Mihàil waited, tapping his fingers on his thigh. Around him, the *donats* dismounted from the SUVs. All wore either black tactical jackets with the Order of Malta patch on the left shoulder or a heavy black military sweater, white collar shirts, black trousers and boots, and a stiff black beret with a red Order of Malta insignia. All wore side holsters with semi-automatic pistols. Some carried semi-automatic rifles. Elias stood next to one of the *donats*, gesturing toward the wooded path along the reservoir. Given the late season, they saw no hikers. That didn't mean that there were no humans, either villagers or tourists, in the vicinity.

The comm chirped in Mihàil's ear. "Sir, there are at least three springs in Odenwald that claim to be the site of Siegfried's murder. The closest to you is a spring named Lindelbrunnen. I've texted the GPS coordinates to you."

"Copy that. And Aerie One? Any news from Giant or *Vir*?"

"Negative, sir. The helo just entered the Valbona Pass. Thick smoke about a klick into the pass obscures visibility."

Mihàil's stomach clenched. "Wreckage from the jet?"

"Uncertain, sir, but the conditions suggest a large area of forest burns. Sir, could András be responsible?"

"Yes." Mihàil inhaled. He needed to focus on his mission. "Going dark now, Aerie One."

"Not before I wish you good hunting," said Olivia in his ear on their private channel. "Come back to us soon, *dashuria ime*."

Mihàil turned away from the gathered *donats*, who'd divided themselves up into two fire teams. "Nothing can prevent me from returning to you, *dashuria ime.*"

He turned back to face Elias, who'd waited until he nodded before approaching.

"Sire, we are ready for your command."

Mihàil scanned the harmonic plane, narrowing his eyes as he fine-tuned his battle senses. "We will proceed along the reservoir about three klicks. When it splits at Hüttenthal, continue north with your team on 460 about two klicks. I will lead my team on the route to Mossautal to approach from the east. Proceed with extreme caution. Luger's spirit and a mass of *daemonia* have gathered at Siegfried's Mord a few hundred meters off of 460."

Elias nodded and gestured to his team to fall in behind Mihàil's team. Although they took off at a jog up the steeply inclined pavement, Mihàil chafed at the slowness of their pace. The wispy fog thickened and billowed along the road as they moved, deadening the sounds and obscuring the low forested hills around them. The sky darkened. Mihàil caught more than one *donat* crossing himself. After a few tense, silent moments, Elias began to chant the *Salve Regina*. A moment later, the *donats* joined in. Two double basses sung a continuous chord supporting the tenors and baritones.

The fog retreated from their cohort.

As they arrived where 460 split from the road to Mossautal, Elias changed the chant to the antiphon *Crucem sanctam subiit*. Power radiated around him as a vivid light on the harmonic plane. The *donats* joined him, their combined voices loud in the eerie silence.

Mihàil led his team north on the lesser road. The fog swallowed their comrades up, quenching the sound of their chanting. His *donats* switched to chanting *Benedicat Nos Deus* in the round. A golden aura limned their forms, illuminating the road a few meters around them. Cold rain began to fall.

The blanketing fog dampened the natural range of Mihàil's battle senses. His neck prickled anyway.

He estimated that they'd gone less than halfway to Mossautal when the assault by possessed humans began. Dark, twisted visages with howling mouths and clawed hands emerged from the thick white and slammed into them.

Mihàil flared, flooding the road and forest around them with a brilliant white light.

The *donats* absorbed the violent energy of the possessed, shifting it away as they encircled their bass singer, who knelt and sang a polyphonic chord to reinforce their harmonics. The possessed flowed around their circle as water breaks on a boulder.

The *donats* continued chanting as they engaged the *daemon*-inhabited in hand-to-hand combat, their harmonies adding power to their punches and defensive moves. Possessed fell, writhing and kicking as the *daemons* inside them reacted to the *donats'* harmonic weapons.

Around them, the harmonic plane boiled. Lightning cracked across the sky, now dark as midnight. Mihàil sped his harmonics and raised his temperature in response.

And then the *daemonia* manifested at the edge of the forest as a massive black iridescent spider with razor-edged legs and multi-lensed eyes.

Otherwise known as an *aranea diabolus*. A *devil spider*.

Luger controlled the manifestation. Mihàil could sink Luger's harmonics here by gaining control of the *aranea diabolus*.

He jumped along a harmonic band, meeting the creature as it raced toward the *donats*, whose chanting faltered as they tired. Possessed began to tear their clothing and scratch their skin, snapping at the *donats* in a mad frenzy. One *donat* fell and possessed submerged him. In the distance, Elias's fire team engaged *bogomili*, who were impervious to the Order's harmonics and required the use of weapons to dispatch.

Mihàil rolled, grabbing the forelegs of the *aranea diabolus* as he did and pulling it over onto its side. The *aranea diabolus* shrieked and roared as Mihàil's heated grip burned through its legs. He jabbed harmonics into the creature's body, twisting to avoid its foul breath and maw filled with rows of pointed teeth.

As he rolled, it managed to plunge a spur from one of its legs into his side. Icy cold burned into him, but Mihàil ignored it to shove both hands into the spider's head, speeding his harmonics and raising his temperature until the *aranea diabolus* exploded. Mihàil, prepared for this, lassoed its disintegrating harmonic energy. He synced it to the harmonics of the ground beneath his feet. Then he shoved the *daemonic* energy into a well far below the surface. The manifestation winked out of sight.

Thirty seconds later the attack ended.

Mihàil, exhausted by his battle with the *daemonia*, collapsed. Overhead, the sun burned away the lingering traces of fog and the afternoon warmed, causing him to shiver. The wound in his side ached with cold.

He closed his eyes, letting himself relax while the *donats* subdued the dispossessed humans, some of whom had lost their minds and walked in circles, foaming at the mouth and scratching themselves until their skin ran with blood.

He'd felt Luger's spirit when he'd sunk the *daemonic* energy underground.

Beta listened as the *bogomili* radioed one of the others with the call sign *Laughing Wolf*. In the distance she heard the *whomp-whomp-whomp* of the helicopter's blades as it clawed its way towards where András waited. Even though it was over two hundred meters away, she recognized his heat signature as clearly as her own. Around him other heat signatures clumped in the chill mountain air, and beyond the warm red of the helicopter next to him, yellow-white flames danced more than two meters above the earth. The heat from the burning grasses extended as far south as she could sense.

Angry Wolf deserved his call sign. The sour expression on his face matched the heat level of his infrared signature, which had no cooler purple or red. He'd taken her karambit and weapon after they'd searched her and stuffed them into his waistband. Beta narrowed her eyes and concentrated on his movements.

She stood between two silent *bogomili* with her hands zip-tied behind her. Someone had forgotten to tell these *křupan* that they should use something stronger than plastic to restrain her. Even if she'd never learned to raise her body temperature at will—and she had, in fact, figured that out—she always ran warmer than the average human, warm enough to soften and stretch the nylon cuffs. She'd already dropped what was left of them to the ground. It wasn't much.

Angry Wolf turned frosty eyes on her.

"Laughing Wolf hasn't responded," he said to the other *bogomili*.

Twelve *bogomili* had dropped from the hovering helicopter, but only three stood around her. The rest had either gone to secure the wreckage of the helicopter that had attacked their jet, to search for *bogomili* survivors, or to gather intel on the Phenom.

Beta cocked her head. "Maybe he is no longer laughing."

Angry Wolf took a step toward her, one hand clenched.

Good. Come closer, my friend, she thought. Her temperature had risen so that the air steamed around them, mixing with the heavy scent of smoke and ash. The two *bogomili* at her sides shifted uneasily.

The radio sputtered. "Laughing Wolf is dead. The giant took him out."

"Who is this?" asked Angry Wolf.

"Lonely Brat," said the voice in Serbian. The accent was flawless. "There are six of us left, four on the east slope above the trail about three-hundred meters from your location. The last two managed to make it into the trees. They're coming to you. Did our fire team reach you?"

András had just told Beta how many *bogomili* had survived from the other helicopter. He was also trying to get a sense for how many awaited him.

"Negative," said Angry Wolf. "They aren't responding either. Looks like there will be more than enough room for you on our helo."

Beta smiled to herself. She'd surprised one of the *bogomili* coming from the south—the one lagging at the rear, of course—and borrowed his automatic weapon to shoot the other four. She'd teach these Serbian *wolves* how a dragon hunted.

"Copy that." Even over the radio, Beta heard the relief in András's voice. They were down to less than twenty-four mercenaries.

"Where is the giant?"

"Inside the helicopter."

Angry Wolf spoke again, this time to the pilot of the helicopter in the air. "Alpha Two, this is Angry Wolf. Target in helo confirmed. Take the shot."

A moment later, the Mil Mi-8 launched a missile. András's heat signature winked out. Beta's heart thumped, hard.

"Lonely Brat, get your squad back here. We leave as soon as Alpha Two picks us up. Priority transport for the package and injured."

"Already on the way, Angry Wolf."

András had shifted harmonics. Beta's heart leaped. He was on his way to her. *And* the *bogomili* had one less helicopter.

Angry Wolf spoke next to the squad leader of the nine *bogomili* on reconnaissance and retrieval. "Gray Wolf, grab whatever and whoever you're going to and get back here. Pickup is three minutes out."

He grinned at her. It was suitably feral. "I can't understand why Command thought this mission required sixty mercs and three helos for one skinny female." He grabbed her arm as if proving his point.

Beta shrugged. "I cannot understand why Command thought that few would succeed. By my count, you are fewer than twenty."

Angry Wolf blinked, struck dumb for a moment.

That's when Beta acted. She struck his jaw with the heel of her free hand, pulling her weapon free of his waistband before his head snapped upright again. She shot the two *bogomili* on either side of her, but the weapon emptied before she could shoot Angry Wolf.

He grabbed her by the hair and punched her. Stars exploded inside Beta's head. The CZ P-10C dropped from her hand. She blinked, tasting blood.

Angry Wolf gripped her chin and forced her to look at him. "That's more than enough, *pička*." The vile slang that he'd called her sent her temperature soaring.

Holding his stare, Beta lifted her thumb and wiped the blood from the corner of her lips. "You would think so. If you didn't know what I am."

Angry Wolf sneered and yanked her closer. His foul breath, a physical sign of his bond with Asmodeus, nearly choked her.

Beta sensed András materializing behind them. At the same time, she snatched her karambit from Angry Wolf's waistband, spiking her temperature in the other hand. Angry Wolf, who'd been distracted by the awful vision of the giant Hungarian emerging like a specter from the conflagration, screamed as Beta slashed his hand holding her chin. She followed it up with a searing punch to the groin. She ended the sequence by slashing the karambit across his throat as he curled over.

András, looking like thunder, yanked the dying *bogomili* away, twisting his neck before dropping him to the ground.

Then he scowled at her. "What the hell are you doing, Gomba?"

"You said not to engage any *bogomili* unless I had to." Beta shrugged. "Clearly I had to distract them from you."

She narrowed her eyes, studying him. His harmonic signature wavered, and although his thermal signature ran hot, he looked exhausted.

She stepped forward and laid a palm on his cheek. "You could hardly get off the ground when I left you. But as soon as you hear that I am in danger, you move heaven and earth to come to me."

András growled and pulled her into a kiss. Beta's head swam in the smoky hot air. She rose to her tiptoes and, wrapping her arms around his neck, kissed him with everything inside her. He responded by tightening her against him. Behind her eyelids, she saw their nimbuses merge. She hummed as their tongues tangled, gripping him by the hair and sending as much harmonic energy into him as she could.

The last Mil Mi-8 beat the smoke as it loomed overhead. András sped their combined harmonics so that he and Beta disappeared from human sight. Angry Wolf's comm crackled.

"Angry Wolf, this is Alpha Two. The fire advances too quickly for us to set down. Be advised that we have to regroup north two hundred meters where the trail widens. How many for pickup?"

András spoke into a comm that he must have confiscated from a dead *bogomili*. "Alpha Two, this is Angry Wolf." He smiled down at Beta as she watched him. She was astonished at how easily he mimicked the dead Serbian *bogomili* after listening to him for only a few seconds. "Let me confirm."

"Copy that," said the pilot.

"Gray Wolf, this is Angry Wolf. Pickup location has moved north of the fire two hundred meters. How many in your party?"

"This is Gray Wolf. We found nothing worth salvaging, and no survivors. We'll meet you at the pickup location in two minutes."

Now András targeted the remaining *bogomili* south of them. "Laughing Wolf, get your squad to the helicopter."

It amused Beta that András had radioed a dead man. But, of course, it was safest to use only recognizable call signs.

One of Laughing Wolf's squad responded. "This is team leader Wild Boar. Laughing Wolf is no more."

"How many in your squad left?"

"I don't know how many made it to the target, but there are only six of us here, two injured."

"Can you get around the fire to a new pickup location two hundred meters north of the original?

"Affirmative. But give us ten minutes. One guy isn't walking, and the other isn't at full speed."

"Copy that." András smiled at Beta as he radioed the pilot again. "Fifteen for pickup."

Alpha Two swore. "Including package?"

"That's a negative on the package, Alpha Two," said András. "Teams should arrive within ten minutes. There are injured."

"Copy that."

"Come." András pulled Beta after him. "We're the welcoming party."

Beta glanced at him as they sped their harmonics. "I like the way you think, Spratek."

They arrived at the pickup location at the same time the last *bogomili* helicopter set down, its rotors churning the encroaching smoke. A *bogomili* gripping the mounted PK machine gun scanned the limited visible area around the helicopter.

"What is your plan?" asked Beta. She had the karambit in her free hand. Without looking, she wiped its wet blade on her tactical pants. Then she began opening and closing it.

"Let me show you something as explanation." András dropped her hand and tugged his shirt over his head.

Despite their situation—or maybe because of it—Beta stared at his upper body, which glistened with a sheen of sweat. His broad shoulders and sculpted torso stole her breath. Muscles rippled as he turned his back to her.

"What is that?" she asked, touching fingertips to the outline of a bird tattooed on his shoulder blade. It fluttered under them, startling her. She pulled her fingers back.

"A redstart." András looked over his shoulder at her.

Beta blinked at that. He'd had a tattoo of her real last name etched into his flesh?

"How long have you known?" she whispered.

He shrugged. "Awhile."

"What is in the ink?" she asked, tracing her fingertips over the bird again. It felt alive. "It gleams like metal."

"That's because it is, Gomba. It's an alloy of lead, antimony, and tin."

Beta darted a startled glance at him. "That is the composition of bullets."

He nodded. "I couldn't melt the fragments from Skopje until our stay at the granary house."

"They have been inside you for three years?" Horror colored her voice.

András turned back and tipped her chin so that she could see his face. "That's in the past, Gomba. See what I can do with my redstart?"

As she watched, the redstart flew up, a fully three-dimensional bird, and perched on his shoulder.

Behind them, *bogomili* came panting out of the heaviest smoke, their faces shiny with sweat. Beta and András watched as they came in groups of four and five. She counted nine.

"I recognize their infrared signatures," she said. "Those are what is left of Angry Wolf's squad."

"I'm surprised that you didn't go after them," said András.

Beta ignored him.

They waited while Angry Wolf's squad loaded onto the waiting helicopter. As the last *bogomili* disappeared inside the belly, another set of *bogomili* stumbled from the haze. Two *bogomili* carried a third man on a makeshift stretcher while an injured *bogomili* stumbled against the side of a comrade.

The final six from the other destroyed helicopter. That made fifteen *bogomili*.

"If you are going to act, now would be ideal," she said to András when he made no move.

"Of course." He continued to stare at the helicopter, whose rotors had begun to rotate faster as it slowly lifted into the air.

Beta ground her teeth and shifted onto the balls of her feet.

"Stay," said András without looking at her. There was something in his tone that warned her not to disobey.

A moment later, the redstart on his shoulder flew and landed on the roof of the Mil Mi-8 where it glowed orange-white as if molten.

"Target painted, Double Eagle," he said into the stolen comm. He looked at Beta's obvious astonishment. "What? You can't hear the other helicopter?"

As soon as he said those words, a missile struck the Mil Mi-8 as it climbed out of the valley north of them.

Twenty-Three

Twenty minutes after the third *bogomili* helicopter had disintegrated in a massive fireball whose flaming shrapnel set more of the dry valley floor on fire, Beta and András stumbled into the village of Valbona. Beta, who clung to András's sweaty torso, darted a glance at what she could see of his set profile. Jaws clenched, eyes straight ahead, skin gray-tinged, and tremors running through him—it was perfectly plain to her human eyesight that András moved forward on sheer willpower alone. But her *Elioud* senses also screamed at her. András's harmonics oscillated wildly, sending Beta's harmonics reverberating out of control. Only his thermal signature, though elevated, remained steady.

They almost ran into a low house in the thick haze. When it appeared in front of them, Beta flinched, pulling András off balance. He staggered, banging his shoulder into the sharp edge at its corner. He sucked in a hiss and would have fallen if a man wearing a cloth over his nose and mouth hadn't emerged from the almost impenetrable smoke and grabbed him.

"*Zotëri!*" The stranger let out a hard grunt as András plowed into him.

"Davud," said András in a hoarse voice. He coughed.

Davud, bracing himself, slipped an arm under András's and accepted most of his weight. "This way, *zotëri.*" The face covering muffled his voice, but he gestured in the direction he wanted them to go.

Beta followed them to a waiting flatbed truck whose running engine alerted her to its location. András leaned against the cab while Beta climbed up into the single bench seat and took the center spot. He waved Davud off and hauled himself into the passenger seat. Davud hurried around to the driver's seat. As they drove out of the rolling smoke, several cars and trucks, including a couple of box trucks and three panel vans, passed them headed the other way. Most of the caravan's vehicles had the Kastrioti Industries logo on their sides. Thermal signatures filled the interior of each vehicle.

Mihàil's people, flashed András, anticipating her question. He'd rested his head against the window and closed his eyes. *They go to battle the fire before it reaches Valbona.*

Beta said nothing. She was still too furious to speak. She wanted András safe inside and fully recovered—and *alone*—before she lambasted him.

They arrived in the small village of Fierzë, north of the Drin River, an hour later. Beta had dozed with her head back against the seat while Davud drove. When she opened her eyes, she saw that the afternoon had turned gray. The earlier smoke from the burning grass at the higher elevation had transformed into low-lying clouds that met fog from the warmer air as they descended out of the Accursed Mountains. Soft white snow weighed down the evergreens and dusted rocky slopes. Slush edged the glistening black asphalt of the highway. Except for the sound of the truck engine and the breathing of the two men beside her, it was very quiet.

Davud drove to a small house where the owners, a middle-aged couple, had hot food and clean clothes, including warm down parkas, waiting for Beta and András. Beta, who normally ignored anything heavier than fleece, slipped the parka on after changing into jeans and a sweater. She ate the *tavë kosi,* a traditional Albanian lamb stew with rice and yogurt, with one hand in a pocket holding her karambit. Despite the fact that they'd made it into Albania free of the *bogomili* who'd been sent after them, unease tightened her neck muscles.

If her harmonic signature had changed as András said, how had Asmodeus found them flying through the Valbona Valley? Could it be as simple as knowing the flight path and watching for their flight? Or was there a more sinister explanation? Had she somehow endangered András? And now brought danger to Olivia and the other *Elioud* and their people?

She looked under her lowered lids toward András, who sat on the other side of the small square table in their unnamed hosts' house. The gray tinge of his skin had been replaced with a ruddier color, though it still lacked a truly healthy vitality.

As she recalled how close he'd come to being killed, her heart leapt into her throat, and her pulse raced.

He'd ordered her to leave him behind and save herself.

And she'd left him there. She'd been angry and hurt, and she'd almost done what he'd told her to do and skirted the wreck and arriving *bogomili*. What if she *had* in a fit of pique? If she hadn't decided at the last moment that she'd show him how wrong he was....

She shivered inside the parka. Her fingers and the tip of her nose were cold. András brought his eyes up and stared at her, his gaze suddenly sharply alert.

What is it, Gomba? He reached across the table and touched the back of her hand holding her fork.

She blinked and willed her breathing to steady. *Nothing. Just reliving that terrifying leap from the plane in a crazy fool's arms.*

András tilted his head, studying her. Then he smiled. It wasn't one of his former heart-wrenching grins dancing with dimples, but Beta's heart soared at the sight. *Of course, your heart patters at remembering being in my arms.*

Beta let his teasing work. He didn't need to know where her true thoughts had been. She shrugged. *It is a good thing your head is so empty or we would have dropped like a boulder.*

Now András did grin. *It is a good thing I am so ... athletic ... to cushion your landing or you would have broken like a twig. Maybe that is what makes your heart race, hm?*

Beta scowled and hunched, dropping her gaze back to her bowl. She gripped the karambit in her pocket, unable to flick it open and slide it closed. By András's continued grinning, she knew that he guessed what she wanted to do.

They finished eating and used the facilities. Before they left, András thanked their hosts, whose expressions bore a mix of awe and affection as he stood in front of them. He took one of the wife's hands between his and declared that he'd never eaten anything more delicious than her *tavë kosi*. As the wife blushed under András's extravagant gratitude and urged him to return soon so that she could cook for him again, Davud leaned toward Beta.

"The Archangel is very wise. You are a good match for the *zotëri*," he said. "He always jokes and laughs, but he has not been so happy as long as I have known him. Just know that you are always welcome among us, *zonjë ime*."

Beta blinked at Davud's use of *my lady*. She didn't know what to say to any of it.

The next moment, the wife pulled Beta into a hug before kissing both her cheeks. She touched Beta's upper arm, an Albanian gesture wishing Beta good fortune, and urged her to bless them with a return visit. Beta murmured *thank you* in Albanian and then hurried out the door to Davud's truck.

It had begun to snow again, big, fat flakes that whirled in the air around the truck and clung to the windshield. Davud turned on the wipers and the heater. The drag of the rubber blades and the sound of the fan blowing filled the silent cab. Beta, though overheating in the down parka between the two men, remained wide awake on this leg of their journey. Despite the growing darkness and falling snow, people began to appear in small groups on the side of the twisting mountain highway. Some waved and cheered, but most stood with their faces tilted respectfully, their hands crossed at their waists. Beta's *Elioud* senses weighed on her. Shifting to look behind her, she glimpsed a caravan of cars and trucks.

"It is a great honor for you and the *zotëri* to pass through here, *zonjë ime*," said Davud as Beta continued to watch through wide eyes. Many feel blessed to have your gaze on them."

András took Beta's hand. "Olivia has made it her mission to visit the people closest to the estate since she became Mihàil's *zonjë*. Most know her on sight. And she knows the names of many of the citizens of this municipality."

Davud glanced down at her, his face radiating happiness. "We are all eagerly awaiting the birth of the *zonjë*'s child. Our people have waited a very long time for this blessed event."

Startled, Beta looked at András, who was watching her.

"Mihàil is much loved. More than that, his people believe that his line will be filled with great warriors," he said. "And fulfill a great destiny."

A dark premonition shot through her. *Asmodeus knows.* She kept the message between them.

He stiffened. *What? How?* A trace of accusation sharpened his words.

It was Beta's turn to stiffen. *Not from me. He showed me a pregnant Olivia not long before you came to extract me from Babyrusk. Before Olivia's spirit came to me.*

We must warn Mihàil and Olivia. He stared at her, his jaw clenched and his eyes a deep-blue agate.

Uneasiness threaded its way through Beta. *Are they not safe inside Albania's borders?*

The land of Albania, especially Mihàil's estate, lends him incredible strength. He also has ancient harmonic defenses in place. He is virtually unassailable here.

But it can be done.

Yes.

Beta looked away, her thoughts in turmoil. András had never answered her earlier question in Lublin about whether Asmodeus could strike at *her* inside Albania. She knew why.

As they climbed toward Fushë-Arrëz, which was elevated higher than Fierzë, an escort of black sedans pulled in front of them, leading them through the town where all the residents appeared to line the main street. At the end, they doubled back to drive north on the highway. The Kastrioti estate sat on a foothill above the town, which nestled in a shallow valley. Their escort drove past the entrance to the driveway. As Davud turned into it, the cars and trucks following them streamed past, heading home.

At the top of the driveway sat a large house made of stone, not nearly as imposing as Beta had expected for a demi-angel hundreds of years old whose people treated him like a medieval lord. And waiting under the portico stood Olivia, her blond hair gleaming in the golden light from the windows, the anxious look on her face lifting as she caught sight of Beta and András.

The one called Sly Wolf, known as Goran before he entered service with the Dark lord Asmodeus, waited until the *drangùe*'s people had finished creating a firebreak to prevent the flames in the valley from spreading. Then he hitched a ride in the bed of a truck whose driver, his face blackened from soot and his shoulders hunched in fatigue, never suspected that he had an unwanted passenger. Sly Wolf remained in the truck until the driver stopped in front of a small house, its lights shining warmly. The afternoon had grown colder, and snow had started falling during the drive, coming down so thick and fast that the tired driver didn't see Sly Wolf until the *bogomili* had grabbed him by the shoulders. And then it was too late.

Sly Wolf slit the man's throat, one hand over his mouth, and then stuffed the body into the truck bed. He did this so quickly and silently that no one from inside the house came to investigate. He'd caught sight of the flat, gray-green Drin River a few minutes before the truck had stopped, so he backtracked to the bridge that they'd crossed.

There, he stripped the dead man's clothes before lifting the body over the low guardrail and dropping it into the river along with his own clothes. He left his tactical knife in one of his boots, which he was forced to keep because the other man's feet were too small. He slipped his weapon into his waistband at the small of his back. The stolen pants were a little short and a little too big, but his belt sufficed to keep them in place. The sweater, though larger than necessary, hid his tactical vest, which was bulletproof and carried extra ammunition. All in all, not a bad haul given the circumstances.

Sly Wolf returned to the truck, holding his smartphone in one hand where he could see a mapping program. From the looks of it, the target had stopped in a place called Fushë-Arrëz—no more than thirty minutes away.

Davud pulled the truck under the portico, and Beta and András got out. Olivia, after hugging them, had taken Beta's hand and led her down the lanai to the door that opened directly into a warm, bright kitchen that smelled of baking bread and roasting meat. Even though they'd eaten only a short time before, Beta found herself hungry again. Pjetër, the Kastrioti steward whom she'd met in Vienna when he'd acted as Mihàil's personal servant and chauffeur, drew Davud and András aside while Beta sat at a small round table next to a large bay window. A fire blazed in the corner fireplace.

After speaking with the two men, András joined Beta. Olivia asked no questions. Instead, she and a young woman served them plates of roast beef with a variety of vegetable dishes, none of which Beta recognized. She suspected that they were American. Olivia herself cut huge slices of white bread with a tender white crumb and golden crust. She also poured them red wine.

Beta took a sip, leery of drinking too much while so exhausted, but the Cabernet Sauvignon, bold and rich with hints of black currant and chocolate, perfectly complemented the meal. She drank it slowly, inhaling each time she did, and felt a deep languor slide through her. Everything that had happened in the past eight hours—the terror, grief, anger, unease, and anxiety—it all moved to the back of her thoughts for worry another time. Now, in the *drangùe*'s home, she could relax.

Beta's head nodded and her eyelids drooped. She struggled to keep them open. She had no idea how long she'd been struggling to keep her face out of her plate when András took her hand and gently removed the wineglass. Standing, he pulled Beta's chair back and leaned down to lift her from her seat. Beta, too filled with torpor to complain other than some mumbling about what he thought he was doing, offered no resistance. András settled her in his arms, and Beta's hands went around his neck of their own accord. She leaned against his chest, letting her head rest in the curve between his jaw and shoulder.

"You smell wonderful," she said as he began walking, "like sweet, ripe berries and smoky evergreens." She closed her eyes and inhaled deeply. "And something else. Like lemon-scented honey. ..."

András laughed. The sound rumbled into her ear where it pressed against his chest. "You must be tired, Gomba. You would never say such things to me otherwise."

Beta sighed. "I *am* tired. So tired," she said, slurring the words slightly on an exhale. She didn't have the energy to open her eyes.

Instead, she tightened her arms around his neck, and András responded by tightening his hold on her. His arms and chest felt so good, so *right* around her. Beta wanted to burrow into his heat and strength, to stay forever inside the shelter of his embrace. She nuzzled him, rubbing the cold tip of her nose against his hot skin. His heart rate picked up, and she felt his harmonics vibrate through her. Dreamily, she realized that her harmonics responded. Humming as she felt him climb stairs, she pressed her breasts, now tight and aching, against his chest.

András groaned.

"Gomba." His voice sounded strangled.

"Mm?" she asked before planting a soft kiss on his jaw and then down the side of his neck.

A moment later, András dropped her legs and pinned Beta against a hard, cool surface before his mouth descended to hers. As his lips encouraged hers to open, a fleeting hope winged through her woozy thoughts that Olivia didn't stand nearby watching. Then she rose to her tiptoes, holding his face in her hands, and tangled her tongue with his.

If Beta had been woozy before, that was nothing to how her thoughts swam from his kiss.

András, growling, flattened one large palm on her buttocks until he held her groin against his rigid erection. Beta moaned and wiggled, trying to get closer despite their clothes. A sharp tingle, in defiance of her intoxication, shot to her core, and her nipples peaked so hard she arched her back, moving her own hands around his hips to clutch him to her.

She *needed* András. She had no more strength to deny or resist that truth.

As soon as she let those explicit words form in her thoughts, her heart pounded, her throat clogged, and her mouth dried. Who knew that love felt so much like terror?

She did, that's who. She'd been terrified for years.

She opened her eyes a slit to see András staring at her, his own gaze predatory and intent.

"Tell me you're aware of what we're about to do." Gravel made his voice rough.

Beta nodded, suddenly wide awake. She swallowed twice before she could manage to whisper. "Yes."

He studied her for a long moment, his deep-blue eyes looking, *really look-ing*, inside her. "After we make love, you will be mine. Do you understand? You can't run away from it, not without consequences for both of us."

In other words, she couldn't pretend to steal a little temporary sweetness and return to her other life, the one where she was alone and on her own.

Under the weight of that reality, Beta wanted to flee.

And then the image of András lying on the floor of the Valbona Valley, driven past his limits and yet still prepared to give more for her, rose up and swamped her. Whatever happened next, she needed this moment now. She'd accept the consequences, not least of which was remembering it for the rest of her life.

Beta moved her hands to András's face. She held his gaze. This time when she spoke, the words came strong and clear and easily. "I love you, András Nagy. I think I fell in love with you when you smiled at me in Mihàil's gym that day after I pulled you down with my chain whip."

His eyes widened. He studied her as if he thought she'd gone mad or perhaps teased. And then he smiled again, that same sweet, wide smile with the dimple that she remembered. An instant later his mouth crushed hers, and he maneuvered her inside the door that only moments before he'd held her up against.

András picked Beta up and carried her across the bedroom to a large bed where he set her down against pillows that smelled like him. She watched as he pulled his shirt over his head, the muscles of his chest moving under his gleaming skin. He kept his gaze on her as he sat on the edge of the bed to pull off his boots before standing again to remove his pants.

The last time that they'd been together, it had been in the middle of the night. She'd denied herself the pleasure of seeing his body, as if that had made what they did together less real. Less important. As if it didn't matter.

Her breath caught in her throat at the sight of him now. His chiseled abdomen and broad shoulders begged to be caressed. His massive thighs and arms made her feel tiny. But the constellation of scars that told a story about his life defending humanity against evil made something like grief mix with her desire.

András helped Beta to sit upright. She raised her hands, and he tugged her sweater over her head. While he folded it, she reached behind her and undid her bra, all while his gaze devoured her. She unbuttoned her pants and shimmied out of them. When she moved to her panties, András's fingers covered hers.

"Let me, Gomba," he said, strong emotion wavering in his voice.

Together they slid her panties down, his fingers trembling on hers. András set them on the chair with her other clothing. She swallowed hard and raised her fingers to his chest when he leaned over her. Then, slipping a large, warm hand between her thighs, András made room for himself in the cradle of her legs. His large hands came to frame her face as he slid inside her.

It was like she'd finally come home.

"I love you, Alžběta Čermáková," he said and began to move inside her, their joining slow and sweet and perfect, and his gaze always on hers.

Twenty-Four

B eta awoke early the next morning to the sound of András's breathing and the feel of his body, heavy and warm, around her. As he exhaled, his breath tickled the hairs at the nape of her neck. She lay captured inside the cage of his arms, one under her neck and the other heavy on her waist as he spooned himself around her. Their harmonic signatures had synced, sustaining high, sweet notes in unison. In the low light, a faint golden glow limned their skin.

For the first time that Beta could ever remember, she felt at peace, cherished and safe. And totally satisfied. Of course, as soon as she thought that, she no longer felt *totally* satisfied. She grinned to herself. Perhaps that was one of the secrets of the ages. A sense of wellbeing lingered long after lovemaking. But as soon as one thought about it, tried to grasp it with metaphorical fingers, it slipped away until the next time.

At the realization, she wriggled her butt against András's groin. Perhaps the next time could be encouraged along....

"What are you doing, Gomba?" growled András in her ear. His big hand rubbed down her hip, causing gooseflesh to rise in its wake. "Do you need to use the toilet?"

"Hmm, maybe," she said a little breathlessly. "Perhaps you should let me go."

"I don't think so." He nipped her earlobe before sucking it into his hot mouth.

Beta gasped. Shivering, she arched into him, giving him more access to her jaw and neck. He responded by licking the side of her throat. His hand, which had moved from her hip to knead her derriere, slid up to cup one of her breasts. She looked down, seeing how his long, graceful fingers engulfed it—fingers that could crush a man's skull if he so chose. He gave a satisfied sigh as he weighed her breast in his palm before he brushed the pad of his thumb over her nipple, which was already firm. It stood to rigid attention, aching and itching as her breasts grew heavy with need. Her temperature rose several degrees as his fingers and palm caressed her, their texture an exquisite abrasion on her sensitized skin.

His thighs parted enough to encourage her to move closer. Beta snuggled in towards his heat, her back pressing into his massive chest. She wanted to crawl inside his skin, breathe with him, their hearts beating as one. András made her feel small and vulnerable yet immensely safe and desirable.

His other arm wrapped around her waist and pulled her tighter against him. His erection lay thick and heavy against her buttocks while his muscular thighs braced her. And everywhere, the scratch and tickle of hair and bristle against her skin, which felt smooth and velvety in contrast. Sharp lightning forked to Beta's core, drenching her and causing her to pant. Sweat sheened her skin.

"I'm never letting you go," he said as his hot, open mouth brushed over her jaw before he blew on her damp skin.

Beta quaked, moaning. She squirmed. She wanted to turn in his arms and wind her own around his neck, pushing her sore breasts into his chest and opening her thighs to him.

"Stop that," he said, crossing his lower hand over her breasts to hold her head against his shoulder while he kissed and nibbled every millimeter of her neck and upper chest he could reach. His other hand pinched and rolled first one nipple and then the other, tweaking them.

Beta's thoughts spun in dizzy intoxication. Nerves danced along her skin where András's warm harmonic fingers stroked her stomach and upper thighs. Her own harmonics purred in response.

"Please," she said, struggling to move. "Let me face you."

András tightened his arm on her chest and moved his free hand down to grip her hip. "No, Gomba. You're staying right where you are. I have given myself, body and soul, to you. I will defend you with everything in me. I will give my life for you, if need be." He paused and when he spoke again, strong emotion roughened his voice. "But now you will submit to me. You must trust me as you didn't in the Valbona Pass."

Suddenly Beta remembered her fury at his order to leave him.

Her dragon lashed out, taking him *and* her by surprise. She smashed the back of her head into his chin. He grunted in pain. Elbowing him in the ribs, she immediately followed it with an elbow jab to his head. He hunched as the air left his lungs, his hold on her upper body loosened. His other hand slipped from her hip. She arched into him, pushing his encircling arm above her and rolling away and off the bed. She sprang to her feet in a ready stance, her heart beating wildly and her hair a tangled mess obscuring her vision.

She didn't need to see, however. Her *Elioud* senses read András's infrared signature, blazing in the early morning light. Anger and desire roiled his harmonics as they vibrated around him in a complex whorl as familiar to her as her own heartbeat.

That whorl exploded to envelop Beta, holding her still. Gentle invisible fingers smoothed her hair from her face, untangling and tucking it behind her ears.

As she watched, András rose panther-like from the bed, which now spread like an impassable continent between them. He stood, embodying his name: a giant who emanated power and authority. His upper lip bled and began to swell. Fixing her in his sight, he raised a hand and wiped the blood with his thumb. Lightning danced in his dark gaze. The air around them shimmered with heat. Beta smelled smoke, but she wasn't sure if it was from her or András.

"Is this what you want, Gomba?" His soft bass voice raked a tremor from her.

Beta raised her chin and narrowed her eyes. She said nothing.

"To fight instead of making love?" he asked. Fury whipped his harmonics. Fury and hurt.

Beta sucked in a breath, anticipating an attack. She tensed.

András's eyebrows lowered. He didn't attack. Instead, he pulled her toward the bed.

Caught off guard, Beta stumbled forward, falling toward the mattress as her thighs hit the edge. Instinctively, she threw out her hands and sent a harmonic shove against it. She righted herself, bringing her hands up again in the ready stance.

She glared at András, who looked fully recovered from their earlier ambush. Well, then, they could certainly spar now.

"Why are you doing this?" she said through a clenched jaw. She still felt the harmonic tug he exerted on her. Something told her that he held back.

It also whispered that she was fortunate that he did so.

"Because we either work this out now where it's safe or next time one of us might die."

She blinked at that. Confused uncertainty filled her. "What?"

"Sometimes you must do what I order you to do without question." András came around the bed and stalked toward her. He stopped within arms' reach—hers, not his.

He was showing no fear. If she had her karambit, her dragon's claw, he'd think twice about standing so close to her.

Beta fisted her hands, tossing her head to free her hair from her ears. She rather liked it in her face. It matched her mood. "Are you my master now?"

The scent of smoke was definitely from her. *He* still smelled divine.

András's face darkened. A muscle jumped at the corner of his jaw. Though his harmonics seethed, they remained tightly controlled around him. "When it comes to battle, I am. You may be one badass fighter, *but I'm trained as an Elioud warrior.* I have decades of experience. And I'm already part of a seasoned team with a defined leader."

"And you will tell me to lie there and take it, Spratek?" she asked, narrowing her eyes.

For answer, András jerked her.

This time, Beta braced her feet and threw a harmonic jab at his head. It snapped back, but he simply shook his head once. Then he stared at her.

Beta redoubled her effort.

András shunted her next harmonic punch away as if knocking a fly aside.

Beta, gritting her teeth, exhaled, sending her fury into her harmonics. She hammered him with a series of invisible strikes.

András staggered, caught himself on the edge of the bed, and then stood upright. He smiled. There was no humor in it.

For the next two minutes, she tried to pummel him. That didn't work, so she focused on moving, but András directed every ounce of harmonic energy that she expended away. She failed to hit him or run from him.

She recognized it as a martial arts technique, specifically from *aikidö*, or the Way of Harmonizing Energy. Worse, she realized that András actually siphoned harmonic energy from her attacks. His harmonics grew more and more steady while she wore herself out.

Beta stopped, her chest heaving. András immediately yanked her into his arms. As he stroked her back, he sent soothing harmonic waves into her.

"Submit isn't the same as submissive, do you understand, Gomba?" he said into her ear. "We're either a mated pair or you're a prowling feline who deigns to visit my bed from time to time. That is not how *Elioud* mates are meant to be. They are meant to become something more than what they are alone. For it is written: a cord of three strands is not quickly broken."

András demonstrated what he meant, meshing his harmonics with hers, which yielded to him. A pure tone resounded through Beta. She recognized it. It had sounded last night, when their lovemaking had reached completion. Their fundamental frequencies had overlapped to create a new, higher frequency. Beta tested it, wonder filling her. In fact, now she felt better. Whole.

András seemed to sense her wonder. He tipped her face up, his thumbs rubbing her jaw as he spoke. "Together, we have the harmonic signature of an *Irim*. And your harmonics no longer clash with our conjoined frequency."

Beta looked at him wide eyed. She'd always thought of herself as a dragon, but she'd never expected to think of herself as an angel.

Swallowing, she said, "I feel it."

András searched her gaze. "But that won't last. It can't."

Beta remembered her earlier epiphany about the fleeting satisfaction that came from lovemaking.

She took one of his hands, and after kissing his palm, asked, "If it is only temporary, Spratek, then why are we standing here talking?"

She followed this by rising to her tiptoes and winding her arms around his neck. András responded by wrapping his arms around her and drawing her against his hot chest. It felt so *good* to press skin to skin. He groaned and closed his eyes. He kissed her, his lips firm and warm until they parted and hers followed along. He deepened the kiss, driving his tongue into her mouth and crushing her against him. And like that, her desire, coiled and waiting in her core, roared to life.

After a long, electrifying moment, András pulled back, laying his forehead against hers. Their harmonics jostled and jumped like a live wire while he struggled to control his breathing. As he did, he controlled hers. Calmness washed through her.

And disappointment.

András held her face and looked at her. Then he shook his head, his face somber. And something else. Fearful? Hopeful? "The only way to make it last, to transform our union into something more, is to bind it before *Elohim* and our friends. Otherwise, discord will eventually weaken it. If that happens, then the Dark *Irim* and their followers will exploit it."

He lifted the St. Michael medal where it rested high on her breast. Beta had the unaccountable sensation that he gathered his courage before he continued. "The Archangel chose not only you, Beta. He chose *us*. Together, we play a key role in his plan to redeem the *Elioud*."

As Beta watched, turmoil again dominating her emotions and her harmonics, András slid down her front and landed on one knee. He held her hands in his. "Will you marry me, Alžběta Čermáková?"

Stasia had given up staring at *La Grandmère*. The old woman's single glaring eye gazing dolefully at the viewer made her look for all the world like a *strega nonna*—a grandmother witch. Instead, Stasia laid curled on her side on the small couch in Saskia's office, where she, Willem, and the art historian had spent the rest of Saturday night and all of Sunday examining the portrait in meticulous detail. Now it was early Monday morning, and she was ready to concede that Yeqon must have the *Codex Angelicus*.

Saskia slept on the floor in front of her desk, an empty bottle of the Dutch liqueur *oranjebitter* next to a half-full demitasse cup of espresso. She'd refused to leave them alone with the painting, even to eat or go to the restroom. They'd had to take periodic breaks to handle her human needs, including escorting her to her apartment for a change of clothes and the bottle of *oranjebitter*, which she said tasted like disappointment sweetened with desire.

Somewhere around two a.m. last night, she'd made a double espresso to stay awake. By three a.m., she'd made a second and added a splash of the orange-flavored liqueur. From there she'd moved to drinking from the bottle. Now, so inebriated that the fire alarm couldn't wake her, Saskia would never know if they carried the painting away. Apparently, Saskia's determination to protect the valuable painting only extended as far as her self-control.

Only Willem remained focused and alert. He had found a tiny clue in the old woman's eye that suggested, to him at least, that the microscopic map there had been a deliberate misdirection by Bernard.

Stasia sighed and pinched the bridge of her nose.

"Willem, *per favore*. Bernard hid a map of Pont-Aven because that is where he painted his grandmother's portrait. It is quite simple. It is also quite detailed, which, frankly, is amazing given that he painted it with microdots in 1887. And it is quite challenging to discern, even for an *Elioud*. If Saskia had not overheard Yeqon discussing it, we would not have even that clue. We must accept that Yeqon has already gone to Pont-Aven and most likely found the *Codex*."

She stood, stretching her arms over her head. "We should retreat to Fushë-Arrëz to plan our next steps. Mihàil returned last night. Miró will join us once he and Miles finish dispersing the *daemonia* in Paris."

Willem, who stared at a digital enlargement of the old woman's baleful eye on a large monitor on Saskia's desk, swiveled his chair around until he faced Stasia. "I think that would be premature. Let me show you why."

He stood and moved closer to Bernard's painting. Stasia, sighing, came to stand next to him. She crossed her arms. As an *Elioud*, she had greater stamina and less need for sleep than the average human, but they had been awake for forty-eight hours. Being around Saskia had also worn her nerves thin. She needed to see Miró and not just for a few stolen hours here and there. If what she thought was coming, then she wanted to be at his side.

She looked at Willem. "I have stared at that painting until I have double vision. I have gone over every millimeter of it. What are you seeing that I am not?"

Willem nodded. "Yes, I know. I have done the same thing. Tell me, how did Bernard encode that information?"

Stasia refrained from rolling her eyes. Clearly, Willem wanted to make his case methodically. "He painted a tiny little map on the canvas using luminous paint that shines through the surface paint."

"Which only an *Elioud* or *Irim* can see unaided, correct?" he asked.

She shrugged. "Of course. He needed to hide it in plain sight. He did not have the ability to change a pixel here or there in a digital image or the necessary software to pull the hidden message out of the binary. This is the modern equivalent of tattooing the bald head of a slave and then letting his hair grow back over it. Or using invisible ink."

He nodded again. "Have you heard of printer steganography?"

Narrowing her eyes, Stasia shook her head.

"That's probably because it's not true steganography. It's the equivalent of watermarking color laser printouts with a machine identification code. Printer manufacturers do this to aid in identifying counterfeit bills. The Dutch authorities used it about fifteen years ago to catch a counterfeiting ring using a Canon printer."

Stasia's instincts began to tingle. This sounded promising. "How does this code work?"

"Small yellow dots, almost too tiny for the human eye to detect, are printed in a spaced pattern in the document. They encode the serial number of the printer along with the date and time of printing in a specific pattern. The pattern is repeated across the printout."

"How are these small yellow dots discerned?"

"A number of ways, including UV light."

"Which *Irim* and *Elioud* can both see."

"Yes, but they have to be looking for them *and* interpret the pattern in which they're arranged. The luminous microdots are much more visible and clumped into a meaningful form. I think Bernard used them as a distraction."

Stasia blinked at that. It was true. She usually only paid attention to the infrared light spectrum. In fact, Miró had warned her that UV light damaged her eyes, which still had the physical limitations of the human organ.

She squinted anyway and studied the painting. Nothing jumped out at her. "What you suggest is that Yeqon saw these yellow dots but dismissed them?"

"I believe so."

"Show me."

Willem nodded and picked up a magnifying glass on the table next to the painting as well as a hand-held lamp with a UV filter. He held it under the old woman's eye, circumscribing a small area of the painting. Familiar yellow dots like sickly freckles riddled the skin.

"I am no artist. Those could just be Bernard's technique for painting flesh," said Stasia.

"True, but then the dots would likely be random. These are in Braille."

Stasia shot a startled look at her partner.

He didn't seem to notice. Instead, he shifted the magnifying glass to isolate a pattern of dots. "These dots correspond to the Latin word *Codex*." He picked up a printout from the table and handed it to her. "Here. That is the internationally standardized Braille alphabet. It hasn't changed much since Louis Braille invented it almost a hundred years ago."

Stasia glanced at the paper. On it, tiny bubbles in groups of six with some shaded in had been labeled with alphabet letters. She recognized the patterned dots, but she'd never learned to read Braille. Quickly she matched the dot groupings that Willem highlighted on the painting with the printed alphabet. He was right. It spelled *Codex*.

Her heart beat faster as adrenaline flooded her. For the first time in two days, she felt alert and hopeful.

She gestured toward the workstation and monitor. "*Dai, non farmi stare sulle spine*," she said. *Come on, do not keep me hanging.* "I know that you have already scanned the whole painting."

Willem grinned. It transformed his face. Stasia blinked. For the most part, the Dutchman lived up to his country's dour stereotype. Grieving Eva hadn't helped. But suddenly she could almost understand Miró's quiet jealousy. Willem's thickly lashed blue-gray eyes under straight brows sparkled with life. His full lips begged to be kissed. Stasia, who'd grown to appreciate her partner's unflappable nature and sharp intellect, sent a silent prayer to the Archangel that Willem might one day fall in love again.

Unaware of her thoughts, the quiet architect returned to his seat and brought up a window with the high-resolution scan of Bernard's painting open in image-processing software. He moused to a toolbox where he clicked on a layer. Suddenly all color left the image except yellow. Dozens of dots scattered over the white space where the image had been.

Willem clicked another layer.

Thin black lines connected yellow dots around the old woman's eye into a network of nodes. Hundreds of other dots were grouped into Braille letters, each labeled with a textbox that displayed the words *Codex in lauandi*.

It was repeated dozens of times.

Willem looked up at Stasia. "This is a map of France, and that node at the top right is Lille where Èmile Bernard grew up. He hid the *Codex Angelicus* in his grandmother's former laundry business just before he died."

Twenty-Five

Beta, awake and restless even though dawn had yet to warm the sky, heard the overhead door on the front garage activate. Someone was up early. Most likely Pjetër, who'd been tasked with driving to the Kastrioti airfield to pick up Helsing, who'd flown back from Warsaw. Stasia and someone named Willem remained in France on a mission Beta had yet to learn more about. Apparently, she'd met Willem briefly three years ago after the *Elioud* had a showdown of sorts with the Dark *Irim* Yeqon. She only vaguely recalled that time. But she did remember that she'd been angry and hurt that Olivia had chosen to leave her in Albania under András's guard rather than trusting her to come and help. Of course, in hindsight, that had been the wise thing to do. At the time Beta had allowed her resentment to fester, which Asmodeus had not only fed upon but used.

She heard no other sounds in the sleeping mansion. Sitting upright, she pulled the down-filled duvet from her and swung her feet to the floor. Despite it being almost December, warm wood met her bare soles.

She padded to the ensuite bathroom. Olivia had stocked the guest bath with products made locally using organic herbs grown on the estate. When Beta moved into the downstairs guest suite yesterday morning, she'd showered the smoke, sweat, and scent of lovemaking from her hair and skin using the verbena-sage shampoo and conditioner along with a mild-smelling herbal body wash.

Other products scented with various blends made from mint, violet, lemon balm, clover, chamomile or eucalyptus promised a spa-like experience if she wanted it. On a glass shelf above the large corner bathtub within easy reach, a row of orange-rosemary-thyme bath bombs and calming hyssop-lavender bath teas joined brown glass vials of essential oils with a warming stand. Aromatic pillar candles stood guard on either side of the tub. Large, fluffy blue towels and a bath pillow completed the enticing array.

Sometime between yesterday morning and this morning, the vanity had been fully stocked with hairbrush, comb, and a dizzying number of hair wraps, clips, and bands. There was even makeup in shades to compliment her hair, eye, and skin color. Beta ignored everything except the mint toothpaste powder on the counter. Rinsing her face in cold water, she brushed her hair and pulled it back into a smooth ponytail.

Olivia never questioned Beta's request to move from András's room. She simply brought her clothes yesterday afternoon, enough to last a week. When Beta tried to help Olivia, whose pregnant belly suggested that she was going to go into labor at any moment, Olivia ignored her.

"We can shop for more later," she'd said as she handed over two large shopping bags containing several sweaters, long-sleeved shirts, jeans, and fleece-lined trousers in several colors. "I instructed Adriana to purchase some underthings for you. She put them in the chest of drawers."

Olivia had watched as Beta slid open a drawer and fingered the stack of underwear inside. "I'm afraid they're pretty utilitarian, so again, we can head into town later. I like to give the local shops my business. If the selection doesn't suit you, the owners are happy to order from their suppliers."

Then she'd grinned and hugged Beta, laughing when her baby kicked the other woman. "I'm over the moon that you're here and safe. Now we just need to get Stasia back here so the three musketeers can have a proper reunion."

This morning, Beta dressed in the single set of tactical clothing, hooking her karambit to a belt loop. Now she felt ready to leave her room.

The breakfast area where they'd eaten upon arriving lay across the hall from the guest suite and up two steps. Gray dawn light filtered into this space from the large bay window. Warm light shone from the kitchen, and someone moved around, the signatures oddly muffled. Beta heard an espresso maker hissing, followed by the refrigerator door. She stepped up into the breakfast area and looked down the length of the kitchen, which appeared to be empty. The smell of espresso filled the air.

A moment later, Olivia came into the kitchen carrying a laundry basket.

"There's an espresso on the counter there for you," she said as if she'd expected Beta.

Beta sat on a stool in front of the espresso. She sipped it. It was still hot. "Thank you," she said.

Olivia said, "Of course." She set the laundry basket on the counter, sighing. "I'd love a coffee about now. Mihàil makes the best decaf espresso, but he's still sleeping. That little excursion to Germany took it out of him."

She said this lightly enough, but Beta knew her friend. She heard the worry in Olivia's voice.

"András described these *daemonia* to me. They sound like a nuisance more than a menace," she said.

It felt good to fall back into easy conversation with her old friend. Although that said more about Olivia than her.

Olivia went to the refrigerator. Though her ungainly belly would have caused another woman to move less than gracefully, she still moved like a dancer.

Apparently, she didn't agree, however, because as she opened the refrigerator door to pull out eggs, vegetables, meats, cheeses, yogurt, and a variety of juices, she said, "Gah! I'm so awkward. *Qifqi* needs to make her appearance. I'm tired of eating for two. And peeing for half a dozen based on the number of times I go to the bathroom throughout the day."

"'*Qifqi*'?" asked Beta, perplexed. She wondered if Olivia avoided responding to her observation about *daemonia* or if she was simply distracted. The *zonjë* certainly seemed hyper-focused on domestic duties.

Olivia answered her question. "It's an Albanian rice ball, similar to the Italian *arancini*. I've craved them so much during this pregnancy that I believe I have a huge rice ball in here." She patted her stomach affectionately.

She set a glass chopping board on the counter and pulled a knife out of a drawer. She continued talking as she sliced a sweet onion.

"I'm due on December first, so really any day now. The nursery has every-thing. The pantry is stocked. And Mihàil is here."

Adriana, the Kastrioti housekeeper and cook, appeared in the doorway from the lanai. A quiet, middle-aged woman, she said little and did much. Now she shooed Olivia away from the vegetables before washing her hands and beginning to chop.

Olivia poured herself a small glass of grapefruit juice. Instead of sipping, she looked at Beta. "I suspect that András was trying to shield you from the realities of our world as long as he could."

She paused, her gaze searching Beta's. "But that ship has sailed. *Daemonia* are *bogomili* on steroids and less smart. Usually, they squabble as much amongst themselves as prey on humans, but now they're forming packs and growing stronger. Mihàil just returned from Germany where he took on a legion. A legion is a vast host. Does that tell you what we're up against?"

Olivia's blue-gray eyes had a crystalline purity to them that made her ros-es-and-cream complexion seem somehow wholesome yet refined. Beta felt drab and dark next to her. And toxic. She said nothing to Olivia's question. She didn't know what to say. She looked down at her hand holding the espresso cup. The urge to pull out her karambit gripped her.

Olivia picked up her free hand, interlacing their fingers. "You and András quarreled."

Tears pricked Beta's eyes, but she squashed the urge by scowling. "He asked me to marry him."

"And you're not sure how you feel about that even though you love him."

Beta brought her gaze up to Olivia and let her friend see the truth there.

"I never saw myself married. I am happy as we are," she said, looking back down. She toyed with the espresso cup, tilting it before lifting it and swallowing the last of the coffee. "Besides, I am not so sure that marrying me will make András stronger. It definitely will not make him safer. Asmodeus is obsessed with me."

Olivia touched a light fingertip to Beta's breast where her St. Michael medal lay hidden under her long-sleeved black shirt. "And St. Michael has chosen you."

Beta started, her own fingertips going to the hidden medal. "How did you know?" she asked in a low voice.

"Because it glows with his blessing," said Olivia gently. "You should wear it outside your clothing where it's visible."

Beta tried another tack. Raising her gaze, she held Olivia's. "You have already lost Roksana and Daněk because of me."

Olivia leaned closer. Something flashed in her eyes. When she spoke, *Elioud* authority sounded in her voice. "Now you listen to me, Beta. Their deaths are not on you. As for marriage, it's up to you, obviously. But I know that Mihàil and I are stronger together. Miró and Stasia as well. It's easy enough to read in their harmonics."

Olivia seemed to have all the answers. Yet she'd been a thoroughly modern intelligence officer when she met Mihàil. One who didn't believe in angels and demons except in the metaphoric sense.

Beta tilted her head. "You will have read our harmonics then." At Olivia's nod, she continued. "András says that our conjoined frequencies won't last without discord disrupting them."

"Human bonds decay. That's part of the corporeal plane. No matter how many times we 'refresh' them," said Olivia.

Beta ignored the allusion. "He also said that St. Michael plans to use us somehow to redeem the *Elioud*. What does that mean?"

"Hm," said Olivia, leaning away and stretching her back. She let Beta's hand go and picked up her grapefruit juice. After sipping, she continued. "Honestly, I don't know for sure, but I can guess. Zophiel—you do remember their guardian angel, don't you?—showed me a painting after you'd been taken by Petrov. She said that the Archangel had commissioned her to paint it as his replacement for the Van Gogh painting."

"The one that Stasia found in that former convent in Umbria?"

Olivia nodded. "*Infatuation of the Watcher Angels (after Caravaggio)*. Zophiel's painting had a plaque on its waiting frame that read *Redemption of the Elioud*."

Beta narrowed her eyes. "What exactly did this masterwork show?"

Olivia sighed and set her empty glass down. "Keep in mind that it was unfinished," she said. "I think it's meant to be hopeful, not prescriptive. Free will and all that."

Beta pinned her old friend under her dragon's predatory stare. "Tell me." Her hand gripped the karambit at her waist, its folded curve hard against her palm.

"Three couples sealed and blessed in the sacrament of marriage."

Cotton dried Beta's mouth and throat. Her heart beat erratically along with her uneven harmonics. "You and Mihàil. Stasia and Miró. András and I."

Olivia, her expression grave, nodded.

A sound behind them drew their attention. Mihàil came out of the master suite into the family room. He was fully dressed in black tactical clothing. Beta frowned. There was something odd about his signatures, but she couldn't determine what. She did, however, recognize the surge in Olivia's. Fear and worry roiled the *zonjë* while a featherlight blue wisp traced through her core, twisting around the radiant orange of her belly.

Her friend slipped off her stool and met her husband halfway.

"You should sleep in more," she said, her hands on her husband's upper arms. Her voice, though low and soothing, sent a tremor of warning through Beta's harmonics.

Adriana set a plate with an omelet in front of her. Beta ignored it, scanning the environment around them.

Mihàil shook his head. "We do not have a lot of time." His hoarse voice echoed around the room.

The hairs on Beta's neck stood.

Above them, something flared brilliant white on the harmonic plane.

A moment later, András came into the kitchen behind Beta, blurring into visibility an instant before she recognized his harmonic signature. When she did, she recognized the András who'd gone into battle mode. His features had all the softness of granite. Smoke clung to him. He radiated heat like a blast furnace.

She slipped off the stool, releasing the karambit from its loop at the same time. It felt warm and alive against her palm. Her harmonics responded to András's.

She too flared. When the light died down, she smelled smoke. She knew the marble tile under feet had scorched and cracked.

Miles Baxter ran into the family room. He had dressed for combat and carried a combat shotgun. He wore a sidearm.

Mihàil looked at Miles. Olivia stepped to his side, and he wrapped an arm around her shoulders.

"Sitrep," said the *drangùe*, now in command mode.

"A convoy of *bogomili* vehicles passed through Fierzë ten minutes ago." Miles paused. His next words hit like a thunderbolt. "Two vehicles stayed behind and killed all of the residents except for Davud, who happened to be out with his sheep when they arrived."

Mihàil nodded at him. "Take the *zonjë* to the safe room. Protocol Five is in effect."

Olivia put her hand on Mihàil's forearm. "I can still shoot," she said. "Let me go to the sniper loft."

"You will be trapped if the *bogomili* get inside the house," said Mihàil.

András interjected before Olivia could speak again. "Asmodeus knows that Olivia is pregnant."

Both Kastriotis and Miles looked at him, shock radiating from their faces.

"Tell me." A muscle jumped in Mihàil's jaw as he spoke.

András looked at Beta. She nodded at his unspoken question.

"He adopted her avatar in Babyrusk," she said. She kept her gaze on Mihàil as she added, "I am a decent sniper."

András shot her a knowing look, a hint of amusement in his eyes. She was more than decent.

Mihàil nodded. "András will show you to the armory and how to access the sniper nest." Then he looked at Olivia. "Take Adriana with you."

Beta read Olivia's frustration in her harmonics, but the other woman only dipped her chin at her husband's command. Adriana, carrying a duffel bag, joined her mistress. The housekeeper now wore a side holster and tactical clothing. Miles escorted both women away. As András led Beta onto the veranda in the back of the house, a couple dozen men ran from the other side of the connected garage headed to the armory as well. They wore clothing identifying them as Kastrioti personnel. The way that they moved confirmed that they had training.

The armory, a stone outbuilding about forty meters from the main house and beyond a pool now covered for the season, had enough weapons and ammunition to hold off a besieging ground force for several days. Beta doubted that they'd face *bogomili* only on the ground, however.

András headed for the display of sniper rifles as the Kastrioti personnel streamed into the armory behind them.

"Which one?" he asked Beta, gesturing to the wall of sniper rifles.

She pointed to the SAKO TRG 42, an extremely accurate Finnish weapon. "With .338 Lapua Magnum rounds," she said. "That is, if you have them."

The .338 Lapua Magnum rounds had an effective distance of fifteen hundred meters. She'd shot through armored glass with one.

"Done," said András, pulling the rifle from its mount and handing it to her.

While she inspected the SAKO, he filled a large black duffel with cartridges. Then he went to the handgun wall. The Kastrioti security personnel moved aside to give him space. András removed several handguns. He shoved one at Beta, who recognized a CZ P-10C and slid the other two into holsters at his sides. She stuck the handgun into the waist of her pants at the small of her back.

"Cartridges are in the bag," he said.

Beta noticed that he wore a backpack. When she tried to pick up the duffel, András growled, lifted it, and pivoted on his heel. She narrowed her eyes but said nothing, following him outside with the SAKO. They returned to the veranda on the back of the house. Instead of going back inside, however, András stopped in front of an innocuous stone wall next to the French door. Apparently, it was stone laminate covering an access door to an elevator. It slid open to reveal a car large enough for her and the duffel.

András dropped the large black bag inside the elevator and gestured for Beta to step in.

She hesitated.

"Go," he said, his mouth tight and his eyes narrow.

Beta stepped into the elevator. As she turned to face András, he leaned in and pulled her into a hard embrace, kissing her. He pulled back, one hand still on her face. His gaze held hers.

"This access door has been keyed to specific harmonics, including yours now. It won't open to any of the *bogomili*. Since you don't have a comm, you're on your own for target acquisition. Wait until one of us flashes the all-clear before leaving overwatch."

When he would have turned away, Beta gripped his hand, her gaze searching his. "How long do I wait?"

"The nest has enough rations to last three days. It's heated and has running water and a toilet as well as a bunk. Wait as long as you can, then set the charge in the bag. You'll have eight minutes to recover Olivia from the safe room and get to safety before it blows. Look for the entrance in the garage. If I can, I will contact you in a week in Vienna."

If he didn't, it meant he was dead. And it would be her fault.

Cold spiked Beta's core. Her harmonics threatened to break free of her will, but she kept her breathing even, imagining that she controlled them as she'd controlled her beloved chain whip. Harmonic energy coiled around her in an invisible deadly promise. She smelled smoke. Heat shimmered in the air around them.

András brought her hand to his mouth and kissed it. Firm harmonic fingers caressed her face and entwined with hers, steadying her.

"Don't worry, Gomba. No *bogomili* can hurt me. Only you can. Now go. I'll herd them into your line of sight. Then you can go *booomm*." A ghostly grin flitted across his face.

Beta blinked. He'd just repeated something she'd said to him years ago in Prague—when she'd asked him to help find the mercenary team that had killed her friend Andrej and seriously wounded his partner, Eliska. He'd even sounded like Beta when he said it. The coldness in her core melted.

Nodding, she stepped back into the elevator.

The last thing she saw before the door closed was András, his expression fierce and *Elioud* power radiating from him.

TWENTY-SIX

András shifted into full battle mode as soon as the elevator doors to the sniper loft closed.

He'd throttled his awareness while getting Beta to her post, but now he trusted that she would be safe and that he could focus on the assault.

Aerie One, this is Giant, he flashed as he sped his harmonics. He was now invisible to ordinary humans. *Redstart has overwatch. On my way to the front entrance.*

Giant, this is Harlequin. I have command of the TOC, flashed Olivia, who had gone to the secondary tactical operations center in the safe room, which was really more of a suite of rooms. *Your nano-origami are offline.*

She didn't question Beta's call sign, but she did sound unhappy that his personal network of molecular drones had disappeared. It would make him unable to communicate with the human members of their security force.

Couldn't be helped, he flashed. *Redstart used them as tiny flares to disrupt an Igla-V missile locked on us. We'll just have to do this old school.*

Olivia rolled with this revelation. *Negative, Giant. I've got your position. I'll send replacements to you. They're keyed to your harmonics, but they won't have your modifications.*

Copy that, he flashed. *I'm at the entrance now.* Bogomili *vehicles have blocked the highway five hundred meters on either side.*

Estimate of strength? she asked.

András closed his eyes to focus on the trucks and SUVs, both the visible and the ones hidden on highway slopes behind them. His angelic sonar combined with his sensitive thermal sensing allowed a highly accurate picture of the number of *bogomili* in the attack force—at least within a five-hundred-meter radius.

Seventy-five heat signatures in the vehicles, he flashed. *In other bad news,* dae-monia *mass on the slopes around the house.* He paused. Olivia was *not* going to like the next bit. *And they've infiltrated the town. They're going house to house.*

Olivia didn't respond immediately. András waited, knowing that she would be communicating with Mihàil. But this was bad. Very bad.

There hadn't been a large-scale Dark angelic assault in Albania in decades, not since World War Two when first the Italians and then the Germans occupied the country. And Mihàil's properties had always been avoided for the much easier human targets around them—one reason that the *drangùe* chose to live in the mountains rather than in any of the more populous cities.

Yet the *drangùe* had insisted on upgrading and expanding their defenses in recent years once he and Olivia had married. His instincts had been correct. It remained to be seen if the *Elioud* general had anticipated just how much Asmodeus would send at them.

Now the *daemonia* sought to draw Mihàil away from the estate....

Giant, Dragon Man will take a team into town. You have command of the estate defense. Your squad has been deployed to the southern perimeter along the highway. Are those nano-origami there yet?

András scanned the harmonic plane around him. The telltale microscopic buzz of the tiny drones reached him before he recognized their unique flying formation. They came deployed in the shape of an eagle.

"Affirmative," he said, directing them around his head and shoulders where they picked up his voice and transmitted it on the frequency dedicated to the TOC. They automatically linked with the system of sensors and batteries in his clothing.

"Be advised, Giant, that Demon Slayer is twenty minutes out. Farm Boy has a NAV squad on the perimeter."

"Copy that," said András, scanning the overcast sky.

Miles, also known as Farm Boy while in the field, would be watching the *bogomili* using Nano Aerial Vehicles, or nanodrones. His squad had two sets of riflemen trained to use the nanodrones as spotters and a practically invisible targeting system. The squad would have scattered around the estate grounds, hidden behind specially designed landscape blinds.

Olivia would also have launched their defensive mesh network of nanodrones programmed to fly the perimeter of the estate as soon as she made it to the TOC. The nanodrones, which took the place of a security wall, would alert them to incursions and could be reconfigured in an instant into tiny defenders until human personnel could arrive. They could even be used to trip defenses, such as sonic mines and thermal flares, that would leave the *bogomili* deaf and blind while distracting and disorienting any nearby *daemons*.

However, from the look of the thick, purple-gray clouds riding low over the slopes around them, the NAV system and mesh network were going to be non-operational soon. Once it started snowing, the molecular machines would be overwhelmed by the icy flakes. The shooters would be left with traditional tactics, such as infrared goggles—which the *bogomili* would have prepared for.

Which reminded him of Beta, high in her perch on top of the house. She had neither a spotter or comms. Soon she'd be blind to all but thermal signatures.

Redstart, snow is on its way.

It makes no difference, flashed Beta. *I can still hunt. They can mask their thermal signatures. They cannot mask their breath.*

András grinned to himself. Of course, his fierce Gomba had already identified a *bogomili* weakness. An idea occurred to him.

Before he could flash Beta, he saw movement among the vehicles on the eastern slope, which was higher than the western.

His grin evaporated as his temperature spiked. He broadcast a message to all defenders. "Eyes on the eastern flank. Let them come to you."

Incoming, flashed Beta.

A puff of smoke flared from the recoilless rifle mounted on an armored Mercedes G-Wagen on the rise of their western flank. András recognized the familiar whine of an M40 High-Explosive shell. The shell hit the attached garage. Designed for anti-tank warfare, it brought down a corner of the stone structure.

An instant later the SAKO popped. The gunner on the M40 went down. A new mercenary took his spot. András had a feeling that there would be an endless line of replacements.

Meanwhile, the lead SUV on the eastern flank, another armored Mercedes G-Wagen, accelerated down the slope, strobe lights flashing on the front grill and a siren wailing. Four trucks and another SUV with a machine gun mounted on its roof followed in its wake.

Go time, flashed András.

He stepped into the space between the twin bollards guarding the entrance, activating the harmonic screen that had been programmed into them and bolstering it with his own harmonics.

Another shell hit, this time on the paver driveway fronting the house. A gaping crater swallowed pavers and the landscaping bed bordering the driveway. Chunks of pavers shattered the large front arched window, leaving holes in others and gouging wedges from the mansion's stone façade.

András ignored that threat. Beta would focus on keeping the M40 from hitting the garage. He trusted that she would keep access to the safe room—and Olivia and Adriana—open.

The lead G-Wagen rammed into the invisible harmonic screen, which absorbed all of the kinetic and heat energy from the SUV and reflected it back into the vehicle.

The armored German SUV accordioned, its fifteen-centimeter-thick windows popping free of the ballistic steel frame and flinging the driver and passengers out. The pickup following close behind swerved so violently to avoid hitting the G-Wagen that its machine gunner was thrown from the bed.

The SAKO popped again.

And then the battle began in earnest.

Riflemen from the NAV squad began firing on the mercenaries emerging from the undamaged trucks and running up the slope toward the house. Box trucks appeared at the crest of the ridge and disgorged more *bogomili* mercenaries.

András grabbed a mercenary who made the mistake of trying to run around the crumpled G-Wagen and between the bollards. He twisted the *bogomili*'s neck and dropped him, reaching the next *bogomili* inside the truck before the first hit the pavement. Thermal flares flashed fifty meters from him as several *bogomili* hit the defensive nano network. The stunned creatures circled. Shots rang out.

András let the fog of war take him. He was simultaneously focused on his immediate surroundings, aware of each and every bogomili that he grappled and fought, and also aware of the metallic, sulfurous scent of gunpowder mixed with the coppery scent of hot blood hanging in the chilly air, the sounds of gunfire, running feet, yelling and screaming combatants, and the noise of automobile engines and squealing tires, shattering glass and crumbling stone, and the piercing tones of sonic mines.

As abruptly as the assault started, it ended. The mercenaries retreated up the eastern slope, leaving their wounded and dying behind. Besides the destroyed G-Wagen and stopped pickup, two other *bogomili* trucks had been left behind. One had veered and crashed into a low ditch when its driver was killed; the other had rolled to a halt on the highway itself, its doors wide and its engine idling. Three of the useless vehicles blocked the easy, direct route to the estate.

And provided ideal cover for Kastrioti shooters.

András slowed his harmonics. He was covered in sweat and gore. He bent, resting his hands on his upper thighs, panting.

"Farm Boy, sitrep," he said, scanning the estate grounds.

There were three Kastrioti security members down, one of whom was dead. The other two had serious injuries based on their harmonics and the amount of blood cooling around them. On the driveway and slopes leading up to the mansion, he counted thirty prone *bogomili*. The defensive mesh network and the NAV system had allowed them to withstand a stronger force.

"We have three casualties, one serious and two minor. Permission to move the serious casualty inside."

"Granted." András looked up at the sky, which had darkened during the conflict. "You're about to lose the NAV system, Farm Boy. Leave a team to defend your rear and take a team to the top of the ridge. It's your job to stop as many of those bastards from reaching the house as possible."

"Copy that," said Miles.

"Get me *bogomili* numbers. My gut tells me we haven't seen the last of the *bogomili* transports from the northeast. And tell your guys to give me some cover. I'm grabbing a couple of injured guys."

"Wilco, Giant."

András waited until he saw one of the NAV teams running to cover behind the abandoned *bogomili* vehicles before speeding his harmonics to reach the first injured Kastrioti guard. A moment later, Miles led the second team at a run up the slope toward the eastern ridge, skirting amongst trees and other obstacles in a leapfrogging forward movement. Almost as soon as András slowed next to the first guard, gunfire sounded behind him. Several bullets whined past, but the Kastrioti shooters responded.

András slung the unconscious guard over his shoulder before heading to the other casualty. Squatting, he lifted the guard one-handed to his other shoulder, speeding his harmonics as he stood. All three of them blinked out of human sight. A shot whizzed through the air where he'd been only an instant before.

"Giant, this is Aerie One. Sitrep." An edge sharpened Olivia's normally calm voice.

"Us one, *bogomili* zero," he said as he reached the relative safety of the front door, which was tucked inside a portico with two stone columns. "I'm bringing two injured to the family room."

"Hammer is waiting," said Olivia using Dr. Armand's call sign. "Giant, Dragon Man's team has met a sizable *daemonic* force. They're pinned down in town."

"Demon Slayer?" asked András, shouldering the front door open and staggering a little down the long hallway.

At best, the American Army Ranger would be ineffective against the *daemonia*. At worst, he'd lose his mind to possession. But he and Pjetër could certainly handle *bogomili*, even these trained mercenaries.

Olivia answered as András reached Dr. Armand. "Demon Slayer and The Saint made it through town. They took up position inside a house three hundred meters behind the *bogomili* on our west. Demon Slayer and Redstart have the western *bogomili* pinned down."

"Estimate of *bogomili* numbers on the west?" asked András, letting Dr. Armand help him ease an injured man onto a cot that had been set up in the family room.

The other cot already held Miles's squad member, forcing András to settle the second man onto a leather sofa. He was jogging back to the front door by the time that Olivia answered. "Demon Slayer estimates fewer than two dozen, but Redstart has the best vantage point of course."

The edge had disappeared from her voice. Too bad he had to bring it back. But he also knew that Olivia needed solid intel.

"I suspect she knows exactly how many," he said, pausing on the doorstep to survey the fat, heavy flakes swirling outside. "Aerie One, it's started to snow."

"That means ..." Olivia's voice trailed off before she infused it with *Elioud* authority. "You know what to do."

"Farm Boy has already moved teams to the ridge and along the highway. They'll do what they can until the snow stops them." It was András's turn to inject *Elioud* authority into his voice. "No one is getting inside this house as long as I'm upright."

"Copy that," said Olivia.

Time to check in with Beta.

Speeding his harmonics until he was invisible to the surrounding mercenaries, he stepped outside as he did. *Redstart, sitrep.*

I thought you were going to herd them to me, flashed Beta.

Mea culpa. Don't want you to have all the fun. Helsing is the shooter inside the house.

I recognized his harmonic signature. The SAKO fired on the tail of her words.

Clearly the mercenaries continued to test their western defenses. And Beta was testing his patience, though he *was* impressed at how far she could accurately read a harmonic signature.

How many bogomili *are left?* he flashed, narrowing his eyes.

There was shadowy movement on the slopes around the house, including across the highway. The snow had thickened so much that he had to rely on his battle senses beyond a couple dozen meters. Prickles ran up the back of his neck.

Massed *daemonia* affected temperature as well as harmonics.

Beta's voice brought him back to his question. *It is tough to say. I keep shooting them. Though that last one popped back into his hole too quickly.*

Guess.

No need to growl. There are eighteen bogomili. *Do you want to know where they are hiding?*

Never mind that. I don't like the looks of the daemonia *on the foothills.*

The harmonic anomalies looming over us that make my skin crawl?

Yes.

Not so innocuous after all? she flashed. She sounded irritated.

They can't come onto estate grounds without being escorted by a more powerful angelic being. I'm concerned about Mihàil. He hasn't fully recovered from taking on a legion, and he's stuck in Fushë-Arrëz.

András had barely finished when Miles spoke into his comm.

"Giant, this is Farm Boy. More vehicles arriving from the north. Best guess is more than three dozen mercenaries."

A moment later, the Kastrioti team on the ridge began firing as trucks crested the ridge and sped downhill. Several trucks stopped just over the apex and began disgorging *bogomili*, who ran toward the house. They wore white camouflage and masks and practically disappeared among the trees.

Behind András, the M40 began firing. Beta responded. A moment later engines revved and several trucks veered around the G-Wagen on the west, driving on the snowy berm before spinning and sliding back onto the highway. Incessant gunfire and violence churned the harmonic plane as far as he could sense. Beyond the conflict, *daemonia* flared and soared, gorging on the swelling dissonance.

They were being attacked on all sides.

András's temperature rose, melting the snow in a wide sphere around him. Steam rose in the air. High-speed ammunition whined around him as he became visible despite his faster harmonics. A round burned across his upper arm. He increased his harmonic buffer to deflect most of the bullets reaching him, but he couldn't stand still.

Yanking the handguns from his side holsters, he sprinted toward the first vehicle from the west, firing as he ran. A shot took out one of the car's front tires.

The car swerved and crashed into the nearest slope, flipping and rolling back onto its roof on the highway. He turned and ran full out toward the east where a truck had made it through the gauntlet of Kastrioti security. That one took most of a clip to stop.

The mercenaries drew back abruptly. Ten minutes later, they attacked again.

The attacks and withdrawals repeated until András lost count. The temperature had dropped twenty degrees already, and heavy snow continued to fall as the afternoon progressed. The *daemonia* roiled and howled, ravenous from the psychic energy that leaked toward them on the harmonic plane like blood in water. Miles and his squad had been forced to pull back where they could rotate into the shelter of the house to replenish ammunition, have wounds tended, and gulp warm liquids. András had covered their retreat and continued to alternate between east and west to block any attacks that made it inside their perimeter.

But his stamina, though prodigious, finally began to wane by mid-afternoon. The snow almost reached his knees, and he no longer had the energy to raise his temperature enough to clear it from his path. After the *bogomili* pulled out in the latest wave, András accepted the painful conclusion.

It was time to abandon the estate.

Gomba, we're going to be overwhelmed soon. Get Olivia out and drive east to Shkodër. Don't stop for anything, no matter what. We'll regroup in Vienna.

It was just getting fun, she flashed. *What are you going to be doing?*

András turned toward the house before answering. *Attracting daemonia. Between a drangùe and me, they won't care about an armored SUV speeding toward the coast.* He paused, steadying his flagging harmonics. *See you on the other side, my love.*

Copy that.

She hadn't said she loved him too. Dread sank like a frozen stone in his gut.

He'd only gone partway when his battle senses buzzed.

A moment later, Mihàil appeared, untouched by the snow whirling around him. He had an odd expression.

Warning knifed András.

"Stay," said his commander in a hollow voice echoing with *Irim* authority. Harmonics clamped András to the earth.

Around them, snow-covered mounds shifted as injured *bogomili* rose unsteadily to their feet, frozen blood crusting their uniforms. The *daemonia*, no longer held at bay, rushed howling and shrieking into these perfect vessels.

Then they lurched toward András.

Twenty-Seven

At the sight of the giant *Elioud* straining to throw off the *daemon bogomili* that launched at him, Asmodeus's glee knew no bounds. Wouldn't Yeqon be displeased if he knew what Asmodeus had accomplished—without the vaunted *Codex Angelicus*? And after breaking the hold his brother *Irim* had on him?

Possessing his old nemesis was just the proverbial icing on the cake.

Asmodeus laughed outright, flexing his vessel's muscles. Startled at the sound, the *daemon bogomili* halted and looked at him.

The *Elioud* took advantage of the moment to slip through Asmodeus's hold. He jabbed several of the distracted creatures, who howled and clutched their heads as they fell. The remaining *daemon bogomili* kicked and walked over them as they followed their quarry. Several gripped combat knives. All fixated on the Hungarian.

Asmodeus laughed again. This was *so* fun. He caught the giant in a harmonic net and slammed him to the ground. The stubborn *Elioud* rolled out of the way of the possessed mercenaries, who slipped in the snow.

Asmodeus let the *Elioud* kick at his unnatural playthings and spring to his feet. Though the *Elioud*'s harmonics wavered like a candle flame in a strong breeze, he gamely lifted his arms in a ready pose. When the possessed minions rushed at him, he grappled and threw fists, elbows, and knees. Finally, the *Elioud* managed to kill a host body and rip the *daemon* free at the same time. The spirit detonated into an infinite number of harmonic particles.

Shockwaves blew snow in a blinding tsunami away from the *Elioud* and his tormentors. Excruciating dissonance buzzed like a chainsaw through Asmodeus.

The *Elioud* broke free of the pack and escaped toward one of the intact SUVs.

Asmodeus, no longer entirely amused, smacked the audacious *Elioud* with harmonics like a cat drops a paw on a fleeing mouse. The weak half-breed's knees buckled to the ground. Vivid red blood brocaded the churned white snow around him.

An instant later, electricity stung Asmodeus.

Clutching his head, he released the *Elioud*, who staggered to his feet. The Hungarian bled from a dozen slashes, but the worst part for him was the drain on his powers of thermogenesis—the prolonged battle in freezing temperatures had sapped his ability to generate heat and cauterize wounds. He didn't have much fight left in him.

Where on this corrupted plane had such a powerful harmonic jolt originated?

Asmodeus massaged his temple, growling at the splitting headache. It was bad enough that remaining in this vessel grew more agonizing by the moment. But this pain had a familiar edge....

The remaining *daemon bogomili* chittered and flinched, backing into the snow drifts and shadows around their master. They were stupid creatures, but even they knew to flee from the agony that the Dark *Irim* would inflict upon them if he lost his temper.

"My love," said a euphonious female voice in Asmodeus's ear. "Fight him."

At her words, the subsumed *drangùe* stirred and fought against his possession.

It hurt like hell. Like a million microscopic suns blazing in his core. Violent tremors rolled through the *drangùe's* body.

Asmodeus gritted his teeth and wrestled with the *Elioud*, siphoning even more harmonic energy from his minions. He didn't have time for this.

"Go, you fools!" With a flick of his wrist, he propelled the *daemon bogomili* to the *drangùe's* house where the insolent female *Elioud* hid, protecting the whelp inside her.

Compelled, the *daemon bogomili* rushed into the house. The *drangùe* redoubled his efforts. Asmodeus writhed and twisted. The snow beneath his feet melted. The air reeked of sulfur and ash.

A moment later, a garage door rolled up. Even before it had fully risen, a Range Rover burst from inside, shattering the door. At the same time, the Hungarian tackled Asmodeus, landing on his vessel's body. Now the *drangùe* took control enough to keep the Dark *Irim* from grappling with the *Elioud* who pinned him to the ground. The Range Rover's engine growled in the still afternoon as it navigated around bodies and slid through the snow. It fishtailed around the corner of the driveway onto the highway heading west. The driver gunned the engine and swerved to miss the mercenary vehicles, driving over several dead *bogomili* as it raced away.

Then the house exploded, throwing a massive ball of heated gas and debris outwards. All of the *daemon bogomili* inside were vaporized. Their individual harmonic signatures winked out, sucking energy from their Dark master.

Enraged, Asmodeus opened himself up to the dissonance. Energy flowed into him.

He gripped the *Elioud* and threw him ten meters. Standing, he stretched the *drangùe's* neck from side to side. His former acolyte had been swamped under the influx of violent harmonics. Asmodeus had full control of his powerful hybrid body. The headache had also disappeared.

The Dark *Irim* inhaled deeply before he jumped harmonics to stand over the Hungarian, whose body lay crumpled, half buried in deep snow.

With one hand, Asmodeus lifted the *Elioud* to his knees. Then he smashed a massive fist into the demi-angel's face.

By *Elohim*, it felt good to slam bone against bone. To feel the reverberation along skin, nerve, and muscle. Physical bodies were wasted on humanity.

Asmodeus gripped the young *Elioud's* jaw, holding the drooping face up so that he could study it. Too young to know that he didn't stand a chance against Asmodeus. And completely unaware of their historic tie.

The Hungarian glared at him from swollen eyes and a bruised face.

It was time to bring his little redstart out to play.

Daughter, come, he flashed.

The command boomed and echoed across the harmonic plane with the force of *Irim* authority.

Power clamped onto Beta. She didn't even try resisting. She just channeled her fury into her core and threw her shoulders back, her karambit in her hand. Her legs walked toward the front of the estate grounds, now a disturbing battleground littered with dead *bogomili*, spent ammunition, and chunks of Olivia and Mihàil's home. The snow had stopped falling, but a slight breeze sent flakes into the blazing ruins. In what had been a landscaping bed in the center of a curving driveway, Mihàil held a kneeling András by the head. The possessed *drangùe* glared at her.

It was all her fault. And it was time to end it.

Beta crossed the highway from the far side where she'd jumped harmonics before blowing the charge that she'd set per András's orders.

She stopped ten meters from the pair. Steam clouded the chilly air around her, but she hardly noticed. In fact, she'd discarded her coat after setting the charge.

András raised his face, and her heart turned over at the damage to his beloved features. She ran harmonic fingers over him. He no longer wore a coat, and his shirt and pants had been repeatedly slashed. All but one of his knife wounds were shallow. Even so, he needed medical attention and to get out of the freezing air.

"Not much to look at," said Mihàil in an odd, echoing voice. Eerie chitters and clicks counterpointed his words. He stroked a finger over András's swollen cheekbone. "But no matter. He will not come between us much longer, my wayward redstart."

Beta ignored the Dark *Irim*. "Yes, András Nagy, I will marry you. I love you." Her words rang with conviction.

And *Elioud* authority.

András's eyes widened. He visibly straightened. His harmonics flared and steadied. Beta imagined supporting them, and he smiled. Emboldened, she stroked his face.

He returned the gesture, soothing her. "Just say when and where, and I'm there, Gomba."

Mihàil threw his head back and laughed. It scraped through Beta's senses like sheering metal. A multitude of invisible insects crawled over her.

"That is the most pathetic thing I have ever heard," he said, grinning at them. It looked evil on Mihàil's handsome face. "No wonder you are so besotted with this hybrid, Daughter."

Beta bristled at the sobriquet.

"I am not your daughter," she said, gripping the karambit and lifting her chin.

She narrowed her eyes at the Dark *Irim*. The scent of smoke filled the air between them.

"Oh, but you are." Mihàil dropped András's head and jumped harmonics next to her. He touched her hair, lifting a strand before rubbing it between his fingers. "Your father was an acolyte of mine. He let me share in his exploits, if you know what I mean."

Beta didn't have to look at András to feel his shock and puzzlement.

Asmodeus's sly innuendo didn't surprise her at all. Somehow, in her heart of hearts, she'd known it all along. Asmodeus was her father. Her mother had told her that she'd had a vision of a scaly, winged beast rutting on her after her father had raped her. Her mother had thought it a figment of her drugged mind, but Beta knew that it explained her own dragon nature.

She never knew why her mother kept her, let alone loved her.

Asmodeus slipped his hand inside the neck of her sweater and lifted out the St. Michael medal by its chain. "Your little token is a joke."

He yanked it from her neck and threw it. It winked in a sudden ray of afternoon sun and then fell among the debris of the destroyed mansion. Wisps of smoke rose from his fingers.

Beta brought the karambit to Mihàil's side before the medal disappeared from sight.

"I love Olivia, so I would prefer not to injure her mate," she said, her words like icy silk, "but she would understand in this instance."

It was Mihàil's turn to narrow his eyes. He inhaled sharply. Heat shimmered in the air around them. His eyes, normally a startling sapphire, glowed against the fading afternoon light.

Beta realized her mistake when the Dark *Irim* leaned forward, a cruel smile curling the corners of his vessel's mouth, and his hand iron around her wrist.

"If you love Olivia, you should kill him, Little Redstart. Because when I am through with the *drangùe*—*if* he survives—he will be a drooling idiot incapable of feeding himself." He paused, a wicked glint in his eyes. "Or a child."

Beta's breath caught in her throat. She barely kept her gaze from darting in terror to András.

Then Mihàil leaned into the blade. Beta felt its tip pierce the *drangùe's* down jacket. She slid the blade shut before it could go into his flesh.

Malicious humor lit his eyes. "Hm. It might be sweeter to torture my former acolyte with the sight of his wife and daughter under my control."

András inserted himself between them.

"That will happen over my dead body," he said.

Harmonics jumped and snapped around them. Beta's harmonics synced with András's, and she gritted her teeth at the effort to steady them. It was like holding onto a fire hose with the spigot fully opened.

Mihàil looked at András, a sneer darkening his features. Instinctively Beta understood that the Dark *Irim* hated having to look up, even a few centimeters, at the other man.

"It will, half breed," he said. His hollow voice rose and fell unnaturally, breaking in the middle of his words and ending on a hiss.

András tilted his head, his lips pressed together as if considering this statement. Then he shook his head. "No, I don't think so. You're outnumbered, *Irim*."

Mihàil chuckled. "My minions might be dead and the *daemonia* dispersed, but it will take more than a puny *Elioud* to defeat me."

Saying that, he flicked his fingers. András flew through the air, landing hard.

Beta reacted without thinking. She headbutted Mihàil, catching him under the chin and snapping his head back. She'd dropped the karambit into her other hand and slid it under his chin before he recovered. He glared at her.

"He is not alone," she said, pricking his skin for emphasis.

András levered himself to standing. Although he'd seemed steadier when standing next to her, the hollows under his eyes and his erratic breathing told her that he was on the verge of collapsing.

"I guess you're not familiar with conjoined *Elioud* couples," he said, shrugging.

In between speaking, he flashed Beta. *Together, they fight like mated alpha wolves. Understand?*

To Asmodeus, he said, "You should ask your brother Yeqon sometime what happened in his Umbrian stronghold a few years ago."

Beta's eyes widened. She and András hadn't been there, but Mihàil and Olivia had. And Stasia and Miró. She'd never thought about how they'd faced a Dark *Irim* in his home and won.

Then I will follow your lead, Spratek, she flashed back.

Read his harmonics. He can't possess Mihàil much longer. It's excruciating. And takes a lot of harmonic energy.

Fury ran through Mihàil's familiar harmonic signature, which was dominated with dark discord. Here and there, dark strands popped free of the tight band, sizzling around him like harmonic live wires. Extreme heat shimmered around them until Mihàil's jacket smoldered and the snow transformed into a muddy puddle under their feet.

Mihàil tightened his grip on Beta's wrist. Her fingers had already gone numb. Now painful electricity ran up her arm to her shoulder.

"I am not my brother," he said. His voice broke completely into individual off-key flat and sharp chords. At the end, it sounded a sweet note, in sharp contrast to the rest.

Oh, *that* was interesting. Beta narrowed her eyes, studying the *drangùe*.

There was something off with him. Something more than Asmodeus's obvious irritation at András's subtle comparison with the Seducer. It didn't surprise her at all that Asmodeus and Yeqon had a strained relationship. They might have colluded in the beginning when the Watcher Angels defied *Elohim*'s orders against mixing with humanity. And they certainly collaborated throughout history. But it always ended in discord.

Live by discord, die by discord.

No, what was off was the single true note. The Dark *Irim* scarcely seemed aware that he had spoken it.

She flashed, *Does that note in his harmonics mean what I think it means?*

Yes, flashed András. *Be ready.*

To Asmodeus, he said, "True, you aren't Yeqon. *He* had a bonded coterie of women who constantly fed him harmonically." False sympathy made his words a mockery. "Like a *daemonic* Italian Dracula."

He was so pale. The deep knife wound still bled and soaked his shirt, and he swayed as if hurricane winds buffeted him. He clearly didn't have the strength to cauterize his wounds. She understood what he was doing, but what if freeing Mihàil didn't work? Or worse, what if Mihàil threw off Asmodeus too late to save András?

Beta shored up their conjoined harmonics as best she could. Fury still burned in her, but she knew that her own stamina waned. Her hand holding the karambit had started to shake. Little rivulets of blood ran down the *drangùe's* neck, but she didn't dare let her hand drop.

Mihàil swore. "Nasty incubus."

Foam flecked the corners of his mouth. The blood dried and flaked from his skin. His clothes turned to ash, scattered by a strong harmonic wind. Harmonic sparks danced in a vivid penumbra. Asmodeus scarcely seemed contained inside his flesh vessel.

When he spoke again, none of the *drangùe's* timbre remained. "He will be quite displeased when he learns that I destroyed you without him and his precious *Codex Angelicus*."

Recognition jolted through András, spilling into Beta.

He knew what Asmodeus referred to. And it terrified him.

Before either responded, Mihàil flicked his hand in a peremptory manner. "Come, *zonjë*. Join your husband."

Beta's gaze darted to András, who looked stunned as Olivia staggered and stumbled from where she'd hidden behind the *bogomili* G-Wagen on the west. Beta's heart thudded as she watched her heavily pregnant friend move as if invisible strings manipulated her limbs. In a way, they did. Asmodeus had taken the thick harmonic strands binding her to Mihàil and turned Olivia into a living marionette. It sickened Beta to see her friend trip over debris and slip over snowy asphalt. Once or twice, Olivia caught herself before planting her belly on the pavement. It took several agonizing minutes for her to make her disjointed—and dangerous—journey to stand before them.

Beta dropped her hand holding the karambit at Mihàil's neck.

He grabbed her hair and wrenched her head back without looking at her. His gaze remained fixed on András.

"You forget that the bond of marriage is a double-edged sword." His voice echoed and wheezed, rising and falling in jerky transition between notes. "And there is no painting imbued with angelic manna for you to draw on here."

Then Mihàil looked down at Beta. Only Asmodeus looked out of his eyes. "You should never have let her stay behind to free the *drangùe*, Little Redstart. Now you will see her die, too."

Beta swallowed. Everything she'd feared was about to come true.

Don't listen to him, flashed András. *He can't take a life. And he can't force Mihàil to take one. He's running out of time.*

So are we, she flashed, well aware that András had sunk to his knees.

His pallor and erratic harmonics told her that his blood loss had crossed into critical. And all of the medical supplies had left with Dr. Armand before she'd blown up the mansion.

In that moment, she knew what she had to do.

To András, she flashed, *He cannot make me take a life either*. Almost simultaneously, she said, "Take me" to Asmodeus.

"No!" The agony in András's voice broke her heart.

Asmodeus chortled. "Harmonics are just brainwaves, Little Redstart," he said, staring into her eyes.

The dark harmonic sparks whirling around them coalesced into a swirling galaxy before diving into her pupils.

This time, when Asmodeus invaded her, she yielded. Instead of a clashing cymbal, a deep reverberation filled her entire being. Her fundamental frequency clicked into sync with his discordant one, like clock gears meshing.

A black veil descended over her vision.

When Beta became aware again, she stood over András. Behind them, Mihàil laid motionless on the muddy ground while Olivia, weeping, stroked his face.

As if from a deep recess inside her mind, Beta watched her hand reach out to lift András's drooping head. Harmonics clashed between them, repelling her fingers from his jaw. Something slithered inside her, up her spine, and out her mouth. A sick glee left a bitter taste in her mouth.

"Now, half-breed," she heard herself say, though her voice had a sibilance that she didn't recognize. "Should I tell you that I knew your mother, hm? Or should I say, how my acolyte knew her?"

A wild light flared in András's gaze. "Don't," he said.

Vicious laughter tore from Beta. "No? You do not want to hear how a Czech refugee raped your mother at my behest?"

András flinched away from her.

She leaned closer, close enough for her heated lips to brush his ear. "Or tell you how I drove her to such despair that she took her own life—but not before drugging your little sisters and pushing them into the Danube?"

Black wings of horror beat at Beta's sanity. The anguish on András's face tore her suffocated spirit. But Asmodeus only chuckled.

"Just think, half-breed. You love my Czech daughter, who tried to kill you once before under my control. "

Beta lifted András's chin with her forefinger. This time, though her touch branded him, he held still.

"You would give your life for her. Ironic that she will be the one to take it, is it not?" A wolfish smile split her face. "Who says fallen Watcher Angels are unable to create symmetry?"

Twenty-Eight

Beta's fingertip burned into the skin of András's jaw, underscoring the malevolent glow in her gaze as she looked down at him.

Or rather, as Asmodeus looked down at him.

It hurt to hear her speak the words about his mother and sisters, her voice warped and grating. But it hurt more to see the woman he loved a mere puppet to the Dark *Irim* inside her.

A tear slipped from his eye. He felt it slide down his face. Asmodeus's gaze brightened when he saw it. Beta lifted her finger to trace its path, the tip sizzling in the moisture.

She lifted her finger to her mouth, a wicked smile curling its corners.

András held her gaze while he spoke, willing Beta to hear him. "My life is yours, Alžběta Čermáková. Nothing changes that."

A crystalline bell chimed. Everything around them halted. Snowflakes, whirling from a chill breeze, hung in the air. Olivia's soft weeping had stopped, tears frozen on her cheeks and her hands cradling Mihàil's head in her lap. In front of him, Beta stared down unblinking.

Next to András, Zophiel clapped her hands together. "Oh, well done, dear boy!" Her sonorous voice instantly soothed the agony in his breast. He felt light enough to fly.

Today his guardian angel was an Amazon, tall and shining with flowing white-blond hair. Large white wings sprang from her back, their barbed feathers a deadly shield. She wore iridescent armor that flowed like liquid silver around her, reforming continuously with her movements. The massive hilt of a silver sword peeked from between her wings.

She bore *Caelistra*, her two-handed sword only unsheathed for angelic battle. Only a few *Elioud* had ever seen the flaming sword. He hoped that he never did.

Zophiel's radiance lit the plane around them for hundreds of meters. The devastation from the battle stood out in sharp contrast against the snow blanketing the mountains. The slow undulation of her wings sent warm air washing over him.

She bent and kissed András's forehead. Around them epic orchestral music swelled, lifting him from his momentary despondence. And then it changed into something quieter, slower, and sadder. He recognized the melody from the Polish woods outside Lublin.

Zophie looked at him, a gentle smile on her face. "I call it 'András's Theme,'" she said, helping him to stand.

She peered at his jaw before touching it. The burn lost its heat. She looked up at him again. "It will leave a scar, I fear."

He nodded, swallowing around a thick throat. "I can live with that."

"Good man," she said. "Now, why have you not flown your redstart, hm?"

She gestured, and the redstart tattooed on his shoulder rose into the air between them.

"I was waiting for the right moment," he said. "But the battle got away from me."

Zophie's eyes blazed an electric blue. She seemed even taller than she had a moment before. "Yes, well, I think now would be the perfect moment to recover what Asmodeus had no right to discard."

András's eyes widened at the hard look on the *Cherub*'s face. Nodding, he sent the redstart toward the spot where the glowing St. Michael medal laid among the still-smoking ruins of the Kastriotis' front hall. The redstart returned a moment later and dropped the medal into his palm before perching on his shoulder, ready to fly again.

Zophiel had disappeared, but András's Theme still lingered in the air, this time with more hopeful notes lifting the melody.

It can be a new theme her voice whispered on the harmonic plane around them. '*The Draka and The Giant.*' *And András, never forget that there is great power in love tempered in suffering.*

The theme trailed gentle harmonic fingers over him. He realized that all of his knife wounds had been stanched and that the bone-crushing exhaustion had lifted to merely tired. He still needed to see Dr. Armand, but for now he could go on.

Beta remained frozen next to him. András lifted her face and kissed her softly.

Then he saw the fingers of her right hand moving out of the corner of his eye. She was tapping her thigh, alternating taps with a sliding movement. He recognized the taps as dots and the slides as dashes in Morse Code.

Beta hadn't been completely subsumed by Asmodeus.

He realized that she'd clipped her karambit to her belt. She wasn't armed.

He slipped the karambit into one hand, pulling her around and against his chest with the other. His harmonics resynced with the plane around them. He felt Beta's chest rise as she inhaled.

She exhaled a hiss as Asmodeus realized that his vessel had been trapped. For the Dark *Irim*, it would have happened between one breath and the next.

"Gomba," András said into her ear, the hooked karambit blade at her throat, "have you forgotten that you said that you'll marry me?"

Beta, her thoughts chaotic and scattered, heard a high tinkling as of glass windchimes far away. Everything stilled, including the Dark *Irim* possessing her. White luminescence flooded the world, throwing it into harsh relief. A warm breeze caressed Beta. Relief flooded her, even if she couldn't move. She had burned, and now cool water bathed her spirit. Order began to knit up the anarchy of her thoughts. The black veil lifted from her vision.

András, however, looked up beyond where Beta's gaze had been aimed. Out of the corner of her eye, she caught a glimpse of quicksilver in the direction that he looked. An ethereal blonde dipped into her line of sight, kissing András on the forehead. Her silver armor flowed and formed around her as if she couldn't be contained inside it.

It must be Zophiel, the guardian angel of the *Elioud*.

Zophiel, archangel of wisdom, understanding, and judgment, who wielded a flaming sword—the one that Beta caught sight of strapped to her back in an intricately filigreed silver sheath embraced by a broad white wing with visible barbs.

In a word, Zophiel inspired awe—especially of the terror kind. If Beta's heart could beat, it would be beating against her ribs like a caged redstart. Next to Zophiel's grandeur and majesty, the ugly darkness of Asmodeus shrank to no consequence.

The guardian angel, taller than András, bent to kiss his forehead. A symphony sounded, resounding from the snow-capped mountains surrounding them. It lifted Beta's spirit, trapped under the heavy burden of dark possession. After a few measures, the music changed to a sweet, tender lullaby that tapped into an aching center that she never knew that she had. It changed again into something dramatic and tense, filled with passion, need, and purpose. But filled mostly with love and respect. It reminded her of those few weeks outside Lublin.

Darling Draka, flashed a mellifluous voice. *Remember, brainwaves are just harmonics. And you, my dear, know very well how to manipulate them. You really should show Asmodeus that you are nobody's plaything, yes?*

The silver-clad angelic warrior disappeared while faint echoes of her last words hung in the air. András turned toward Beta. On his shoulder perched the redstart, the one made from an alloy of the bullets that he'd taken while saving her life another lifetime ago. He bent and kissed her. And her frozen harmonics began to reverberate from the touch of his lips.

She didn't have much time.

She focused on moving just the fingers of her right hand. Quickly she signaled that she wasn't completely under the Dark *Irim*'s control.

András didn't respond. Instead, he slipped her karambit from its clip at her waist before wrapping his arm around her and holding the blade to her neck.

"Gomba," he said into her ear, "have you forgotten that you said that you'll marry me?"

Asmodeus, who'd lain quiescent like a coiled snake inside her, struck.

She bit down on András's forearm. Hard. Not enough to break his skin through his padded jacket, but enough for it to hurt.

He grunted in pain but didn't release her.

Instead, the redstart on his shoulder flew into her face, its tiny beak delivering harmonic shocks all over its surface.

Asmodeus thrashed and snapped. The redstart fluttered around her head, its tiny wings stirring up a harmonic eddy that made her head ache. Her jaws released his forearm.

The redstart landed on her exposed collarbone. Familiar harmonics jolted through Beta's nervous system. She twitched.

Asmodeus stilled for a moment. Though dizzy, Beta read uncertainty in his harmonic signature.

András bent his head close to her ear. "This will hurt me more than it hurts you," he said before snagging the top of her shirt with the hooked blade of the karambit.

Beta felt the sharp tip of the karambit kiss the skin of her collarbone as András's hand moved. The incision stung. Hot blood ran down her skin, steaming in the freezing air.

Hissing, Asmodeus raised Beta's temperature precariously, sealing the cut. She began to shake as though she had a fever. Her teeth chattered.

The redstart returned, flitting so quickly around her head that it was practically invisible. It wove a harmonic web. A moment later the web flared into a brilliant white. Inside this visual cocoon, Beta—and therefore Asmodeus—heard and saw nothing. Beta, though unable to throw off Asmodeus's full authority, regained a bit more control of her own harmonics. She imagined them sinking in his power like a willful child suddenly going limp in a parent's arms.

What are you doing, Little Redstart? droned a nasty voice in her mind. Did it sound weaker?

I am not your redstart, she flashed back. She added a white barb to the words. They left a vivid contrail in her thoughts.

Asmodeus's spirit flinched away from hers. Beta's harmonics rushed into the gap. A moment later, she felt the tip of the karambit blade digging inside of her chest. She shuddered.

Asmodeus shrieked. The harmonic cocoon exploded.

Blinking her streaming eyes, Beta realized that the dark veil that had descended over her vision now resembled a fine screen of black dots.

"Protecting this?" András held a tiny metal disc on the tip of the karambit. "Naughty Petrov hid your consecrated tracker under the port." He grinned. Then he turned serious. "You left your own token on her, Asmodeus, but she belongs to the Archangel Michael, who has entrusted her to me."

András held up the St. Michael medal. A golden ray from the lowering sun, now visible in the clearing sky, struck it and bounced into Beta's eyes. Asmodeus screamed and threw an arm over them. But it was too late. The dark veil had disintegrated.

At once Beta used her harmonics to repeat the melody that she'd heard earlier when Zophiel had manifested next to them.

Asmodeus's harmonic signature, previously thickly corded with minute spikes that burrowed into his victim's spirits, decomposed into the fragile strands of his fundamental frequency. Beta hummed the melody, stretching her fingers before pouring all of her love, regret, hope, sorrow, and joy into it until it was entirely her own composition. She let it swell and carry her spirit. Then she narrowed her eyes, concentrating on compelling the last of Asmodeus's discordant harmonics from her very pores.

Though Asmodeus fought, snarling and clawing and biting her, Beta exhaled and, bolstered with András's harmonics, rolled with the dark vibrations as Asmodeus expended the last of his energy. After he subsided, she conducted the Dark *Irim*'s harmonics into her own, taking some of the spiked chords and braiding them into her signature.

Harmonics are just brainwaves, Asmodeus, she flashed. *And I refuse to think about you anymore.*

What remained of the Dark *Irim*'s harmonics exploded into an infinite number of dark sparks inside her. Beta exhaled them into a dark penumbra. She raised her hand and dropped it, sending a harmonic tidal wave over what was left of Asmodeus. His spirit was scattered far on the harmonic plane. Beta's own spirit soared, finally free of the Dark *Irim*'s malign influence.

Triumph filled her. She held out an open hand.

"May I have my medal back?" she asked András.

Beta stood before him, scratched, bitten, and bloody from her final fight with Asmodeus, pride shining on her face and her hand raised in an expectant manner.

András grabbed her and kissed her instead.

She melted against him. He didn't have to open his eyes to see their nimbuses meet and flare or to see how their individual angelic light melded. He plunged his tongue into her mouth, inhaling the scent and taste of her as if he'd been starving and dying of thirst in a wide desert until this moment. Wrapping his arms around her, he pressed her against his chest.

Sweet Zophiel! She felt *so good, so right* there.

This, this possession by Asmodeus, was never happening again. He'd do whatever it took to keep Asmodeus a harmonic league from Beta.

And, clearly, she would too.

When he read the drastic changes in her harmonic signature, András wasn't surprised. Where Beta's fundamental frequency had been unstable and chaotic before, it had become steady and secure. She'd cleverly incorporated some of her angelic progenitor's dissonance into her harmonics and made it her own.

Not unlike Zophiel. So beautiful, yet so incredibly tough and resilient.

Beta was nothing short of angelic. András was every bit in awe of her as he'd ever been of his sublime guardian angel.

Their harmonics synced as they kissed, winding tighter. Spicules in the dark chords that she'd claimed from Asmodeus latched onto his own chords, binding them in a way that they could never have been without those shared notes of pain, sorrow, and despair.

As if understanding this new integration—or perhaps responsible for it—Beta flashed, *I am never letting you go, Spratek.*

In response, András hummed his theme, pulling Beta's harmonics into the melody.

She hummed, catching the tune and expanding upon it.

Her variation felt familiar. She'd hummed it just before vanquishing Asmodeus. For a breathless moment, the music elevated András until everything around him faded, and he saw the vast reaches of the dark and starry Heavens around them.

And then she exhaled and the vision vanished.

Reluctantly, he pulled back from her, slipping his hands on either side of her face, and kissed the tip of her nose. It was cold. She shivered.

It was time to leave.

He held her gaze. Her dark-gray eyes gleamed with vitality despite the frigid temperature and the destruction around them. "Ready?"

She nodded.

"First, let me put this back on you." He held up her St. Michael medal, its blessing a faint luminosity in the waning daylight.

Holding her hair away from her neck, Beta turned in his arms. András held each end of the broken chain that held the tiny disc and brought them around her throat. He held them close while he directed the redstart to donate some of its alloy to fastening the two ends of the chain together. When it finished its repair work, the redstart settled back on his shoulder.

He kissed the back of her neck. "There, Gomba. Better than ever."

She turned back to face him.

"Are you forgetting something?" she asked, her eyes narrowed.

It was such a familiar—and beloved—expression that András nearly kissed her again.

Instead, he grinned. "Of course not. Here."

He handed her the karambit, which she held as if an extension of her hand. Which it was. A dragon's claw for a dragon.

They turned to find Olivia on her knees, helping a scowling Mihàil to sit upright.

By tacit agreement, they set off for the *drangùe* and his *zonjë*. The wellbeing that had carried András through the final confrontation with the Dark *Irim* and the resulting euphoria from his defeat had faded, and now his anvil-like feet threatened to bog down in the freezing mud.

Beta slipped her hand into his. Soothing harmonic fingers massaged the cramps in his calves. He squeezed her fingers in silent thanks.

When they got to the prime *Elioud* couple, Beta dropped András's hand and went to help Olivia to her feet. András gripped his commander's hand and tugged him to standing. The effort made András dizzy. For his part, Mihàil swayed dangerously.

"Sitrep," said the *drangùe* in a voice rough with more than fatigue.

If András knew the demi-angel who'd been like a father to him, Mihàil's anger and disgust were self-directed.

Before András could answer, the grumbling sound of engines disturbed the harmonic plane beyond their eyesight, sharp as it was. They waited to see whether it was friend or foe who approached from the direction of Fushë-Arrëz.

It was Ryan driving a battered pickup clearly commandeered from a local farmer. In the front seat rode Pjetër. As they got closer, András recognized the combat shotgun that Mihàil's loyal retainer carried across his chest. The man's expression said that he was fully prepared—and capable—of using it.

"The cavalry is here," said Olivia in a faint voice. When Mihàil twisted as if to go back to her, she said, "I'm fine, I'm fine. Beta won't let me fall."

Ryan drove the pickup on the berm, navigating deftly around bullet-pocked vehicles and what was left of disintegrating *bogomili*. Once their spiritual over-lord had been scattered like so much harmonic ash, his power over them severed, their bodies had decayed rapidly.

Behind the pickup came Olivia's Range Rover, driven by Miles. In the seat next to him sat Dr. Armand.

Ryan parked the pickup and jumped from the driver's seat. He sprinted the short distance to where they stood.

"Sir," he said as he halted in front of Mihàil. He refrained from saluting; the *Elioud* commander had made it clear that a respectful nod was enough.

"Helsing," said the *drangùe* through a tight jaw. "Sitrep."

András knew without reading the older *Elioud*'s harmonics that his unyielding duty to his people warred with his almost preternatural devotion to his mate.

"No one died," said Helsing, his voice grim. "But more than a few are suffering from *daemonic*-induced psychosis, and about a dozen sustained injuries, two serious. I called in a team from Shkodër to handle triage and transportation to the hospital there."

"Good." Mihàil dipped his chin sharply. "Now take the *zonjë* to shelter before reporting back here."

While they spoke, Miles and Dr. Armand had begun looking for surviving Kastrioti security personnel. Beta stepped aside as Ryan picked Olivia up. She, András, and Mihàil watched as their security chief slid the heavily pregnant *Elioud* into the passenger seat and then ran to the driver's side before driving away in a controlled hurry.

At last, alone with his commander and his fiancée, András turned and said, "Casualties still being determined, my lord. But Asmodeus has been turned into a mote in St. Michael's eye. And Alžběta Čermáková has agreed to marry me."

Twenty-Nine

In the end, Miles and Dr. Armand found five gravely wounded Kastrioti security members, and one who died before they could transport him. Ryan had driven Olivia to their local Fushë-Arrëz facility where her employees transformed wild-harvested herbs into a myriad of culinary and spa products. All of the local injured people as well as the wounded Kastrioti team members would be treated there by Dr. Armand until they could be transported to Shkodër.

When Beta arrived an hour later, she found her friend wearing a borrowed dress and apron, her blond hair pulled back into a loose ponytail, directing the able-bodied in putting the wounded on cots in their large storeroom. Pjetër, also wearing an apron over his still-impeccable suit, managed the volunteers setting up the main room as a cafeteria. In the small kitchen, Adriana led a couple of volunteers preparing dishes. Women from the town streamed through the entry door bearing pots and casseroles filled with hot food. Cases of bottled water reached the ceiling near the long folding table that had been set up in one corner of the room. Everyone not already using both hands on some task held a mug of hot tea or coffee. They all looked somber. No one spoke except when necessary and then only in low voices.

A woman pressed a steaming cup of *salep*—a rich, hot Albanian drink made from the flour of wild orchid tubers, milk, and sugar—into Beta's hands as she stood waiting for Olivia to make her way to her. The whole scene, coming after the nightmare at Olivia's home, moved Beta in a way that she couldn't have foreseen. Olivia had loved her home and filled it with valuable material possessions, but it was clear that the people of Fushë-Arrëz meant more to her than the stone mansion that she'd lost. She'd gotten into her Range Rover and driven away without looking back.

Beta wanted that. A craving for home and hearth hit her so hard it weakened her knees. She sipped at the *salep* to hide her sudden desire and was surprised when the sweet, rich drink made her feel better immediately.

"Sugar helps after a drop in adrenaline," said Olivia next to her.

She held up a ceramic mug with the Albanian words *E ka në gjak*, or *It's in the blood*, printed over a nosegay of tiny purple flowers surrounded by blades of silver-green leaves that she'd told Beta came from the *salvia officinalis*, or sage plant, from which Wise Herb, her company name, had been derived. Albania was the world's top exporter of the culinary and medicinal plant.

Olivia went on. "This is my third cup. Dr. Armand's got his eagle eyes on me, but I'm not sitting down until all the injured are taken care of."

"I want to help." Beta's voice came out rough. She cleared her throat. "Please."

Olivia laid a hand on her forearm. "I know you do, *milovaná*." *Beloved*. Olivia had called her *beloved*. "It would help me a lot if you would sit with the injured Kastrioti personnel."

She lifted her chin toward the far corner where a door led to the storeroom.

"Not all of them are Albanian. Mihàil recruits from all over the continent. Only those who have already served the *Elioud* cause in an exemplary manner are invited to audition for estate security. There's a young Czech recruit in there who hadn't even earned a spot on the team yet."

"Will you sit down sooner if I do?" asked Beta, studying her friend with a side glance.

Olivia seemed strangely energized from her role, but there was something odd about her harmonics.

She laughed. "Yes, Beta, I'll sit down with you once I check with Pjetër. He's making a huge pot of *lakra me mish*. It's a spicy beef and cabbage stew that I've got a craving for. Would you like some, too? I asked him to put in extra chili flakes. I suspect that a *draka* will appreciate the added heat." She smiled.

Beta fingered the St. Michael medal lying over her sweater. It warmed to her touch like encouragement. "It *has* been a few hours since I ate one of those tasteless dust packs that you call redimeals in the sniper loft." Her stomach grumbled to underscore her words.

Olivia laughed again, this time the sound pealing, and slipped her arm through Beta's. Beta felt the harmonics in the room lighten and noticed the relief washing over the faces of the townsfolk. Soft, soothing music resonated in the warehouse. It was amazingly rich and full, as if the music inhabited the air around them.

As they walked toward the storeroom, Beta surveyed their surroundings. She didn't see speakers, certainly not anything capable of such complex stereo sound.

"It's a mesh nanospeaker system," said Olivia, reading her curiosity. "I designed it myself using the nanotech that Miró developed a few years ago. You've probably sensed András's personal nano-origami system. We use it to monitor vitals, communicate securely, and store excess heat as electricity in micro lithium batteries in our clothing and boots. It's flexible, adaptable—in short, very powerful—tech in our arsenal."

They'd reached the storeroom by the time Olivia finished speaking. Inside the long room wooden shelves filled with plastic bins of dried herbs lined the walls. Between the long walls, two rows of cots had been lined up for the ten wounded whose injuries could either be treated by Dr. Armand or could wait until they could be transported to Shkodër. Several comfortable chairs had been dragged from the breakroom and the visitors' lounge. Olivia led Beta to one in the far corner near a young man lying with his eyes open staring at the ceiling.

"This is Jan," she said, smiling at him when he looked at her. "He lost his hearing during the combat this afternoon. Fortunately, Mihàil developed new nano earbuds for our team members that also protect against the worst of the battle noise. Dr. Armand thinks Jan will get his hearing back in a couple of days. He just needs to rest and avoid loud sounds. Now, let me go get some of that *lakra me mish* for us."

"I will get it. You sit," said Beta.

Olivia shook her head. "No, thank you. I can't sit yet." This time, when she smiled, it was a little lopsided. "Nerves, I guess. Don't feel bad, Beta. You did more. You need the rest. I'm pregnant, not traumatized or disabled. I can handle a few bowls of stew."

Beta sat down, scowling, and crossed her arms. Jan had only glanced at her and then returned to staring at the ceiling. If he couldn't hear anything, what was Beta supposed to do, Czech or no Czech? Olivia clearly wanted to humor Beta rather than give her something to do.

Before she got too far down that road of thought, she sensed András entering the warehouse. Her neck tingled. He searched for her. Closing her eyes, she imagined him, his harmonics a vivid whorl around his infrared signature. When he found her, their harmonic bond activated, sending a strong current through her that was part desire, part recognition, and pure relief.

She was complete now. Her body relaxed of its own accord in the chair.

Focusing, Beta identified András's voice among the bustling activity in the other room. He'd started toward her, but every few meters someone would stop him, first to press a cup of something hot into his hand, or to clasp his shoulder, or, in the case of an older woman by her signature, to hold her hands up until he bent so that she could grasp his face with both and kiss him several times.

She waited patiently. He might not be a Kastrioti, but the people in Fushë-Arrëz regarded him as a prince nonetheless. A prince who would defend them with his life. Deferring to their gratitude was a price she must pay for loving András. He would find her when he had fulfilled his duty to them.

Olivia returned, her harmonics oddly jittery as though anxiety or excitement roiled her. But when Beta looked at her friend, her serene face belied whatever deep emotion stirred her.

The *zonjë* stopped next to Beta's chair.

"Here you are," she said, holding out a bowl of stew. In her other hand she had a mug with a spoon inserted.

Beta accepted the bowl. Olivia had stuck a spoon into it as well. She sniffed the beef and cabbage. Spicy steam wafted into her sensitive nostrils, making her eyes water. Extra chili flakes, indeed.

She took a careful bite as Olivia sat in the chair next to hers. It was good.

Without looking at her friend, she said, "You are either anxious for Mihàil to return or you are in labor."

"Can it be both?" asked Olivia, a brief smile lifting the corners of her mouth. She spooned some of the stew and ate it.

Beta said nothing. They ate in companionable silence until Olivia, sighing, let her spoon drop into the mug with a soft *chink*.

"That was very good, but I can't eat any more." She glanced over at Beta. "Pretty soon, I think, eating will be a bad idea. I've learned that laboring women often vomit, either from the pain of transition or hormonal shifts. I've already noticed that the contractions strengthened from dehydration."

"So drink more," said Beta, finishing her own stew.

Sleepiness descended. She set the empty bowl on the floor so that she wouldn't drop it.

"Hm," said Olivia. She set her mug on the floor beside her. "I've been trying to get more fluids to slow things down since Ryan dropped me off here. But Adriana just told me that spicy foods and exertion speed things along. I'm just hoping that the more gravely injured have been transported before everyone's focus shifts to me."

"When will Dr. Armand return?" asked Beta, surveying the injured lying quietly around them. Some had visible wounds, though they'd been treated enough to stop the bleeding, and IVs. More than half had clearly been given sedatives.

"Not long. Less than hour, if Miles's update is accurate."

Beta narrowed her eyes. "Should it be?"

Olivia nodded. "Yes." She looked over at Beta. "András will be here any moment. He passed the last of the adoring gauntlet."

"I can wait." Beta held her friend's gaze. "I am not going anywhere."

Olivia searched her gaze a moment, her clear blue-gray eyes far wiser than her years explained. "Good. Because if Asmodeus can't dislodge you from András, I'd say you're stuck with the big guy."

"Of course she is," said András, appearing behind them still wearing his battlefield clothes. His bruised face, on the other hand, had already turned purple-green as it healed.

Warmth filled Beta at this sign of eagerness. He bent his head briefly toward Olivia, who nodded once, before kissing Beta.

Olivia stood, her belly leading the way. "Well, that's my cue to leave. András, someone will bring you food and drink. Just stay there so we can find you."

"You won't find me anywhere else," he said, his gaze on Beta.

After Olivia left, he sat down, taking Beta's hand and playing with her fingers.

Beta swallowed. Time to own up.

"I am sorry for improvising with Olivia. It clearly was a mistake."

András said nothing for a moment before slipping his long, elegant fingers between her much smaller ones. He raised her hand and kissed it.

Then he cupped her cheek with his free hand, his thumb brushing over her cheekbone. A shiver stole down Beta's spine. She pressed her face into his palm.

"There is nothing to apologize for," he said at last, his voice gruff. "No plan survives contact with the enemy. You know that."

"But you ordered me to take Olivia to the coast," she said, persisting.

They needed to clear the air between them, and now, if they were going to marry on the right footing.

"No plan survives contact with a superior with different ideas," he said. "Besides, the Archangel writes straight with crooked letters."

Beta frowned. That didn't make any sense. "What?"

András dropped his hand from her face and leaned forward, tucking her hand into his chest as he did. His dark-blue gaze captured hers.

"I would never have found that micro tracker on you as long as you wore your medal."

"Are you saying that the Archangel not only left the micro tracker in me, he blocked its presence with his own medal?" Skepticism made her voice sharp.

"Are you saying that you would never have taken that medal off?" he countered.

Beta squirmed. She still didn't understand, but she was certain that she would have eventually removed the Archangel's gift, feeling unworthy of its blessing and forgetting how he'd been a light in the darkness when she'd been all alone.

"No," she said, slowly shaking her head as she answered András. "You are saying that the Archangel wanted the tracker to lead Asmodeus to me."

"You cannot outrun who you are," he said, still holding her gaze. "You had to face Asmodeus. Either you removed your medal, in which case you'd chosen to reject me and your place with faithful *Elioud*, or the Dark *Irim* removed it in an effort to claim you."

"In which case, we would face him together."

He nodded. "As mated alpha wolves, remember? Alpha wolves don't have commands. They have a mystical bond, moving in tandem to take down their prey."

Beta pulled her gaze down. She wanted to slip her karambit into her hand and work its mechanism. Instead, she breathed deeply, steadying her harmonics. She felt András's support, but he didn't soothe her. On the contrary, he waited patiently.

"I integrated some of the Dark *Irim*'s harmonics into mine," she whispered at last around the catch in her throat.

"I know, right?"

Hearing the humor in András's voice, Beta looked up, startled. He was grinning, dimples notching his cheeks. The bruise from Asmodeus's blow had faded a lot while they talked, and he looked almost himself again.

"What?" she asked, bewildered.

This whole conversation had been unpredictable and confusing. She did not do well with unpredictable. In the field, yes. That had its own set of rules. Social interactions? Not so much, especially between her and András. It was going to take a lot of practice on her part. And a lot of patience on his.

"Leave it to you, Gomba, to demonstrate the wisdom of an angel," he said.

When she still looked confused, he relented.

"When we were in Lublin, Zophiel came to me. She showed me how she absorbs a lot of inharmonious energy from her wards. Namely, me." He grinned again. "It's part of her superpower. It's like the Archangel writing straight with crooked letters. Understand now?"

Beta nodded. She supposed that she did. But she'd have to turn this insight over later along with all of the day's events.

Adriana entered the storeroom with a tray that held two bowls of stew, a loaf of fresh bread, flatware, napkins, and steaming mugs of coffee. She came over and handed the tray to András, who took it with obvious relish. His stomach grumbled. They laughed.

"This stew smells unbelievably delicious," he said, aiming a flirtatious look at the older cook. "But two bowls of your cooking will hardly be enough."

Adriana clearly knew him because she rolled her eyes.

"One of those bowls is for him, *Arush*," she said, gesturing to Jan, who'd sat up and swiveled on his cot to face them with a bright gaze. "You will have to bring your empty bowl back to the kitchen for more. I have too much to do to wait on you hand and sole. And bring all the empty dishes to the kitchen. Do *not* leave them in here for me to gather."

She said this last bit with a pointed look at András, whose face flushed in guilt.

"*Bear*?" asked Beta, translating the Albanian endearment as Adriana handed one of the mugs to Jan.

She picked up the other mug and sipped. Hot, sweet, and black. She took another sip.

"It's her nickname for me," said András, tearing a hunk of bread and dipping it into the stew.

Adriana turned back to them.

"It is what we call little children. Little children with big appetites," she said, lifting the second bowl from the tray and handing it to Jan, who'd perked up after slurping half of the coffee in his mug. "Now, *zonjë ime*, please to come with me. My mistress has gone to her office where there is a couch. She says that it is time and asks for you at her side. You know of what I speak?"

Beta's heart tapped in sudden recognition. Her brief sleepiness fled. She nodded, then finished the rest of András's coffee. She held the empty cup out to the older woman.

"Please bring *Arush* some more coffee." After Adriana nodded and took the cup, Beta looked at András, who'd stopped shoveling stew into his maw and watched them with an alert gleam in his eyes. "Olivia is in labor."

She felt his gaze on them as she and Adriana left the storeroom. Adriana led her through the maze of long benches where workers processed wild-harvested herbs and packaged them for wholesale distribution. This evening, they doubled as food bars where townsfolk and Kastrioti employees stood to eat or relaxed on stools while sipping coffee or tea and chatting with their neighbors, the afternoon's terror already receding. Except for Mihàil, Ryan, and Miles, everyone needing food and aid had gathered inside the warm building. Since Beta had arrived, the somber mood had lifted. Somehow, the noise level never rose above the soft music still resonating around them.

The management office where Olivia lay on a comfortable leather sofa, her head resting on a plump rolled arm, was at the front of the facility through a short hallway off the main room. It would be a quiet corner, but Beta realized as she stepped inside that Olivia had dampened the harmonics even more so that no sounds from outside reached her.

And no sounds from the office would escape.

The *zonjë* glanced back as Beta came in. Even in the dim light, her face gleamed with a sheen of sweat. Adriana, remaining outside of the office, pulled the door shut behind Beta with a soft *snick*.

Beta crossed over to the sofa and knelt.

Olivia smiled briefly at her. She smoothed one restless palm over the seatback above her and then shifted into a sitting position. When she made to stand, Beta rose with her, steadying her. The front of her dress had a large dark wet stain. Beta's nose said it wasn't urine.

"I tried to hold off as long as I could, but I'm afraid the extra chili flakes in the *lakra me mish* have worked their magic." Pain threaded Olivia's voice and vibrated through her harmonics. "Has Dr. Armand returned?"

"Yes, *zonjë ime*," said Beta, taking Olivia's hand. "He and Miles are eating some food now before taking the remaining injured to the hospital."

Olivia groaned, hunching over as a powerful contraction hit her. A moment later, she turned and vomited, splattering the carpet beneath them.

When she stood upright again, sweat drenched her pale face. "Please send him to me. I'm not sure I can make it to Shkodër now."

THIRTY

*B*ring *Dr. Armand,* flashed Beta to András as she helped Olivia to sit in one of the two armchairs facing the large desk on the other side of the room.

To Olivia, she said, "I will stay with you until Dr. Armand comes. I know nothing about childbirth. I am no good to you now."

She strode to the credenza where Adriana had left bottled water, a pot of herbal tea, a bowl of ice, and a stack of clean kitchen towels. She brought one of the water bottles to Olivia, who rinsed her mouth and spat into the clean towel Beta handed her before sipping a little.

Olivia raised a flushed face as she handed the soiled towel back to Beta. "My mom said that her labors were fast. I just never imagined how fast. Or painful."

Groaning as another contraction hit her, she curled over, her hands clutching the chair's armrests. Beta looked at her watch. Two minutes between contractions. Her internal clock had timed it accurately.

The office door opened. Dr. Armand came in, András trailing. He shot Beta a concerned look.

What is wrong? András glanced around the office, his gaze sharp. *I smell vomit.*

Her contractions are very strong. Dr. Armand will tell us if throwing up is normal.

The doctor had gone directly to Olivia, who answered questions for him as he checked her pulse, pupils, and temperature. András came to stand next to Beta. His presence alone steadied her, but his harmonics lent her a bulwark upon which to lean. Armed combat made her less nervous than the visceral pain emanating from the other woman.

Another contraction doubled Olivia over. Again, two minutes. Surely, they didn't come so quickly so soon?

They waited what seemed like forever but was in reality only a minute for the contraction to peak and ease. Olivia panted a little through it.

Dr. Armand addressed all of them.

"The *zonjë*'s labor is much faster than the typical first-time mother," he said. "She is very fit. Today's activity plus her dehydration caused her early-stage contractions to move the baby down enough that her water broke. I will examine her, but she has already transitioned to active labor as evidenced by her vomiting and the strength and length of her contractions."

Olivia's eyes widened. "That *is* fast. My water only broke half an hour ago."

"Yes." Dr. Armand nodded. "I advise against transporting you to the hospital. You're very healthy and low risk. And I have everything I need even if an emergency arises, which we knew was a possibility. You'll be more comfortable here than in a moving vehicle driving through these twisting mountain roads. And it has started to snow again." He paused. "In addition, moving you will likely speed your labor further."

"What about the injured waiting for transport?" asked Olivia, her eyes hard. "You will not prioritize me over them."

It was a command.

Dr. Armand didn't seem bothered by it. "They're all stable, *zonjë ime*. I'd already planned to advise you to wait until morning to move them."

Olivia nodded.

"How long?" asked András, his gaze narrowed in a calculating manner.

The Swiss doctor shrugged. "My guess? Five or six hours total."

On cue, Olivia clenched the armrests and her teeth, holding her breath. No one said anything until the contraction ended. Then Dr. Armand asked András to carry Olivia to the sofa where he examined her. A soft mewl of pain escaped Olivia as he did.

They waited for his conclusions, Beta fingering the hilt of her karambit while András stood with the alertness of a panther.

Dr. Armand stood, removing his nitrile gloves and tossing them into a nearby waste can.

"Four centimeters and eighty percent effaced. Contractions are sixty seconds and three to five minutes apart," he said. "I will check her again in half an hour."

Beta didn't know what 'effaced' meant, but as a measure of labor progress, eighty percent sounded advanced.

Dr. Armand directed his next words to Olivia. "*Zonjë ime*, please remember what we discussed. Uterine contractions can be managed. Move about freely, and don't tense any of your other muscles, as you did just now when gripping the armrests. Of course, the more relaxed you are, the more your body can focus on its job to deliver this baby."

He paused, letting Olivia absorb his words. "Remember: breathe. Get comfortable. Massage or a lukewarm shower can help. It is too late for an epidural even if we were at the hospital, but I can inject you with Demerol to take the edge off for a little while, if you prefer."

"Until it's time to push?" Olivia laughed. It sounded shaky. "And even then, it doesn't sound very effective."

Dr. Armand shook his head. "It's not."

"Then no thank you," she said, sitting up and swinging her feet around to the floor. "I'd rather not buy myself a little chemical relief at the risk of exposing my baby to something she doesn't need."

She? Beta caught András's equally curious gaze.

"Beta, you know the best way to learn about childbirth?" Now Olivia sounded a little breathless. "Help a friend in labor. I wish I had."

She began to lever herself to her feet. András practically leapt to support her.

Beta narrowed her eyes. Perhaps he had. There was a lot she still didn't understand about the *Elioud* control of harmonics.

Olivia smiled up at him. Another contraction caught her, twisting the smile, but she didn't tighten her grip on his forearm. Instead, she sighed, letting her palms lay flat as she flexed her fingertips. Beta swore that the pain thrumming through Olivia's body flowed down her arms and through her hands, pulsing into the warm air.

She'd heard the unspoken plea in Olivia's statement.

"I will stay," she said, as though deciding for herself. "It is much quieter in here than out there. Besides, Jan is not much for conversation."

She walked over and took Olivia's hand, sending soothing harmonics through their clasped fingers and along the other's woman's back. Olivia squeezed her hand in gratitude. They began to pace, navigating the open space between the sofa and the armchairs in front of the desk.

During Olivia's next contraction, Dr. Armand slipped from the room to retrieve some medical supplies from the van parked outside that they'd used as an ambulance earlier. She had three more contractions in the span of time it took him to return. He seemed impervious to Olivia's pain, setting out his medical tools on a clean kitchen towel in the middle of her desk before leaving to check on his other patients.

András found supplies in Olivia's private washroom and cleaned the carpet as they paced. Then he left and returned with a fresh pot of herbal tea, a full bowl of ice chips, and coffee and pastries for Beta. He even found a pair of slippers embroidered with the Kastrioti eagle somewhere for Olivia.

He moved around them soundlessly, almost invisibly, a lodestar to their peripatetic wandering around the office, which was thankfully half again as large as the main production room where a good number of the village still gathered, by now aware that their lady labored. He'd served his lady with efficiency and care, even though he must have been exhausted from their long day.

A long day that was only going to get longer.

At first, Olivia chattered about her plans for Wise Herb between contractions, but it was obvious that it became a struggle to speak after another twenty minutes. Eventually, she muttered as she walked, going completely silent during a contraction as she focused on shunting the pain outside herself. Her damper on the harmonics in the room began to waver.

At that point, Dr. Armand washed his hands before checking Olivia and announcing cryptically that labor was progressing. Then he asked Beta if she had the energy to keep Olivia company so that he could eat and steal a catnap in the breakroom before it was time to deliver the baby. When Beta hesitated, he assured her that unless Olivia insisted that she had to push, nothing much more interesting or challenging would happen for several hours.

Olivia, alert for the moment, turned to her and said, "I trust you, Beta."

Beta nodded at the doctor then and resumed her post next to her friend's side as Dr. Armand left for his much-needed respite as the only doctor.

Where is Mihàil? Beta flashed András, who'd slipped from the office to give Olivia freedom to disrobe if she chose. *You have been here more than an hour.*

He and Ryan just arrived. They scoured the estate and drove north to Fierzë. It had to be done before the snow covered the evidence of the assault.

Good. Olivia needs him.

Beta began to hum the melody that she'd composed at the end of her encounter with Asmodeus. She felt Olivia's harmonics shift and sync with hers, and she took some of the jagged throbbing into her own harmonics, staggering a little at the intensity of the pain.

Almost as soon as she'd started, however, Mihàil appeared inside the office next to Olivia. The *drangùe* looked awful. Hollows darkened his blue eyes. Rough stubble bristled on his cheeks. His clothes, torn and dirty, reeked of gunpowder and blood.

As long as the day had been, only a few short hours ago the powerful *Elioud* warrior had been possessed by a Dark *Irim*—perhaps for days.

But the ferocity and love shining in his gaze belied any fatigue or lingering damage from hosting Asmodeus. Instead, the *drangùe* looked like the last few hours had only hardened his considerable resolve to protect and defend his wife.

Mihàil didn't say anything or touch Olivia. Instead, he watched as she and Beta made another circuit around the room, weaving around the armchairs and the coffee table in front of the sofa. Olivia, lost in a contraction, seemed unaware of him. When the contraction ended, however, she lifted her gaze to her husband's.

"*Dashuria ime,*" she said on an exhale that was almost a sob. Her relief at seeing her husband resonated in the thick atmosphere of the room.

Beta stepped back as Olivia stepped into Mihàil's arms. She wished that she knew how to speed her harmonics to disappear, but in reality, her own skill at moving unobtrusively paired with the couple's reunion meant that they never looked her way as she padded out of the office.

András sat in the main room on a stool next to one of the long work benches that had been used as dining tables earlier. Next to him sat Pjetër, and across from them sat Miles and Ryan. All were eating.

Beta came and squeezed onto András's lap, reaching for his drinking glass, which apparently contained beer. She drained the glass while all of the men watched in silence, then set it down with a decided *thunk* before wiping the back of her hand over her mouth.

She smiled at all of them.

"Thirsty?" asked András mildly. He wrapped one arm around her waist, shifting her so that she sat more firmly on his thigh.

"Not anymore," she said. "The next one I will drink because I want to taste it, however."

Everyone laughed, including the reserved Pjetër, who passed his glass down to András while continuing to eat. His neatly folded apron laid on the table next to him.

"How would you feel about toasting our nuptials?" asked András before taking a bite of something inside a flaky crust.

He lifted his chin in the direction of Adriana, who'd come out from the kitchen and surveyed those still eating and drinking. The rest of the villagers had either gone home or curled up where they could: the floor, one of the workbenches, or the sofa from the breakroom. Adriana, who'd been on her feet all day, seemed indefatigable. She nodded, wiping her hands on her apron, and returned to the small kitchen.

Beta waited until the cook had disappeared before answering. Then she plucked what was left of the savory pastry from András fingers and plopped it into her mouth.

Ryan, who'd watched, nodded toward them. "Like the legendary crocodile bird, she is. You know, the little Egyptian plover said to clean the teeth and gullet of the crocodile, who opens its jaws in gratitude." He took a bite of food.

András picked up his beer and raised it. "To my redstart, who braved the teeth of the devil Asmodeus and found them not so sharp."

He took a drink before turning and kissing her. Ryan whooped. Miles and Pjetër smiled.

"I've seen that wicked little karambit she twirls around," said Miles, setting his fork and knife onto his plate and picking up his beer. "If I were a *bogomili*, I'd run from her. Fast."

He winked at her before finishing his beer.

Beta blushed. She'd never blushed before in her life. But somehow it felt good to be sitting here with these men laughing and joking in the aftermath of their battle. Like she'd become a part of something. A family maybe.

Adriana returned carrying a tray with a plate of food and a glass of beer. She set the plate in front of András and the beer in front of Pjetër. Ryan and Miles began discussing their similar American military background while Pjetër took a long swallow of his fresh beer, gifting Beta and András a little privacy with their casual inattention.

Beta snagged what looked like an Italian *arancini* from the plate. Holding it up in front of her, she asked, "Did you tell Adriana to bring these for me?"

"The *qifqi*? Yes." His voice rumbled in his chest.

He popped an entire *qifqi* into his mouth and chewed.

"And the beer for Pjetër?"

He nodded.

The *Elioud* could send private messages to humans as well. Good to know.

"As for your question, I will toast our impending nuptials here and now if you can have Adriana bring me another beer."

"Done."

Adriana, who'd been clearing empty dishes from the workbenches and stacking them on her tray, acknowledged András with a tilt of her head and left.

András shifted Beta's weight to the side as he pushed his stool from the workbench, his arm around her waist steadying her. He looked at her. His face had almost completely healed from the devastating blow that Asmodeus had delivered. A dumpling rose in Beta's throat as she recalled seeing his swollen and bruised cheek after Asmodeus had compelled her to come to him.

"What I was asking, however, Gomba, is whether you're set on a big wedding with a flouncy white gown and meters of fresh flowers," he asked, searching her gaze with his deep blue one. "Or whether I can find the local priest and have him marry us now."

"Now?" she asked, dumbstruck.

Adriana arrived at that moment and set a beer next to Beta's hand.

She ignored it. András regarded her with a stillness that made her suddenly conscious of everything and everyone around them. She didn't need a beer; she needed whiskey.

"Perhaps not right now, but after Olivia has the baby," said András. "Would you like a Trebitsch while you think it over?" He grinned, dimples making him look impossibly young.

Beta's qualms fled. This man knew her. Really *knew* her.

"No, Spratek," she said. "I do *not* need to think it over."

She paused dramatically while she flashed a message to Adriana, not at all certain that it would work.

After several long moments in which his harmonics began to tighten in worry, Beta picked up her beer, stood, and stepped away from the workbench.

"Attention!" She pitched her voice so that it rang through the room even though she didn't raise it.

Everyone who wasn't sleeping sat up and looked at her. András studied her with a thoughtful gaze. Ryan leaned back in his chair, his arms crossed over his chest while Miles watched with a smile curling the corners of his mouth and eyes. Even Pjetër, who'd stood and gathered the empty dishes on their workbench, paused and waited. Adriana appeared with a tray of filled beer glasses and began handing them to everyone who waited to hear Beta's announcement. Once everyone had a glass, including Adriana, Beta addressed them.

"In the Czech Republic, whenever one drinks a toast to celebrate, it is crucial to hold the gaze of those drinking with you," she said, taking the time to look at each one, holding each gaze. She stared at András last. "This is so that you will not have seven years of doom. Or bad sex."

There was a little bit of laughing and cheering at her words. Ryan whistled.

Beta refused to flush or cross her arms. Crossed arms spoiled one's luck.

She raised her glass. "To *Zonja Jonë* and the *drangùe*. May their happiness be multiplied a thousandfold and their family increase in proportion."

Now the cheers broke out in earnest. Ryan shouted, "Hoo-ah!" while Miles yelled, "Oo-rah!"

"And to András, whom I have agreed to marry."

The room fell silent. All Beta could see was András's glittering eyes.

She raised her glass again. "To the man I want by my side, whether it is on the battlefield or the bedroom or giving birth to our children. I will marry you as soon as it can be arranged with the priest."

This time, everyone raised their glasses, even the sleepy ones who'd awakened enough to find any available container and ask someone else to share their beer.

She looked around the room again, touching every gaze with her own. "And I want you all there to witness. *Na ex!*" *Bottoms up!*

Beta drained the beer from her glass. When she'd finished, András stood next to her. Wrapping his arms around her, he kissed her to the raucous cheers of the room.

Thirty-One

Stasia and Willem had nearly reached the French border before Miles called with the news that the Kastrioti estate was under attack. They'd made it to within 75 kilometers of the original *First Book of Enoch*, the text delivered to Enoch himself from the Watcher Angels. The document containing detailed descriptions of the illicit technology that the rebellious *Irim* had shared with humanity—and not a few angelic abilities with their progeny.

Stasia had synced her phone via BlueTooth to the VW Jetta's sound system so that Willem could hear what Miles had to say. Willem's harmonics, already taut with adrenaline and excitement, thrummed at Miles's news, but he said nothing. Which was a good thing because the tires rhythmically hit striations in the asphalt. Belgian drivers had complained for years about the noisy highway.

"Should we abandon our search for the *Codex* then?" asked Stasia, looking over her shoulder to move into the center lane over the viaduct in preparation for exiting. "Are there any assets in Belgium who can fly us? We are outside Ghent at this very moment and can be in Brussels in forty-five minutes. Or less."

"Negative," said Miles. "You won't reach Fushë-Arrëz in time. What's the status of your search for the package?"

No need to get off the E17 in Ghentbrugge then. Stasia looked into her side mirror again before returning to the left lane taking them south into France. As she did, she glimpsed another car in the center lane move with them. She narrowed her eyes. Her neck itched. She'd learned as an operative never to dismiss an itching neck.

Stasia briefed Miles on their Amsterdam visit, including the likelihood that Yeqon had seen *La Grandmère*.

"However, Willem found a code hidden around the obvious map of Pont-Aven in the figure's eye," she said. We believe that Yeqon failed to see the second code and now *caccia le mosche*."

"It would be perfect if all he caught were flies," said Miles, answering her quip about hunting them. "But if any of the Dark *Irim* knows what's in the package, it would be Yeqon."

Willem finally added something to the conversation. "Saskia said the 'art lover' brought an ugly friend. That description does not match the usual companions with which he surrounds himself."

Stasia abruptly changed lanes, moving all the way into the farthest right lane. The silver BWW moved to the center lane a moment later, and then into the right lane too smoothly for a typical Belgian driver during mid-morning traffic.

With her eyes on her rearview mirror, she said, "I, too, am concerned about who Yeqon brought with him to view *La Grandmère*."

Up ahead, she spied the exit sign for E40 towards Brussels. It would add considerably to their trip, but perhaps she could throw their tail off, either now or in Brussels.

She doubted it, however. If they'd been heading to Paris, they wouldn't have taken a route through Ghent. No, the route through Ghent led to Lille, where Bernard had been born. Whoever followed them knew that.

Miles brought the call to an end. "I'll update Dragon Man and Harlequin as soon as the situation here allows. For now, you're on your own. I've alerted local assets in Brussels and Lille that you're in the area and may need support. I've also texted the address of a safe house in Roubaix on the outskirts of Lille. Good luck and Godspeed."

Stasia kept her gaze focused on the highway, driving a little too fast for the right lane and letting the car drift left. Next to her, Willem placed a palm on the dashboard but wisely said nothing. She waited until they'd almost passed the exit to the E40 before swerving right. Horns sounded behind her.

The silver BMW executed the same move.

Whoever drove the German sportscar had excellent training.

"We are being followed?" asked Willem. Although he didn't raise his voice, she heard him clearly.

"*Sì.*"

She repeated her previous maneuvers, acting undecided as to which lane she wanted before taking the exit east toward Brussels. The silver BMW exited as well.

They drove in silence for ten minutes before Willem asked, "Do you know whether this is simply surveillance or ..." His voice trailed off.

Stasia glanced at him. "Or a team sent to engage us?"

At his nod, she said, "No, I cannot yet tell."

A sign for Karus Hospital at the first exit on the E40 caught her attention.

"But perhaps we can find out," she said, darting a look at her partner before swerving onto the exit ramp.

The silver BMW managed to exit as well, though it cut off a driver, who was then rearended by the car behind. Stasia confirmed that there was only a single occupant in the car. Better and better.

"It is an individual, no team," she said, watching the silver BMW, now exposed on the ramp behind them. "If I had to guess, a tail not a hit squad."

"That is a relief," said Willem. He dropped his hand from the dash. "I have never been in a gunfight."

Stasia looked at him. "That will change, sooner or later, *bello*. Perhaps now is the time for a little first blood, eh?"

"What are you suggesting?" Both alarm and excitement rippled through Willem.

"The roundabout ahead." Stasia gestured with her chin. "I will drive slowly. Shoot one of her tires."

"Her? Willem's harmonics tightened.

Stasia, approaching the entrance to the traffic circle, kept her gaze on the road. "She hid her distinctive hair under a jaunty hat, but I recognize Gina Orlandi's Roman nose."

His harmonics resounded as if they'd been plucked. Stasia hummed, smoothing the air inside the Jetta. Too much more of Willem's adrenaline in such close quarters, and she'd have a massive headache—not good for driving sedately. Terrible for high-speed maneuvers.

Willem pulled his handgun from the glove compartment, checked the clip, and lowered his window.

Stasia slowed at the entrance to the roundabout to yield to a car on her left. Gina's BMW coasted to a stop behind her. Stasia raised her hand to her side and waved once. The Art Squad officer scowled.

She also clearly expected Stasia to try to lose her in the circle because when Stasia drove forward, Gina crowded in behind her. More honking ensued as another driver was forced to stay in the inner lane.

Willem rose through the open window and fired back at the BMW, which veered into the berm in the center as its front tire exploded. Gina, caught off guard, spun out, blocking all traffic in the circle.

"Bravo!" Stasia grinned at Willem, who'd slid back into the car with a satisfied smirk.

Even though she'd stayed in the outer lane and should have exited at the first right, Stasia continued around the circle until she came to the exit back to E40. As soon as the Jetta cleared the roundabout, she accelerated. From there, they could head east to Brussels or west, returning to the E17 and heading south to France. Gina, too far behind them to tail now, would just have to guess.

"As repulsive as she is to me, I do not think Signora Orlandi is *L'amante's* 'ugly friend,'" said Willem, raising his window. He kept the handgun in his lap, however.

Stasia agreed. "Neither do I," She took the ramp toward E17. "We will have to be aware that whomever it is may be waiting for us in Lille."

After they'd gotten back onto the route south, Stasia called Miró.

He answered. "Go for Blackbird."

Stasia ignored the comm protocol. Who knew when she'd see her husband again? "*Moja ljubavi.*" *My love.* "Have you been recalled to Fushë-Arrëz?"

"Not yet." He sounded grim. "Harlequin told me to stay and finish my task."

Stasia checked her rearview while signaling and simultaneously moving into another lane. Still no sign of Gina. But she was now using her tactical driving skills to their utmost. Thank the Archangel that Miró had developed a harmonic cloaking device to mask their speeding from law enforcement. She did *not* need to outrun pursuit by a police car.

"*Molto bene.* Willem found another code in Bernard's painting. We believe that he hid the package in Lille in his grandmother's former laundry. There is a record of him going there a few months shortly before his death in 1941."

"Which would have been risky in Nazi-occupied France to say the least," said Miró. "I will see what I can dig up on his time there to narrow your search."

"But we have picked up a pesky Italian *mosca*. *Sfortunatamente*, she has become aware that we spotted her. I have lost her for now, but she must know where we are headed."

"Ah." Miró didn't have to ask who the 'fly' was. They'd been describing Gina as a fly clinging to stench ever since the Umbria mission. "I have finished here. I will go to Italy and wait for you."

"Copy that. We will contact you once we have secured the package." Stasia paused to focus on weaving among slower moving cars. "*Amore mio*, Yeqon has an 'ugly friend.' Do you have any idea who that is?"

Miró's response, when it came, was far from reassuring. "Sounds like a *daemon* or Dark *Irim*. The chance to recover the original knowledge contained in the *Codex* will bring more than a few Dark flies to the party."

Stasia swore rapidly in Italian.

"It will be fine, *Duša*," said Miró when she took a breath. "You are a *bushtër* who has already bested Yeqon. Never forget what you know about him."

"*Naturalmente.* He will never work with another that he cannot manipulate," she said, glancing at Willem. Eva had been very malleable.

"And I have confidence in Willem," said Miró. "I trust no one outside of myself more."

Although Willem said nothing to that, Stasia felt the change in his harmonics.

Miró ended the call without the standard comm protocol. "*Alla prossima.*" *Until next time.*

Stasia sighed as the left lane opened up ahead of them and floored the gas pedal. The Jetta jumped forward before settling into an agile run toward the border. Although the Belgian authorities had started tightening border controls due to the influx of migrants from the Middle East traveling into France to reach Calais or Dunkirk, for the moment there were none on the highways. After her extensive work with Europol's counter-terrorism center, Stasia suspected that free travel among the 27 European Union countries—known as the Schengen Area—had a limited future. Especially given the increasing presence of *daemons*.

Forty-five minutes later, they entered Lille. Miró had sent them a synopsis of his research into Émile Bernard's early life. Some of this research came from *Elioud* archives that he had started long before humanity in the form of Charles Babbage had conceived of anything resembling a computer. In fact, Miró met Babbage in the late 1820s when the English mathematician traveled Europe. It would be more than a hundred years before computers resembled Miró's early archives, now an advanced network shared with Light *Elioud* throughout the world.

As a non-*Elioud*, Bernard had only a minor entry in the archives. But whoever had entered his biography had noticed the pattern of interactions with other known *Elioud*, such as Van Gogh, Cézanne, and Gaugin. Bernard was watched.

In 1941, the French artist returned to Old Lille, north of the Boulevard de la Liberté, where Bernard's grandmother had a laundry in the mid-1800s. Lille, known for manufacturing cotton, supported a number of commercial laundries, and Bernard's grandmother, a canny businesswoman, had thrived. The archives placed her business not far from the Cathédrale Notre-Dame-de-la-Treille à Lille on the Rue Basse, but an actual address was lacking.

They reached Lille around mid-morning. As it was a Monday in December, many of the shops in Old Lille hadn't opened. They grabbed an early lunch in a small café and drove the length of the narrow one-way cobblestone street considering likely locations for the elder Bernard's laundry.

Stasia grew frustrated at the lack of obvious choices—and yet the number of possibilities given the historic buildings now home to boutique clothing stores. Uncharacteristic pressure had started to set her on edge. Miró had heard no updates from Fushë-Arrëz, not even from the new Kastrioti chief of security, Ryan Helsing.

Rolling to a stop at the intersection with the next street, she hit the steering wheel. "*Dai!* We cannot search them all!"

Willem, his handgun in his lap ready to use, asked in a mild tone, "Why not?"

Stasia blinked over at him.

The Dutch architect shrugged. "Rue Basse is not that long, and there are two of us. Moreover, the archives specifically mentioned the cathedral. If we start on the portion of the street west of Rue du Cirque, especially on the side closest to the park around the cathedral"—here he pointed to the row of shops on their left—"we have only a handful of buildings to search.

"After that, we move to the opposite side"—now he pointed to the buildings behind him. "If we find nothing, then we can decide how to proceed."

He showed her the map on his tablet even though she recalled it very well. He was right, of course.

Stasia swallowed her frustration, both a little chagrined at her outburst and grateful for Willem's steadiness.

She turned south until she came to one of the parking garages for the Opéra de Lille where they could leave the Jetta and return to the Rue Basse on foot. For the next three hours, they broke into and searched the north side of the street, alternating shops. Each building had another two stories with apartments, which they avoided. Except in the two instances where they identified potential candidates for a deeper inspection. Stasia, whose *Elioud* gifts paired with training as an intelligence operative made her a skilled cat burglar, returned to the two buildings while Willem began assessing the south side of the street.

She'd just finished with the second building when her *Elioud* battle senses alerted her as she crossed the deserted street. Something had disturbed the harmonic plane since she'd gone inside.

"Orangeman, sitrep," she said over their comm.

"Gina, so good of you to join us," he said.

Stasia scowled and sped her harmonics, scanning the buildings for Willem's personal beacon. *E li*! *There*! Inside that vintage clothing shop halfway down the block.

Hurrying, she passed through the glass entrance door. It was one of her favorite *Elioud* abilities, this ability to vibrate the molecules of her being in time with those of something inorganic (as long as it wasn't for long or the barrier was thicker than a few centimeters).

It wasn't difficult to find where Willem and Gina faced off among the racks. To Stasia's left, harmonics—mostly Willem's—writhed and seethed in a tight vortex. He literally gave off vibes of barely contained violence.

Stasia moved invisibly toward them as Gina spoke.

"Where *is* your partner?" asked the older Grey *Elioud*. "I doubt that she has wandered farther than flash distance. In fact, based on your harmonics, I suspect that she's already here with us."

Stasia had almost reached them when Gina flared.

Not only did she flare a brilliant white light, but the other woman also emitted a sonic boom that disrupted Stasia's harmonics. She fell to the floor, stunned and blind, with her heart racing painfully in her chest.

For a terrifying moment, Stasia thought she might be having a heart attack.

When her harmonics returned to something approximating their normal rhythm and rate, Stasia realized that Gina had bound her and Willem together. She tried to heat the cord around their wrists and ankles to free her hands and feet, but the material refused to melt.

"Fire-resistant cord," said Gina from three meters away. "Firefighters and soldiers use it. I also dosed you both with histamines, which affects the human body's temperature regulation. It might be a few moments—or even hours—before you can raise your temperature enough to burn through the knots. I'll be gone by then, however."

Stasia, lying on her side among a mess of clothes, twisted her face toward the Art Squad officer.

Gina stood watching them, a steady weapon aimed at Stasia's head. Willem's handgun, in fact. He moaned and stirred next to her.

"I should thank you for leading me to the *Codex Angelicus*. I never would have found it without your *Elioud* resources."

Stasia tried to keep the Grey *Elioud* talking while she struggled to raise her temperature. If Willem joined her, they might have a chance of getting free before Gina left....

"That is because you only think of yourself, *Raggio di sole*." Stasia laced the nickname *sunshine* with heavy sarcasm, pushing doubt-laden charisma at Gina. "When you are part of a team, everything is easier. You are not on your own, doomed to failure."

Gina ignored the gibe and the subtle suggestion of uncertainty in Stasia's words. Instead, she knelt and reached toward something beyond Stasia's line of sight.

"Or perhaps I'm free from encumbrances," she said, lifting her chin toward Willem, whose harmonics signaled that he'd come around fully. "I'd say Willem here is more of a *raggio di sole*. His expression radiates at least."

She laughed at her own wit. Then she bent again. Scraping and shuffling sounds disturbed the harmonics around them.

Stasia closed her eyes, calming her breathing, and focused on reading the harmonic plane. After a moment, a ghostly sonar image floated behind her lids.

On the wall in front of them, she discerned the outline of a mantel. From the harmonic reflection above it, a large mirror hung on the wall. Gina's wraithlike image quivered as she pried on the fireplace screen. Her harmonics keyed in to the harmonics of the metal just as Stasia became aware of an alien hum inside the fireplace.

Or more precisely, a *celestial* hum.

She'd only ever heard something like it when Zophiel appeared.

Gina stood, holding the object that produced the otherworldly vibration. "*Che magnifico!*"

Then she walked around and squatted down to show Stasia and Willem what she held. Though Stasia couldn't read the script on the aged leather, it was clearly a book.

Gina had the *Codex Angelicus*.

Later that night, more than 2,300 kilometers away in Fushë-Arrëz, Olivia Kastrioti delivered a seven-pound, two-ounce daughter after six hours of labor. After Dr. Armand had cleaned, weighed, and assessed the red-faced newborn, he wrapped her in a soft blanket, and Mihàil brought her to the waiting group in the main room.

As they took turns peeking at the *drangùe's* firstborn, he accepted their well wishes with a tired nod, his handsome face drawn and rough with whiskers. Ryan and Miles peered at the baby's delicate features and pronounced her beautiful like her mother, the former Army Ranger and the former CIA officer subdued with uncharacteristic awe. Adriana beamed, while Pjetër simply nodded.

After the others had faded away to their beds or the kitchen, Mihàil stopped in front of András and Beta. He held each one's gaze for a moment. When he spoke at last, his voice was thick with emotion too tangled for Beta to resolve.

"Olivia wants to name her *Luljeta* after my first wife." He swallowed. Tears sheened his eyes. "It means 'Flower of Life.' Her middle name will be Emily after her cousin."

The one who'd been murdered.

Then he held Beta's gaze. "But we will call her Yeta, in honor of you, the sister of Olivia's heart."

Beta nodded, too moved to speak.

Outside, the wind howled as a blizzard buried them in drifts of deep snow, sending an unexpected presentiment through her.

She shivered and said nothing as Mihàil took his sleeping daughter back to her mother.

Thirty-Two

When András awoke the next morning, it was because the strong winds of the snowstorm had died. The silence weighed on him. He sent his *Elioud* senses ranging beyond the Wise Herb facility into the rugged mountains beyond. The eldritch glow of the Kastrioti estate beneath meters of fresh snow drew his *Elioud* gaze like an unearthly beacon. Lingering chaotic vibrations disturbed the harmonic plane for kilometers around the site of yesterday's battle. At odd moments, fresh violence seethed across the low valley as though the Dark angelic energy hadn't been vanquished, just temporarily subdued.

Every spike and surge sent a tremble through Beta, who slept curled against him. Closing his eyes, András dipped his nose into her silky hair and inhaled her scent. *Black Orchid*, wild and sweet yielding to a heavy richness. She smelled like life and home.

The thought brought up an image of his lord holding his newborn daughter, so full of gratitude, love, and awe that it overflowed into András. Mihàil had been the father that he never had, but Mihàil deserved to have his own children with the woman that he loved.

That's what András wanted with Beta.

He brushed aside the glossy dark strands hiding the silky skin of her neck, nuzzling her as his hand stroked down her side and along the curve of her hip. His own body responded at the touch, his erection demanding attention, but he savored the feeling of his desire without letting it take control. There would be time enough to love his wife once they'd sealed their union with the sacrament of marriage.

That and they needed privacy, not the common room of a manufacturing facility populated with a couple dozen people in various states of consciousness.

But he wasn't going to wait long. He'd already waited what seemed like forever to make her his. If he had to plow through the roof-high mounds of snow outside to get to the village priest using nothing but his heated body, he'd do it.

And *that* was before he used thermogenesis.

"That feels good, Spratek," said Beta, pressing her back into his chest.

Though she still wore the bulky sweater and loose jeans that she'd donned the night before after discarding her battle-worn tactical clothing, the heat from her body lured András.

"Hm, *you* feel good, Gomba," he said, kissing the column of her neck and gently squeezing her breast.

She shivered, practically purring.

They were both silent for a long moment, sharing the heated bliss of their embrace. Her harmonics danced and tangled with his. Where their nimbuses kissed, they blazed and settled into a warm glow.

But this interlude had to end.

"There is something out there," he said into her ear.

"I feel it."

"Yes, your harmonics are quite jittery," he said, sighing and rolling over before standing.

Adriana had brought them some pillows and several quilts so that they could make a rough bed on the concrete floor. It was a good thing that he'd learned to sleep in all kinds of environments. All he needed was a decent pillow wedged under his head and a place to set his boots. He only felt a little stiff this morning. Nothing coffee and thermogenesis wouldn't combat.

Padding to the kitchen in his socks, he found Adriana already up cooking. A large urn of coffee percolated. András nodded at the Kastrioti housekeeper as he went to grab two ceramic mugs from the dishrack and filled them for Beta and him. He made them both extra sweet, adding a little cream to his.

When he returned to their sleeping area, Beta had folded the quilts and stacked them against the wall topped with their pillows. She sat on a low bench, tying the laces on her boots. Setting her mug next to her, he sipped his as he watched her graceful, spare movements.

She picked up her mug, audibly inhaling before taking a sip. "How do you always know what I want even before *I* know it?" she asked, her gaze pointed and suspicious.

András laughed. "You're not that difficult to read, Gomba."

As he finished his coffee, Mihàil joined them holding his own mug. The *drangùe's* face had smoothed with sleep, but a short beard now darkened his cheeks. He'd wet and combed his hair and changed into a clean shirt. Beta said nothing, but András sensed her approval. Jealousy tweaked him. He sat down next to her, pressing his thigh against hers.

The little minx began running soothing harmonics down his side, but when he glanced at her, her face had a studied innocent look.

You are not that difficult to read, Spratek, she said, laughter in her words.

Before András answered, Ryan joined them. The American soldier had also washed and dressed in clean clothing donated by a local resident. He stood with his arms crossed next to his commander, nodding to them, his gaze alert and focused. It was a very different posture from the previous night. This was no impromptu confab. Mihàil had already put his security chief on notice.

Next to him, Beta straightened and tilted slightly forward, ready to listen to the *drangùe's* news.

The words and tone when Mihàil spoke were those of the *Elioud* general.

"Yesterday we won a battle. But we did not drive the enemy from Albania. I fear that the attack on my home was just a feint. The blizzard that followed Asmodeus's defeat masked activity from his forces. Even though Ryan and I went as far north as Fierzë yesterday, we stopped too soon."

Suddenly András understood. "The Shalë Valley."

Mihàil nodded, his face grim.

"What is it?" asked Beta, her tone razor-edged.

She glanced back and forth between them.

Be my guest, said Mihàil to András's questioning look.

"We think that the dissonance convulsing the harmonic plane comes from a *kulshedër*," said András, answering Beta. "In Albanian mythology, *kulshedra*—fire-breathing, eight-headed dragons—plague humanity. As you probably can guess, *drangùes* are its primary opponents."

Beta's gaze sharpened. "It is not only a myth, is it?"

András shook his head. "The *kulshedra* are Dark *Irim*. After the Archangel Michael sentenced the guilty *Irim* to penance or punishment, the leaders chose punishment. One of those was Kôkabîêl, known as the Star of God. The Archangel Gabriel shackled Kôkabîêl and buried him in the Shalë Valley."

"And stationed *drangùes*, including my father, throughout the highlands to guard against Kôkabîêl breaking out," said Mihàil. "In 1937, an Albanian friar wrote the epic poem, *Lahuta e Malcís*. In one canto, he describes how a *kulshedër* escapes from a cave in Shalë to seek revenge against a *drangùe*. A force of *drangùes* defeat the *kulshedër*, and afterwards they celebrate their victory with a group of *ora*, protective spirits. Or you might say guardian angels."

"Let me guess," said Beta, looking between Mihàil and András. "This friar wrote about combat between Kôkabîêl and some *Elioud*, including you."

"I was there with Mihàil and Miró. The fighting lasted weeks. Several *Elioud* died."

In fact, András, a teenager at the time, had nearly lost his life when Kôkabîêl's tail knocked him into the jagged foothills where the dragon then tried to roast him alive. If Mihàil hadn't managed to pull András to safety, the maddened Dark *Irim* would have.

"And not nearly as glorious as Friar Fishta proclaimed," said Mihàil. "Although we managed to trap and chain Kôkabîêl again, some of his army of spirits escaped into the world. These are fallen angels whose powers have been contained for millennia with a thirst for retribution to match. They make *daemonia* look weak and tame."

András said, "Given that there are 365,000 of them, we're fortunate that so few did break free."

Mihàil shook his head. "Even so, Hitler invaded your country"—here he looked at Beta—"a year later. And then Kôkabîêl's soldiers rampaged through Europe."

"And you think that our battle with Asmodeus and his forces disturbed Kôkabîêl's prison?" asked Beta.

"Yes," said Mihàil and András together.

She stood as her hand went to the karambit at her waist. "When do we leave to confirm this?"

Mihàil shot a startled glance at András, who read the admiration in his commander's harmonics. That was good because Beta was going to be a full team member from this point forward.

"As soon as the highway is cleared. The snow stopped around four a.m., but it will be mid-day before plows can get through to us. Until then, we get our gear ready, go over the terrain, and settle on a plan of action. Miles has topo maps showing where we engaged Kôkabîêl in 1937."

Miles came from the supply room where he'd set up a small office using the Wise Herb server and a laptop that he'd recovered from an intact Kastrioti vehicle. Like Ryan and Mihàil, he'd changed shirts and combed his dark hair. He glanced toward Olivia's office on his way to the group. András read the concern in his harmonics, but the man—an exceptional CIA field officer—was very skilled at masking his emotions for a human. Nevertheless, András tucked the insight away.

Mihàil looked at the human who'd largely become indispensable as his operations manager and nodded as he joined them. Miles nodded back.

"Stasia and Willem arrived in Vietri sul Mare last night. They'll make their approach after they've gone over Miró's intelligence."

András's battle senses engaged. The hair on the back of his neck spiked. He'd missed some intelligence overnight.

Mihàil looked at him. It was clear from the *drangùe's* expression that he'd assessed András's reaction correctly. András narrowed his eyes. Next to him, Beta stiffened. Her harmonics tightened until they thrummed.

"I made the command decision to let you sleep," Mihàil said, "because we had a long day yesterday. Today will be longer."

He paused. Startled, András read uncertainty in his commander's harmonics.

"Gina Orlandi ambushed Stasia and Willem in Lille, France, yesterday after they discovered the hiding place for the *Codex Angelicus*. She took it to Yeqon on the Amalfi coast."

András had to keep himself from flaring. They didn't need him to lose his cool at this moment.

"*Codex Angelicus?*" asked Beta, holding herself still. Before anyone could answer, she said, "That does not sound like the kind of book that Yeqon should have."

"That's because it's not," said András, growling.

His temperature rose enough that sweat beaded on Ryan and Miles's foreheads. They ignored it along with the strong ash scent that swirled around the five of them.

He turned to Mihàil. "It can be no accident that Asmodeus attacked us here while Yeqon's ally brings him the original *First Book of Enoch*."

Beta gasped softly next to him.

Mihàil nodded once. The grim line of his mouth matched András's mood. "Stasia and Willem learned during their search that Yeqon brought an 'ugly' friend with him. It could be Asmodeus. Regardless, the timing could not be worse. And now Olivia and the baby ..." He let his voice trail off.

András suddenly understood Miles's concern.

Before he could say anything, Mihàil cleared his throat. "My first priority is my wife and newborn daughter. No matter how much I would try to shut them from my mind, I fear that I would fail, and it would cost us all."

He paused and then looked at each of them in turn. "Asmodeus used Luger's spirit to bait me in Germany. While I dealt with it, an *aranea diabolus* injected me with its venom. That is how Asmodeus possessed me. I am not yet fully recovered. András, I need you to lead the search into the Shalë Valley."

It was a request, not a command.

I am with you, Spratek, no matter what you decide. Beta slipped her hand into his.

The other two men watched, their expressions so laser focused they could have cut diamond.

András straightened his shoulders and held Mihàil's gaze. Then he said, "I'm honored, *Uram.* I won't let you down."

Miró waited for Stasia and Willem in a sea-facing ristorante in the marina area of Vietri sul Mare, the gateway of the famed Amalfi coast. It kept his attention focused on the soothing harmonics of the moving water rather than the foul miasma at the top of the hill in Dragonlea, the hamlet where Yeqon in his Angelli avatar had bought existing houses to tear down and replace with a palazzo, now under construction. Miró had checked the zoning and property records. Angelli had friends in local government. The palazzo should never have been approved.

Miró felt the change in harmonics when Stasia entered. He closed his eyes, inhaling. Her warm, sweet scent, though faint, always hit him like a punch in the gut. His harmonics reached for her of their own accord. Hers met him with fierce passion.

Duša, he said.

Amore. Gentle harmonic fingers caressed his jaw.

A moment later Stasia and Willem joined him at the table. They sat.

Miró nodded at Willem and took Stasia's hand.

"I am afraid that we do not have time for pleasantries," he said, looking at each for a moment. "Our mission has just gotten more urgent. Miles called this morning. Mihàil and András sense harmonic turbulence from a known *kulshedër*, an eight-headed dragon, in the Shalë Valley north of Fushë-Arrëz."

"A Dark *Irim*," said Stasia. A fine tremor ran through her harmonics.

She looked exhausted. Purple shadows darkened her lovely hazel eyes. She'd pulled her hair back with a soft headband and wore no makeup. Even so, Miró drank the sight of her in.

He nodded at her guess. "The condemned Dark *Irim* Kôkabîêl, chained beneath the Accursed Alps." He paused and then freighted his next words with subtle *Elioud* emphasis. "He broke free once before."

Stasia shot him a sympathetic look and squeezed his hand.

Willem finally spoke. The Dutch architect always listened and appraised everything. It was one of the things that Miró respected about the man. "The timing is not a coincidence, I gather."

Miró shook his head. "Not likely. And with the theft of the *Codex Angelicus,* Mihàil suspects that Yeqon and Asmodeus have allied against us. Which means that Asmodeus will soon have access to some of the power and secret knowledge in the *Codex* to release Kôkabîêl, ancient enemy of the *drangùes.*"

Stasia narrowed her eyes in thought. "Somehow, I do not think that this partnership is a match made in Heaven. Both are too self-centered to give way to the other for long. Perhaps we can exploit their differences, *sì*?"

"That would seem to be our only play," said Miró, "As for your pitch, I have done as you asked. The package has been delivered and the site prepared."

"Then it is up to me to convince *L'amante* that I have something that he wants," she said, looking at both of the other *Elioud*. "Is there somewhere that I may change?"

That was the part of the mission that Miró didn't like. But this time, he wasn't going anywhere. He would be right next to Stasia when she approached Yeqon.

Miró lifted his chin at the owner, who'd hovered not far behind a counter filled with a display of local wines. The man hurried over and bowed.

"*Per favore, signora,*" he said. "*Vieni con me.*" *Come with me.*

Stasia followed the man through a doorway. After she left, Willem leaned back in his chair and studied Miró.

"You have more self-control than I do," he said. "Every fiber of my being shouts that I should confront Angelli regardless of the cost."

Miró sipped his espresso, keeping a tight rein on his harmonics. He studied the other *Elioud* before measuring his words. Nevertheless, the air heated.

His lips pulled back from his teeth in a simulacrum of a smile. "That thought had occurred to me," he said, his voice harsh.

Understanding passed between them.

Willem nodded. The owner returned with two espressos, setting them down and leaving as quickly and unobtrusively as he could. Anxiety churned in his harmonics.

Miró sympathized. The man's daughter, only eighteen and beautiful, had been targeted as soon as Angelli selected the site of his palazzo. The only thing that had saved her, in fact, had been the Dark *Irim*'s absence while construction occurred.

But Miró's local asset had alerted him to Angelli's return three days ago. In exchange for *Elioud* help, the ristorante owner had agreed to let his daughter lure Angelli here. Afterwards, Miró's asset would relocate the owner and his family with permanent harmonic cloaking. And the daughter would receive a course of targeted music therapy.

He and Willem sat in silence until Stasia returned.

Amore, she said, familiar harmonics caressing his back.

Her transformation quite took Miró's breath away. Willem blinked several times, the muscles in his jaw working.

Before them stood an unfamiliar beautiful young woman whose wide eyes projected naïve sexual allure.

"How do I look?" she asked in her own voice.

"You lack only one thing," said Miró, holding up a bracelet with embedded nano-origami keyed to the young woman's harmonic signature. It would direct Stasia's own harmonics to match.

Stasia held her delicate wrist out. Miró fastened the bracelet, his thumb rubbing a warm line on her forearm when he finished. She trembled once before her harmonics adjusted.

Miró dropped her wrist.

Stasia bit her lip and played with the bracelet before adjusting her stance in a nervous sway. Then she smoothed her long dark hair behind an ear.

"By the Archangel!" said Willem, standing.

"Indeed," said Miró drily.

"I will interpret that to mean the mission is a go," she said. Her voice had modulated into a high, soft soprano to sound like Gianna, the ristorante owner's daughter.

Except for the bracelet which modified her harmonic signature, Stasia had managed the transformation on her own. Individual *Elioud* warriors had never been able to achieve this ability before. Only since the two married *Elioud* couples had gained dynamic signatures had it even been possible. Add in some very clever human technology, and the field against the Dark *Irim* and their cohort had just gotten a whole lot more level.

"Neat trick," said a cultured male voice behind them.

Miró's anger spiked. So did Willem's next to him.

Before either could flare, a powerful harmonic wave washed over the three *Elioud*. Miró moved with it as a sailor would on a ship's deck, while Willem caught himself on the table in front of him. Stasia, however, staggered and fell into the chair that had moved behind her.

Harmonics clamped and turned them toward the voice.

Angelli, eyes narrowed and lips compressed, watched them with the cold gaze of a predator. Gina Orlandi stood next to him, a smirk lighting her expression.

Between them stood Gianna, her arm linked through Angelli's and her other hand on his forearm. The young woman detached herself from her angelic seducer and walked to Stasia. She slapped her impersonator hard. Blood trickled from Stasia's split lower lip.

Miró clenched his jaw to contain his fury at the assault.

I am fine, amore, flashed Stasia.

The Dark *Irim* said, "Now that I am here, you really must tell me how you accomplished it."

Stasia licked the blood from her lip before speaking to Gianna.

"Return to *tua babbo*," she said without looking at the young woman, who looked terrified and confused now. Stasia's lower lip had already healed.

Gianna pivoted and stumbled toward where her father waited in the passage leading into the kitchen.

Then Stasia looked at Gina, whose peevish expression failed to mask her sudden deep unease.

"*Per favore*, sit," said his wife with a gracious smile and graceful gesture filled with *Elioud* authority.

Authority amplified by him and Willem, who both stood behind Stasia as she set the stage for her offer. Gina had no power to resist. Or interfere.

Stasia turned back to Angelli, who'd watched with a slightly bemused expression. Good. She'd already begun to entice him.

"You have discovered us. What will you do now?" she asked, softening the question as though she feared his answer. Her continued appearance as the teenaged Gianna only added to the ploy. Miró loved how his wife's mind worked. The Dark *Irim* himself had given her the opening. Desire, after all, was a two-way street, and he desired Gianna.

She tilted her head before setting the hook. "You have the *Codex Angelicus*. Your ally attacks the *drangùe* as we speak. What more do you desire?"

Miró felt the subtle bait his wife infused into her words as it drew the Seducer, her target.

Angelli's eyes widened. Anger sharpened their vivid blue. As Stasia had suspected, the Dark *Irim* didn't know that Asmodeus had launched an offensive on their enemy without him. Gina's unease spiked. Even Willem looked stunned at Stasia's gambit. The Dutch *Elioud* had learned his craft well. The other two had no idea that Stasia's little slip had been calculated.

Miró kept his pride under control. He didn't want to sabotage his wife's play.

"What I desire is what is mine," said Angelli in a silky voice, leaning toward her. "Rembrandt's *Judgment of the Watcher Angels*."

Stasia pulled away as if startled at his request. Miró marveled at her control. Her masterful performance would have fooled even him if he didn't know better.

"It is not mine to give," she said. "The *drangùe* protects it in a special vault."

"Perhaps the *drangùe* would be willing to part with it in exchange for the *Codex Angelicus*," said Angelli, watching Stasia as he insinuated his harmonics into hers.

Miró clenched his jaws against the feeling. The Seducer had lost his touch. The clumsy effort was best used on eighteen-year-olds, not happily married women.

In particular a happily married woman who brought more of the Dark *Irim's* harmonics under her control as a result.

Stasia bit her lower lip, signaling both confused worry and simulating a sexual response. "He does not have the time or ability to oversee such a complex trade. He is fighting for his life even now."

Her pouty reply had snared Angelli's gaze, which glazed over. Miró simultaneously wanted to cheer and beat the crap out of the Dark *Irim*. He felt Willem's sympathy but refused to look at the other *Elioud*. He controlled his harmonics instead, sending heat into his soles and strength into the bond with his wife.

Which secured the Dark *Irim's* agreement as the unfaithful angel lost the tug-of-war with her.

"Surely you can influence the *drangùe's* plans for the painting," said Angelli, a magnanimous smile spreading across his handsome face, "if I give you the *Codex* as a sign of my good faith."

Miró allowed a small smile to curve his mouth. How like Stasia to win the battle and make her opponent think that he had ended with the upper hand.

Stasia, playing the ingénue, let her eyelashes fall in gratitude as she sighed. Then she smiled, wrapping the Dark *Irim* in a binding cocoon.

"As you desire," she said, dipping her head.

Thirty-Three

B eta wanted to strip out of the winter camouflage that she wore. As hot as her internal temperature ran, she felt as though she'd started to cook in her own juices in the specially designed suit, which captured all of her body heat. It both protected her against the negative temperatures high in the Accursed Alps and concealed her from the humans and *daemons* below. Mihàil's private military research company, Shqiptek, had taken the nano-origami developed under Miró's direction and extended it in astounding ways. Not even the Americans and Russians had developed material as advanced, though they had come surprisingly close.

They, like the Dark angelic forces, required constant surveillance for their capacity to harm humanity.

Beta ignored the itchy rivulet of sweat creeping down her spine. Instead, she peered through the eyeglass in her helmet, which displayed data on the scene below. Scoffing, she pulled the helmet off.

Her own *Elioud* senses were much, much better at identifying temperature anomalies—not just the thermal signatures of the enemy *bogomili*, but also their *daemon* allies, who showed up as negative temperatures. And her keen eyesight had no trouble seeing targets or the landscape around her for a thousand meters. Factor in her previous experience as a sniper, and her *Elioud* senses gave her an edge in assessing target information and environmental data that human tech had yet to replicate.

It was true that the Shqiptek camouflage had helped her to understand and train her *Elioud* senses, efficiently and broadly. Already she had a better grasp on what transpired in the valley than she would have if she'd been forced to assess it without the cutting-edge camo. But she wasn't going to be shackled to it. Let human defenders like Helsing and Baxter benefit. They needed all the upgrades that they could get.

Because what she saw froze her to the marrow.

In the heart of the forbidding Albanian Alps, whose craggy peaks embraced a wintry sky, an unholy wound yawned in the Shala River valley. An invisible meteor had crashed into the thick carpet of snowy trees on the valley floor, spewing snow, ice, boulders, and black earth in raw, violent destruction. *Bogomili* crawled in and around this massive opening like black ants, carrying more dirt and boulders on their backs. *Daemons* hovered in opaque black mists over the desolate landscape, obscuring details. An obscene, low thrumming sent chills rolling down her spine.

Beta closed her eyes and sucked in a fiery breath. It burned all the way down her esophagus, but she held it to keep herself alert and clearheaded.

Something monstrous waited deep underground. It called to her, hypnotizing her with wordless promises of power, pleasure, and domination. It fixed her to her perch on the mountainside.

András's voice rang like a clarion in her thoughts, piercing the heavy thrumming. *Gomba, your thermals have spiked. Is everything all right?*

Then the St. Michael medal under her winter camo warmed, glowing in her *Elioud* vision like a beacon. She touched a fingertip to the spot over it. Almost immediately the external vibrations muted. Beta released her pent breath.

Yes, she said, searching the harmonic plane for András's signature. As she scanned the slope behind her, his harmonics synced with hers in an almost audible click.

Thank the Archangel that she could still sense him.

What do you see? asked András. As her commanding officer, he should have berated her for removing the helmet, which recorded whatever its camera saw—and disguised her dark hair from any overhead observers.

On the heels of his question, magma shot from the gaping hole in the earth, sending *bogomili* into the air before gushing over the ground. The hundreds of *bogomili* moving around the blast site disappeared in a thick, steaming river of molten rock.

Not the worker ants any more, she said, drily. *Or should I say the ones that had been digging until thirty seconds ago. Magma swallowed them. However,* bogomili *continue to arrive from the river. A lot more. They have set up camps and divided into smaller operational units in a five-hundred-meter perimeter around the dig.*

I didn't think that Asmodeus had it in him to be so deceptive, said András.

He is here. How is that possible? Beta shivered as Asmodeus's unique dissonance spiked the harmonic plane beneath them.

My guess? He tethered himself to a bogomili *that he left here before attacking us earlier. The tether acts as a homing beacon for his spiritual energies. He's feeding off of the* daemonia, *who are feeding off of the energies released from Kôkabîêl's prison.*

There are so many of them. Beta winced at the despair in her words.

Without Kôkabîêl, they are no match for us. András sounded confident.

How long? Beta didn't clarify.

But András understood her anyway. *If you're seeing molten rock, then perhaps thirty-six hours.*

Perhaps?

Perhaps. His sigh vibrated through their comm, sending a warning shiver down her back. *More likely half that time.*

He didn't have to tell her that they needed intel to share with the other defenders.

Beta pulled the helmet back on and rotated the eyepiece back in place, aiming its camera at the landscape below. The camera livestreamed the scene to the makeshift TOC back in Fushë-Arrëz where Mihàil and Olivia both waited for updates.

Once she'd thoroughly documented the enemy's position, strength, and the state of their efforts, she backed from her perch toward András, who waited at a narrow plateau fifty meters behind her. Then they climbed backwards down the tree-covered slope, staying low. Should one of the dark creatures flying overhead suspect that they had infiltrated the perimeter of the enemy's operation, their progress would be easy to mark through the deep snow.

But the creatures patrolled the area over the cavernous maw, unaware of the incursion. As Beta and András descended the mountain, András swept their tracks away with harmonics.

They made their way to the small hotel that András had commandeered as their base camp east of the *daemonic* excavation along the steep southern bank of the Shala River. Given that it was December, only the caretaker and his wife occupied the two-story wooden building nestled among the bare trees. At first the couple refused to cooperate with the Kastrioti forces, but when András appeared, his skin luminous and the snow melting under his boots, they acquiesced.

Which was a good thing because the Kastrioti forces needed shelter from more than the elements. *Bogomili* and *daemons* traveled the frozen river continuously.

A small Kastrioti team in winter camouflage slipped through the heavily wooded slopes along the river, setting harmonic relays for intrusion detection. Other Kastrioti teams, familiar with the local terrain, evacuated residents as quickly and quietly as they could. It was little enough that could be done to protect the villages most at risk. Already some residents had sickened from drinking water polluted by the presence of *daemons*. And the dark energy leaking from Kôkabîêl's prison blighted the flora and fauna in an ever-expanding concentric ring for hundreds of meters beyond it.

By the time Beta and András returned from scouting the dig site, Miles had set up a field communications array. Miró had worked with his French materials engineer to create lightweight display screens on collapsible graphene sheets. As computer monitors, they were terrible. As intelligent whiteboards, however, they were brilliant. Miles had expanded three large sheets, supporting them in stands on a table in the dining room. Around them, he'd added a sophisticated system of nanospeakers with dedicated channels for the field.

As Beta and András entered the makeshift communications center, Mihàil and Olivia's ghostly images peered back at them like a poorer version of angelic sonar. But it was the best they could do. Even Mihàil, almost a full-blooded angel, had limited battle senses. The secure, rapid-deploy tech gave the *Elioud* and their allies eyes and ears where they had none—powered by nearly inexhaustible micromovements and ambient temperature.

Miles sat in a straight-backed chair, a keyboard in front of him, tapping rapid-fire. He nodded at Beta and András as he slid his chair and keyboard to the side. Beta's keen hearing picked up the faint sound of speech from his earwigs.

Mihàil, his arms crossed, went straight to the point. "The clock has started on our response, Giant. The *bogomili* are human and will need to rest overnight, but Asmodeus will drive them hard once the sun rises. I do not believe we will get another night to prepare. We need to be ready to move on them as soon as our forces have gathered here. Elias Klum and five hundred *donats* have landed in Durrës and Vlorë along with enough armored civilian vehicles for half their number. The first platoon should arrive in Fushë-Arrëz in the next two hours."

As the *drangùe* spoke, a map of Albania filled one of the three screens. Details of the movements of the Order of Malta troops followed his description. The final screen listed the call signs for all of the squad leaders currently in the field, their task, and their current GPS coordinates.

Mihàil continued. "Two hundred more *donats* will muster in Tirana this evening from various Order enclaves in southeastern Europe. Some will join the *donats* from Vlorë. However, they lack enough transport. Demon Slayer is working on that as we speak."

András crossed his own arms and nodded. "Copy that. What about Flower, Blackbird, and Orangeman? We could use their special talents."

Mihàil dipped his chin. "Understood, Giant. Our trio of wandering warriors will reach Durrës later tonight. They will hitch a ride with Elias to Fushë-Arrëz."

Olivia, who'd said nothing until this point, spoke. "How much longer before your teams have evacuated the locals closest to Kôkabîêl's prison?"

"My lady," said András, bowing his head briefly. "There are still residents in the two villages within a kilometer north and west of the site. They're aware of the danger, but at this time of year, the snow prevents the older and infirm from escaping without help. My team members have had to travel house-to-house and carry some of them out."

"All without attracting notice," said Olivia. The mediocre display obscured the *zonjë's* expression, but the excellent acoustics of the nano-speakers conveyed her worry quite clearly.

András chuckled. Both Mihàil and Olivia blinked at the sound. "The *bogomili* are hardly interested in the odd farmer and his family when they can ogle a crazy hot tourist taking a polar plunge downriver."

"Beta!" said Olivia, shocked but laughing.

Beta shrugged. "This camo retains heat very well."

"Careful that you do not engage before we are ready," said Mihàil.

"No danger of that," said András, slipping a hand around Beta's. Invisible harmonic fingers tucked loose hairs behind her ears and then ran down her back as he went on. "For once, Asmodeus keeps a tight rein around his playthings. They're only free to act on clear threats, not their lust."

"Good." Mihàil glanced over at his wife, who shifted closer to him.

The *drangùe* cleared his throat and continued. "Giant, Draka, once you have overseen the last evacuation, confirm that the intrusion detection system has gone online before returning to Fushë-Arrëz. I have asked Father Bekim to christen Luljeta tomorrow morning, after everyone has assembled. Father Bekim will bless all the warfighters before they deploy."

Gomba? András didn't look at her, but Beta knew what he asked.

Yes, if they have no objections, she said. *I will already be wearing white.* She touched a fingertip to her jacket.

András glanced at the gesture.

Winter camo? I like it. Beta heard the humor in András's words before he said aloud to the Kastriotis, "And we will ask Father Bekim to marry us before the blessing. That is, if you will allow it."

Beta added, "Little Luljeta will be my flower maid."

Olivia smiled, joy radiating through the blurry outlines of her image. "Of course!"

"I look forward to toasting to your future happiness, *Stuhi*," said Mihàil.

After the Kastriotis faded from the graphene display, Beta asked, *Tempest?*

András grinned, dimples appearing on each side of his full mouth. Beta knew that she shouldn't want to kiss him right now, but she did.

He answered her aloud. "I was a rather difficult twelve-year-old when Mihàil adopted me." He paused. "And my cat, Gomba."

Beta blinked at that, but she said nothing. Just as it wasn't the time to kiss him, it wasn't the time to probe for more about the boy he'd been. But she was a patient woman. And a skilled interrogator. She'd get it out of him later, when they were alone and had all the time in the world for love and revelations.

They spent the next twenty minutes with Miles testing all of the nodes in the intrusion-detection system. After identifying three malfunctioning nodes, or clusters of nano-relays, András left to repair or replace the nodes while Beta returned to the Shala River for another "polar plunge" to cover the final group of evacuees, which included an elderly woman who had to be carried on a stretcher until the first switchback in the river to the north where they would transfer to a shallow-bottomed boat and navigate east to the larger Drin River.

The sun hovered on the horizon as the team made it to the bare trees edging the north riverbank when a dark mass of flying creatures—András called them *volantem diaboli mures* or *flying devil mice*—rose above the lookout point that bordered Kôkabîêl's prison.

The *volantem diaboli mures*, squeaking and chittering like hell-spawned bats, arrowed toward the team and the terrified grandmother. From the southern ridge came the voices of *bogomili*. By the sounds of it, at least a couple of squads.

Beta reacted without conscious thought.

Send the redstart! she flashed to András as she undid her wet bra and stepped out of her wet panties to stand naked in the icy water. Steam rose from her heated skin, whose temperature had risen several degrees as her battle senses engaged.

The redstart flew above her as the *bogomili* crested the southern ridge. Beta's harmonics snagged it, flinging the animated tattoo at the colony of *volantem diaboli mures*, now massed in a thick cloud over the Kastrioti team. The dark creatures dispersed in a confused exodus of beating wings and shrieks.

Meanwhile, the *bogomili* fell silent, watching Beta as she bent to scoop water and dribble it over her head. As she did, a ray of setting sun reflected from the St. Michael medal on her breast. A moment later, the *bogomili*, muttering and grumbling, turned away from the river and disappeared back down the shadowed slope leading to the cavernous pit. The Kastrioti team, not waiting for an all-clear from Beta, picked up the stretcher and began moving as fast as their snowshoes allowed.

After that, Beta hurried to dress in dry winter camouflage, heading to the hotel porch where she was met by Miles. They rendezvoused with András, who waited in the woods along the switchback. Though the light faded fast in the mountains after sunset, they hiked due east over steep terrain, Miles using the enhanced night-vision setting on his helmet's eyepiece to see. András and Beta focused on their thermal vision and innate angelic sonar to keep them oriented.

It was a long slog through deep snow as the temperatures dropped below zero in the shade of the heavily wooded mountain. For once Beta was grateful for the advanced thermal properties of the Shqiptek suit that she wore.

The three of them reached the Wise Herb facility after the last of the Kastrioti security personnel had checked in with Ryan. Mihàil greeted them, asking András for a sitrep and then quizzing Beta and Miles for specifics before sending them to Adriana for food. They were eating in ravenous silence when Miró, Stasia, and Willem arrived with Elias Klum. Though Beta's curiosity about the German pricked her, she only watched as the three *Elioud* and the Order of Malta knight entered Olivia's office, which had been turned into a war room.

A little while later, Olivia, carrying Luljeta, found Beta in the employee locker room where she'd showered and now dressed in borrowed clothing. Stasia followed close behind.

Olivia halted next to the bench while Stasia sat next to Beta.

"I told Stasia you had some great news to share," said Olivia, holding her daughter in the crook of her elbow and swaying gently. Her harmonics hummed, sweet and low. "Something more important than where you've been for the past three years or that horrible fiend that Asmodeus is digging up."

Stasia, whose hair and skin carried trace scents of sea minerals and marine gas oil, leaned close. "*Non avere pelli sulla lingua,*" she said. *Do not have hair on your tongue.* "Speak! *Per favore*, tell me that you have finally tamed that *velký smradlavý býk.*"

Beta, narrowing her eyes at her friend, sniffed. "That 'big bull' is not so stinky now."

Stasia smiled, the warmth lighting her hazel eyes. "That is because your nose has become accustomed to him."

Beta shrugged a shoulder, tilting her head. "Perhaps. Either way, I will marry him tomorrow morning so that we will go into battle as husband and wife."

Stasia's broad smile widened, if possible. She briefly squeezed Beta's upper arm. "*Felicitazioni, dolce amica.*"

The warmth of Stasia's congratulations, and the endearment *sweet friend* filled Beta's heart in a way that she hadn't expected. She was not as close to the Italian officer as she was to Olivia, but in that moment, gratitude and happiness made tears prick her eyes. Before she could stop herself, she wrapped her arms around Stasia and hugged her, hard and fierce, and then sat back.

Stasia looked a little stunned. She raised her gaze to Olivia, who was smiling. Then she looked back at Beta. After a moment, her fingers hovered over the St. Michael medal lying on Beta's chest.

"May I?" she asked.

Beta dipped her chin in response.

Stasia lifted the medal between two fingers. Her harmonics crackled and sparked as her own St. Michael medal glowed in response. Beta felt a strong magnetic pull between the two medals. A moment later, Olivia gave a little surprised yelp and then laughed softly. Her medal gleamed in the warm fluorescent light of the locker room, adding its own harmony to the high, sweet song now echoing between the three of them.

"The Archangel chose all of us," said Olivia, "and brought us to this moment. No matter what happens tomorrow, we have all been blessed beyond our merits." She gazed down at her newborn daughter as Luljeta made faint suckling sounds against her tiny fist. "And I have been blessed beyond my imagination."

"I have been blessed with a family when I believed that I would spend my days alone," said Beta, emotion thrumming in her voice.

She rose to her feet. Stasia followed.

"The Archangel writes straight with crooked letters," Beta said, quoting András.

She finally understood him.

THIRTY-FOUR

At dawn the *Elioud*, Miles, Ryan, Elias, and a senior *donat* met in the war room to go over their battle plan. And to hear more from Stasia and Miró about their encounter with Yeqon and Gina Orlandi.

Pjetër and Adriana moved quietly around the large office, carrying trays of hot coffee and hearty sandwiches. No one objected when they set filled plates on any nearby surface; no one rejected a steaming mug. It would be a very long day with field rations and icy water-filled canteens. They all knew it was better to eat real food now, even if adrenaline had killed their appetite. All were experienced war fighters, so no one suffered nervous nausea at least.

Beta, who stood in a corner eating one-handed while sliding her karambit open and shut, scanned the harmonics in the room around her. Miró, also standing, did the same, his icy blue eyes piercing and intelligent. Of the three *Elioud* warriors she'd met in Vienna four years ago, Miró was the least clear to her—beyond his devotion to Stasia, which was obvious and binding. She felt his deft harmonic touch, so slight that she doubted that many would be aware of it.

She, however, was.

She paused in her surveillance, holding the Croat's gaze. Energy jumped between them as they each took the other's measure.

Harmonics whispered over her St. Michael medal, tracing over the faint scar beneath her collarbone where Asmodeus's consecrated token had hidden under her skin.

Beta narrowed her eyes, her upper lip curling. The air around her heated. She scented ash. Harmonics buzzed along her skin. Another moment and the Croat would learn what kind of harmonic control *she* had when she zapped him.

Before Beta could respond, Miró did.

I would not try that if I were you, he said, apparently accurately reading her.

The harmonics between them thickened until Beta felt as tightly drawn as a bowstring. Electricity played a warning along her skin. His electricity.

Without looking at her, András said, *He can't help it. Being a plaything of the Ottomans for a decade will do that to you.*

As long as you remember that, we will get along, said Miró, his gaze never wavering from hers.

András reached up and took the karambit gently from her hand. Beta blinked, startled to see that the hooked blade had been extended. He handed her a cup of coffee.

András glanced over at the Croat. Instantly the tension surrounding Beta dissolved as his harmonics synced with hers, displacing Miró's.

Mihàil may be a father to me, but Miró is my brother. An annoying, overbearing, pain-in-the-ass older brother. And despite his overt hostility, you should know he advocated for you when the Russians took you. I wasn't so sure I wanted to go after you, but he told me to give you another chance.

That surprised Beta. She looked at the Croat, who merely dipped his chin in acknowledgement.

Tucking that insight into the aloof *Elioud* away for later, she nodded back and lifted her coffee, sipping it. András had sweetened it as she liked.

Mihàil stood at that moment, looking around the office at the serious faces surrounding him.

"Now that everyone has broken their fast and gotten reacquainted"—here he looked at Beta, Miró, and András—"it is time to face what the day has in store for us. First, Miró will tell us what happened when he, Stasia, and Willem went to recover the *Codex Angelicus* in Vietri sul Mare."

This Beta had to hear more about. She'd been with Stasia in Prague three years before when they'd been tracking *L'amante*, the infamous art thief, who'd been hired to steal a Caravaggio painting of the Watcher Angels. She'd seen the way that *L'amante*, the earthly manifestation of the Dark *Irim* responsible for seducing Eve, had been taken with Stasia. Stasia had disappeared with *L'amante* for more than eight hours.

Beta suspected that the Dark *Irim* had tried, and failed, to seduce the Italian officer during that time. Denial was a powerful aphrodisiac that the self-absorbed angel lacked the ability to counter. Stasia had always had the upper hand.

"It was our Hail Mary," said Miró, addressing the obvious question about why his team thought they had any hope of getting the long-hidden first edition of the *First Book of Enoch* from a Dark *Irim*. "All the credit goes to Stasia. She doubted that Yeqon wanted the book for himself or that he wanted to share it with his 'ugly friend,' Asmodeus."

Stasia spoke, smoothly taking the lead from her husband. "He could have kept it all those years ago." She shook her head. "No, what Yeqon wants—has wanted for the past three years—is the painting he commissioned from Rembrandt."

"The *Judgment of the Watcher Angels*," said Mihàil, "which I have kept safe."

Olivia, who'd quietly nursed Luljeta while sitting behind her desk, now spoke. "Until the time was right."

Miró nodded. "Stasia used all of her considerable charisma to let Yeqon believe that he manipulated her into offering up the Rembrandt in exchange for the *Codex Angelicus*."

"In fact, I convinced him to give it to me before we left Italy," said Stasia, a full, sincere smiling lighting her face. "Because I tapped into his envy of Asmodeus, who had double-crossed Yeqon when he came to free Kôkabîêl alone."

"He gave you the *Codex* without exchanging the Rembrandt?" asked Beta. She let skepticism color her voice.

"*Sì*, but Yeqon believes that he, how shall I say it, convinced me to move the location of the Rembrandt, which he will be unable to resist stealing."

"What about Gina Orlandi?" asked Olivia. "She went to a lot of trouble to get the *Codex* only to have Yeqon give it away. I bet she wasn't happy about that."

Miró glanced at Willem, who nodded and said, "My lady, with your permission, we would like to include Ms. Orlandi in our operation against Yeqon."

Olivia nodded. "Granted."

Mihàil brought the topic to a close. "That plan will be made when the time comes. However, the here-and-now requires us to determine whether this gift is useful against Kôkabîêl's army. The *zonjë* and I spent a lot of time with the *Codex Angelicus* last night. Learning to apply its secrets requires more time than we have, however. But at least we know that Asmodeus will not be able to use it against us today."

Elias Klum, who'd stood with the senior *donat* to the side while the *Elioud* discussed the recovery of the ancient book of scripture, cleared his throat. "Our *donats* have all assembled on the grounds of your estate. Our chaplains are hearing their confessions now. We will be ready to move out after Father Bekim's blessing."

"Good." Mihàil nodded.

He turned to the others. "Helsing, Beta, I believe that you two are the only ones who have not been introduced to our allies in the Order of Malta. Elias, Antonio, this is Ryan Helsing, a former American Army Ranger, and Captain Alžběta Čermáková, Czech military intelligence."

Beta read curiosity in Ryan's harmonics about the two men, clearly warriors, dressed in anachronistic black robes with the six-sided Maltese cross on the chest, but he refrained from asking any questions and shook their hands instead.

When Beta would have done likewise, she was startled as both Order of Malta warriors went to their knees in front of her.

"My lady," said Antonio, looking up at her with shining dark eyes, "we wish you great joy in your upcoming nuptials. My *donats* and I pledge ourselves to you, the beloved of the Archangel Michael. We will defend your life with ours and serve you on the battlefield against all enemies, *daemonic* and otherwise."

Panic surged inside Beta, whose gaze darted around the room, first to Olivia, and then to András, who'd come to his feet and watched the scene gravely. Neither of them said anything, however, leaving Beta the center of attention.

She swallowed, bracing her harmonics against András's, and, lifting her chin, acknowledged the pledge as gracefully as she could.

"Thank you," she said, her voice husky.

Then Elias spoke. "And, if you will accept it, we would gift you these rings to stand as the token of your troth to András Nagy, and he to you."

He held out a small black-velvet-covered box, opened to reveal two gold bands embossed with tiny Maltese crosses separated by three raised dots on a beaten gold field.

Beta reached for the box. András stepped up next to her, reassuring heat radiating from his solid bulk. She shifted slightly until her thigh brushed against his before taking the smaller gold band from the box. It was heavy.

"Thank you," she said to Elias.

András gripped the German knight by the hand and hauled him to his feet. Then they clapped hands on one another's shoulders as old friends. Antonio stood, beaming.

"And on that note, our time draws short. The sun has risen," said Mihàil. "Father Bekim waits for the baptism and blessing as well as the wedding ceremony."

Beta slipped the small band back into the box and then slipped the box into the side pocket of her tactical pants. András took her hand as they walked out of the office. Five minutes later, they joined all of the residents still in Fushë-Arrëz as well as the Kastrioti security forces and the Order of Malta *donats*, who lined up on the Kastrioti estate grounds along the highway.

Nanospeakers had been dispersed in a fine veil over the entire area where the participants stood, keyed to the individual *Elioud* nanosystems, which would relay sound from the ceremonies. Father Bekim, a small, gray-haired priest, wore a microphone.

Olivia and Mihàil stood at the edge of their driveway, the blackened ruins of their stone mansion backlit by the fiery rising sun. They wore white camouflage, but baby Luljeta was clothed in a traditional, long white christening gown and cap, edged in soft white lambswool. Just before Father Bekim began speaking,

Zophiel appeared sitting on the ruins in full battle dress, the massive handle of a long sword peeking from a silver sheath on her back.

Beta, whose palms had started to sweat, nevertheless watched, fascinated as Olivia and Mihàil responded to all of Father Bekim's questions. When the short ceremony ended, the townsfolk cheered as Father Bekim anointed the baby's forehead with holy oil, while the *donats* and warfighters stomped and clapped, their expressions intent and focused.

A shiver raced down her spine at the sound.

And then it was time for her and András to vow love and fidelity until death parted them.

Olivia and Mihàil stepped up beside them to witness, the *zonjë* on Beta's left side and the *drangùe* on András's right. Miró and Stasia filled out the wedding party.

Zophiel called in a clear voice that reached everyone below with no distortion. "You will want to speed the rite, good Father." She held her sword across her lap now.

On the heels of the guardian angel's advice, an invisible tsunami flashed over them from the north. No one could speak or move as it buffeted them, although several people among the town residents lost their footing and fell, their faces transfixed by soundless screams. Something ancient and discordant attacked Beta, calling to her very spirit to flee this gathering and make her way into the Accursed Alps where her dragon nature could break free.

Cold lust, anger, hatred, and bitter envy rolled over her. Beta quaked.

Then a massive growling rent the morning. It came from the north. Jagged lightning forked the sky far behind Zophiel. Purple-black thunderclouds blotted out the rising sun. Unnatural darkness shrouded the formerly bright morning. The temperature fell fifteen degrees in as many seconds.

Zophiel raised her sword to pierce the harmonic wave, which dissipated immediately.

"Now would be an excellent time to start," she said.

Father Bekim remained equanimous despite the turbulence roiling the harmonic plane and the urging of the terrifying *Cherub* dressed in liquid silver armor and wielding a massive sword.

"Please hand your witnesses the rings," he said, "so that they may warm and pray over them while you say your vows."

Beta, who'd been warned by András about this addition to the ceremony, pulled the box with the gold bands from her pocket and handed it to Olivia with shaking fingers. András took her hands in his, his harmonics soothing and steadying hers. Their nimbuses blazed as they met, spotlighting them in a warm glow.

And then Father Bekim asked András, "Do you, András Nagy, take Alžběta Čermáková to be your wife?" His voice broadcast over the silent residents and warfighters.

András answered in a strong, steady voice that brought tears to Beta's eyes as it rang out. "I do."

An indigo harmonic chord wrapped itself around his heart, entwining with Beta's harmonics in an unbreakable bond.

Lightning flashed, closer this time.

The indomitable priest continued, his voice steady and sure. "Do you promise to be true to her in good times and in bad, in sickness and in health?"

András said, "I do."

Another sweet, pure harmonic chord braided their harmonics tighter. Love filled Beta's heart so full that she feared it would overwhelm her.

Father Bekim's voice had gradually risen as the gravity of the vows had increased until now his voice echoed over the nearby mountain slopes.

"Will you love and honor Alžběta all the days of your life?"

"I will." The ground under their feet shook with the intensity of András's vow. Infinity shone in his dark-blue gaze.

The third and final harmonic chord rose from the earth beneath their feet and raced in luminous joy around their forms, integrating within their harmonics so deeply that nothing would rend them without great pain and loss.

And then it was time for her, the *draka,* to be bound to her husband on the celestial plane, before *Elohim,* the *Angeli Fidelis*, and humanity.

"Do you, Alžběta Čermáková, take András Nagy to be your husband?"

Beta lifted her chin and, holding András's glittering gaze, answered. Emotion threaded her voice. "I do."

At her answer, a glistening harmonic chord shot delicate tendrils through their nimbuses, tiny buds of golden light unfurling along its length.

Lightning cracked overhead, underlighting heavy clouds in its glare.

"Do you promise to be true to him in good times and in bad, in sickness and in health?" Father Bekim's voice was almost gentle now.

In contrast, Beta's voice had strengthened. "I do."

Another pure harmonic chord sounded inside her ribcage before rising from her in a gold filigree, adding texture and detail to their conjoined harmonics.

Ominous thunder rumbled. The morning darkened farther until it resembled early evening.

"Will you love and honor András all the days of your life?"

Beta inhaled, taking in András's scent, running harmonic fingers over his resolute face, down his shoulders, and to their linked hands. His warm, firm fingers held hers. They breathed in union. For a moment, time stopped, and she knew it was because she'd stopped it.

Then she spoke, infusing her words with *Elioud* authority so that they rang through the mountains.

"I will."

The final white-gold harmonic chord from her vows, anchored in the unshakeable harmonics of Creation, rose through their united harmonics as a glittering mesh. From this moment forward, they would share a single harmonic signature from which to live their married life together.

Beta expected another lightning strike, this time a massive one overhead. But an unnatural and ominous stillness settled over everything.

Then Father Bekim said, "It is time to exchange the rings."

András accepted a gold band from Mihàil, and then, holding Beta's left hand, he said as he slipped the ring onto her third finger, "Beta, receive this ring as a sign of my love and fidelity. In *nomine Patris, et Filli, et Spiritus Sancti.*"

Beta, no longer afraid that she would be unable to speak, accepted András's gold band from Olivia. Heavy and warm like living flesh, its harmonics resonated a pure musical tone with theirs. She saw the blessing on it, the one given to her by their friends.

She took András's left hand and said, "András, receive this ring as a sign of my love and fidelity. In *nomine Patris, et Filli, et Spiritus Sancti.*"

Father Bekim, beaming now, said in a ringing voice, "I pronounce you husband and wife. D*eus Vult!*"

He blessed them, his hand sealing their vows with the words "in *nomine Patris, et Filli, et Spiritus Sancti. Amen.*"

The cheering this time bounced off the rolling slopes around them as even the reserved Order of Malta soldiers joined in.

And then the eight-headed *kulshedër* emerged from the roiling purple-black clouds in the distant mountains, shrieking in fury and clothed in brilliant white lightning.

Father Bekim, to his credit, hadn't forgotten that he needed to bless the fighters, the *donats* and the Kastrioti forces, as well as the *Elioud*.

As thunder rumbled around them and many of the Albanians appeared ready to bolt, he called, "*Benedicat nos Deus, benedicat nos angeli! Sit lux tenebris superare!*"

May the light overcome the dark!

Zophiel, who'd stood while Father Bekim spoke, acted as an amplifier for his words, muting all other sounds for a precious interlude.

The blessing had scarcely ended when a thick swarm of *volantem diaboli mures*, harbinger of the greater flying beast, attacked the citizens of Fushë-Arrëz.

A *donat* began chanting *Crucem sanctam subiit*, his bass voice a clear call to action. After a couple of measures, a squad of *donats* joined him as they calmly encircled the screaming Albanians, now covered in the *volantem diaboli mures.* Pure light shone in a column from the heavens on the writhing scene. Then *daemonic* hordes flooded the mountain slopes around them, pouring over everything. *Bogomili* couldn't be far behind.

Olivia wrapped herself and Luljeta in an impenetrable harmonic cocoon created from the nanospeakers that had covered the estate. Miró and Stasia stationed themselves around mother and newborn, their harmonics ringing. Heat shimmered in the air around them.

Mihàil and Elias ran toward the *daemonia*, the *drangùe* flaring as he came into contact with the horde. Elias chanted, power radiating from him on the harmonic plane. *Donats* streamed after him, the *daemonia* breaking on their golden forms as waves break on cliffs.

"Stay with me," said András, his face terrible.

He flared, and Beta followed suit. *Daemonia* disintegrated, buffeting the harmonic plane around them.

Beta lost sight of the other warriors when the *kulshedër* loomed overhead, its eight heads alternately breathing fire and shrieking. On its back rode Asmodeus. Spectral planes and lines obscured their obsidian forms, which gleamed amid the fiery light and swirling gray smoke. Asmodeus laughed, and the sound screeched down Beta's spine like shorn metal.

And then an infinite number of dark spirits crawled, slithered, climbed, burrowed, jumped, buzzed, and flew in every open space on ground and sky—and into mouths, eyes, ears, nostrils. The cacophony drowned the chanting from the *donats*. The pure light winked out. The stench of death mixed with the foul scents of unnatural creatures and the caustic miasma exuded by Kôkabîêl.

Daemonia surged over Mihàil and András.

And Beta.

She fell to her knees, clutching her head and choking, but the *kulshedër*'s harmonics seemed tuned especially for her. Clashing dissonance on a spectrum beyond normal hearing pierced her mind, resetting her fundamental frequency. Her veins iced over. Tears coursed down her cheeks.

The *kulshedër* landed, its massive weight and heat melting the asphalt of the highway. Asmodeus jumped a harmonic band to loom over Beta.

The Dark *Irim*'s voice cut her in a thousand places, pouring vitriol over the bleeding lacerations. "Daughter, you belong to the dragon."

He reached for her.

Thirty-Five

A beacon of cold celestial fire cleaved the smothering darkness.

It was *Caelistra*, wielded in a two-handed grip by Zophiel, magnificent white wings spread and glowing against the purple-black thunderclouds. Her quicksilver armor danced as it reflected *Caelistra's* flames.

A choir of angelic voices rang from the skies. *"Sit lux tenebris superare!"*

Zophiel hung in the sky over the *kulshedër*. The silver blade flashed, and the dragon screamed, so high and piercing that a wide crevice opened in the highway. A single head fell, smoking, to the earth, followed by a sonic boom.

The *volantem diaboli mures* burst into flames in a million points of fiery light.

Now melodies swirled through the cacophony and violence, and blue sky shone in patches among the storm clouds. Somewhere a lone baritone chanted the *Salve Regina*.

Daemonia rushed toward the angel. Invisible spirits from the Star of God's army manifested warped and twisted bodies with dozens of eyes, fangs, claws, and wicked bladed weapons. Possessed humans, both Albanians and Kastrioti special forces, began attacking each other. *Donats*, impervious to possession, engaged them all in hand-to-hand combat with knives, grenades, combat shotguns, and handguns.

Beta, blinking, barely took in the change in the battle around her. She felt the ice melt in her veins. Asmodeus, whose horned fingers burned the tender skin of her throat, pressed an enormous stony thigh between her legs. A mad gleam glazed his eyes. His thorny tumescence seared the camouflage from her, scalding her with his vile lust.

It was clear that the Dark *Irim* was totally consumed with what he was about to do to her.

Beta's dragon broke its chains.

Her searching left hand found her karambit, sliding it off her waist and open as Asmodeus braced a hand on her throat and thrust his pelvis forward.

Only to find Beta's blade.

"I would not if I were you," she hissed, her voice breaking into discordant notes.

Smoky steam filled the air between them. Her nostrils flared as she inhaled.

Asmodeus's eyes widened. He growled. His temperature rose until Beta thought her skin would melt from her bones.

Instead, her temperature rose to match the Dark *Irim*'s. She growled back, her lips pulling away from her teeth, and sliced into Asmodeus's groin. He grunted and his arm loosened over her throat. In an instant, she reversed her grip and thrust upward into his arm with the hooked blade before throwing an elbow into his temple. As it connected, she pulled the karambit back, taking a chunk of flesh with it.

Over the Dark *Irim*'s shoulder, she glimpsed Antonio and a squad of *donats* fighting their way to her. Zophiel rose in the air, blood and gore defiling her luminous armor, the white feathers of her wings weighed down. Another of Kôkabîêl's heads erupted in a sonic boom.

Gomba.

Spratek. Having fun with the daemons? she asked.

A little.

Daemons exploded outward in a spectral fountain from where András stood, his camouflage hanging in charred strips from his body. He pivoted and grabbed one of the deformed creatures hanging on Elias's back, twisting its neck and snatching another before the first hit the ground. Then he turned and hauled Asmodeus off Beta.

Instantly hideous malformed creatures lunged at András, and he disappeared in a tangle of arms, legs, and tails.

Asmodeus laughed, returning to stalk Beta. The sparkle in his gaze sent chills down her spine.

I *am having fun*, he flashed.

He'd violated the sanctity of her intimate communication with András.

Fury burned Beta. She slashed at Asmodeus's face, but when he blocked with his arm, she tossed the knife to her other hand and reversed the hawksbill across his torso.

Asmodeus is not enjoying being my sparring partner, she said, changing hands again and jumping clear of the Dark *Irim*, slashing his face this time.

That's because he has no sense of timing. None of them do.

András ducked inside the reach of a creature with a bladed weapon, gripping its arm and twisting until it broke. Then he snatched the weapon as it fell and slit the creature's throat with it.

After András said this, Beta caught her husband's battle rhythm, its gravity and skill. She inhaled, letting it dictate *her* timing. She consciously reset her fundamental frequency so that her harmonics meshed with András's again.

She belonged to a dragon all right.

Herself.

Beta began to weave around Asmodeus, who jumped and flitted around her, looking for an opening in her defense. The expression on the Dark *Irim's* face said he toyed with her. He'd even manifested a body no larger than a large human male, as if giving himself a handicap.

Vûl. Idiot. She'd had enough of his antics.

Antonio and his squad of *donats* reached them as thousands of whirling stars surrounded Kôkabîêl. The Order of Malta warriors formed a defensive shield around Beta, their golden auras keeping *daemonia* at bay as long as they chanted.

Which wouldn't be long. Hissing, snarling, and snapping grotesqueries surrounded the warriors.

Another sonic explosion shifted the world around them. Zophiel tumbled away from the five-headed dragon, whose newly severed neck sprayed acidic blood. The whirling stars winked into pinprick black holes and followed the

Cherub across the sky where they caught the angel and clung to her armor, dimming its brightness and weighing her down. The weapons, whatever they were, disrupted Zophiel's fundamental frequency. *Caelistra's* flame winked out and the massive sword dropped to the ground like a silver anvil.

Mihàil and Elias fought back-to-back now while Ryan and Miles led a group of Kastrioti security personnel to a small island of innocents being defended alone by shiny-faced Willem, who looked like he channeled his Viking ancestors. Stasia and Miró moved around the dense harmonic cocoon in which Olivia sheltered her baby, fighting the attacking creatures with a precision that suggested hours in the gym together.

Hours Beta and András hadn't yet spent.

But she could sense where her husband was as he moved, and his harmonics tethered her. Focusing on him crystalized the harmonic plane for her. She saw all of the *Elioud*, *donats*, and human fighters as bright pools of harmony, but her own activity provided the melody linking it all together into a jazz symphony—one in which *she* could direct the next measure.

She anticipated Asmodeus's move an instant before he made it.

In a heartbeat, Beta jumped on the Dark *Irim*, smashing the butt of the karambit into his jaw before pulling the hooked tip across both his eyes. Aqueous humor spurted, burning her hand. He thrashed and grabbed for her wrist, but the redstart appeared and flew at his now blind face, shocking him until he twitched. Beta switched hands with the karambit and pulled its blade across the Dark *Irim*'s throat. Black blood spurted over her, so cold it took her breath away.

"That will teach you to manifest a body," she said, panting.

A hoarse cry pulled her attention to the trio of *Elioud*, who stood alone, trapped inside a meter-high barrier of corpses. Olivia's nanodrone cocoon had disintegrated, and now Kôkabîêl threatened them, the dragon's five remaining heads focused on the adult *Elioud* with a preternatural intensity, its tail flicking like a great cat's as it gathered itself to spring. Lightning crackled around the dragon's heads, and clouds obscured the valley, so that only Beta realized what had happened as the conflict moved away from the isolated group.

At the same time, a vicious-looking humanoid with iridescent sable skin covered in knobs and scales, rows of razor-edged teeth, and intelligence sharpening its gaze engaged Antonio, who only had his combat knife and his wits. The other *donats* in his squad had been wounded or devoured while Beta fought the Dark *Irim*.

Asmodeus disappeared.

A sickening realization hit Beta's stomach. She turned and threw up.

It had all been a feint to get the fighters away from Olivia and Luljeta.

Luljeta, an incandescent pearl of love and perfect harmony whose existence called everything Asmodeus and Kôkabîêl were a pernicious lie.

Beta jumped to her feet, speeding her harmonics as she moved towards her friends, praying that her stunt would take her closer to the action before they were roasted alive.

Spratek, Olivia needs us, she flashed, landing on her feet behind Kôkabîêl.

The dragon's sulfurous stench gagged her. Worse, its armor-plated hide had no chinks or visible scales. Beta had no idea how she could distract, let alone attack, the *kulshedër*, whose harmonics whirled around it in overlapping ellipses with distinct frequencies. It existed both now and a moment before and in the future.

Kôkabîêl leapt, spraying jets of flame and acid. Yet Stasia and Olivia stood next to Beta, who felt a whisper in the harmonic plane between one blink and the next, as if time had stopped and started again.

Another *Elioud* trick that she'd missed out on learning.

Miró, on the other hand, appeared under the dragon's feet. András materialized on the other side of Beta, vicious short swords in each fist, wet with monstrous blood. He tossed one of the swords to Miró, who swung it at the dragon's nearest foot. András did likewise. The weapons, manifested from the Star of God's own army, each sliced a clawed toe off.

Kôkabîêl's five intact heads shrieked and flailed. Its tail slammed into the ground, quakes radiating out from it that cracked the frozen earth in a spiderweb of destruction. The corpse barrier disintegrated.

Then the *kulshedër* urinated.

Miró and András had already moved away. The hot poisonous liquid dissolved a pit under the creature deeper than a man. Battlefield debris fell into it. In moments, the landscape had transformed into a surreal hellscape.

The *kulshedër* lumbered as it turned in search of its antagonists.

But this time Mihàil met the beast. He wielded *Caelistra*. Though the great sword didn't flame, its sharp edge sank into another of Kôkabîêl's necks before the dragon could get airborne. Mihàil lacked the angelic strength to finish cutting through the sinewy muscle and bone. As he strained, the dragon clamped onto his shoulder with one of its uninjured feet, holding him still to torch him.

Olivia screamed, fury and pain echoing around the valley. The monsters and the defenders arrested in mid-action as her *Elioud* authority gripped them.

Kôkabîêl halted. Mihàil collapsed to the ground, his skin blackened. *Caelistra* fell to the earth, the *kulshedër's* head partially severed.

Olivia handed Luljeta to Stasia and strode to her husband. She knelt, tears running down her cheeks, but she didn't touch him.

Time started again.

A thousand things happened at once, floating on the harmonic plane like a constellation of bright stars on a dark field, spinning around a central axis threatened by entropy.

Beta saw and understood each and every one.

Donats, Kastrioti security personnel, and civilians bleeding out and dead for five hundred meters.

Antonio hanging on the blade of an evil-looking basalt weapon, his eyes wide as the reptilian monstrosity embraced him, its jaws open.

Elias, Ryan, and Miles trapped with a group of injured inside the ruins of Olivia and Mihàil's home.

Willem, bloody, bruised, and alone, with an arm hanging useless.

Daemonia and monsters swarming toward Stasia and Miró and the newborn Luljeta.

The *kulshedër* wrapping its tail around Olivia and Mihàil.

Then András materialized at her side, the redstart fluttering around their heads. He took her hand and hummed their theme, its melody sweet and hopeful and filled with trust. When he looked at her, his gaze said that he saw only her. And she was everything.

Beta flared for the second time that day.

This time, she transformed into a dragon. An actual dragon.

A *kulshedra* with eight heads.

She roared, and the world trembled.

Next to her, András radiated so much heat that he appeared to Beta's dragon gaze as a man-shaped white supernova.

Kôkabîêl hesitated, his four uninjured heads turning to look at Beta.

She hissed and spat venom. It landed on the *kulshedër's* flank with a sizzle. Then she launched herself at the other dragon, knocking it onto its side. She attacked it with all of her teeth and claws, ripping and gouging until Kôkabîêl bled from dozens of wounds. She urinated over the other dragon's body, the toxic liquid acid-washing the once-invincible hide until it looked raw and fragile

While Kôkabîêl struggled with Beta, András ran and gripped the monster's mangled head. Roaring, he twisted it off. Smoke and the scent of charred flesh filled the air.

In the midst of this noisome carnage, Zophiel appeared above Kôkabîêl, her magnificent armor whole, if less luminous. She gripped *Caelistra*, which burst into flame, and slashed off another head.

The Star of God's army rallied around their general, who now had only three heads and five bloody stumps.

But Zophiel was merciless. She hacked and stabbed, *Caelistra* spinning about her in a mesmerizing kaleidoscope of flame and silver. A magnificent choir of angels accompanied her graceful maneuvers, overcoming the chaos and dissonance with a soaring hymn. *Daemons* and Dark angelic spirits evaporated under the cleansing celestial fire.

For her part, Beta rampaged in a musical composition of her own.

She flew over the battlefield, scorching and blasting monsters, while András destroyed *daemons*, their redstart a blur as it attacked faces and hands. First they cleared a path for Olivia and Mihàil, who stumbled but managed to follow his wife. Then they dispatched members of the Star of God's army in a symphony of destruction.

The other *Elioud* contributed minor variations on this theme. Stasia played hide and seek with the manifest spirits, mixing harmonic jumps while using her personal nanosystem as a cloaking device. Miró, tethered to his wife's harmonics, wielded harmonics as if they were grenades and cannons, moving in a syncopated rhythm against the manifest spirits, who never matched his complex timing.

When Olivia and Mihàil reached their lieutenants, the four *Elioud* activated what was left of the defensive mesh network, turning the drones into molecular landmines whose shrapnel maimed thousands of the Star of God's army. And then they erected an impenetrable harmonic barrier.

Willem managed to keep his feet until Elias initiated a foray to rescue him with Miles and Ryan, who whooped as he discharged an automatic weapon at the monsters. Where they'd been large and savage, most of the manifested creatures had shrunk into vicious dog-size monsters, who were still capable of ripping out a victim's throat.

As soon as it had started, the battle was over. The *daemonia* and Dark spirits vanished. Kôkabîêl, his wings struggling to carry him aloft, rose briefly above the valley. But Zophiel took no pity on the renegade *Irim*. Instead, she avoided the weakly snapping jaws and plunged *Caelistra's* burning, singing blade into the dragon's chest.

This time, instead of a sonic boom the *kulshedër* mewled once and then plummeted. The ancient being imploded before impact. The Star of God had received his final judgment for his role in the original Watcher Angel rebellion.

Easter brings crowds to Rome, the *Urbs Aeterna*, the *Eternal City*, which had been ancient at the time of the first holy day. This April in the year two thousand nineteen was no different.

If shadows marred the faces of the small group of tourists visiting the famed Spanish Steps and admiring the vases of fresh azaleas there, they were fleeting. And what young friends, so obviously loved and loving, with proof of the goodness of life in the form of a gurgling baby girl in their midst, would have much to trouble or worry them?

If every now and then the eldest of the group, a handsome man with dark hair and piercing eyes who seemed to command respect and attention from the others, looked at the horizon with a troubled gaze, surely it was only the weight of fatherhood intruding on a formerly carefree life.

Because his ethereally beautiful wife looked at him as if the sun and moon set on his shoulders. And the little girl, whose name meant *Flower of Life*, adored him despite the rivalry for her affections from two of her more boisterous 'uncles.'

Their friends, which included two other happily married couples, and a trio of bachelors, enjoyed their first candlelit procession around the Colosseum for Good Friday. One of the couples, the one with a playful giant and a slender, sharp-eyed wife, disappeared into the darkness to kiss while one of the bachelors, as broad and nearly as tall as the playful giant, called out loudly teasing them. And the other couple, holding hands, gazed again and again at the baby with the secret joy of impending parenthood.

On Holy Saturday, the nine friends visited the Doria-Pamphilj Gallery, a large Renaissance and Baroque art collection housed in the private Palazzo Doria-Pamphilj in the historic center of Rome. Anyone within earshot of the group knew that they intended to view a little-known painting by Rembrandt, which had been stolen four years before but recovered. Now the gallery displayed the arresting artwork in a limited exhibit in a small mirrored room off the palazzo's central courtyard.

The group entered the room to find a couple already there, a man exuding sexual magnetism so dense it was visible as a fine black net and a smug gray-haired woman in a designer suit. Despite being together, they were definitely not linked by love and romance. The Rembrandt transfixed both. In fact, they looked like they'd been standing before the *Judgment of the Watcher Angels* for some time and had no plans to tour any of the other galleries.

While the three bachelors stood guard in front of the door, their hands crossed at their waists and their faces impassive, the three couples stepped closer to these patrons.

"An astounding masterpiece, wouldn't you agree?" asked Olivia, the baby's mother. "It's incredible to think that it's been kept from sight all these years. Almost as if it's too explosive for the world to know about."

She smiled at the man, apparently impervious to his appeal. The baby laughed and reached for the stranger's lapel. His eyes widened, but he said nothing and remained motionless.

"I rather prefer the *Redemption of the Elioud*," said Mihàil, her husband, taking Luljeta from her arms. "But I am afraid it will not be shown to the public for some time."

Stasia sidled closer to the haughty woman, whose eyes had started to show strain in the corners. "Gina! *Sputa il rospo!* Or would you rather keep 'the toad' inside your mouth?" The Italian laughed at her play on words. "*Naturalmente,* you intend to keep quiet about sharing some of the *Codex Angelicus* with Asmodeus, *sì?*"

Now Miró, Stasia's husband, stepped up next to his former rival, crossing his arms as he studied the captivated male. He shook his head, looking grave. "I rather think that Yeqon has been puzzling over his predicament. How, after all, can an *Irim* be imprisoned?"

Behind them, one of the guards, a Dutch *Elioud*, answered.

"Perhaps he needs a lesson in the physics of a Faraday cage," said Willem.

Miró, whose face had been rather somber, smiled. It transformed him into an exceptionally striking male, whose cold blue eyes burned with passion. Stasia could be forgiven, then, for the sudden warmth that flushed her at the sight.

"It *is* rather technical for an angel, especially one most interested in desire and seduction," he said to his wife, the smile still playing around the corners of his mouth. "Not in the ability of his descendants to develop technology that enables them to compete—even overcome—fallen angels."

Willem didn't smile. He watched *L'amante* with an unforgiving gaze. "Suffice it to say, you have been trapped inside this room, which isolates you from the harmonic plane and blocks all harmonics transmission or reception."

"Powered by your own manna," said Mihàil, gesturing with his chin toward the painting.

"And your own charisma," added Miró. "Which is quite extensive, I have been warned."

Luljeta, who'd been growing a bit cranky as her naptime approached, began to fuss. Olivia, bouncing her a little on her hip, looked at the others.

"Well, I've enjoyed this meeting with our old acquaintances—really, it's been such a pleasure seeing them caught up by the spectacular brushwork of an Old Master—but we must be going now. We have a long evening ahead of us at the vigil."

Mihàil nodded, murmuring, "*Lux tenebras vincet.*" *The light will overcome the darkness.*

Clearly he relished the upcoming rite, which featured a bonfire and candles being lit.

After they left the mirror-lined room, a statuesque blonde entered. Her sleek hair had been pulled back into a glossy roll, and her snowy-white skirt suit showed off her hourglass form as she strode on high heels toward the painting.

She stopped next to *L'amante*, tapping her chin with a glossy red fingernail. At last she said, "Hm, well, I think perhaps this painting would benefit from a contrast with my own masterpiece."

Another painting featuring the *Elioud* couples, surrounded by numerous children, appeared on an easel next to the Rembrandt. Indeed, the contrast between the somber portrayal of the punishment of the unfaithful *Irim* and the joy-filled depiction of *Elioud* couldn't have been more stark.

Zophiel, the head *Cherub* known as God's Spy and the Commander of the Watch, grinned at her wayward underling, whose gaze reflected the deep agony of his portrait.

"Perfection, if I do say so myself."

About the Author

Liane Zane is the cover identity of a novelist who is an expert at hiding in plain sight. She has spent time interrogating a former Army intelligence officer and engaging in Open Source Intelligence (OSINT) activities related to Italian slang words for naughty body parts and the proclivities of Eastern European criminals. She spends her days drinking New England chocolate-raspberry coffee and gazing at the magical brook in her back yard as she plots her romantic thrillers or walking her monstrous dog along mountain trails near her estate-like home.

THE DRAKA & THE GIANT is the third and final book in her series, *THE ELIOUD LEGACY*, which includes THE HARLEQUIN & THE DRANGÙE (Olivia & Mihàil's story) and THE FLOWER & THE BLACKBIRD (Stasia & Miró's story). All three books tell the underlying legacy of the *Elioud* descendants and are best read in order.

Liane is currently writing the prequel series, THE UNSANCTIONED GUARDIANS, which narrates the genesis of the Wild *Elioud* (Olivia, Beta, and Stasia) into a disciplined team of covert advocates for innocent victims, especially of sex trafficking and assault. THE COVERT GUARDIAN (Book One), Olivia's transition from idealistic college student to tough CIA operative, releases wide in print and ebook in July 2023.

Visit www.lianezane.com for updates and to buy merchandise related to the series.

ALSO BY

The Elioud Legacy series
The Harlequin & The Drangùe
The Flower & The Blackbird
The Draka & The Giant

The Unsanctioned Guardians series (a prequel series to The *Elioud* Legacy)
The Covert Guardian (forthcoming)

Available in paperback, ebook, and audiobook online at all major retailers or through your local library by request. Check the copyright page for the ISBN numbers to expedite ordering.

www.ingramcontent.com/pod-product-compliance
Lightning Source LLC
Chambersburg PA
CBHW030737310726
48969CB00005B/1249